Phil Murphy
Photo by Karen Atkinson
https://www.karenatkinsonphotography.com

The Pavelić Trap

To Sue,

With love and very many thanks for your help with this

[signature]
xxx   *8/10/25*

PHIL MURPHY

Copyright © 2025 Phil Murphy

The moral right of the author has been asserted.

Apart from any fair dealing for the purposes of research or private study, or criticism or review, as permitted under the Copyright, Designs and Patents Act 1988, this publication may only be reproduced, stored or transmitted, in any form or by any means, with the prior permission in writing of the publishers, or in the case of reprographic reproduction in accordance with the terms of licences issued by the Copyright Licensing Agency. Enquiries concerning reproduction outside those terms should be sent to the publishers.

Although based on real events, this is a work of fiction. the author seeks to represent authentically historical events featured in the novel, but characters, businesses, places, events and incidents are either the product of the author's imagination or used in a fictitious manner. Any resemblance to actual persons, living or dead, or actual events is purely coincidental.

Troubador Publishing Ltd
Unit E2 Airfield Business Park,
Harrison Road, Market Harborough,
Leicestershire LE16 7UL
Tel: 0116 279 2299
Email: books@troubador.co.uk
Web: www.troubador.co.uk

ISBN 978 1 83628 392 8

British Library Cataloguing in Publication Data.
A catalogue record for this book is available from the British Library.

The manufacturer's authorised representative in the EU for product safety is Authorised Rep Compliance Ltd, 71 Lower Baggot Street, Dublin D02 P593 Ireland (www.arccompliance.com).

Printed and bound in Great Britain by 4edge Limited
Typeset in 12pt Jenson Pro by Troubador Publishing Ltd, Leicester, UK

This book is dedicated to my father, Robert 'Bob' Murphy who gave me the two greatest gifts – a love of reading and a love of learning.

CONTEXT

The years that saw the fall of Yugoslavia witnessed one of the most baffling series of episodes in recent European history. How was it that a federation that had held together independently of the Soviet Union or the West for forty-five years could implode so dramatically? How was it that ethnically diverse communities that had lived side by side largely in peace sometimes for hundreds of years could suddenly turn on each other? What could explain the depths of depravity that scarred much of the inter-ethnic horror? And how can we, when viewing the beautiful landscapes and experiencing the warm hospitality of the people of Croatia, Bosnia and Serbia, make sense of what happened?

This novel seeks to bring these questions to life and also to spell out to the world beyond Bosnia in particular the human cost to hundreds of thousands of mainly innocent people caught up in the conflicts. Their pain and loss was due to appalling acts sanctioned by leaders at national, regional and local level – leaders who effectively granted low-life individuals 'permission to persecute'; but the pain and loss were perpetuated by acts of omission by some Western leaders who let the conflicts drag on until it ended with the genocide of thousands in a small town in South-East Bosnia, Srebrenica.

It was perhaps unsurprising that, after holding Yugoslavia together implausibly for thirty-five years with an iron fist, President Tito's death in 1980 should have been followed by a decade of decline. Structural issues and competing priorities across the six component parts of Yugoslavia – Serbia and Montenegro, Croatia, Bosnia, Slovenia, and Macedonia – created chronic economic problems, not least rampant inflation that consumed the savings of many who had expected to live comfortably into retirement.

When Croatia and Slovenia, resentful of funding the costs of some of the poorer areas of Yugoslavia, moved to secede from the Federation, the match was struck, lighting blue touch-paper that would blow up into four years of devastating conflicts. As it often does in times of strife, nationalism had found roots in the soil of the late 1980s and early 1990s – in Serbia and Croatia in particular - and contributed to the 1991-5 conflicts that would be marked by rape, torture, inhumane incarcerations, ethnic cleansing episodes and genocidal killings. They would represent Europe's worst atrocities since World War II.

Yet this was rarely a war with a conventional aspect to it: one big army pitched against another, fighting it out between them. Because of the nature of Yugoslavia with its mixed populations, much of the combat was localised with paramilitaries joining or replacing state armies in crushing their enemies. As the central character in the novel, Mick Morrison, says: "This was often a war where journalists were not rather than where they were." Much of the action went unwitnessed by outsiders. Indeed, Commander-in-Chief of the Bosnian Serb Army Ratko Mladić observed drily that, while the outside world was watching his forces as they besieged Sarajevo, he was able to do whatever he wanted across the rest of Bosnia largely without witness. Or as political leader of the Bosnian Serbs Radovan Karadžić liked to quip: "We are skinning the cat while the world is watching."

What is difficult to grasp is how it was that the Yugoslav National Army (JNA) effectively triggered the conflicts in 1991, when this was an army made up of professional soldiers and conscripts from across the six states that made up the Federation. As its forces piled into Vukovar in Croatia backed by some fearsome paramilitary forces, the claim that the JNA was merely protecting Serb communities and reclaiming a city that was historically Serbian just did not hold water. A glorious Baroque city was destroyed.

The reason why the JNA was able to act as it did in Vukovar and later in besieging Dubrovnik, which had few Serb settlers in need of protection, was because in the years running up to the outbreak of conflicts, Serbs had taken a firm grip on the army, placing their people in all key roles. These initial assaults were designed to try to persuade Croatia from seceding. They did not work.

And the contradiction of a Yugoslav Army allegedly protecting Serb communities beyond Serbia could not hold. Youngsters called up from outside Serbia increasingly refused to fight or dodged the draft, unwilling to turn on their compatriots in Croatia and Bosnia in particular. Eventually, a new Bosnian Serb Army, led by Ratko Mladić, was carved out of the JNA as the focus of the conflicts shifted from Croatia to Bosnia.

I examine the background to these conflicts in more detail in blogs on my Website: www.philmurphyauthor.com

These explain Yugoslavia's background, who Tito was, how the conflicts broke out, how Slobodan Milošević manoeuvred himself into the leading role, and what was special about Bosnia. Readers can enjoy the novel without reading this background, but the experience may be more complete with a knowledge of what went before and how the conflicts broke out.

Because of the availability of material on the conflicts and because there are hundreds of thousands of pages of transcripts from the International Criminal Tribunal for the former Yugoslavia, I can state confidently that every substantive episode described in the novel either happened or was said by credible witnesses to have happened. I have made every effort to ensure all historical details are accurate, though, where participants are still alive, I have often changed names to protect them.

Mick, Saša, Lucy, Petra and some other characters are my fictional creations through whom I tell the story of 1991-5. While Mick's encounter with former Foreign Secretary Douglas Hurd is fictional, Hurd's words are lifted verbatim from a statement in the House of Commons in a debate about the Balkans about one year into the conflict. Overall, I have endeavoured to make this as accurate an account of the conflicts as possible – one designed to ensure that no-one can say they did not know what went on and to guarantee these never become Europe's 'forgotten wars.'

Pronunciation Note:

In the use of Bosnian, Croatian and Serbian names, location and dialogue, 'ć' is pronounced as 'ty', as in the English tube ' 'č' is 'ch', as in cheetah, 'c' is 'ts' as in cats, 'ž' is 'zuh' as in azure, 'i' is 'ee' as in keen, 'o' is as in pot, 'u' is 'oo', as in spoon, 'đ' and its capital 'Đ' are pronounced like 'd' at the beginning of the word dew, and 'j' is pronounced as 'y', as in yellow.

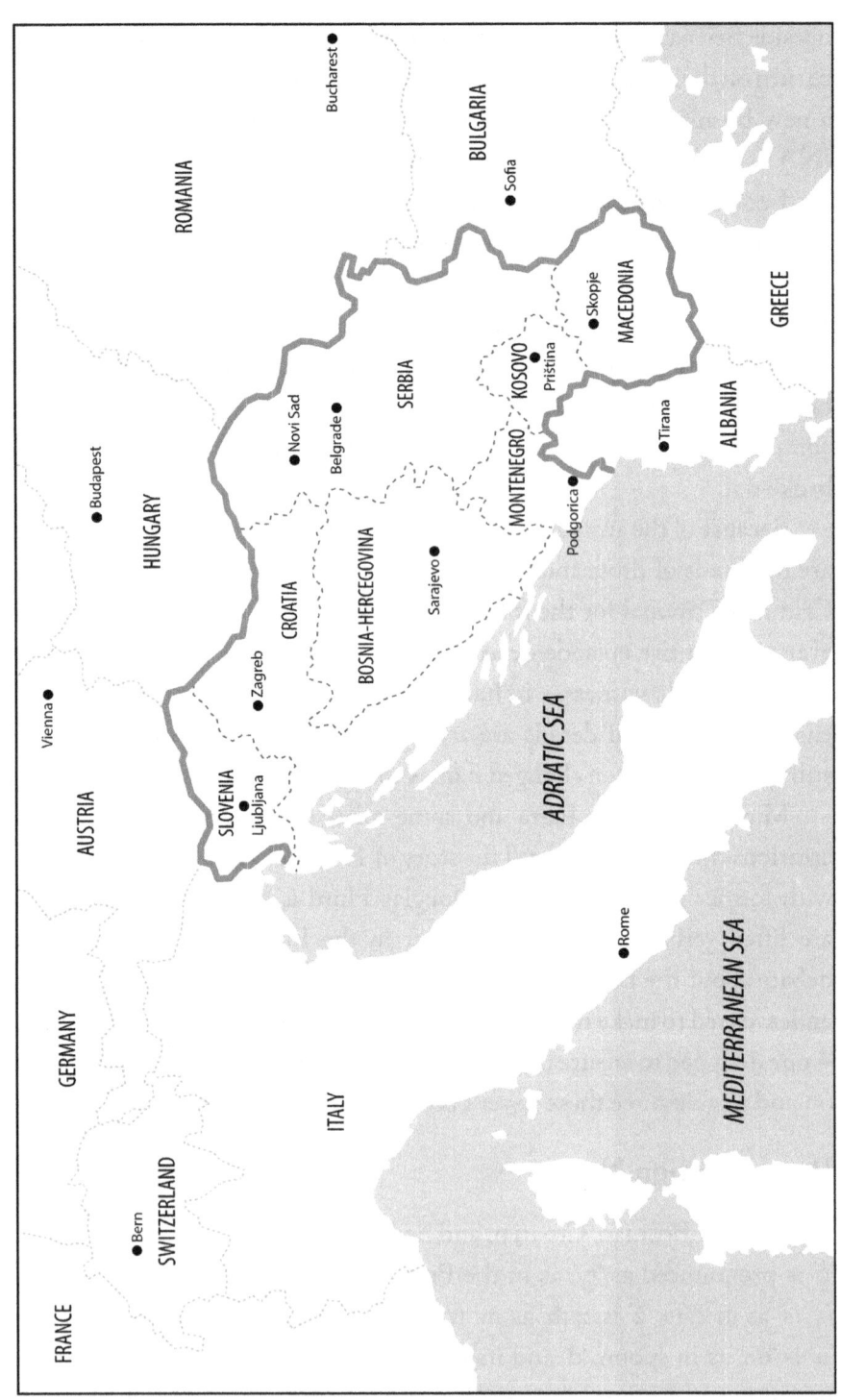

Yugoslavia 1991-5 – location within broader Europe

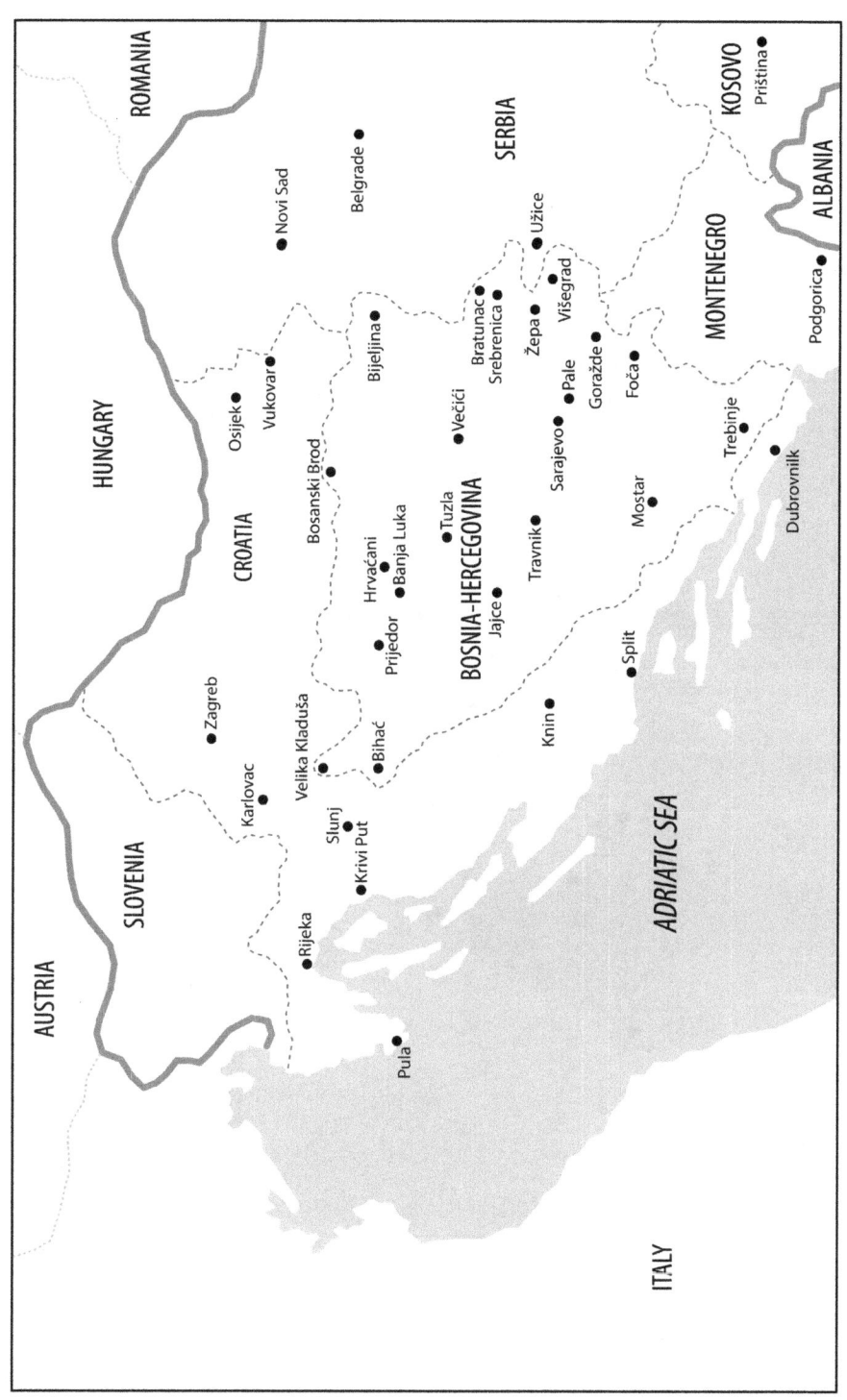

Yugoslavia 1991-5 – town and villages referred to in the Pavelić Trap

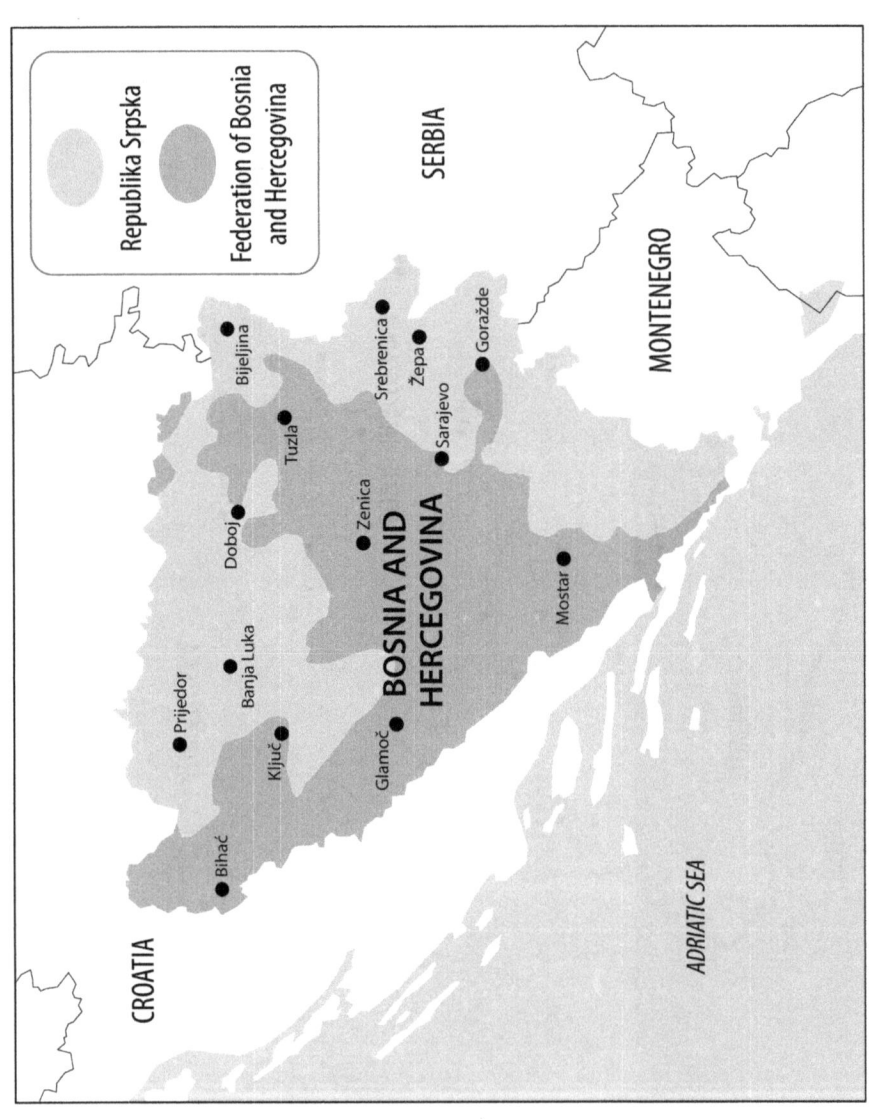

1996 – how Bosnia was separated into Bosnian Serb (Republika Srpska) and other Bosnian areas in the Dayton Agreement

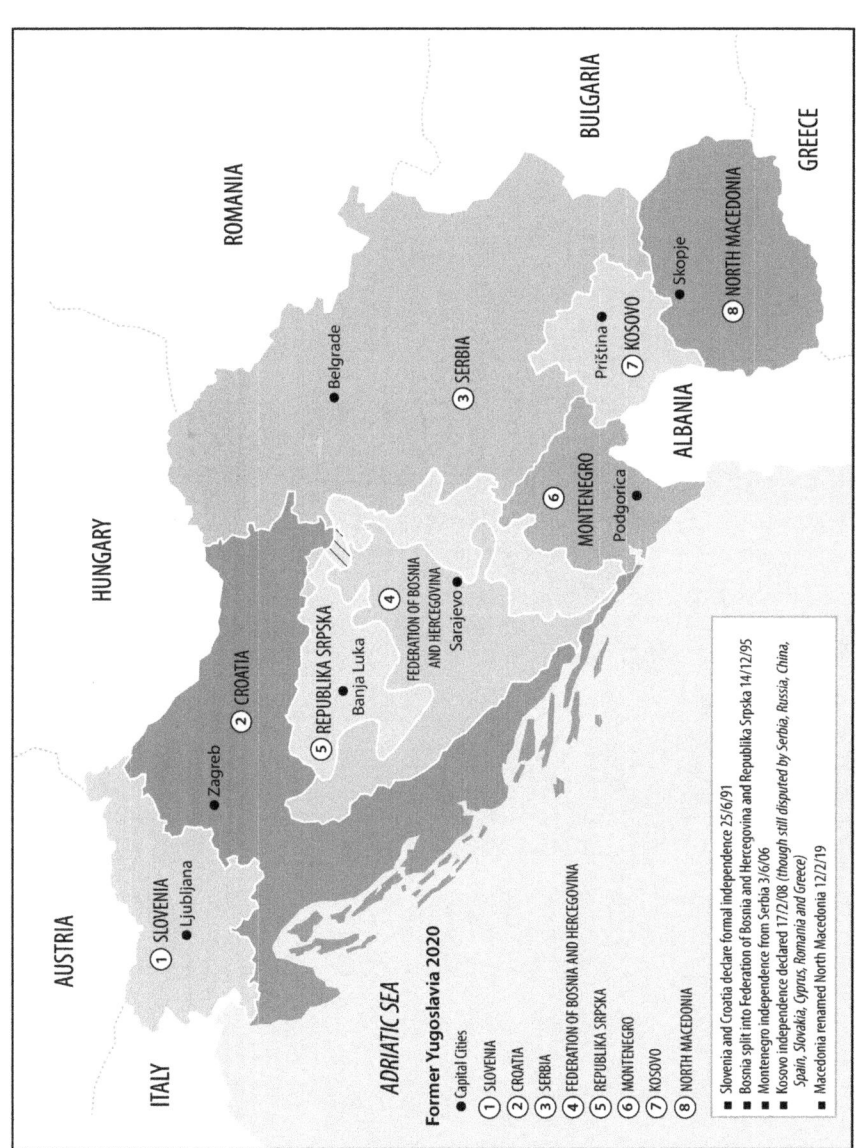

Former Yugoslavia 2020

1
OCTOBER 2018

I had been in an antiques shop. I had been digging around for globes of Planet Earth. I had to. It had become a compulsion that stopped just short of an obsession.

I had been checking whether the globe I had located featured Yugoslavia and so pre-dated 1995, or whether it featured the six post-Yugoslavia republics – Serbia, Croatia, Bosnia, Slovenia, Montenegro and Macedonia – and hence post-dated 1995.

It mattered because the transition from one to the other marked a hinge point in my life. And it matters because, towards the end of my Balkan journey, it was as if a new chemical element had been injected into my bloodstream, affecting me profoundly. It was an element to which I had thought I was immune.

When I found myself, a British journalist, dropped almost by chance into the former Yugoslavia as hostilities broke out in 1991, I suspected that I would struggle to deal with fear and to summon up bravery. I had not prepared myself to deal with shame. Why should I have?

I learned over time that fear was like an accident: you never knew it was upon you until it happened. And I learned that bravery was how you reacted in the face of fear. I called it instinct. Third parties told me I was brave. I never felt brave.

Shame was – is – something different. Although I was just twenty-four when I embarked upon this adventure, I had sufficient belief in my own moral compass. I had developed such a clear vision of what I believed journalism should and shouldn't be that, had you presented shame to me as a potential vulnerability, I would have told you confidently that I offered it no entry point. I had built my reputation on reporting the shameful actions of leading players and lowlifes in the dirty wars that broke out as Yugoslavia broke up, yet now shame was in my own bloodstream and proving impossible to purge.

For I had learned that shame – self-inflicted, unfortunate, or vicarious – was malarial: upon you in the time it takes a mosquito to bite, shattering in its impact upon your constitution. Even when you believed that you had rid your system of it, you could never be sure it wouldn't return – particularly in my case, when my critics or, God forbid, my foes chose to resurrect it. Just a single clause in a single article, reminding readers of my backstory, could bring it all back. My cheeks would redden and sting. I would try to shrug it off as the malice of the malevolent, but the arrow would have found its target.

Now my wife is sitting at the breakfast bar, quiet in concentration over a newspaper, my children, seven and five, are playing and occasionally squabbling in the room next door, and I present a picture of a man orthodox in every way unless you know that I am an award-winning war reporter.

Out of the jumble of causes impossible to unravel without the range of an academic dissertation, I had cut through the complexity and captured the conflicts in Croatia and Bosnia, as the British Press Awards' judges had said, "through real people and their stories – an Ivo Andrić of his day".

That comparison with Bosnia's only Nobel Prize-winning novelist had sent a thrill through me the likes of which I had never felt before, nor since. With my best friend, Saša, all the way from Zagreb, beside me in a penguin suit applauding as I went up to receive my gong, it was the perfect evening.

My subsequent shame could never eliminate that memory nor dispel the thrill, and I hoped I still pursued the truth with the same integrity as I had in my twenties; but I was never the same again after my 'revelation'. Where before I would have presented myself with self-assurance, now I skulked. On the fringes, I still endeavoured to consume facts, interpret motives, and explain developments with a facility that my colleagues told me was nigh on unique; but the experience of being humbled quietens one. From front foot to back foot.

Lucy closed her newspaper, stepped down from her stool, and walked over and ruffled my hair. She knew what I was thinking when I fell silent like this. She knew that she didn't need to say anything. I hope she knew how much it meant to me when she reached across and touched me like that, as if I were her third child. Her touch said "It doesn't matter to me. You have no need to feel ashamed." But I had been marked by shame and there was no gainsaying it.

And I thought back to the moment some twenty years earlier when I had stepped into that stairwell in the apartment block in Madrid. What if I hadn't pressed on and climbed the stairs? What if I had turned on my heel and walked away, leaving the question unresolved? Would I have found peace? Or would the revelation that was awaiting me upstairs have haunted me to this day, as dangerous for being open-ended as it had proved devastating in the unfolding?

But I knew I could never have walked away. And there was no such thing as a 'what-if'. There were things that happened and things that didn't happen. All that remained in play was my interpretation of what it all meant.

2
JUNE 1991

I had landed in Yugoslavia four months before the siege of Dubrovnik broke out and, shortly afterwards, an episode occurred that was so brief it could have been inconsequential; but it had depth-charged my memory and kept resurfacing. It was the moment when I stopped avoiding the question and allowed it to ask itself out loud: "How the hell did you end up here?"

I had swung my hire car off the road on an impulse. I had pulled off the main Zagreb to Belgrade highway and had just driven through the small Serbian town of Ruma, as I was considering whether to drive on to Belgrade or turn back. I had seen in the distance a car heading west at speed. My instinct was that I would be better off tucked out of sight behind a thick clump of bushes as the car passed rather than draw attention to my Zagreb number plates and risk a confrontation.

I had sensed from the propaganda contained in TV broadcasts coming out of Zagreb and Belgrade that the mood was darkening and that the tinderbox of ethnic conflict sparked by Serbian and Croatian leaders was flashing out to fraternities who knew few constraints and needed little excuse to draw a knife or a gun. I was far from alone in feeling that the atmosphere in mid-1991 risked a conflagration capable of consuming multiple victims – combatants and innocents alike.

The battered car sped by, with Belgrade plates and turbofolk music blaring from its open windows. I would learn later that its two dangerous-looking occupants were 'Chetniks' – extreme Serbian nationalists, who dressed like Hell's Angels and lurked on the fringes of army or paramilitary activities, hoping for a chance to mete out some violence of their own on Croats or Bosnian Muslims.

I felt relief and then regret as they disappeared into the distance. If I was going to do what I was sent here to do – or rather do here what I'd chosen to do – there could be no hiding in the shadows. I was more likely to attract suspicion, to be seen as a sympathiser towards 'the other side', than if I made my way about confidently and relied on my Press credentials to protect me. Yes – easy in principle to rationalise and adopt as default behaviour. Harder to do.

In answer to the question that had posed itself, I knew episodically how I had ended up there but I didn't fully understand the forces that had driven me. More importantly, I certainly didn't yet know whether those forces had driven me to the right place or whether I was way, way out of my depth.

If that was the fundamental question at that moment, had I thought it through precisely before setting off solo from Zagreb that day I might have realised that I was trying to prove myself by putting some distance between myself and the inert section of the Press pack. These were the hacks who hung around hotel lobbies in Zagreb, Belgrade and Pale, hoovering up briefings from the various official sources, be they Yugoslav, Serbian, Croatian, European Community or other, rather than venturing out into conflict zones.

Had I been totally honest, I might also have admitted that I was trying naïvely to impress my mentor, Saša, by embarking on an independent excursion. Given his experience, I should have known there was a fat chance of achieving that.

But did my parking up behind a bush at the first whiff of a Chetnik mean that I had failed my first test? That I wasn't brave enough for this?

The question was enough to prompt another episode in a chronic internal conflict over which I appeared to have little control: two voices at odds with one another, whispering away incessantly. One that I called 'top dog' would judge me harshly: "You're hopeless, you're craven, you're not cut out for this." Occasionally, on a good day, he would be crowded out by the gentler voice of 'underdog': "Don't be so hard on yourself! Anyone would be afraid in a place like this at a time like this." These were debates inside my head that would ping-pong infuriatingly.

As to my original question as to how I had landed there, I knew that two people were largely – though entirely unwittingly – 'responsible' for my finding myself in Yugoslavia as wars were breaking out: a delightful sexagenarian I had met by chance at a Press conference, who turned out to have been a war correspondent for *The Daily Telegraph*; and my Croatian mother, who had spoken to me in Serbo-Croat as a child until I absorbed the language.

I would never forget the elegantly named Ray Massingham-Byrd, though each recollection served as something of a rebuke. An Oxfam press officer by the time I met him, he had uttered the line that so many press officers come out with: "I used to be a journalist, you know?"

It normally meant that they had worked for *The Grocer* trade paper or *Horse & Hound*, and a newspaper journalist like me could feel a slightly sneering sense of superiority. The unwritten professional canon decreed that a failed hack who had become a PR man for a charity, however worthy its cause, was clearly down the pecking order from a bona fide journalist like me. Fortunately, it was a view that I had not articulated at the time.

Which was just as well, because Massingham-Byrd's career as a war journalist on *The Telegraph* had begun with the Six-Day War in the Middle East, then the Prague Spring, then Belfast to cover 'the Troubles'. He had had a significant stint in Beirut, reporting on the civil war in Lebanon, then had moved to the foreign desk and sent his reporters to the Falklands and other war zones.

I had been working for a regional newspaper in the north-east of England at the time and I can only inadequately articulate the effect this encounter had upon me. I was aware of the allure of London and the national newspapers but I may have lacked the courage to make the leap. I had probably been drifting towards a future of scaling the ranks of my newspaper, perhaps even ending up editing it, when Mr Massingham-Byrd had jolted me out of drift. But it was I myself who took up a challenge that he had never laid. *I* allowed our meeting to reshape my life. *I* chose to try to overcome my lifelong risk aversion and follow in his footsteps, a seductive voice in my ear whispering, "You could do that, you know."

Instead of my saying "No, I couldn't", a few months later, having freelanced for *The Times* in the interim, I found myself by the desk of the paper's foreign editor. It was thanks to my mother that I was able to explain to him why I was the right person to stand in for his Eastern European correspondent, Dan, who had broken his ankle in a game of five-a-side football just as Yugoslavia appeared set to blow up.

"I know it's a bit of a long shot, Paul, but… I speak a bit of the lingo."

It was as if words had come out of my mouth without my weighing them or even deciding to issue them.

The foreign editor had looked at me with an expression still heavy with the irritation prompted by Dan's situation.

"What do you mean 'the lingo'?"

"Serbo-Croat," I said. "My mum was Croatian and I did a Master's in Serbo-Croat. She died when I was a teenager and I wanted to keep the language going."

"So, when you say, 'a bit of the lingo', what do you mean? Are you fluent?"

"I can get around. Actually – I can do better than just get around."

There was a brief silence and words again emerged from me spontaneously: "As I say, Paul, I know it's a bit of a long shot but, if you wanted me to go out and try to fill a gap, while Dan's out of action, I'd be happy to give it a go."

Paul was a friend of mine. He had helped me with a dissertation when he was a Paris correspondent and I was a journalism student. I had made sure I kept in touch with him and he had helped me land shifts at *The Times*. Nevertheless, mine was still an audacious offer from a freelancer. But, as I spoke, I was simultaneously upbraiding myself: "What are you saying? You know nothing about war reporting. You're risk averse! You'll hate men shooting guns around you! You'll run a mile!"

But it was said. It was out. Offer made.

I couldn't recall a time when I hadn't felt fearful and hadn't made choices designed to avoid risk. In the schoolyard, the park and the back lane, I had probably spent an unreasonable amount of time and energy working out how to avoid violent situations. Perhaps I had been too successful. Perhaps, if I'd ended up squaring up to a bully, with classmates in a circle egging us on, and swung out a fist and felt bone on bone, then the ring of fear might have been cut and its spell over me broken. But I didn't and it wasn't.

I hated the fearfulness. It cocooned me. I could be extrovert around the family meal table, making everyone laugh with my observations of characters and with the way I verbalised stories from my day-to-day encounters and experiences. I seemed to spot details others didn't. Without being pompous, it was most likely the analysis and articulacy that over time would translate into my journalistic gift. But beyond the home, the fearfulness dialled up my introversion and dialled down my extroversion.

The fearfulness wasn't anything I'd inherited from my father. If, over the years, he had become a little more cowed, a little more reluctant to challenge the status quo, his tough upbringing in a mining town had given him a harder edge than I had acquired from my more middle-class upbringing.

I remembered as if it were yesterday his leading me by the hand into the boxing tent at the annual fair when I was just eight years of age. Walking through the curtain into the tent took me into a kind of hell unlike any I had experienced: a big gypsy in white vest, brown leggings, and calf-high, laced boots raining blows on his challenger; the proximity and power of the action shockingly brutal; the thump of glove on flesh remote from the elegance of those televised, professional heavyweight bouts.

And, as the challenger was helped away just about intact and the referee offered ten pounds to anyone in the audience who could step up and beat the champ, I could feel my father's palms twitching and I swear he was having actively to quell the desire to stick up his hand, climb in-between the ropes and strap on the gloves. I felt an admiration for his perhaps ill-judged courage, but I felt sheer dread at the prospect too. Had my father, who had boxed in the army during national service, not been the sole adult in charge of an eight-year-old on that day, might he have climbed into the ring? And in what state might he have returned home to my mother?

For the most part, my fearful childhood evaporated in a world in which adults largely kept their fists to themselves and where analysis and words were king. When it came to analysis and words, I was cock of the walk.

But, having reached that tranquil place, why was I now contemplating stepping back into the ring of fear? And not just any run-of-the-mill, playground ring of fear but a big, ugly, grown-up ring of fear populated by gun-toting men, unfettered by social rules and – as I would discover just weeks later south of Dubrovnik – granted permission to persecute.

When I dug deeper into the reasons why I seemed to be ignoring my instincts of self-preservation, I began to realise that there were reputational ambitions close to the surface. One was an ambition that Ray from *The Telegraph* had fulfilled and that he had passed on to me like a contagion.

I wanted the kind of respect he had earned for analysing and explaining complex political developments and conflicts. To be brutally honest, I wanted family, friends, and readers of a serious newspaper to notice my pieces and marvel at their clarity and elegant prose. I wanted them to think "Now I understand" and also "Wow! I couldn't do that." I wanted them to think "You know – he's the best."

There may have been a large dollop of intellectual vanity in there, but it was hardly malign.

Alongside the conflict between fear and ambition, I was aware that I would carry in my war reporter's knapsack behaviours and instincts that were not all transferred genetically from my parents. Some were adapted, reactive. For example, from my father, admirable man though he was, I had learned a harsh lesson about the need always to question the myth.

'Mythical'. It was a fascinating word. How was it that it could mean 'heroic and inspirational' and describe actions by legendary characters that mortals might seek to emulate, yet at the same time mean 'fictional and, therefore, not real'?

Thanks to my father, I had come so close to building my life story around a myth that I was intent on ensuring that I never risked doing that again – about my own life or anyone else's. I would go so far as to say the episode not only confirmed my inclination towards a career in journalism, it also put an indelible stamp on how I would report once accepted into the profession.

Although family legend had it that our strand of the Morrisons were Irish in origin, we knew of no living relatives in Ireland. Only a vague story about the family sailing for Liverpool during the potato blight and famines of the mid-nineteenth century and settling in what was then Westmorland until the exhaustion of Cumbria's lead mines led them east to the coal mines of Northumberland.

My father had repeatedly told us that the family originated in County Kerry, but when one of my uncles had heard this line being pedalled on a visit to our home, he immediately corrected his brother, my father: "No, it wasn't County Kerry. It was County Cork."

And my father had shrugged it off, as if it were a minor detail. He made no effort to defend his version. And I found myself having to suppress a sudden pang of rage. What if I had begun to build my own mythology around County Kerry? What if I had sought out some old 'truths' seventy kilometres north-west of where I should have started looking?

It felt like a lucky escape. It became a lesson in the sanctity of facts that would define my journalism: never portray guesses, hunches, or rumour, however plausible, as truths. A lesson learned inadvertently at my father's knee would be one for which I became deeply grateful as I built and garnered my journalistic reputation – but it was one for which my father deserved little or no credit.

I hoped that my legacy from my late mother was more direct, more genetic. I could never strive to emulate her, but I hoped that I had inherited from her something of what my father described at her funeral accurately and unsentimentally as her 'uncomplicated integrity'.

I often felt that my father's holidaying in Yugoslavia as a student, meeting Nada, having a summer romance, and then inviting her to Britain, was a chapter in his relatively mundane life so out of character that I struggled to conclude anything other than that fate could have brought it about. My mother had accepted his invitation, arriving in Britain one year later, and then stayed for the rest of her life.

"I had a crazy friend with a motorbike, who somehow persuaded me to ride pillion across Europe to Croatia and the Adriatic coast as far as Split. Ron, he was called," my father said.

I remembered thinking that 'Ron' wasn't a particularly heroic name.

There were no figures in mythology – that word again – called Ron. Shouldn't he have been called Brett or André – something with a note of daring or sophistication to add flavour to the story?

When I first asked my father why he thought my mother had made what back then would have been a dramatic relocation at a tender age, he had replied Delphically: "She had her reasons."

When I pressed him further, he suggested her decision was perhaps driven in part by her own father's refusal to join the Yugoslav Communist Party.

"From all accounts, as a result, theirs was a pretty miserable existence. You and your family got no privileges, no plum jobs, no holidays funded by the party if you refused to sign up. Maybe it wasn't so surprising that, when I gave her the chance to get away, she took it. Both of her parents died before you were born and, after that, she seemed to have no inclination to go back."

It seemed to me an implausible explanation for a lifelong self-exile, but I sensed he either didn't want to talk about it or was perhaps irritated by my failure to see his own personal attributes as sufficient justification for her quitting Croatia for good. Something troubled me about the incompleteness of his response but I'm afraid I let it lie.

Like a large majority of Croats, my mother was a devout Catholic and, in my younger days, I sometimes blamed the Church's strictures for making her a dispenser of advice to her children that was cautious and, dare I say it, uninspired. However, over time I came to appreciate that that advice was in fact measured and, more importantly, almost always right.

Her cancer had descended upon her abruptly after a lifetime of good health and took her away in the precise eighteen-month period that her doctor had forecast.

Sometimes, when I had visited her in the hospital and in the hospice, she had been out of reach, exhausted by blood transfusions or in a zombie state, as specialists tried to juggle pain-relief drugs with consciousness. But, in those conscious moments, she had never complained or despaired. What, as a child, I had seen in her as meekness and a lack of assertiveness, I saw then as a humble acceptance of her place in the firmament. It was excessive humility but it gave her a quiet strength. And those around her felt her goodness. It rippled out from her silently, lapping over them in benign, liquid pulses.

At times of stress and challenge, I often turned to a guttering but inextinguishable flame of her that I held in my soul. If my anxiety and circumstance allowed me pause for reflection, she could sometimes bring me succour, composure, and more balanced judgement from beyond the grave.

When Paul called me at the friend's flat where I was lodging two days after I had stood by his desk and made my pitch, he said I was being sent to Yugoslavia for a trial period of at least three months – shorter if the potential conflict blew over. I received the news with an equanimity that surprised me. I realised then that, subconsciously, I had had a sense that this was meant to be, that the events and my linguistic suitability represented an irresistible coincidence. Fear and self-doubt could wait. It was as if, invisibly, Mr Massingham-Byrd was propelling me down a route I could never have envisaged even a few months earlier.

Paul insisted that my first priority was to meet an old friend of his, Saša Našica. Saša had been the Associated Press's regional correspondent for many years, his patch stretching from the Balkans to the Middle East, as events dictated.

'AP', as it was known in the trade, was a renowned international news agency, and a prestigious employer for a journalist who could work swiftly, precisely, and factually. It wasn't quite my bag. I was more interested in the confluence of the personalities, the exceptional circumstances, and the dynamic that had produced a situation, rather than bare facts. Having said that, my respect for the AP output was enormous. And it suited Saša to the ground because, as Paul confided, he was a superb reporter but "as a writer, he's no James Joyce".

Paul and Saša had operated alongside each other on some big stories over the years. Hearing how Paul spoke of Saša, I had little doubt that they had forged a soulmates' bond. It was a small niggle but, though I was grateful for the connection, I lacked something of Paul's extroversion and feared Saša might find me a less fulfilling companion.

"He'll show you the ropes. He might take you out a couple of times, but then you'll need to stand on your own feet. He won't let you shadow him permanently," Paul said.

"Of course. I understand."

Paul paused, as if silently recalling some episode from the past with Saša which he chose not to disclose.

"But he's a great character. Great sense of humour. Mind you – if you had an attractive fiancée, probably best not to park her with him for too long."

"Okay. I haven't, but I know what you're saying."

"He's Serbian, but you'll find he'll be scrupulously balanced in his reporting. Certainly, the kind of nationalism that seems to be being pushed by some Serbian leaders would be anathema to him," said Paul.

Whenever he was in Zagreb, Saša stayed at the Hotel Astoria, a comfortable hotel not far from the railway station. It was one in which staff showed their clientele an old-fashioned style of respect that exhibited itself in ways that ranged from starched white linen napkins to excessively polite forms of address. It was something which I surprised myself by rather liking.

A week after learning that I was bound for Yugoslavia, I found Saša in the bar at the Astoria. The scene – his sitting in a winged, red Chesterfield armchair, two fingers of his right hand either side of the stem of his chunky, crystal brandy glass – was one that would be repeated time after time over the next four years. In his late forties, Saša had black hair, receding only slightly, swept back from his forehead, and running into curls where it reached the back of his shirt collar. His hair glistened in a way that made me wonder whether he might wax it. He wore gold-rimmed, pear-shaped glasses.

From the moment I met him, I liked him enormously. Initially I was so in awe of him that I risked falling silent and gawping as he recounted episodes from his war reporter's past. However, I knew that I needed to convince him that I was a credible player and potentially a useful colleague who could ride shotgun.

Part of my awe lay in the fact that in many ways he was everything that I was not. He swept up admirers and friends everywhere he went. Gregarious, witty, always at the heart of any debate when a gaggle of journalists got together, he would often be the first to suggest an initiative or an outing to try to track down the story. He could be ingenious in finding a way to the truth, often via what Paul described as his legendary contacts book.

Where I might shuffle about shyly before going in to make a contact or conduct a vox pop, Saša was straight in, as though his Press credentials gave him the same rights to question as a policeman or a bailiff. Few could resist him, his easy charm so natural that even those he interviewed who were intent on holding back would wonder afterwards how he had persuaded them to sing like canaries.

Yet this facility came with no arrogance. Self-assurance, yes. Firmness in framing and expressing his views, yes. But, as I would discover, he was a generous counsellor to the young and the new. The upper limit to his tolerance was an inclination to puncture with humour the pretensions of any pompous cub reporter who might arrive on the scene with a swagger to which he had not yet earned the right.

With women too, as Paul had alluded, he had something that I appeared to lack. Many were drawn to him irresistibly and, if he didn't quite take full advantage of his appeal, Paul intimated that there was many a female journalist who had ended up naked under a duvet with him. And many a female politician. And policewoman. And waitress.

When I looked for any cracks in the façade, I detected an occasional short span of attention that spoke of a man living on his nerves, despite impressions to the contrary, despite a set of magnificently pared, unbitten fingernails.

Given that his contacts ranged from Austria to Montenegro, from north-east Italy to the furthest reaches of Turkey and the Middle East, perhaps he was simply impatient to learn what the next development would be, the zone to which he would next be dispatched, after covering the East European beat for twenty years. Or might there have been some hidden insecurity beneath his composure? Since becoming a journalist, it was a question I had taught myself always to ask about the confident and the assured. In Saša's case, at this stage, I was far from coming close to an answer.

"It's a bit of a fluke that I'm here, to be honest, Saša," I told him, sipping at the Croatian red wine in my glass that was every bit as good as Paul had promised it would be. "It just so happened that my mother was Croatian and that she spoke to us as kids in Serbo-Croat. Without that, I wouldn't be here."

Saša looked down at his drink and then back at me directly. He had a way of fixing his interlocutor with his deep brown eyes which all but forbad him or her from unhooking and looking down or aside. In those early days, I found it uncomfortable; I would become accustomed to it.

"I don't think you're right there, Mick," Saša said. "Paul said he had had his eye on you for some time. Your speaking Serbo-Croat might have clinched it – but you should know he felt you had potential. He told me he'd always planned to pinch you from the general reporters' pool. He was just waiting for the right opportunity for you."

"Really?!" I was taken aback.

"Yes – really. He liked the fact that you never went for the easy analysis. He liked the fact that, when the news desk asked you 'Well, what are you saying in a sentence?', you weren't afraid to say 'I can't tell you in a sentence. I need at least a paragraph.' He feels that you can't describe where Yugoslavia is now in a sentence. It needs a paragraph... at least."

"He said that?!"

"He did, Mick. And he said you write beautifully..." He paused and then added with a smile, "Which pissed me off big time, because he always told me my writing was shit!"

Saša burst out laughing, as did I – out of relief and out of sheer surprise.

In that moment, Saša had repositioned me: from raw, timorous rookie to someone with promise to fulfil and a reputation to construct. Simultaneously, I was thrilled and daunted.

A few glasses of wine later, as I lay in my bed in the Astoria, glowing at the tribute I had heard, I thought to myself *Less of the daunted, more of the thrilled, please!* And, after the psychological challenges of the day, I fell into a deep, deep sleep – daunted but thrilled.

3
OCTOBER 1991

The wars didn't begin here but the start of the siege of Dubrovnik was where my war began. This was when and where men with guns and missiles first began firing, if not directly at me, then within my vicinity and without any concern for my safety or peace of mind.

I had watched on TV as much of the Baroque quarters of the handsome town of Vukovar in north-east Croatia had been reduced to rubble. It had been too dangerous to get close to the action, Saša had insisted. And, on my way down to Dubrovnik, I had seen the devastation wreaked on the village of Kijevo, just south of Knin in Central Croatia. Knin was a town that had recently become the informal capital of 'Krajina' Serbs – those whose ancestors had settled in Croatia more than five hundred years earlier.

Reports suggested that Kijevo's entire 1,250-strong Croat population had been driven out by a combination of Serbian paramilitaries and the JNA, the acronym everyone used for the Yugoslav National Army. TV footage from Belgrade had shown JNA jets strafing the hills above the village – an act designed to instil in the final stragglers fleeing their homes that it was probably best that they never went back.

Any homes that I could see from the road were uninhabitable, blackened with scorch marks, not a pane of glass intact, tiled roofs with gaping holes. On the hill where I'd been told the village church should have stood, its simple belfry set against the backdrop of a mountain ridge, only the backdrop remained.

The scale of the devastation suggested heavy pounding from the JNA;

but whether the Yugoslav Army was responsible for the devastation or Serbian militia, one thing was certain: this was not the level of artillery required to clear Croats from a village which, through no fault of its own, was too close to Knin. It was excessive force and, I suspected, almost certainly gratuitous.

But, on the road past Kijevo, I had been witnessing an aftermath. Now, in a group of around two dozen journalists squeezed into a convoy of hire cars that had driven south of Dubrovnik and across the border into Montenegro, I sensed that my baptism as a war reporter was upon me.

Trepidation didn't capture how I felt. I suspected I would have been paralysed with fear, had I not had to put on a pretence of surface calm in the presence of other reporters alongside me in our car. I hated my fearfulness and lamented my lack of bravery, but were the others brave, sanguine, or just more experienced at concealing their trauma? Was their swagger and gallows humour real or an act?

The JNA had given us permission to make the trip a couple of days earlier, as rumours of the start of the assault on Dubrovnik from the south had begun to spread. Earlier that morning, before the JNA allowed us onto the main highway that led back to Croatia, it was clear some kind of assault was underway. We had heard the singing and crunching of rocket fire on targets somewhere not far over the border into Croatia.

I had tried not to flinch each time the roar of a fighter plane tore into the silence and a jet then zipped overhead. Each time it was a shocking, heart-jumping assault on the senses. I was waiting, tense, for each new sortie, beginning to relax just as another would jolt me to my core. I was already questioning how much of it I could take. Maybe I wasn't cut out for this? Maybe I'd been deluding myself in thinking I could become accustomed to rockets and shells and bullets falling and flying around me?

"It's okay, you'll find a way through it," one of my inner voices said quietly, reassuringly. I wanted to believe it.

As the car headed back in the direction of Croatia and Dubrovnik, the answer to one of our questions was resolved. Multiple reports had suggested that the JNA had been facing a crisis of manpower, with many young recruits deserting and others simply dodging the draft as it became clear that Yugoslavia was breaking up.

Although the leadership in Belgrade in the couple of years before war broke out had succeeded in placing Serbs into most of the key senior roles in the military, this was still a Yugoslav army, drawing recruits from all six states. That meant that young Croat soldiers were being asked to attack their own people. And why would a Bosnian mother allow her son to die in battle for a cause that might have made sense to those seeking to further Serbian aims but risked squeezing her country between the competing ambitions of Serbia and Croatia?

So how could the Yugoslav National Army mount an effective attack on Dubrovnik without enough new recruits? The solution would set a sickening stamp on how parts of the war across Yugoslavia over the next four years would be conducted: on occasions the JNA, and then their Serb and Croatian and Bosnian successors, would simply contract out parts of their operations. In this case it was to paramilitaries, who piled over the border from Montenegro, looking for loot and a macabre kind of fun.

As I framed the thought, I corrected myself. In this instance 'paramilitaries' was too dignified a word for these men. At least paramilitaries had some loose set of beliefs that prompted them to act in the way that they did, however misguided their principles and however repulsive the scale of their violence. These two thousand or so Montenegrin young men, who had been invited by the JNA to act as a force that would sweep away all the Croat communities between the Montenegro-Croatia border and the coastal town of Cavtat, just south of Dubrovnik, were – we suspected – almost entirely from the criminal fraternity.

Once our convoy was on the main highway into Croatia, the bargain struck with the Montenegrin mob became clear: you flush these villages of Croats and you are free to loot and pillage whatever you find. Violence and theft that, before the war, would have led to extended jail sentences were lifted from any putative charge sheet. Norms of civilised behaviour were suspended. It was as if these volunteers had been told "Anything goes in that stretch from the Montenegrin border and Cavtat." And, as I witnessed, everything went.

Although I experienced horror at what I was seeing, I found it an absorbing, fascinating spectacle. Every dwelling, every building in every village on the road north had been shelled or blasted after their most valuable contents had been emptied into hatchbacks, pickups, and flatbed trucks.

Every mile or so our convoy would cross a laden truck, heading back south, with long-haired, grubby men hanging out of its windows or sitting in the back wedged between looted items piled so high that no more could be inserted. Check shirts, dirty jeans, teeth missing, they were the kind of men you would cross the road to avoid even in more normal situations. I could not take my eyes off a single truckload of these alarming, compelling, fascinating wild men.

Recognising the Press logos that we had hoped might offer us some protection, each of their drivers without exception would hammer the horn and each truck's passengers would offer the obscene fist gesture and heckle, usually around a theme of "Fuck you, Nazi media scum!" Now and then a driver would swerve intentionally at our cars, trying to force us off the road. I could sense the exhilaration from every returning truck and, if I could have got close, I suspect I would have picked up a powerful smell of alcohol, even though it was early morning.

These were men on the fringes of society who would never normally have responded to a formal call-up. But they could never have imagined that 'war' would be like this: free rein to discharge guns and grenades; free rein to menace and terrify and even shoot to kill; free rein to correct at a stroke the imbalance between their dire, mountain-dwelling poverty and the wealth of Croatians in one of the country's most affluent regions. And all wrapped up and adorned with a ribbon guaranteeing immunity from prosecution – for now at least. For the fraternity that had responded to the call of a JNA desperate for backup, this was likely to have ranked amongst the best days of their lives.

Beside me in the back of the car was a French journalist. I sensed him shrugging his shoulders, as if to register that, if I was enthralled by the scenes I was witnessing, this was nothing new to an experienced, international journalist like him.

"These mountain guys. They're the same the world over. Fucking crazy. You can't reason with them and you can't deal with them. I've seen them in Afghanistan, in South America. Shit, I've even seen them in Austria... They're all the same."

I bristled at the sweeping, normalising nature of the assertion, though I tried to show no visible reaction. This was the antithesis of my mission. I needed to know the precise dynamics of how these abnormal circumstances had unleashed this terrifying rabble force. What were the clan and family systems, what were the economic and climatic conditions from which these hardy, terrifying people were hewn? And how did they differ from or resemble the men of the Afghan mountains?

If our French friend wanted to suggest that everyone was the same, that they all fell within a given band of the spectrum, for me the whole point of our craft was to differentiate within each band. Was that ochre or tangerine and, having decided which, how did I differentiate between shades in my description?

As we headed north, it became clear that the Croatian villagers must have been warned of the approaching hordes and had chosen flight way before fight. What might be the state of mind of these people, now effectively refugees?

The Dubrovnik authorities would tell us later that their estimate was that around eight thousand people had fled the thirty or so villages of the Konavle region south of Dubrovnik. I imagined them piling into their cars as many light valuables as they could before they headed off to family or friends in and around Dubrovnik or Split or over the border into Bosnia just twenty kilometres away. One day living a quiet life on a coastal stretch of paradise, the next uprooted and shuffling around, embarrassed to be a burden in the homes of others, wondering what might have become of their properties, none of them yet aware of the scale and the uniform efficiency of the devastation wreaked on their properties and their contents.

After the sweeping away of humanity and the looting of Croat properties had been entrusted to the wild men of the mountains, the JNA launched a more leisurely but more orthodox style of warfare from behind, its forces beginning a slow march north from Montenegro's Bay of Kotor.

We saw on our journey shell damage inflicted on Croatia's southernmost town, Vitaljina – no doubt from the missiles we had heard flying overhead earlier that morning. But, as we drove north, we also witnessed JNA jets launching missiles apparently haphazardly into villages that had already been cleared. Naval bombardments added to the destruction. The word 'wanton' kept forming in my mind.

By the time our convoy made it back to the outskirts of Dubrovnik, JNA MiG fighters had targeted Komolac, the source of the city's water and power, cutting off supplies for the next three months.

I'd found in most of my vox pops, in the fortnight running up to the start of the siege, a reluctance among the people to countenance the possibility of their city being attacked. Many of them seemed to believe that their town, their city, was so special that no one would dare to attack it. Now the assault was real. As I wandered through the streets, as dusk was on the cusp of turning to darkness, many of those I came across appeared frozen into incoherence by the speed of their transition from free folk of one of Europe's most privileged and elegant cities to besieged.

I made for the Revelin Fort by the gate at the south-east of the Old Town after a tip off that those Konavle people unfortunate enough to have no kith or kin to billet with had found sanctuary in the cellars of the building.

I felt ghoulish, an uninvited voyeur of the misery of people I had never met, as I picked my way from subterranean room to room. Each was carpeted with brick flakes and draped with years-old cobwebs. Here and there a single naked bulb would hang from the ceiling, powered presumably by a generator somewhere on the ground floor. So early in their ordeal, these were the best-scrubbed refugees I had ever seen in the flesh or on screen.

Some had found, or brought with them, fold-down or deckchairs and gulped nervously at bottled water, clenching the fringes of their blankets. There was a plump, squat man with improbably gleaming skin, the product of years of expensive moisturiser, wearing a leather jacket that probably cost him four figures. There was a handsome woman in her forties with a blonde rinse teased up on top, shards of hair spilling out of her imperfect knot.

I read an abruptly suppressed vivacity in that face and craved meeting her in normal times. I identified an irrepressible dinner companion, no doubt with stories of exotic travel, excess, and sexual encounters – now drained of that joie de vivre and quietly desperate, silently pleading with her god to make this a brief interruption to a life lived to the full.

Most of these Konavlians wouldn't speak to me when they learned that I was a journalist, but the few who did dwelt on trivial concerns, in order, I sensed, to try to dilute their deeper anxieties. One investment banker feared for his four-berth cruiser, aware that JNA marine forces were off the coast and might be attracted by a spot of mindless, spiteful target practice. An elderly lady regretted leaving behind her cage of finches. At least, so far, they were not mourning any dead.

Unlike Jelena Milišić, whose husband had died in her arms, one of the first victims – some said the first victim – of Yugoslav National Army shelling of the Dubrovnik area. The JNA could not have hand-picked a more inappropriate victim, had they tried: a celebrated Serb poet and playwright, Milan Milišić, whose successes had included the daunting tasks of translating into Serbo-Croat the poems of Robert Frost and Ted Hughes and Tolkien's *The Hobbit*.

When I learned of his death the day after the siege began – a former member of Belgrade literary salons whose parents were Bosnian killed by a Yugoslav Army shell in his front room in a residential area of a Croatian town – what became all too clear was the daunting scale of the challenge of explaining how and why this conflict had erupted, who was shooting at who and why. But even so early in the wars I was beginning to feel I had a duty to try.

4
SEPTEMBER 1991

It was my first visit to Dubrovnik and, in the fortnight between my arriving there and the descent of the wild men of Montenegro onto the villages of Konavle south of the city, I had seen and learned enough to conclude that Byron's description of it as 'the Pearl of the Adriatic' was probably inadequate.

It wasn't just that its peerless setting meant that any group of inhabitants would have been hard-pushed to have made of this city something banal; my crash course in local history taught me that for topographical as well as historical reasons Dubrovnik had represented a largely impregnable barrier to external empires and religions. Only Napoleon had broken the spell since the Venetians left in the fourteenth century and he had been 'invited in' as a more palatable alternative to the Russians.

As would-be invaders had marched or nibbled their way in its direction, through foresight, ingenuity or judicious use of their enormous wealth its citizens had managed to retain their autonomy for virtually all of the last six hundred years. Cultural and social anarchy had been kept at bay.

Even as malign forces were gathering to the south, the city and its Old Town in particular appeared to be clinging onto a calmness and a serenity that reflected well centuries of self-confident dignity. Its people were largely unrufflable, it seemed to me, though I couldn't be sure from my conversations whether their confidence was genuine.

Might they have been being glib – as in "It'll never happen to us"? Might there have been some cowardice there, as in "If we don't face up to it as a possibility, it might never happen"? Might they believe that their sacred patron, St Blaise, still cast a protective veil over the city one thousand years after he first saved it? Or did I find little concern that Dubrovnik might become the next Vukovar because bad blood between Serbs and Croats was measured in millilitres in this part of the country?

It had been a chance meeting that revealed to me that not everyone shared the calm and the sense of serenity, not everyone believed that the city might be saved by some ancient magical properties. I had met Branko Komlenac when he had emerged on his back on a roller board from beneath a jacked-up motor car in a side-street mechanic's shop, oil stains on his face as if a make-up artist had prepared him expertly for a film set.

The hire car I had travelled down in had started to whine as I homed in on Dubrovnik and I was hoping an expert could reassure me that it wasn't about to give up the ghost. After Branko had lifted the bonnet, made some tweaks and explained in vocabulary beyond my Serbo-Croat what he had fixed, the conversation took a turn once he realised that I was an international journalist rather than a tourist. I had become in an instant someone with the potential to help his and his fellow citizens' cause rather than a simple customer to whom he needed to be polite.

As we sat an hour later in his small, neat flat, half a kilometre north of the Old Town, his pregnant wife Ivana next to him on the settee, cards from guests at their recent wedding still on the windowsill behind them, he insisted I hadn't just got lucky in bumping into him.

"You could have chatted to any one of a couple of hundred men of my age around the town and you'd have found that we're all just waiting for the sign. Then we quit our jobs, we join forces with the local military police, and we become the defenders of our city," he said.

"So are you sure they're going to attack Dubrovnik?" I asked.

"We know the JNA are out there," Branko said, pointing south-east, in the direction of the hills above Dubrovnik, towards Montenegro and Eastern Hercegovina.

"Our people have seen activity from at least three brigades since July. And they've been calling up youngsters and reservists and training them out in the wilds. We don't know what their plan is – but I doubt they're picnicking in the woods."

Ivana chipped in. "Branko, tell Mick about my friend, Maja."

"Yes, Maja… Well, you know, Mick, Maja was one of Ivana's oldest friends – she was my friend too," said Branko. "She was Serbian. She was all teed up to be one of the maids of honour at the wedding and then, three days before the event, she just disappeared. Her and some of her Serbian friends and their families. Vamoose! Just gone."

"What? Did somebody kill them?"

"No, no. They did a runner."

Ivana explained: "She – they – obviously know that something is going to happen. And so they've vanished – but without a word of warning to any of us. I don't even know where she is now."

Branko shook his head with a look of barely disguised disgust on his face. "The most generous thing you could say is that Maja and her friends felt something in the air. They might not have had a tip off. But, as I say, that's being generous… and I don't really believe that."

"Call themselves friends…" Ivana left the comment hanging in the air. Branko looped an arm round her shoulder and gave a squeeze of reassurance.

Together they made an attractive couple: Branko tall and broad, lean but muscular, his dark brown hair cut fashionably, short at the sides, collar-length at the back; Ivana's straw-coloured hair was parted in the centre and tied back and, if some might have found her plain, I found her beautiful. Her pale blue eyes, thin lips, clean features and calm demeanour meant that an Old Master could have captured her as an angel and dropped her into a crowd scene in a biblical canvas.

At that moment, I felt a warm pang of affection for them, for their allowing me into their space.

They told me that they were both twenty-three years of age, had been at school together, and Ivana was now five months pregnant. I could imagine what a striking couple they would have made, walking down the aisle after their union had been blessed, Branko with a barely suppressed smile on his face at the prize he had claimed and Ivana, just shoulder-high against him, glowing and basking in her new status, proud of the man for whom she had no doubt faced significant local competition.

Yet here they were, just weeks after the happy day, at risk of being torn apart. They represented a stark example of hundreds of innocent people across the city under threat of becoming collateral damage in a conflict that wasn't theirs. I didn't need to articulate the thought that Branko could be killed in action even before their child was born; it was clear that he had weighed up the options and concluded that the right thing to do was to defend their city.

He looked across at Ivana. "I think we're going to get her well out of here, if it looks like things are kicking off… And this one too." He patted Ivana's bump. "We've got a plan."

"It won't come to that, I hope," said Ivana.

I mentioned to them that I had heard reports of large scale JNA desertions and draft dodges.

"I mean – will they really be able to mount a viable attack?" I asked.

"None of us has any illusions about the scale of the challenge we're likely to face," Branko said. "To be honest, if you include volunteers like me, together with the military police, we probably only add up to about a thousand men. Depending on what they plan to do, the numbers they'll have around Dubrovnik are likely to be a multiple of that. They'll definitely outman us."

As I stood up to leave after a lengthy conversation, Branko offered me open house. I should drop by at any time with questions or intelligence. He would update me on any developments, and he hoped I would take any opportunity I had to tell the outside world the true story.

As I made my way up the hill to my digs, it was already becoming clear to me that the way to capture this conflict was not by trying to explain the multiple moving parts of the political drama driving the threat of violence; it was in capturing the Brankos and Ivanas of the wars, if that was what these conflicts became. These were normal, decent people living in one of Europe's finest cities – no different to the citizens of Paris, Barcelona or London. So why were they set to have their lives torn apart?

Before I had left London, Paul had taken me aside. "Lots of people think Yugoslavia doesn't affect their lives and that the Southern Slavs just like fighting each other. It may not be true but that's what you're working against. So, Mick – people and their stories. That's how you tell it. People and their stories."

"Yes. I can do people and stories," I had said.
I had nearly added "I think." I was glad that I hadn't.

5
OCTOBER 1991

When, a week later, Yugoslav National Army forces were seen mobilising to the east of Dubrovnik and one of their leading officers quit to join his native Croatian forces and become commander of the 'Defence of Dubrovnik' unit, Branko signed up formally to the 116 National Guard Corps brigade that would form the unit defending the city.

"They won't roll in straightaway – but it won't be long," Branko forecast. As September turned into October, hordes of young Montenegrins swarmed over the border, backed by JNA artillery, air and sea bombardments. Dubrovnik's centuries of peace were over.

After witnessing the rout of Croatian villages south of Dubrovnik, though it was late and I was in a state of mild shock, as I picked my way out of the Old Town and headed north I decided at the last minute to knock up my new-found friends rather than head straight back to my guest house. The power was out but the couple had two chunky candles on the coffee table in front of the sofa and the flames cast elastic shadows across Ivana's face.

Branko listened with some bewilderment and no little concern as I described the demeanour, the methods and the scale of the devastation wreaked by the men from Montenegro and their JNA supporting cast. Then, without articulating it in too obvious a way, Branko began oozing reassurance that I soon realised was aimed at Ivana.

His was a maturity beyond his twenty-three years, one that I had witnessed before in several characters I had come across in a range of different environments. These were self-sufficient individuals, brought up by parents who loved them unstintingly but unfussily, people who were allowed by their fathers to take controlled risks, to learn bravery, and to regard fear as a stranger so rarely encountered as to be unworthy of consideration. Regrettably, I was not one of them.

"We're not sure quite where they landed but, early this morning, there were rockets whistling over us. I suspect that Mokošica has taken a hit."

I knew that Mokošica was one of Dubrovnik's most chic suburbs. Just as the wealthy and privileged Konavlians had been treated with contempt, was this another example of the JNA targeting those who had the most to lose, those who inspired in non-Croats the most envy?

"I'm not tempting fate, but we're fortunate here in the layout of our street. You couldn't angle a rocket in that would do us any damage," Branko said.

After Ivana excused herself and slipped off to bed, I picked up the point.

"You're lucky, then – if that's the right word – if you can't be hit by shells or rocket fire here."

"Well – not really." Branko paused. "It isn't true. I made it up to make Ivana feel safer. The only thing protecting us, if they target this district, is old Ma Popović in the flat above us… Sorry if that sounds a bit callous. I don't mean her any harm."

"It's what we call in English 'gallows humour', Branko," I said.

As the clock ticked on, the chunky candles held up robustly, just millimetres of wax softening and running to a sludgy halt down the circumferences or folding in towards the flames. Branko explained that the defenders of the city believed that their best hope of holding the enemy at bay was the Fort Imperial. Part fortress and large-part bunker, the fort was virtually impregnable except in the event of an invading army rolling right up to its front door.

It sat on the western extremity of Srđ Hill, the block of rock that towers above the east of the Old Town. Fort Imperial was Napoleon's attempt in 1806 to protect Dubrovnik from Russian and Montenegrin threats, at a time when long-range guns were beginning to be introduced.

"We need to get up there and occupy it before the JNA get hold of it. That way, we might be able to hold them at bay – because anyone trying to cross the open mountain top from the south will be a sitting duck we can pick off. Even with our limited weaponry," said Branko.

Branko explained that a group of the city's defence force would make their way up to the fortress during the night in the next twenty-four to forty-eight hours and try and dig in.

"Once we're in, it should be pretty difficult to shift us, even if we are just holding the JNA or your crazy Montenegrins at bay rather than pushing them back. We'll get a sense of how it is up there and, if it's safe enough, I might be able to smuggle you up one night to give you a first-hand view of the scale of the fight."

I said that I would welcome the opportunity. Having heard only the distant pounding of rocket fire and witnessed only the aftermath of the rout of villages so far, I wondered with what kind of dread I might scale that hill in the dark. Then I suppressed the thought. There would be plenty of time for fear in due course.

Back in my guest house, illuminated only by candlelight, I slipped under the covers. Physically I was spent, but my mind was humming. I still felt I was a 'war virgin' – every spectacle of devastation I had witnessed had been in the aftermath rather than as it was wreaked – but the images of the day, from the coast road to the catacombs, jostled for space. And I wasn't proud, though nor was I surprised, that a big, buzzing current of exhilaration coursed through me until exhaustion tipped me into a deep sleep. And I slept until the rockets and the shells resumed. Six in the morning. Whistling and thumping, some distance away, north of the city and onto the hills to the east, I sensed.

At seven o'clock, I got up, ate an apple, and decided to head for Mokošica to see whether it was true that that had been the district targeted by the JNA. Though I knew it would be a long walk, my hunch was that I would be safer on foot than in a car that would be more visible from the skies and more easily tracked and shelled.

The sky was colourless but hinted at sunshine working to burn away the thin cloud. The air was cool and the breeze was negligible. My route took me up through the district of Gruž, past the port that in normal times welcomed ferries from Bari, Split and the small islands just off the coast north-west of Dubrovnik: Šipan, Lopud and Koločep.

The mouth of the estuary south of Mokošica was crying out for a bridge, but this would require a not insignificant feat of engineering with over five hundred metres of water to span. My landlady, a kindly woman in her late fifties with greying, curly hair, had given me directions to Mokošica and said that plans had been drawn up just a couple of years earlier for just such a crossing.

"Pray God we can soon get back to thinking about progress – not survival. I was anticipating a big fight between people like me whose businesses benefit from better transport links and those locals who can't stand change or disruption. Now it all seems trivial. Maybe when it's all over, we'll be better able to appreciate the luxury of our peacetime differences. We'll be closer as a community – so, instead of an argument, we might just be able to have a debate. I don't know. Maybe I'm wrong…"

"You're not wrong, Marta," I said. "It's good that what's happening around you isn't making you cynical."

The word prompted Marta to look up at me.

"Cynical? No, no, Mick. We must never resort to cynicism. A cynic sneers at the world. A cynic sneers at people like me who believe in humanity. Even here – now – I believe in the goodness of people. I believe that goodness will prevail. There's a logic to goodness. Evil has no logic."

I looked at the small, silver cross round Marta's neck. But I knew her words were more than the words of the devout, learned from the pulpit. I had hated the easy categorisations of the French journalist who had shared my car the day before, who had claimed that "mountain guys" the world over were all the same. I sensed in Marta something finer: a refusal to make sweeping judgements about individuals or groups of people. I hoped that it was fair to say that I shared Marta's greater generosity and subtler analysis. In the coming months and years, we would both discover whether our faith in humanity was justified – or whether the cynics had called it right.

By the time I reached the mouth of the estuary on the north bank of which sat Mokošica, the temperature had climbed to the mid teens of Celsius and the clouds were gone. I had had to take the south road and then loop back beyond Komolac. I drank in the view of the glistening stretch of water, reflecting on how war changed every perspective. Weeks earlier, my excursion would have been tourism. The siege meant it was now a mission.

In a café on the main road through the town, a waiter confirmed that the district had been targeted the day before.

"Some of the rockets went into Malo Selo. It's an area just up the hill from here. One old dear took a direct hit. The rocket just went straight through her window. By all accounts, she didn't stand a chance. A couple of other houses took a hit. Their roofs were damaged, but everyone survived. But then quite a few missiles fell short into the fields and trees on the hills behind us."

Malo Selo was just a five-minute walk away and I picked my way through the side streets until I found a house with its roof shattered and a window blown out, black scorch marks caked around where the frame had been. A young man with frizzy pale brown hair and a Mexican moustache, dressed in a white vest, black tracksuit bottoms and flip-flops, was leaning on a gate a few doors down, smoking a cigarette.

I introduced myself and asked if this was where the old lady had been killed.

"Yes, yes. It was here. Poor thing. She didn't stand a chance," he said, echoing the waiter's phrase. He paused. "Mind you, she wouldn't have even known it was happening. We were all just lying in our beds, then there's this weird whistling and a thud and then a huge explosion."

I asked about the victim.

"There's no justice, mate," the man said. "Brought up three children, reared them nicely. They move away. Her husband dies a few years ago and then she's gone. Like that. Brutally. Spent her whole life thinking about others and then she cops it for no reason. I mean what do these fuckers think they're doing? Pick a fight with someone else's army if you like. But lobbing shells into the suburbs. It's just cowardly."

I mooched around a few nearby streets, looking for more damage but finding none. People were beginning to emerge from their homes, sensing at least a lull in the bombardments. Some ventured into the streets, heading for shops or church. I decided to head back to the main street. As I turned into a street called Kitoš Street, my attention was caught by a woman ahead of me, carrying her purse in an old-fashioned blue string bag. She made to cut across the courtyard of a small church by the roadside.

I heard a faint pop in the distance behind me, there were ten seconds of silence, then a whistle above me that lasted just two seconds, then a huge thud followed instantly by a massive, ear-splitting explosion. I fell or dived onto the ground and, instinctively, curled into a bundle. Around me were tingling sounds, as if it were raining little drops of metal. It was. I would realise soon after that this was shrapnel. There was a brief silence. Then a baleful wail rang out.

"Moja noga! Moja noga! U pomoć! U pomoć!"

I raised my head, tasting dust on my lips. The lady with the blue string bag was sitting by the corner of the church seventy metres ahead of me, separated by three metres from the lower part of her right leg.

"My leg! My leg! Help me!" she was shouting. The shell crater was ten metres beyond her. A piece of shrapnel must have sliced off her leg just below the knee.

For the first time I understood what being paralysed with fear felt like. All the strength had drained from my legs. The woman needed urgent help but, momentarily, I could do nothing. I couldn't even move.

As I froze, a door opened on the first-floor veranda of a white house beyond the churchyard and a man in his fifties burst out. He swung over the railings and let himself drop down to the ground. A floor below, a younger man, most likely the son of the household, shot out of the front of the house. Within seconds they were beside the woman, the elder man quickly seeking to calm her. Within a minute, a woman who I presumed was the elder man's wife and the mother of the younger man rushed up the slope from their house with a blanket and a towel. The older man wrapped the wounded woman in the blanket and gestured to his son. The younger man took the towel and, without revulsion, wrapped the leg in it, as if he were bagging an everyday item.

Finally, I found the strength to get to my feet and move towards the group. I was trembling uncontrollably and surprised that my jelly legs could bear my weight.

"Is there anything I can do?" I managed to say.

The wounded woman was in her forties, with black hair and pale skin. "Oh, Mary, mother of Jesus, pray for me," she was muttering.

The elder man had his arm around her back. "Don't worry, my love. We'll get you to hospital. You'll be okay. Don't worry."

He looked up at me. "Are you okay, son? Did you take a hit?"

"Er, no… I don't think so," I said.

With just five minutes having elapsed since the shell had exploded, the shocking burst of a siren blasted the air and an ambulance shot up Kitoš Street.

I was a little ashamed of my relief as these figures of authority emerged from the ambulance and took charge. Though physically I had been unable to jump to the woman's aid initially, shouldn't her plight have trumped my fear? And this man and his son – they had shown compassion without hesitation.

The ambulancemen gave the woman a sedative injection, placed her on a stretcher and popped the lower leg into a plastic crate full of ice. Then they were gone with another ear-splitting blast from the siren.

The woman who had brought the blanket and the towel had gone back inside. I stood with the other two men in an uncomfortable silence on the church courtyard, a puddle of blood beginning to congeal on the ground to our left.

"Will you have some coffee, son?" said the elder man. "Might be wise."

I accepted the offer and, as an armchair took my weight, it felt like the most comfortable chair I had ever sat in. The strength had been sapped from me and I felt that I would like to stay in that chair for a long time.

The conversation between the three of us was halting. I had lost temporarily my journalist's intelligence-gathering instinct, and the man and his son uttered only the occasional platitude about the injured woman's plight, the folly of war and, above all, their hopes that normality could resume sometime soon.

When the elder man asked me if I'd like a lift back to Dubrovnik centre, I really wanted to say yes but, when his wife suggested that it was too dangerous to drive when there were rockets overhead, I knew I had to decline. I dreaded the two-hour trudge back but I knew I had to lever myself out of the chair and leave these people to their privacy.

I thanked them and set off, still a little trembly, my mind returning time after time to the sound of the shell exploding, the wind-chime tinkling of the shrapnel, and then the heart-rending cries of the stricken woman.

Relief came in prose. That soothing, absorbing process of searching for the words that would adequately – perhaps even comprehensively – capture the events of the past thirty-six hours. For me, it wasn't hard. Painstaking, yes – but painstaking was satisfying. And I had developed a discipline of weighing every descriptor and patiently throwing out any word that was anything other than precise, digging and fishing until I found a fit or something superior. I knew I would thrill at the sense of achievement when I was happy that my pieces were complete. And I knew I would thrill again at reading them in print over and over again, usually satisfied that I'd done the subjects justice, occasionally disappointed when a better word or turn of phrase might come to me belatedly.

After a short career during which speed of reporting was critical, it was strange for me to have to come to terms for the first time with the fact that, in a war zone, there was no guaranteed immediacy about reporting. On day one of the conflict, JNA jets had knocked out the communications masts on the top of Srđ Hill, wiping out most of the telecommunications links. But a telecoms engineer had climbed up to the top of the hill in the gloaming, brought down a shattered junction box, fixed it and replaced it, restoring one phone line to the city post office for a few days at least.

I filed my stories, spoke to Paul telling him of my lucky escape, and then called my father to let him know I was okay. I hadn't thought ahead in any detail about how he might respond but, had I done so, I probably could have predicted it. Like many of his generation he was modestly travelled and, for him, there was physically near 'foreign', namely Western Europe, and there was culturally near 'foreign', namely the USA. He could be comfortable with both. I knew that my father's reaction to my finding myself besieged and having been seventy metres away from a potentially fatal hit was based on paternal concern but, for him, the Balkans were just too 'foreign'.

"If I were you, I'd just get the hell out of there, Michael," he said. "You're in a wild place with wild people. They don't play it by our rules."

He paused and added, "I don't really think the readers of *The Times* want to read about them either."

The last comment felt like a rebuke and I had to resist an urge to snap back; but I realised later that his words had clarified two things. First, given that he was a target reader, I couldn't rely on my conviction that intelligent *Times*, readers should be interested in events in Croatia. I had to interest them. But second, I was struck by the extent to which, just a few weeks into my 'mission', I was buying into these places and these people.

Branko, Ivana, the widow killed randomly in Mokošica, the lady who had lost her lower leg – I was taking their sides, and a sense of duty was growing within me, obliging me to reveal how this situation had come about and who was doing what to whom.

Another correspondent was hovering behind me, and I knew it was time to hand over the phone, now that my key calls had been made.

"It's okay, Dad. Don't worry. I'll be okay." I paused. "I guess that's the challenge, isn't it? To get the readers to want to read about this stuff." I didn't wait for the answer.

6
OCTOBER–NOVEMBER 1991

While JNA spokesmen had always insisted that Dubrovnik's Old Town would remain untouched provided its defenders didn't seek to use it as a launch pad for their attacks, picking my way through the streets some days into the siege, the damage was all too visible. And it was unlikely that the damage so far was entirely down to stray shells.

Storefront windows the length of the central promenade, the Stradun, had been shattered, as well as on the top floor of Dubrovnik's 640-year-old synagogue. There was a hole in the roof of the Rupe Museum, the Renaissance carvings that had decorated the Onofrio Fountain had been taken away and concealed in a safe place, and statues in the streets that local people were unable to remove were surrounded by planks to protect them from shrapnel damage. Sandbags were everywhere, shock absorbers that may or may not protect precious buildings and features.

A woman standing in the doorway of a house with blown-out windows in Boškovićeva Street, adjoining the Stradun, was keen to show me the extent of the damage done, once she learned that I was an international journalist: shrapnel holes in her walls, the staircase and even her bed. Her husband was stuck on one of the islands off the Adriatic Coast and couldn't break the blockade.

"And this is what we have to live on for a whole week – me and my four children."

She revealed, under the staircase, a box containing two tins of meat, two tins of fish, half a kilo of bread, half a kilo of potatoes, and small bottles of milk and cooking oil – her share of food supplies topped up intermittently by a ship sent from Split that the JNA tolerated on some days and blocked on others.

"They even shelled the Catholic cemetery when people were putting flowers on the graves of their loved ones. Can you imagine? Tell the world that! Put that in your newspaper, sir!"

"I will, I will," I promised as I left – the only succour I could offer.

Outside the walled city, there wasn't even the flimsy protection of a poorly enforced protectorate. It meant Dubrovnik's citizens within and beyond the Old Town were in a state of paralysis. They knew they were besieged but it didn't appear that the JNA or their agents were planning to take control of the city any time soon. Yet they could still be killed – randomly.

I did begin to wonder how long it might be before nearly everyone came to regard the abnormal as normal, just as the townsfolk of the quarantined, plague-infested town had in Camus' *La Peste*. Not long, I suspected.

If this was by far the strangest environment I had ever found myself in, it was the absurd, the vaguely ludicrous and the touchingly human aspects of the siege that at the same time appalled and appealed to me most, as a journalist and chronicler of human behaviour.

The absurd was best played out, as if in a West End theatre production, in and around the shorefront Hotel Argentina, set on a prime coastal location just half a mile south of the Old Town. Although the hotel had taken some early hits from JNA naval vessels, life went on within its whitewashed walls as if in some irreverent parody of normality.

It enjoyed some protection from full-frontal JNA assault due to the residence there of journalists and half a dozen European Community monitors but it was still exposed to the occasional random strafing. Nevertheless, the Argentina's staff endeavoured to keep up business as usual. They served breakfast on starched linen tablecloths, somehow conjured up three-course meals, raided the seemingly bottomless wine cellars and coolly switched from generator power to candlelight when the nine o'clock curfew kicked in.

For me, there was something slightly distasteful about wristy barmen in white jackets and black bowties shaking up a 'sex on the beach', the clunky ice-cube rattle an unlikely counterpoint to the whizz of the occasional rocket across the terrace. Not that I didn't avail myself of the wine list from time to time, as I popped in to hoover up the latest gossip from fellow journalists and from the glib EC monitors. Two thousand kilometres from Brussels, the monitors' sense of entitlement appeared to be undimmed but their value on the ground I found questionable.

The sense of absurdity probably reached its peak one day when, after one female journalist found herself stranded neck deep in the sea off the hotel terrace for three hours after a JNA naval assault interrupted her dip, I walked into the bar to witness one of the Konavlian refugees, the English wife of a Croatian from Čilipi, belting out 'It's a Long Way to Tipperary' to a barman's piano accompaniment.

I shook my head in bewilderment and heard myself saying out loud in staccato fashion, "THIS is ri-dic-u-lous."

A man with slicked-back black hair, wearing a Hawaiian shirt, bleary-eyed from red wine, looked up from his seat and said, "Chill out, kid. What are we supposed to do? Sit around and wring our hands?"

I didn't much appreciate being called 'kid' and I couldn't stay there to witness anymore of that pantomime.

If the absurd was played out at the Hotel Argentina, the vaguely ludicrous took place on a near-daily basis as the city's leaders mounted what I described in print as "a campaign of innocents". It was a scattergun attempt to rally support from any and every international figure they felt they could access, as if somehow Václav Havel or, one year after her political demise, Margaret Thatcher could knock some sense into leaders in Belgrade and Zagreb.

My sense of irritation at what I saw as a poorly focused campaign with minimal chance of success threatened to upgrade to outright scorn – targeted principally at Dubrovnik's mayor.

As a fifty-four-year-old agronomist, Pero Poljanić's laughter lines suggested a man accustomed to warmth and engagement rather than someone equipped to handle the impact of conflict on his citizens. I accepted that a city did not choose its representatives expecting to be the target of a military attack, but I found jarring Poljanić's total failure, despite his unquestionable articulacy, to make any attempt to boost the morale of his citizens.

He failed to keep them informed of any potential ceasefire negotiations that might give them hope and launched misguided initiatives, such as trying to ban alcohol sales to ensure the defenders of the city stayed sober. At this time, Dubrovnik needed different leadership.

My attempts at remaining patient and biting my tongue finally foundered at a Press conference at which Poljanić was flanked by a well-meaning but equally naïve Oxford University philosophy professor, a regular visitor to the city who had made it her mission, after landing in Dubrovnik just before the siege, to remain and to help prompt an international backlash. As if the outrage of the great and the good might provide some protective umbrella against bombardment.

"I can announce today that we have sent a fax to His Majesty, the Prince of Wales. We are inviting Prince Charles to visit our city to help prevent its destruction at the hands of Yugoslav federal troops," said Poljanić.

"In our fax, we say – and I quote: 'We would very much appreciate if you would help us preserve this city, which is part of the European and world cultural heritage.'"

I put up my hand but, before being called, heard myself launch into an outburst that could not conceal bewilderment edged with irritation. "Prince Charles?! Do you honestly believe for a nanosecond that Prince Charles: a) would even contemplate coming to Dubrovnik while the siege is on; and b) if he did, would have any impact at all on the situation. The skies are raining missiles and you're faxing Prince Charles! Really!

"We need to shame Europe and America's leaders into stepping in with hardware – not run through a who's who of global dignitaries."

As my comments hung in the air and an electric pulse appeared to course through me, I realised that my emotions had bled into my question. It was a heart-on-the-sleeve style to which my fellow journalists were becoming accustomed. Sometimes it was admired for its frankness; sometimes it was deemed inappropriate.

Poljanić took a moment to reply, his bloodhound eyes appearing to take on a further degree of sadness before he spoke.

"Sir. You are no doubt aware that His Royal Highness has already spoken out against the threatened destruction of Dubrovnik's Old Town.

If he chose to come, he would have to share the bombs and grenades with us. We may be housing thousands of refugees, but I personally will find him a safe place to stay. But let me say to you, sir. He is not a child. He knows the risks."

I raised my eyebrows skyward and exhaled in exasperation but chose to leave any follow-up questions to someone else. As I made my way out at the end of the Press conference, one of the British journalists passing me in the crowd shouted, "Good question, Mick! You really stuck it on him!"

"Thanks, mate," I replied. I couldn't help but think it would have been more useful if he had followed up with another question highlighting the folly of the mayor's approach, but perhaps it was my role to be the principal irritant to the inept and the incompetent.

But if I was irked by the absurdities of the Hotel Argentina and frustrated by the mayor's 'campaign of innocents', I was moved and inspired by the human sorrow and suffering that manifested itself in cameos snatched within and just beyond the Old Town. And I became convinced that, exceptionally, it was boredom that sharpened the trauma of Dubrovnik's citizens.

Normally, boredom is a numbing force. Here, far from numbing, boredom froze people in a perpetual anxiety about their plight: trapped, unable to go about their day, turned constantly inward, never able to let their consciousness drift into a comforting, neutral state of mind for much more than a minute before being pulled back into the reality of their enforced inertia by the click of a door handle, the cough of a partner, or the trill of a bird somewhere on top of a neighbour's house.

Normally boredom could be nullified by activity, but here it stretched out endlessly, punctured only by sporadic shelling – shelling which brought a strange, split-second relief to the besieged, until they came to their senses and realised even boredom was preferable to fear, to ear-splitting blasts or, heaven forfend, to the loss of one's loved ones. With no electricity, there was no light to read by after dusk, the daily trip to collect water rations the only pursuit that resembled activity – and one that, itself, could be risky.

"Paralysis that silences a gilded city's caged songbirds" ran the headline of one of my pieces, the sub-editor having lifted and highlighted one of my flights of prose. And I drew for my readers prose pictures of the woman with the blonde rinse sheltering in the catacombs, of Marta's struggle with the 'illogicality' of evil and her hopes for a more tolerant kind of civic disagreement in a post-siege Dubrovnik. And I tried to capture the grinding of the gears of relationships under strain, like that of the couple in their fifties in my neighbourhood who I heard through an open window, suddenly thrown together for twenty-four hours a day with none of the safety valves that work, walks and external friendships normally provided.

"Marko, calm down. Don't get so angry. There's nothing we can do. Don't make yourself feel worse," I heard the woman plead.

"Calm down?! Calm down?! I can't calm down, woman. I'm going mad in here."

It was a snatched moment, but I felt I could sense his wife's delicate diplomacy. I sensed it was a skill honed over years, securing their relationship by a sanguine acceptance of his volatility and by the pressure release of the hours each day they normally spent apart. If this reflected an imbalance experienced all over the world's male-dominated societies, the circumstances were exacerbating the violence of this man's swings of temperament and testing to the limit his wife's ability to dampen these upward and downward lurches and still remain standing.

When I told her the story, Marta said she knew the couple and bore out much of my intuition. She told me that, at one point, a young couple in their apartment block had had to knock at the door, concerned that the husband's violent language might risk tipping into a physical assault.

"Thank you for your concern, my dear. But we're fine. He's just frustrated. Don't worry. He'd never lay a finger on me," the lady had said at the door of her flat.

The intervention had appeared to have punctured her husband's aggression and silence fell within.

"I just hope he doesn't blow at some point and do her some real damage," said Marta. "He's not a bad man – but he's hot-headed. If I see him out and about, I'll let him know I'm watching and that, if anything happens to her, he'll have me to answer to."

It was a threat that I knew I would heed, were Marta to feel the need to point her moral compass at me.

And if small family units were under pressure, the broader community did not always hang together in solidarity either. Early in the siege, a group of residents broke down the door of the Saint Jeremiah Seminary, accusing the monks inside of hoarding water. They shouldered the rector aside and filled their urns before parting with volleys of abuse about the brothers' lack of self-sacrifice, empathy, and Christian charity. It was another breakdown of community morale that could have been avoided, had Mayor Poljanić and his gang had more gumption about uniting and rallying the community, I reflected. Or had I reached a conclusion and was now simply looking to heap blame for everything on the civic leader?

In the lulls between the shelling, when I met people sliding discreetly through the streets, seeking out relatives and friends to complain to or console, I found exasperation the only emotion threatening to dislodge the boredom. People knew that their forces were massively outnumbered and outgunned and yet this was a strange kind of siege that lacked the scale and the violence of the destruction of Vukovar. Was the JNA trying to take the city or was it not? Would things get better or dramatically worse?

Soon enough I would discover what was behind this on-off campaign and its almost painful sluggishness. Saša popped up one day at the daily Press conference, having been smuggled into the city overnight with a couple of journalist colleagues in a small boat whose skipper, for a price, had defied the blockade of the port.

Chipper as ever and with the swagger of a man you might have thought had just risen from an eight-hour sleep and emerged from a piping-hot shower, Saša clasped my hand, smiled, and said, "Michael! How are we? How are we in this gilded cage of songbirds?"

I glowed. I not only felt that Saša's arrival meant that the grown-ups had landed, I was thrilled by the thought that Saša had read my article, even if he was teasing me for my florid prose.

"Bastard!" I growled at him with a smile on my face. Our subsequent mock tussle was likely to have fooled nobody. This was a man hug, masquerading as fun fight.

Coming afresh to the situation from outside the Dubrovnik cocoon some of us had been living in, Saša highlighted the flaw in the reporting of the siege to date: we had been reporting the story only from the point of view of the besieged. We needed to get some insights into the minds of the invading forces – in large part to understand why their siege lacked the components of a traditional siege, such as forces in a tight ring around the city and coordinated attempts to take control of it using superior firepower.

Typically, Saša already had a plan in his back pocket and I felt privileged to learn that I was part of it. I felt less comfortable as we edged our way in the dark towards Trebinje, a pro-Serbian town just over the border with Bosnia, in an old car he had borrowed from a local hack.

It was the closest I had come physically to groups of Chetniks. They hung in and around the doorway of the Tri Šeširi club, most sporting long hair, beards, and T-shirts bearing the words 'Freedom or Death' and a skull and crossbones design. They appeared to be hoping someone might bump into them, spill their beer, and justify a rumble. But, despite his relatively diminutive size, Saša disarmed them with a confident "Zdravo, druge!" – "Hi, guys!" – and I picked my way through carefully in his footsteps.

We were meeting Arian, the nephew of one of Saša's high-grade contacts – a senior Belgrade security official. Arian's uncle, unusually, had made it to the top despite being of Kosovo Albanian descent.

As Arian tucked away the military pistol he had placed on the table like some kind of bizarre speed-dating symbol to identify him to us and to warn off troublemakers, he explained why he hadn't fled to Germany to dodge the draft, as two of his cousins had.

"Uncle advised me not to do a runner. 'If they catch you, they'll kill you – and, if you escape, you can't come home again,' he said. He told me just to do my eighteen months and, as best I could, keep out of trouble."

Arian explained that, like most Kosovo Albanians, he had never bought into the concept of Yugoslavia. His mother had adored Albania's late leader Enver Hoxha and the family had toasted the death of Tito in 1980.

Two years ago, he and his college friends had had to carry away one of their classmates from the barricades in the city streets of Mitrovica after police used live ammunition against a student protest at the removal by Slobodan Milošević of Kosovo's twenty-five-year-old autonomous status.

"His leg was shattered and he was screaming in agony but we had to carry him away in case the police moved in and beat him to death," he said. "So, as you can imagine, I wasn't wild about signing up."

When I expressed my bewilderment at JNA tactics which were imposing a kind of paralysis on Dubrovnik's citizens without appearing to have any clear goal, Arian said there were clear reasons for what he called 'Foxtrot War'.

"It's slow-slow-quick-quick – but without much of the quick-quick," he said – and he laughed.

The plan had been to seize a big slab of Croatia from south of Dubrovnik right up as far as Split, he told us.

"But further north I'm told we had recruitment problems and we ran into better-organised Croatian forces. So, we're the bottom half of a pincer movement with no top half to our pincer!

"The idea originally was to pile pressure on Zagreb and get them to rethink their push for independence. But is there a chance of that happening now? No way, no way."

Poor leadership and the lack of a just, easily explicable war aim capable of rallying disparate recruits from across Yugoslavia's federal republics were also to blame for a less-than-smooth descent upon Dubrovnik, he said. I could see now that the random nature of the shelling in and around the city spoke eloquently of a campaign in which individual initiatives prevailed and clear tactics and coordinated action were not so much relegated as virtually non-existent.

I told Arian about my experience of the men from the Montenegrin mountains, as the siege had been launched. He said he had been in one of the units following behind.

He said, "When we were moving through the Konavle district, we came across one young Montenegrin. He can only have been fourteen or fifteen years of age. He was herding six magnificent, fat cows back south. 'Where the hell are you going, kid?' I asked him. Cool as you like, he replied, 'I'm going back home. My war objectives have been achieved.'"

But Arian said it wasn't just the wild men from Montenegro who were looting. It was JNA captains too.

"It was as if they saw those out-of-control kids making a killing and thought they should have a slice of the action too."

By the time Arian's unit reached an airport south of Dubrovnik at Čilipi, they realised the leadership was out of control.

"It was pretty much a free-for-all. We were too late. We missed what some of the guys described as the party of a lifetime. The duty-free had been stripped and drunk dry. The place was a scene of devastation. And one of the guys told me that, before the real mayhem broke out, his captain had stood on a box of vodka bottles and warned his officers, 'Anyone getting stuck in before I've filled my boots will get a bullet between the eyes.'"

Saša and I laughed. Arian creased a thin smile, as if he were not really amused. He paused.

"It was pretty despicable, to be honest. These were our leaders, after all. We'd been trained not to loot, and here they were, cashing in. These are weak leaders and pretty poor human beings. These are not leaders you want to die for. This is not a cause you want to die for. I mean, who are we fighting for? Yugoslavia? Serbia?

"The irony is me and my tight group – six of us – we're an example of the best of Yugoslavia. We trained together, we laugh together, we fight together, and we look after each other. There's me – a Kosovo Albanian – two Bosnian guys, a Serbian guy and, before they refused to fight their own people, two Croatian guys, one from Split and another from Zagreb. We're like brothers. We'd die for each other.

"We wouldn't die for the Federation – none of us. We might fight for our states but only if their freedom was threatened. But we'd die for each other. No question. So far, for me, these friendships – they're the only good things to come out of this whole senseless episode."

Arian said he fully expected the JNA to complete the move north eventually and to surround the city, but there would be no attempt to breach the Old Town and occupy it.

"Once you get into hand-to-hand combat, that's when you start racking up the casualties. We've got way more firepower and manpower than the Croats but, if you go hand-to-hand, you level the playing field.

"But we'll have to do some kind of deal. We can't sit up on the hills around Dubrovnik and have potshots taken at us. Let's hope even our idiot leaders are working on a ceasefire or some kind of demilitarisation.

"There's already an agreement – I don't know how formal or informal it is – that we won't fire into the Old Town, if they don't use its walls and its ramparts to fire at us. And, I think, so far, so good."

I thought of the damage I'd witnessed first-hand in the Old Town but chose not to contradict Arian's 'so far, so good' assessment.

The conversation wound down. It was time for us to make our way back. Navigating the group of Chetniks was a still more delicate exercise, given the additional alcohol they had taken on board since we landed, but soon Saša was driving us out of town, each kilometre put between us and this town's undisguised menace bringing me a degree of relief.

Apparently unruffled by our experience, Saša said, "You know, Mick, I don't mind them being called up for a spot of harmless national service, but these kids should be off to college, travelling abroad, spreading their wings. Not involved in a stupid conflict that our leaders are incapable of justifying. I just hope this madness is stopped before an entire generation is lost."

But something else was happening in that car. My heart was warming as I sensed that this risky episode, which initially had seemed to me to have all the elements required of a wild goose chase, represented a deepening of my friendship with Saša.

I didn't quite understand why my experienced, self-confident colleague was offering me a free ticket to experiences that only he with his extensive contacts and local knowledge could generate. If it was more than simple generosity, I hadn't yet identified what it was.

The following morning, when I came downstairs, Marta looked relieved to see me.

"You were out late, Mick," she said.

"Yes, it was a bit of a crazy night." I paused, then qualified. "I mean, it was work… Don't ask, but a couple of us hopped over the border to Trebinje to see how the mood is on the other side."

"Well, I won't ask you how those people justify what they're doing but I'm glad you're back and safe."

Marta was referring to claims that some of the shelling of Dubrovnik was coming out of Trebinje.

I was beginning to feel increasingly like a surrogate son to Marta, her own two children in their thirties now, educated and established and far away in 'safe' cities in Britain and the United States. And no doubt generous, well-rounded citizens, I suspected, having been reared by Marta and a father that she never mentioned but who lived on, looking kindly out of black and white photos on the sitting-room wall and the sideboard.

I had told her about how I had lost my Croatian mother, and her unspoken, waxing surrogacy touched me. She brought me a different kind of assurance to Saša's presence and support. Even to Saša, I still felt I had to exhibit a certain bravado that I didn't possess, though I guessed Saša knew that in my case it was at best superficial and an attribute on which I placed no value.

Male reporters never talked to each other about fear; but at that moment, in Marta's kitchen, I wondered whether I might find some comfort in sharing my self-doubt with her. Admitting vulnerability to a surrogate mother emerged out of the blue as an attractive option: a secret I was tired of keeping allowed out, admitted to.

The question to her might be couched between the lines, but it would sound something like "It is okay to worry and to be afraid, isn't it?" And what might Marta say? Would she say simply, "Yes, it is, and we're grateful to people like you for telling the world about what we're suffering." Or would she say, "For the love of God, Mick, get yourself out of here and save your own skin. We have to be here. You don't."

I wasn't quite ready to ask her the question but, alongside the sense that she might provide me with support, another realisation was dawning. I had noticed that I was beginning to have to fight for space in the paper. Events such as Middle East peace talks in Madrid and the mysterious death of the soon-to-be-disgraced UK newspaper tycoon, Robert Maxwell, were threatening to crowd out the slower burn of reports of a city under siege. But I knew that I was not giving up on this complex conflict. I would only leave Yugoslavia if ordered to or if the whole drama fizzled out. Whether I would situate myself anywhere near the firing lines was the real question to which I currently had no answer. Perhaps like an accident, like fear, those lines would come to me.

How much danger might I expose myself to? How brutal might this war become? What might I have to witness or hear recounted, if the first signs of an excessively forceful response to complicated, often invented, sources of conflict were anything to go by? Was it inevitable that I would acquire Saša's subtly calibrated ability to assess risk: no to trips to bombarded Vukovar; yes to a late-night trip into the den of dangerous Serbian nationalists? Or might I stumble into trouble through inexperience?

I suspected I would never acquire the addiction to war that was the hallmark of some of the best-known war reporters, but I was undoubtedly experiencing a deepening empathy towards a war's victims: one that might place on me obligations to stick around and do my bit to help, wielding the flimsiest of weapons – prose.

"That friend of yours was round last night, when you were out," said Marta. "Branko Komlenac. Lovely man. I was at their wedding, you know. Lovely couple. He told me to tell you that Ivana's gone."

"She's gone! Gone where?!"

"He managed to get her on a Red Cross relief boat and she's headed for Pula. They've got relatives there. She'll be safe. She didn't want to go but Branko persuaded her it was for the best. What with the baby coming."

My instantaneous reaction was of shock – but, as the shock of the news ebbed, the sensation felt to me more like loss. I had form in falling head over heels with women I barely knew, I admit. My affections latched onto their objects precipitately; but if all I had was a crush on Ivana, it was creating within me something akin to mild panic.

"It can't be… I have to see her again," was the loop repeating in my mind. And I ached inwardly at the thought of her hair parted and neatly tied back, those clean, plain, beautiful features and that aura of calm and quiet contentment.

"He wants you to go round and see him. He said something about going up the hill. He said you'd know what he meant."

"Okay, okay… Thanks, Marta."

If Marta sensed that I had tuned out, she didn't let on. I excused myself and took to the deserted streets to brood a while and to try to dull the emotional shock that had hit me quite out of the blue.

I wasn't ready straightaway to go and talk to Branko. Nor did I want a great internal debate about what was and was not a reasonable reaction to the news. Instead, attempting to dislodge introspection, I went first to Gruž port and then to the peninsula of Babin Kuk, a chic area that I had rightly forecast would become a target of JNA missiles.

It was clear that, as well as military casualties on both sides, the number of civilian casualties was ticking up – close to fifty in the first few weeks of the siege, according to the Red Cross. The random scatter of bombed-out houses and shops spoke of innocent victims whose stories would be told by no journalist, whose senseless tragedies would be recounted in coming years only by family and neighbours.

By early evening, I had rallied sufficiently to enable me to call on Branko without revealing the bruises on my heart. I could barely imagine the sense of loss that he would be undergoing, though I knew he would show none of it.

"I know you'll miss her, Branko, but I'm glad you were able to get her away to safety. It makes sense, doesn't it?" I said.

"Yes," said Branko. "They're letting out the odd boatload of women and children now – but any male aged eighteen to sixty is stuck here. Not allowed to leave. It took some doing, persuading her to leave – but I managed it in the end."

But Branko moved quickly onto his reason for dropping in to find me at Marta's the night before. He and his fellow defenders of the city had now established a routine for manning the fort at the top of Srđ Hill and a timetable for swapping out shifts.

"I've been up a few times, Mick, and we've got it all off pat now. If you're up for it, I think we can take you up there. The JNA are gradually massing forces up there, but our experience is that the fort is really solid. We can do just enough to stop them getting up much closer. And they can't really dislodge us at present. So, you should be pretty safe.

"I've talked to the other boys and they agree with me: if we can get some coverage in the international Press, then I think it might be good for us."

"You mean 'Plucky defenders of the city, holding the Yugoslav Army at bay against the odds'? That kind of thing?" I said.

"Well, it's your call, Mick. We're happy to show you how it is up there. Then you do with it what you think is right."

I said I would gladly take up the offer. If things didn't change, there was only so long I could go on finding new angles about random shelling with no apparent strategy and about gloom turning to despair at the mounting death toll in the city.

Two nights later, about an hour after dusk fell and the shells stopped flying, I stood at the foot of Srđ Hill, dressed in dark, warm clothing borrowed from Branko's wardrobe, cuffs and trouser legs rolled, given that Branko's frame was considerably more athletic than my own. As well as Branko, another five men were gathered there in combat jackets and helmets, three of them around Branko's age, another around ten years older, and the final member of the team a solid, squat man in his forties with a thick, neat moustache. A donkey laden with full baskets manoeuvred quietly behind them, occasionally lifting and replacing a hoof delicately without any sense of specific direction.

"Hi. I'm Dragan. You'll be needing this helmet," whispered the man with the moustache.

I shook hands with each of the men and slipped on the helmet. Dragan then picked up what looked like a rifle but with a barrel wider than any gun I had ever seen – a weapon I would come to realise later was a grenade launcher. I must have let my discomfort at handling any kind of weaponry show in my expression even by torchlight because Dragan laid a gloved hand on my shoulder affectionately and said gently, "Don't worry. You just need to carry it up the hill. I won't ask you to use it!"

I was just beginning to still the question in my mind as to whether it was ethical for me to carry weapons for either side, when Branko whispered with urgency, "Come on, guys. Let's get going before the shells start flying again. Ante, have you got Sherlock?"

"Yes, I've got him," said Ante, wrapping a rope attached to the donkey's bridle round his wrist and patting its nose. Ante was a small, squat man with a dark moustache and beard, a crumpled haircut and sleepy eyes.

Branko turned to me. "Ante's donkey is called Sherlock. He's named after your great English detective. He's not very bright – but he's good as gold. Quiet as a mouse. Loyal as a lapdog."

Several months earlier, had you said I would find myself in southern Croatia in the dark in combat helmet, holding a grenade launcher, at the foot of a cliff with a donkey, I could have imagined no circumstances that would have taken me there. Here and now, somehow it felt less than preposterous.

The climb up to Fort Imperial was steep and hairpinned. It was impossible to move too quickly, but I was nonetheless pleased I was able to keep up with these fit, mainly young men. Thirty-five minutes later, we were slipping into a small gap in the entrance to the fort and swapping places with another six men, who unloaded and reloaded Sherlock's baskets and set off back down the hill with the donkey.

I felt alive with exhilaration, as I sat in a dark room the size, I imagined, of a top division football club's dressing room. The room contained a couple of dozen Croatian soldiers, some of them rolled in blankets and trying to sleep, others sitting with their forearms resting on their thighs, reflecting inwardly on who knew what. I just wanted to sit quietly for a while, unnoticed. I didn't want day to dawn. I knew that the material for my next piece would take shape in due course. There was no need to force it. I felt safe in what appeared to be concrete rooms tucked below ground level. I hadn't understood earlier Branko's explanation of Fort Imperial's near-impregnability, but I did now. Thrill briefly outdid fear in what felt like a unique, privileged place in the middle of an unorthodox war. A man thrust a tin cup at me, and the hot, sweet, black coffee in it tasted like the best drink I had ever had. I felt a fresh pang of exhilaration.

But, of course, dawn did begin to break. And before the light sharpened, Dragan sought me out and led me to a vantage point within the fort that offered a view that I calculated stretched beyond the southern tip of Croatia as far as the mountain tops of Montenegro. Beyond stretches of woodland beneath Srđ Hill, south of Dubrovnik, there was an exposed range of hills – just an expanse of creamy-grey rock tinged with veins of purple. I could pick out a hairpin track jagging its way up and down the middle of the grey rock, but it looked like a makeshift trail rather than part of the road network and any vehicle using it would be exposed.

"That's not great territory for the JNA beyond the trees. We could reach them with our best weapons, if they were to be visible from here," said Dragan. "South of the town, it's not great terrain for tanks either – so that's slowing them down as well. We just look out for where their shells are coming from and then have a pop back at them. Just try to pin them down and stop them from getting too close. We try to use the minimum amount of ammunition – just enough to stop them from getting too cavalier.

"When their shells fly, sometimes they overshoot the fort and land on the scrubland behind us; sometimes they explode on the hill in front of the fort."

"Do you get used to them?" I asked.

Dragan paused. "Hmmm. Good question," he said. "I haven't really asked myself that for a while. I think, mainly, they've just become part of the soundtrack of the town for the last few weeks."

I registered the phrase 'the soundtrack of the town', making a mental note to recycle it in my next piece.

"But then you'll get one that lands really close and it feels as if it's shaking the foundations of the fort. And that does shake you up. Reminds you it's real war – not just some kind of game," said Dragan.

He then led me to a vantage point at the opposite side of the fort.

"You just need to see this, Mick," he said.

"Why? Do they bomb from the north too?" I asked.

"No. There's shelling of the suburbs north of the town but not much that gets this far – but you just need to drink this in. It's such a beautiful view… as day dawns."

I was momentarily taken aback by Dragan's abrupt shift from soldier and leader to sensitive, bucolic observer. But then I did drink in the view: a breathtaking palette of grey tones, the islands of Koločep, Lopud and Šipan nestled like the outlines of Mesozoic beasts in a gently trembling surface of sea that the wind was barely caressing. Above, the clouds rippled out concentrically from cream to dark grey around a slim oval of sky just beginning to acquire shades of blue. It was cloud that sunrise would gradually but inexorably burn away, but this was a magical transformation, happening more slowly than the brain could compute or the eye clearly register.

Someone had tied two pieces of wood into a makeshift crucifix and laid it against a pyramid of rocks that tourists had built up, each adding their own individual stone over the years. There was a poignancy to its simplicity and the way in which it had been laid casually: the sacrifice of the Cross fighting for space against a paradisean, littoral panorama that sought to absorb entirely the viewer's attention, fighting too against the thought ever present in the back of the mind of the advancing forces and the threat they represented.

"It's quite magnificent, isn't it?" I said.

"In peace and in war, it's a life-enhancing sight. This is what we're fighting for. The right to enjoy our land. When this is all over," said Dragan, gesturing with his right arm in the direction of the JNA forces south of the city, "I'll come up here every dawn or dusk, just to revel in the fact that this is ours. No one will take this from us."

"And you don't entertain the prospect of defeat?" I asked.

"No, I don't, Mick… I just don't."

Dragan's lyricism had emerged from within quite unexpectedly. And when we went back into the heart of the fort and I watched him firmly but sensitively exercising his authority over the younger soldiers, advising, cajoling, directing, I felt like the holder of a sacred secret. This experienced, effective soldier kept a candle burning within him that glowed unseen. His sensitivity fastened his soul to his landscape. He had that priceless gift that not everyone shared: a soul that swelled at the sight of natural beauty, a man diminished were he to be deprived of his landscapes. And I wondered whether he might be a painter – or perhaps wrote poetry that he shared with no one.

Over the next three days I went after my task with vigour, greedily devouring every personal detail I could elicit from the professionals and amateurs who had banded together to mount the resistance. As well as the trained soldiers and policemen, the volunteers who had signed up to the 116 Brigade were largely young working men: mechanics like Branko, farmhands like Ante, barmen, a baker. The lack of either a butcher or candlestick maker would enable me to avoid cliché, I reflected wryly.

If I was becoming weary at my own interminable, internal questions about bravery and what it constituted, I found little clanging heroism in these ranks. None of the volunteers appeared to be out to prove anything. They were simply young, fit, practical men intent on preventing their city from being overrun. Theirs was matter-of-fact resistance, not one paraded with a view to garnering plaudits or gratitude. They imbibed with earnestness the lessons in weaponry, positioning and timing that the likes of Dragan passed on and, over the three days that I was there, I witnessed episodes of quiet satisfaction as the baker delivered a well-targeted grenade or the barman developed a facility for handling an automatic rifle. I could only imagine the warm glow within that each triumph kindled.

For these men, bravery was not something they oozed or appeared anxious to exhibit; it was a natural reaction to the dangers to which they were exposed. A reservist or volunteer would only fail the bravery test if he fled in the face of fire. None of them fled, as the grenades and the shells and the rockets whistled and crashed beyond, adjacent to and in front of the fort.

For me, the explosions that began about forty-five minutes after my tour d'horizon with Dragan were variations on my Malo Selo experience, the incoming whistle, crunch and bang shockingly close and ear-splittingly loud at times, at others more muffled and rumbling. And I came to hear each missile in a volley as a note in an unlikely cadence. They came in spates and then there was silence. Sweet silence. Silence that sometimes endured but sometimes was abruptly punctured by another volley. And as soon after a volley as Dragan and the other leaders estimated that it was safe, a counter volley of grenades and artillery ammunition was sent back from the fort with a view to pinning down and holding back any further advance of the JNA.

Inside the fort, as down in the streets of the city and its outskirts, at moments time stretched out tediously. But at least there was a tightening bond of camaraderie in this bunker. Volunteers-turned-soldiers would swap stories, discover mutual acquaintances, and grow closer without the claustrophobia that plagued many cooped up in apartments and houses below.

And then the baker would emerge with delicious meals extraordinarily conjured from the most basic of ingredients. A break in the tedium. A flood of compliments, as the men eagerly cleared their plates, the act of sharing food communally, just as in families, bringing them still closer.

After three days, I felt I had captured the essence of this hastily assembled but increasingly coherent resistance group. I was now keen to see out my last day and then find a means of filing my stories and share with the world my exclusive peek into the world of Dubrovnik's defenders.

But, with the JNA's frontlines nudging closer to the city, the most advanced perhaps just a few hundred metres away, on my final morning Dragan was keen to try to put some more space between Srđ Hill and the Yugoslav Army. Five men were firing off volleys from automatic rifles, hidden behind the battlements of the fort, aiming in the direction of where they suspected the JNA frontline was concealed; but Dragan and Branko had rigged up a grenade launcher behind the fort, ready to deliver a riposte after the usual early morning shelling of the fort had eased.

The six-foot barrel, propped at an angle by two folding legs and sitting on a circular baseplate, hardly looked high-tech to me.

"Hundred-and-twenty-mill shell, nearly sixteen kilos," said Dragan, and he let me feel its weight before he held it over the barrel. "It's all very well our snipers pinning them down but this might give them something more to think about. I'm going to drop this in and then you turn your back and drop down to your knees because it'll go off pretty much straightaway."

"How far will it fly?" I asked.

"A couple of miles. We've calibrated it as best we can at an area where we think there's a JNA group massing – but it's guesswork. We're mainly just looking to put the wind up them."

Dragan paused. "Ready?"

"Yep."

Dragan dropped the shell into the top of the barrel and turned away. Branko and I did the same a split second later. Within three seconds there was a huge bang, a puff of smoke, a short silence and then a distant crump as the shell landed in the distance. But no sooner had that sound begun to echo than another explosion took place. We looked up and out across the hills. Then there was another explosion and another, as smoke billowed and fire flashed in the target area.

"Holy shit!" Dragan shouted. "Bullseye! I think we've hit an ammo stockpile!"

Dragan and Branko high-fived. I grinned.

"Was that brilliance or a complete fluke, Dragan?" I asked.

"It was brilliance… with a bit of fluke added in!" Dragan laughed.

"Quick, let's get this away before they fire back."

Yet if this was a little triumph for the resistance, we wouldn't know for some time that it was a strike that would have inordinate consequences for Dubrovnik. The captain leading the unit hit by the shell witnessed his best friend being blown up as the ammunition in the back of a lorry took a hit and exploded. If there had been already some shelling of the Old Town – by accident or on purpose – this captain would now actively ignore the order handed down from above not to attack the area within the city walls and would begin lobbing a sustained and deeply damaging bombardment of shells and grenades into the heart of the city with predictable consequences.

Later that day, after the JNA shelling stopped and dusk thickened into dark, I shook hands with the men staying in the fort, Branko included, and set off with a small group back down the hill, Sherlock's hooves clopping quietly but reassuringly at the back of the crocodile line.

I let myself into Marta's and slept deeply, the exhaustion of three days of exhilaration, absorption and tension tugging me deep beneath the surface of consciousness. I was aware of some distant explosions in the early hours but didn't surface properly till the middle of the bright, sunlit November morning. I ate an apple – apples were everywhere, the one commodity the people of Dubrovnik never ran short of – and I set about composing my pieces for *The Times*, plunging again into that creative reservoir that gave me such stimulation, such satisfaction.

When friends said to me that today's newspapers were just tomorrow's fish and chip wrappers, I didn't care. For me, it was as if each story were carved on discrete little tablets of stone. Once polished, completed, and submitted, though they were gone, for me they continued to exist, hanging somewhere in the air like holy offerings. Aspic-preserved. And, though there was a lady in the newspaper library with feline spectacles and an irrepressible addiction to tobacco whose job it was to snip and file on microfiche every article of substance, for me each serious composition added to a choate body of knowledge out there, however patchily readers scanned their papers. All the more important, then, that my version was as close to the truth as I could possibly make it, each shade and nuance identified and described, their significance weighed in the most sensitive of balances.

7
NOVEMBER 1991

A couple of hours after waking, I stepped out into a street still drenched in sharp November sunlight, the air entering my lungs like a refreshing drink. My scripts were folded inside my jacket pocket. I felt as though I was delivering precious cargo.

As I walked down towards the Old Town, heading for the office in the Town Hall where I could file my copy, a man in his fifties on the other side of the road, hugging the wall as if in fear of gunshot, shouted over.

"Careful how you go, sir! They've been shelling the Old Town today. There's a fair bit of new damage. Casualties too." He paused. "Bastards!" the man added, then headed back up the hill away from the Old Town.

"Thank you. I'll mind how I go."

Given the warning, I decided to slip through the side streets rather than take the most direct route down to the Old Town. As I turned the corner into a narrow street, I noticed charring around the space where the first-floor window of a house across the road had been. It was reminiscent of the house in Malo Selo in which the old lady had died from a direct hit from a shell. In this instance, thin ribbons of smoke drifted sporadically out of the hole in the wall. I crossed the road and peered through the mesh fencing, past the straggly, untamed buddleia bushes in front of the house.

Was this one of the places that the morning's shells had struck? Almost certainly, I thought. Between the bushes I saw two little girls sitting on the front step. Eight and five years old, I guessed. I edged to the right of the main bush and stood at the gate to the property. I heard the elder girl saying to her little sister, "No, Azra. We're not going back into the house."

"Hello?" I called across to the girls. The elder sister looked round, stood up and walked towards me, gripping her sister's hand tightly, as if it were essential to keep her from the house.

"*Gospodine, da li biste nam pomogli? Bomba je pogodila našu kuću.*" Sir, are you able to help us? A bomb hit our house. The girl was faultlessly polite and showing no signs of trauma.

"Sure, sure," I said. I unclicked the gate and stepped through.

I was aware of my heart rate picking up rapidly. A controllable but creeping, invasive sense of panic began flooding through me — as if it were a real tide flushing gradually through me. The sensations preceded my crystallising the thought *Hell! What am I going to find in here?*

I walked towards the threshold of the house. "Are your mum and dad not here with you?" I asked.

The elder sister, walking a pace ahead of me, turned and said, "I'll show you."

She stopped, unhooked her hand from her little sister's and, pointing a finger at her, said sternly, "Azra, you stay here! Right? I have to show the man."

Azra said nothing but stopped. I wasn't convinced she would remain obedient.

The elder sister opened the front door, releasing billows of smoke. After the smoke had ebbed, I followed her into the house. Though the ground floor was largely intact, there was a big gap in the ceiling and rubble and dust was strewn and sprinkled across the floors and the furniture. The girl beckoned to me and scaled the staircase to the right of the front door. It was undamaged but for the top two steps, a gap which the girl skipped over.

Outside the bedroom at the top of the stairs, she whispered, "Mummy and Daddy are in here — but I don't want Azra to see them."

I stepped into the room. Light streamed in through the huge hole punched in the left wall by a shell or a rocket. There was a man lying flat on the floor, chest down, to the left of the bed, in trousers and a patterned jumper. His head had been blown off completely. Only the blood and the plasticky mush of melted flesh pieces smeared on the floor and the walls nearby remained of it. My body was convulsed in a spasm but I stayed on my feet, aware that the little girl was just a step behind me. I looked to my right and saw a woman in a dress and cardigan lying on – or most likely knocked onto – the double bed. She was on her back. Her head was still attached to her body but it had spread out, its features indistinguishable, like a huge watermelon that had dropped, smashed and pulped on the ground.

"*Oh, my God!*" I couldn't stop the exclamation. I wanted to shout, "*No! No! No!*" but I managed to suppress the words. I wanted to wind back the clock, send the rocket into reverse, undo the damage, resurrect these parents, make so that this mindless violence targeted at no foe had never happened. I wanted too to step out of this role of responsibility into which I had walked. But I couldn't. I wouldn't. No one would.

All of a sudden, my stomach heaved. Searing, acid liquid rushed up my windpipe into my throat and spewed onto the floor, its lumpy, half-digested, vegetal contents sprinkling at the foot of the bed. There was an intense pressure in my head but without pain. I gasped to pull in some air, tried to slow my breathing. I had to regain some composure for the girls.

I wiped the vomit from my lips with the bedspread and turned to the elder sister just as Azra's head peeped round the frame of the door.

"Are Mummy and Daddy going to be okay, Delila?" asked Azra. She spoke out loud instead of with what would have seemed more appropriate – the whisper of the devout in a consecrated space.

"Azra! I told you not to come in!" said Delila in a harsh whisper. She paused. "No, they're not okay. They haven't got heads anymore. Now come away."

Delila led Azra away from the threshold of the room. I couldn't tell what Azra had or hadn't seen. Before I turned to follow them, I heard Azra asking matter-of-factly, "How can we get heads back for them, Delila?"

Delila let the question hang in the air. The silence may have been just seconds, but I had time to ask myself, "What will she say?"

Delila replied coolly but with unmistakable compassion towards her little sister, "I don't think we can, Azra. I think we'll need a new mummy and daddy."

The girls picked their way down the staircase and, trembly and weak,

I followed shortly after. I wasn't able to frame quite how I might handle the situation but, as I followed the girls out of the house, I turned and pulled the door to.

"Here, girls. Let's just sit down here for a minute. I sat on the front step and gathered the girls to me, Delila under my left arm and Azra under my right. I gave them a squeeze.

"So – you're Azra and you're Delila. Right?"

"Yes," said Delila.

"Well, I'm Mick… And how old are you, Delila?"

"I'm seven and Azra is five."

"I'm five and a quarter," corrected Azra.

"And when did the bomb come, Delila?"

"It was about two hours ago. The clock said nine o'clock when it happened. But then it stopped working so I don't really know. We were playing downstairs and there was this big crash. And I grabbed Azra and ran out of the house. There was fire and smoke. After a while, I went back in and found Mummy and Daddy."

"Okay, okay. You were very brave, Delila. And clever." I paused. "And you too, Azra. So – listen. We're all going to be okay. Right?"

I wasn't sure whether this make-it-up-as-you-go child psychology was what was needed. Delila seemed to be holding it together for Azra. Azra may have been too young to understand. I hoped she hadn't had a sight of the corpses, hoped she'd be spared the recurring nightmares of those images.

"Now, do you have any aunties or uncles round here, Delila?"

"No," said Delila. "Once we went to see my auntie in Germany. But that was ages ago. When Azra was just a baby."

"And what about your neighbours? Are they your friends?"

"Sort of," said Delila. "But one is an old lady, and there's a man, but we don't see him much."

"Okay, girls. I'll tell you what we're going to do. We're going to go and see a lovely lady and she'll look after you, while we sort out your house… and your mummy and daddy."

I didn't know how to phrase it, but I had no other words. And I couldn't leave the girls' parents unacknowledged.

"Has the lady got a doggie?" asked Azra.

"Azra!" Delila looked exasperated. "She's always talking about dogs… We were going to get one. Before they started the bombing."

"No, Azra," I said. "She hasn't got a dog but she knows someone who has. We can go and see him. Maybe later. Maybe tomorrow."

And I took each girl by the hand and headed back in the direction of the hill out of town. They were beautiful girls. Chestnut hair and strong, wide-set brown eyes. They couldn't have been anything other than sisters, Azra a miniature Delila. Delila was in jeans and a white cotton top with a big violet '9' on the front. Azra was in a flowery print dress and a lemon cardigan. Smears of brick and mortar dust marked their clothing.

My heart swelled at the feeling of their hands in mine, Delila holding on firmly but not too tightly, as if she were comfortable there, perhaps relieved that an adult had stepped in to fill the parental space after her hours in sole charge of her little sister. Her trauma had not kicked in yet, though I did wonder for how long she'd be able to keep it at bay. Azra's hand was minute and still had a baby-like softness.

I kept the conversation going with the girls. Trivial details might keep them relatively calm until I had piloted them to Marta's.

"So, Azra, what kind of dogs do you like? What kind of dog will you get?" I asked, as if her owning her own pet was only a matter of time.

"Little ones… well, not too little. Fluffy ones," she said.

"She'd like a miniature poodle. But not a poodle. You know, those white ones with the curly coat… and, like, a bit of a fringe up here." Delila pointed to her forehead just above her eyebrows. "They are pretty cute," she added.

I didn't know the Croatian words for a bichon frise so I said, "I know the kind you mean. Have you met one before, Azra?"

"Yes, a man let us play with his dog in the park. He was lovely," she said.

I opened the gate. "Right, girls. Here we are." I let myself into the house.

"Marta!" I shouted. "I've got a couple of friends for you to meet."

Marta emerged at the end of the hallway.

"Marta – this is Delila and Azra. They've had a bit of a shock. And their house is damaged so…"

"Come in, come in!" Marta beckoned the girls in the direction of the kitchen and I followed them in. The sun was still shining into the garden beyond the kitchen window and my heart leapt a little as I saw Marta and Delila and Azra slip easily into familiarity, the girls detecting intuitively Marta's warm heart and easy way with children.

The idea of taking the girls to Marta wasn't so much thought-out as blindingly obvious. And here was this saintly woman shifting effortlessly into surrogate grandmother mode.

"And who would like hot chocolate?" she shouted, having settled the girls on chairs at the table.

"Yeah, me!"

"I would!"

As Marta dug out a small Calor gas stove and began rummaging in cupboards for a hot chocolate tin that would have not seen action for many years, I guessed that she would be sacrificing most of her week's ration of UHT milk on the drinks, her way of beginning to settle the girls into a completely new environment.

"Well, we'll have some hot chocolate and then I'll see if I can find some crayons and colouring books," Marta said.

After the girls had wrapped their hands round their cups of hot drink, Marta slipped into the hall and I gave her a brief version of what had happened.

"You did well, Mick. And they can stay here as long as they need to. You know that."

"Yes, of course. I'll pop back into town and let the police know about their parents. Then I'd better file my stories before I miss tomorrow's deadline."

We stepped back into the kitchen. "Azra, Delila. I have to go into town, so you stay here with Marta." I nearly added "So, be good" but I held it back. It would have been a redundant comment in the circumstances.

Delila looked up at me from the table with her stunning eyes and said, "But you will come back later, won't you?"

"Yes, yes. I'll be back. Don't worry."

As I made my way down the hall, I heard Azra say, "Marta? Can we go to see your friend with the doggie?"

"Who's been telling you about my friend with the doggie?" asked Marta in mock surprise.

I didn't wait to hear the answer, but I smiled and stepped outside.

In the police station, the officer logged the details of the deaths. He expressed relief at Marta's willingness to look after Delila and Azra until 'the authorities', as he called them, found somewhere appropriate for them to stay.

"Maybe they'd be best off in Germany with their auntie," he said.

"Maybe. We just can't know, can we?"

I made my way to the office in the Town Hall where the phone was located and filed three pieces from my handwritten scripts, recounting my experiences at Fort Imperial and including a graphic description of the grenade launcher's bullseye on an ammunition pile.

Then I said to the copytaker, "I've got another piece, Mary. It's just I haven't written it – so, bear with me. I'm going to have to do it off the top of my head."

It was a skill that I rarely had to deploy, usually enjoying the time to weigh and winnow my words, checking and re-checking once they were on paper. But the power of the narrative prevailed on this occasion. I proceeded to tell the story of the girls and the bombed-out house, the bodies in the bedroom, and the lodging of Delila and Azra with Marta.

I didn't use their real names. I didn't know who might read the piece, and I might have been being overcautious, but I didn't want a relative to learn first of the orphaning of the girls from a newspaper article. There was probably only one family in Dubrovnik whose young girls were called Delila and Azra.

"Good heavens, Mick. Did that happen to you or was it someone else who told you the story?" asked the copytaker.

"It was me, Mary…about three hours ago."

"Oh, my God. Are you okay? Are you going to be okay?"

"Am I okay?" I echoed the question back to her, feeling as if I was walking round the question and examining it. "Well… I'm not quite sure yet. I've not stopped to think, since I found them."

"Well, look after yourself, Mick. That's a terrible, terrible thing to happen to anyone. I do hope those little girls will be all right."

"They'll be well looked after by my landlady – but whether they'll ever get over what happened... well, we'll see." After I had uttered the words "well, we'll see", I realised that what they meant was "probably not". I paused. "Listen, Mary. Tell Paul I'll call him later to see if everything's okay with my pieces."

"Okay, I will. God bless." Mary hung up the phone.

I made my way out of the Old Town and wandered into Park Gradac with its views down into the bay, out to sea, across to Lokrum Island, back to the city walls. There was no one about. It was not long before dusk and I knew there was no point in going back to Marta's till Paul had read my articles and I'd checked in with him.

The view was as spectacular as ever, the colour of the sea just deepening from a greeny-blue to something more inky as the dazzling November day slipped away. And then, without my being aware that it was upon me, I bent down onto my haunches and it was as if a dam inside had broken. Fat, hot tears broke out, big enough to splash on the ground as they tumbled from my cheeks. I wept and sobbed and, this time resisting my first instincts, I didn't try to squeeze back the tears, to pull myself together, to get a grip. I wept until the dam was empty.

When the tears stopped – after three, perhaps five minutes – I tried to steady my breath. To the voice in my head that whispered *Calm down*, I said out loud, "I don't want to calm down. I don't need to calm down." The sound of my voice was still distorted in the aftermath of tears. These were pent-up tears of fear – oh, so much fear over days and weeks – tears of living too long on my nerves, tears of anger at this ridiculous geopolitical situation, anger at those unidentified, cowardly killers, tears for those orphaned girls, tears for kindly, golden-hearted Marta. These were tears that I needed to shed.

As I began to stabilise my breathing pattern, and a sense of relief at having let that dam burst began to inch through me, I said with the laughter that often concludes a fit of crying, "You're not supposed to cry if you're a war journalist." And then, still out loud, "Well, I am a war journalist and I have cried."

But, as soon as I had said those words, I knew I would never tell anyone about the episode – not even Marta – though I wasn't sure why not.

At that moment, there was a rumble rising in volume to a roar as a JNA jet shot up the coast from south of Dubrovnik. As it swooped over me with ear-splitting volume, it let off a couple of missiles apparently randomly into the suburbs. I looked up at the sky and screamed, "Oh, fuck off! Why don't you just… fuck off!"

The jet spun away as anti-aircraft fire from Fort Imperial tried to bring it down. And then it was gone, over the hilltops in the direction of Bosnia.

Paul was fulsome in his praise of my articles. He liked the description of the guardians of the city in Fort Imperial, he liked the phrase I had stolen from Dragan, "the soundtrack of the town", but, naturally, he had been most affected by the tale of Delila and Azra.

"It's a shame you didn't have a photographer with you," he said.

I recoiled in shock at the suggestion. The thought would never have crossed my mind. I thought the idea inappropriate given the scale of the tragedy, but I didn't say anything.

Paul went on: "Listen, Mick. Are you sure you're okay to stay? If it's getting a bit much, we can try to get you out. Dan's ankle is just about fixed so, if we needed to, we could swap you out."

I bristled slightly at the idea of Dan replacing me, as if this were now my exclusive patch.

"No, no. I'm fine, Paul." As the words were uttered, an image of myself on my haunches, shedding fat tears in the park, firmed up.

"It's just that a lot of the other papers and TV crews are pulling out, as it drags on." Paul paused. "Mind you, you've always managed to find strong angles so…" His voice trailed away.

"Paul, let me stick with it. I kind of wonder whether it might be building up to some kind of showdown. I mean, why would the JNA be inching up towards the city, if they weren't going to try to force a surrender? It doesn't make sense." I paused. "Mind you, not much of this makes sense."

I was keen to get back to see the girls before it was late, but I felt I owed Saša some of my insights into the defence of the city and my experience in Fort Imperial, given the favours he had done for me.

In the bar of the Hotel Argentina, the first sip of Croatian red wine was as shockingly good as if it were the first time I had tasted it. The cellars appeared to be bottomless. They weren't saving the best wine till last, and they clearly weren't yet running short of the good stuff.

"As for your girls," Saša went on, "just make sure no idiot from the council puts them in an orphanage."

I glowed inwardly at the description of Delila and Azra as my girls.

"No, I think Marta will chase them off with a stick if they suggest anything she's not happy with," I said.

I went on to recount my Fort Imperial story and Saša scribbled the occasional note in his little black pocket book.

"It's a great tale of citizens rallying to the cause," he said, "but you should know they've got some outside help too."

While I had been up in the fort, he had been investigating and he had established that not only had seventy reinforcements been sent from a brigade one hundred kilometres north of Dubrovnik, they also appeared to be receiving so far unspecified help from the HOS, the paramilitary arm of the right-wing, nationalist Croatian Party of Rights.

"Mick, you need to know that these guys are not an offshoot of the Boy Scouts. They are admirers of the World War Two Ustaše. Their motto is 'Za Dom Spremni.'"

I knew that, though this literally meant 'For the Homeland', it was the equivalent of the Nazi 'Sieg Heil'.

"They were a raggle-taggle bunch," said Saša, "but, in a matter of months, they've become better equipped, a bit more professional." He paused. "But they're maniacs. One of the boys told me he'd seen one of their leaders in a village not far away. His nickname is 'Barba' – or 'Uncle'. But he's no chummy, avuncular guy. If you're a Serb in a backstreet, you don't want to come across Barba."

Sometime afterwards, I would come across a photo of him, a slight man with a vulpine look: big ears, a Roman nose, bushy eyebrows and the extravagant moustache of a San Francisco homosexual. Just a couple of years later, he would be accused of threatening women and children at gunpoint as he evicted inhabitants of Split from an apartment block to which he had taken a fancy, moving into one of them himself and dealing drugs from another.

Saša went on: "So, you know, Mick, I like the sound of your baker and mechanic. They're brave boys and I hope I'd have the courage to do what they're doing, if I was in their place."

I sensed that there was a 'but' coming along.

"There was one time when I was covering the Middle East and I was with a group of journalists in jeeps on the West Bank. We'd left our base hotel and gone out to get a feel for what was happening on the ground right in the middle of the latest round of the troubles. All of a sudden an open-top lorry carrying PLO fighters with automatic weapons swung by. The PLO flag was fluttering from the back. And one of the journalists, a French guy, raises a clenched fist in a 'victory to the PLO' salute.

"And I'll never forget it: the guy next to me in our jeep – he was one of your paper's most famous Middle East reporters, Robert Fisk. He just said out loud in earshot of the French journalist, 'There are no good guys in the Middle East.' It was a beautiful put-down. And the French guy, who had thought he looked cool, blushed with embarrassment. He didn't know where to put himself."

If I had had my own concerns that I was being drawn into siding with 'the victims', here was Saša gently advising me not to buy into any side's story. His was a delicate warning, but it stung nevertheless.

I attempted a weak pushback. "Branko and Dragan are good guys – and, for that matter, Arian too."

"I accept that, Mick. The problem is that these HOS guys enable the Serbs to say that the Croats are Fascists running amok. It plays into their narrative of how Serbs across Yugoslavia need protecting from these guys who, just a few decades ago, were fighting alongside the Nazis."

Saša paused and then expanded on his thesis. "What I'm saying is that, in the Middle East – and almost certainly in Yugoslavia, if this plays out as I expect – everyone is a perpetrator of violence and everyone is a victim of it. Not every individual but… You know what I mean: no nation's hands will be unstained."

Saša left the forecast hanging in the air portentously. I drained the last drops of wine from my glass and, having got the taste for alcohol, I wanted another glass.

"Better go, Saša. Better catch Delila and Azra before Marta tucks them up."

As I walked into the hallway half an hour later, I heard singing coming from the kitchen. Marta and Delila and Azra were singing Croatian nursery rhymes, the girls now barefoot but dressed in pyjamas that Marta had borrowed from a neighbour.

I doubted that the girls – and Delila in particular – could keep their trauma at bay for much longer, but Marta was deploying every ounce of her experience and intuition to delay the crash for as long as possible – or, at the very least, to soften the fall.

"Mick!" shouted Delila, as she spotted me. My heart leapt.

In what felt like a lucid ten minutes before the exhaustion of the day pulled me under, I thought about what Saša had meant in recounting his episode from the West Bank. Even if it seemed obvious in this case that the ordinary citizens of Dubrovnik were blameless, the pro-Serbian Radio Titograd was claiming that the city's forces were firing at the JNA from within the walls of the Old Town in an explicit breach of the deal to which Arian had alluded: that the JNA would not fire on the Old Town if they didn't face rockets from within. The same station was claiming that the people of Dubrovnik were exaggerating the damage done to the Old Town in order to provoke international outrage. And now, if Saša was right, often unrestrained HOS paramilitaries were in the vicinity, ready to carry out atrocities on Serbs and the JNA that might match the excesses of Serbian Chetniks on Croats.

"All I can do is report what I see and what I know to be true," I reflected. And I tipped off to sleep, having invested that banality in my own mind with a near-philosophical profundity.

8
NOVEMBER–DECEMBER 1991

As November slipped into its final days, there was a sense of a noose tightening, an increasing rain of fire from sea, land and air suggesting that the commander of the unit attacking Dubrovnik from the south, Admiral Miodrag Jokić, might finally have been framing some coherent tactics for his forces to implement.

In the streets of the Old Town, I saw increasing debris and fewer intact windowpanes, and there were reports of further casualties. The death toll in the outskirts kept ticking up too in the face of random but more sustained shelling and grenades.

A spokesman for Mayor Poljanić told me that Belgrade and the JNA were leaning on the Croatian leadership and on the mayor to agree a ceasefire.

"But they're not really looking for a ceasefire; they want capitulation," he said. "The mayor says these are conditions we couldn't accept because it would mean surrendering the city, surrendering our men, surrendering the area. If we agree to this, it's over for us.

"My sense is the JNA is losing patience. UNESCO observers are piling on the pressure and the European Community is threatening Belgrade with sanctions. But I can't see this all just fizzling out."

"No, it doesn't feel like it, does it?" I replied.

A few days after Delila and Azra had been delivered to Marta's, I returned to the house to find it in silence. In the kitchen, Marta was sitting at the table and I could see that she had been crying.

"Oh, Mick. I'm so sorry you weren't here. I wanted you to be consulted before they went." Her voice trailed away.

"So where are they? Are they okay?"

"Yes, yes. I think so. Two women came – one from the council and another an experienced foster parent. Nice lady. In her thirties. Seemed very kind. I went with the girls to her and her husband's house in the Nuncijata area. They've got two older daughters who made a fuss of Delila and Azra as soon as they arrived. I think the girls liked the idea of having big sisters." Marta paused. She looked up apologetically at me. "Mick, I thought it was for the best."

"Yes… I'm sure you're right," I reassured her, but I felt hollow. I'd become accustomed to their chatter, to Marta's subtle, maternal steering and her delicate handling of the girls in their fragility; but I knew that Marta couldn't have looked after them indefinitely and I was pleased that council officials had had the resources and good sense to identify experienced foster parents amid the mayhem of the city's current situation.

"We can go and visit them whenever we like," said Marta, still sounding apologetic, as if she'd made a grave error.

"Good… good," I said. I smiled at Marta. "I don't suppose these guardian angels had a dog, did they?"

Marta's face lightened, as if she felt she had needed and had now been granted forgiveness. "No, no. Unfortunately not."

I leaned down and wrapped my arms around Marta. It was an instinctive action but, as I hugged her, I knew that that was what she needed – a physical sign that I felt she had made the right choice. I felt Marta's right arm being laid gently around my waist.

"Oh, Mick," she whispered. "When will this madness end?"

"I don't know, Marta. I just don't know."

In fact, it was the start of what would be a decisive week for the city. It was the first of four consecutive days of bombardment and, if the main target was Srđ Hill and Fort Imperial, it became increasingly clear that the JNA tactic was changing and direct attacks on the Old Town were now regarded as legitimate.

On Sunday, the first day of December, four mortars fell into the Old Town, one blasting a hole in the wall of the convent. On the Monday, for the first time, shells crashed into the city walls as, down the coast at Kupari, the once elegant Grand Hotel with its Austro-Hungarian-style architecture went up in flames and, on Tuesday, the JNA launched a sustained assault, using what I would later learn were Soviet-manufactured, wire-guided missiles.

As if in some kind of oversized space invaders game, they blasted boats and buildings in the Old Port area and set fires burning. Even the relative anomalous tranquillity of the Hotel Argentina, till then largely spared because it housed EC monitors, came under fire. Saša laughed as he told me of how those monitors were sent scuttling from the hotel terrace as gunfire whistled around them, and they then had to spend hours pinned down, crouching beneath a window indoors.

"They just about crapped themselves. It was hilarious," Saša said with a wheezy chuckle that made no attempt to conceal his contempt for the officials from Brussels.

As the sun set that evening, I could see from the hill above the city near Marta's house smoke plumes twisting artistically above the walls of the Old Town against a vivid orange sunset. Even in tragedy Dubrovnik was displaying a ridiculous kind of elegance.

In the event it was a British TV crew, from ITN, that probably made the critical contribution to sparing the citizens of Dubrovnik from being crushed completely. They were the sole international TV crew left in Dubrovnik, the latest having beaten a retreat due to the risk of the intensifying bombardment, many others having quit earlier out of a sense that this enduring saga could no longer compete with fresher newsbreaks more easily explicable to viewers.

My appeals to Western leaders to step in and intervene more dynamically were restricted to packages of several hundred words a time in cold print to a limited readership. I was competing for attention with the power of moving pictures that could be shared across international networks. And the ITN team managed to capture the drama of the heightened assault on the city in a powerful piece edited to eleven minutes – an unusually long bulletin for a TV news slot.

It was to have a decisive impact internationally, having been smuggled out of Dubrovnik during a phoney ceasefire on Wednesday and Thursday of that week and screened the night before the heaviest blitz on the city to date on the Friday. At last, the international outrage broke – the outrage that Mayor Poljanić had been trying to generate for so long: outrage at clips of people huddled in the catacombs of the Revelin Fort; at shells like regimented, equidistant fireflies streaming onto Srđ Hill; at wire-guided missiles thumping into the city walls and destroying pieces of the Old Port; at nuns cowering in the convent, pointing out the shrapnel holes in the wall; at a monk grimacing with shock as a mortar exploded by the monastery.

After a war of words, Belgrade and Zagreb contradicting one another on every detail of the siege of Dubrovnik, here was the definitive proof of the JNA not just lobbing missiles randomly into the suburbs but now engaging in an outright assault on the Old Town.

Fires still burned here and there but, for no evident reason, the scale of the bombardment was dialled down on Wednesday and word spread that the JNA would be allowing women and children to leave the city by ferry on Thursday. As before, no men of fighting age would be allowed to accompany their families.

Down by the port at Gruž, what could in other circumstances have been scenes of happiness and relief were submerged beneath the waters of uncertainty. Would that mother with her two small children ever see her husband, their father, again? Was it better to stay or go? And how might the Red Cross and the city officials overseeing the exercise sift and assess the competing needs with only sixteen hundred places available onboard? Which children were most traumatised? How to judge how heavily one family's desire and need to leave weighed in one pan of the scales against another's?

For me, it was a brand-new kind of distress and despair, a new variation on weeks of perpetual, sense-numbing human trauma. Yes, there might be some relief, once the boat had sailed safely and vulnerable people were removed from this existence frozen by siege: mothers glad to have saved children, fathers concluding that they had done the right thing to send their families away. But these were overwhelmingly miserable scenes. Vales of tears, waves of self-doubt, torrents of internalised self-recrimination.

I watched, but no tears came to my eyes this time. I felt rather a boiling anger at the way in which the JNA, Belgrade, or whoever was responsible had constructed out of the attrition they had delivered to the city this bogus act of magnanimity – as if the people of Dubrovnik should thank them for their humanity and compassion.

"They are shits, just total shits," I said to myself out loud as I stood on the dock, watching streams of diminished people mill and bustle by. I was aware of the inadequacy of my spoken words in capturing the moment, but I would capture it more skilfully later in prose, I told himself in consolation.

I had asked Marta if she wanted to go. Predictably, she didn't. "There's no one to keep on the business if I'm gone," she said. But we both hiked up to the Nuncijata area to ask Delila and Azra's foster parents whether the mother was thinking of quitting the city with the four children in their care.

I liked the atmosphere in the house. I noticed first a clean, fresh smell to the property and I warmed instantly to 'my' girls' foster mother, a woman with wiry, shoulder-length blonde hair, shaped as if by a topiarist. She had a kind, open face and an apparently effortless manner that blended warmth towards the children with a certain firmness. I felt no reason to question her decision to stay.

"I think you're probably right," I said. "We may not be at the endgame, but let's hope this is all going to tip into a proper ceasefire. I think it just might."

I had been touched when, when I saw Delila for the first time since she left Marta's, she sat at my feet and wrapped her arms round my leg. "Mick!" she exclaimed.

"Delila! How are you?" I wondered to what extent she might feel I had helped make her safe.

After the elder girls took Delila and Azra off into their playroom, I asked their foster mother how the girls were.

"They're good. They're pretty resilient. Delila sometimes wakes up crying in the night. She doesn't say whether it's nightmares or just loss… but we've put one of my girls in with each of them at night to try to keep them calm. So far, so good. Little Azra – well, I'm not sure how much she understands."

"Or what she actually saw on that day," I added.

"I think she might be expecting her parents to reappear at some point. I think she might think this is just some kind of holiday." The foster mother paused. "But they're lovely, lovely girls. And, you know, we're in no hurry to move them on. We're here for as long as it takes."

I realised that I had not so much suppressed as never framed the thought that the girls might still be in transit and that this apparently perfect fit of a family might not be their final destination. It was an important realisation; but it wasn't one I needed, or was able, to dwell upon just now.

On the Friday that would prove to be critical to the future of the city, despite the ceasefire of the previous two days I had risen early, guided by Branko's convincing hunch that, with international pressure rising against them, the JNA would try one last decisive push to seize the fort and force the surrender of the city. Slipping alongside walls and down narrow streets where I could, scurrying like a nervous fox, my head swivelling at each sound, it was clear as early as 6.00am that the JNA were on manoeuvres. From a street just north of the Old Town, I could see a major JNA bombardment of Srđ Hill.

I would learn later that, helped by a counter bombardment by their own anti-aircraft batteries and mortars, the defenders of the city would hold firm. Despite the size of the foe lined up against it, miraculously Fort Imperial would not fall.

The paramilitary leader that Saša had mentioned to me, Barba, would be mentioned in dispatches for his bravery on Srđ Hill that day. He and a small group of HOS colleagues had been asked to smuggle themselves up to the fort the night before to help the locals. Colleagues of Branko would attest to his leadership qualities. If Barba was a maniac, as Saša had suggested, at least he was a fearless maniac.

But, if the fort held in the face of that early morning bombardment, it led the JNA to redirect its fire onto the city and the Old Town in particular. In the gap in the JNA's bouts of shelling, I had slipped into the Old Town through the Pile Gate and was there as the missile-fall turned from sporadic to steady.

I had been in the Old Town in previous weeks and days when mortars had fallen within the walls – an explosion here, a bang there, a fatality when one poor individual just happened to be exposed in a place where the narrow streets could not protect and a mortar penetrated. This was different. It was by far the most concerted fire to which I had been exposed, and I scraped along the walls and winced each time a shell exploded or a missile smashed into a roof or a wall anywhere nearby.

I couldn't gauge whether the need to be perpetually alert made me feel more or less afraid. Fear kept rushing at me, but I couldn't dwell on each pang. As each flared and eased, another would replace it. *Save your skin*, a voice inside said. But, having stepped into the Old Town, I didn't know how to precisely.

The action soon appeared to be focused on Dubrovnik's famous main street, the Stradun, and the area north-west of it. I began by trying to count the number of explosions as I slipped west of the Stradun, hoping that the narrowness of the streets and the height of the three-storey buildings might act as an umbrella against the missiles. After counting to thirty, I stopped. Official calculations subsequently put the shells, mortars and wire-guided missiles that fell in the Old Town on that day at seven hundred and twenty-six.

Thirteen civilians would die in the city that day yet, thanks to the robust construction of the houses, each with their own four walls, only nine would be totally burned out.

I looked on as the home and studio of the artist, Ivo Grbić, on Od Puča Street had burned through floor by floor, each level crashing down onto the floor below with the inevitability of a cartoon catastrophe. Neighbours acting as firefighters told me how, when the first bomb hit his roof, the sixty-year-old grabbed his ninety-nine-year-old mother from her room on the first floor, slung her over his shoulder and gave her a fireman's lift down the stairs and out to safety.

"She's sitting in an armchair in my front parlour now. I'm amazed the shock of it didn't kill her," a neighbour said.

Once it had become clear that nothing could be done to save the house, another neighbour had brought Ivo a thick orange-and-cream checked blanket, wrapped it round him and tried to persuade him to come away from the blaze and sit with his mother, out of sight of this scene of devastation.

Reluctantly, he had agreed, though he insisted later in the day, once the flames had subsided, on walking back into the street and striking a pose of defiance that was caught on a neighbour's camera: right fist clenched, as if in victory, an upturned metal cooking pot on his head acting as a makeshift helmet, the blanket still wrapped around his shoulders.

"It may only be papers and art. And I can make more art," Ivo said to me. "But we must never forget this day – these days. No one must ever forget this mindless aggression against this blameless place, these blameless people."

I nodded sagely. "Yes, of course." My words were inadequate but what more could I say?

We would learn the following day that, alerted to the brutality of the bombardment, UNESCO and European Community officials had called Belgrade and demanded that the bombing stop.

"It will stop at 4.00pm," an official had promised. And it did.

Not before fire had broken out in the Inter-University Centre just outside the Old Town's walls, destroying a 20,000-volume library. Not far away, having bombed the Libertas Hotel, the JNA targeted the firemen attacking the blaze. Some lost their lives.

The day after the bombardment, Mayor Poljanić received a delegation from the JNA to inspect the damage to the Old Town. JNA representatives promised an inquiry into who was responsible; but few in Dubrovnik or Zagreb expected to see such a report pursued, let alone published. And, if the JNA delegation and the phone call with Belgrade suggested that this was ceasefire, it was a ceasefire only of sorts. The guns were largely silenced, but there was no visible withdrawal of JNA forces from the area surrounding the city. If the sea blockade eased, there would be no restoration of electricity until the end of December. If the people of Dubrovnik ceased having to be on red alert, their guard was certainly not down.

And, barely had the JNA representatives left the city than into this uncertain environment stepped Ivana.

Branko sought me out at Marta's to give me the news. Ivana had set sail from Pula even before she knew that the siege was set to ease.

"I couldn't believe it, Mick. The boat's just sailed taking sixteen hundred women and children out of harm's way, and she's letting herself into the flat with her key, having made the journey in the opposite direction.

"I mean, I was delighted to see her, of course – but I said to her, 'What are you doing here, you crazy girl?' And she said she just couldn't take it, hearing about us still under fire. She said she just had to come back. And, Mick, you'll see. She's huge! Looks like that baby could burst out any day now.

"And she said to me, 'Branko, I hope you got my food parcels. I sent one every week.' Well, of course, I hadn't. I didn't."

If Branko was concerned about Ivana returning to a city without power and precious little fresh water, he could barely keep a smile from his face. Perhaps it was ending. Perhaps it would be okay. Perhaps Ivana and Branko's baby would be able to grow up beyond the shadows of war.

"If it's a girl, you must call her 'Nada' – hope," I said. "It was my mother's name…"

"Mick, you know we might just do that." Branko paused. "Except it's going to be a boy… and he's going to play football for Hajduk Split."

My heartbeat took a fast, momentary kick, as I walked into the flat and saw Ivana. I had feared I might never see her again.

"Forgive me if I don't get up." Ivana smiled. Branko was right: she was beachball huge.

"They say if it's very prominent, it's usually a boy," I said, as I leaned over and laid a gentle but purposeful kiss on Ivana's cheek. "It's lovely to see you, Ivana," I said, "but you're crazy! Coming back with the siege not even over."

"I know, Mick." She shrugged. "But you can't know what it feels like, when you know you've escaped but your people are just stuck there. It was eating away at me. I was more afraid of the stress affecting my baby than if I came back. And, you know, Mick? As that boat sailed from Pula, I felt this weight lift."

A few days after she returned, the first of Ivana's food parcels arrived. No doubt the others would follow.

A few days after that, Ivana went into labour and Branko drove her in the early hours of the morning to the hospital still starved of mains electricity, where a generator could only provide a small amount of equipment with power. Nevertheless, the baby was born safely. Ivana and Branko called her Nada. And, of course, she was beautiful.

But it was time to go. Time for me to leave Branko, Ivana, Nada, Marta, Delila and Azra.

"I'll be back to see you all soon," I said as I did the rounds. And I hoped I would and I hoped I could – but who could know? I welcomed this latest imperfect ceasefire in and around Dubrovnik and I expected the immediate crisis here to subside, but I suspected the overall situation across Yugoslavia would become murkier.

As I waved to Marta as the boat pulled away from the port at Gruž, tears filled my eyes. I doubted that Marta would have spotted from the dock those tears reflecting in the light, but this time these were tears of regret at leaving friends I had come to love, not the tears of fear that had wracked me in Park Gradac that day. It was another sign of the centre of gravity of my life shifting.

9
FEBRUARY 1992

Although Bosnia's President had reassured his people that they could sleep peacefully, as there would be no war in Bosnia even as shells were falling on Dubrovnik, I was back in the Balkans a couple of months later because it appeared inevitable that the contagion of conflict would be spreading into Bosnian territory.

In fact, it would emerge later that, as early as spring 1991, Serbia and Croatia's leaders Slobodan Milošević and Franjo Tuđman had met in one of Tito's old hunting lodges at Karađorđevo in north-west Serbia to discuss how they might share Bosnia between them. They had reached no agreement but the writing was on the wall.

Saša had listened patiently as I had ranted at the TV in the Astoria in Zagreb at reports that British Prime Minister John Major had done a deal with Germany, which would help swing the European Community behind independence for Croatia and Slovenia before any further package had been put in place to find a bloodless solution for the rest of Yugoslavia.

He listened as I accused Major's Foreign Secretary Douglas Hurd of actively discouraging other players from intervention, and he nodded diplomatically as I pointed out that a so-called peace plan put together by the US's Cyrus Vance not only failed to resolve any of the territorial disputes that had erupted over the previous year, but at least temporarily it froze them in place.

For good measure, I had pitched into the author of a lazy article about the conflicts in Yugoslavia in the *Daily Express*, accusing him of being heavy on hyperbole and light on analysis. He wasn't within hearing distance so there was no bravery involved.

"If you can't get readers' attention by simply describing what's happening here objectively, then you're not much of a journalist," I had opined.

"Hmmm... 'Objectively,'" Saša had replied. "That's a big word."

I left the comment hanging in the air. It was one to gloss over or to have a two-hour debate around, and I didn't feel up for two hours' worth at that point.

While Bosnia teetered on the brink, I did have a plan, though I sensed that its substance didn't appeal to Saša: head south of Zagreb to see whether the terms of the Vance Plan's ceasefire were being respected in disputed parts of Croatia, and then tip up to the north-western tip of Bosnia where a maverick Muslim politician was claiming he could save his country from an unnecessary war.

I was intending to make my trip solo, until an ITN producer, Lucy Plunkett, who had overheard our conversation in the bar, asked if she could come along for the ride to help her scout some filming ideas and locations.

Despite my selectiveness about companions – '*Daily Express* journalists need not apply' – and although I knew her only slightly, I heard myself say "Of course" without a moment's hesitation.

And there I was the following day, in a dark green VW Polo hire car, heading south out of Zagreb with Lucy in the passenger seat. She was easy company and I was quickly reassured that I had been right to respond positively to her request to hitch a ride. We were soon into a conversation about the feelings, fears and vulnerabilities we experienced in covering these conflicts. And I felt so much more comfortable with this kind of exchange than with the swagger, bravado and puerile humour behind which so many of the largely male travelling Press pack veiled their feelings.

Within twenty minutes, we were discussing our frustrations at the swirling, multiple sources of strife that made this conflict so difficult to analyse and explain and our concerns that mini-wars might be going on out of range. And we discussed what was one of my favourite themes:

my sense that this war might be a war where journalists were not, rather than – as I'd always assumed would be the case – where journalists were.

I may have sounded naïve as I admitted I had somehow expected the protagonists to act out their battles so that I could chronicle them like the man known as 'the First Special Correspondent', *The Times*' William Howard Russell, observing some of the battles in the Crimean Wars from hilltops conveniently situated adjacent to the battlefields.

When Lucy asked me directly, "So how do you deal with your fear, Mick?" I realised it was not only a question that none of my male colleagues would have dreamed of framing, let alone asking, it was also a question that, without my fully realising it, I had been yearning to be asked – ever since the shell landed at Malo Selo, the woman had lost her leg, and I had been sprinkled with minute pieces of shrapnel. I'd been yearning to be asked it because I was intrigued to hear the kind of answer that would come from my lips.

"I'm not sure that I do deal with it, Lucy. Basically, I'm a coward and I have to fight with myself not to avoid every potentially dangerous situation. I suppose I force myself into locations where there is conflict but I suspect I won't be in mortal danger."

And I told her of the moment in my first days in Yugoslavia, when I had driven my car off the Zagreb to Belgrade road to avoid crossing a car travelling north, containing Chetniks who might have taken exception to my Croatian number plates. If I had felt shame at the time, admitting to this episode now felt like a kind of relief. Lucy hadn't even coaxed the confession out of me; I had volunteered it because of how I felt in her company.

"Maybe it was the right thing to do… But it made me realise that I couldn't stay one hundred per cent safe. If I wanted to be totally safe, I needed to go home. And I don't want to be home. I want to be here, trying to unpick this conflict and, to be honest, to get people back home to care about what's going on." I paused.

"But there's one thing I have learned about fear. And it does offer me some comfort. And that is that you don't seek out or choose your fear. It comes to you."

I had rehearsed the line to myself a thousand times over the past three or four months, but I had never shared the thought. If it wasn't profound, it certainly wasn't banal or obvious.

"It's like having an accident. You don't realise you're having one till it's happened. So, fear is on you all of a sudden, and you just have to deal with it.

"And each brush with fear has felt as if it has added something to me. And I don't just mean that these have been new experiences. It's as if they've thickened me up; each episode given me an additional, invisible few ounces of substance."

I paused, wondering whether I was at risk of rambling. "Am I making sense, Lucy?" I asked.

"Yes… I think so."

"Perhaps before all of this, I felt a bit lightweight. I'm not the full ticket yet. I'm no Saša… but maybe each episode does just give you a little more."

And I told Lucy of an article I had read a couple of years earlier, written by a journalist who had made herself sit through the entire trial of Peter Sutcliffe, the Yorkshire Ripper, and, hence, had heard the unimaginably gruesome details of the murder and mutilation of his multiple victims.

"She said she wished she hadn't done it, Lucy. She said she felt diminished as a human being by the experience. I'll never forget her use of that word 'diminished'. And that piece of her that she felt she'd lost – maybe it was a kind of innocence – she didn't believe she could ever get it back." I paused again.

"Whatever I witness out here, I don't expect to feel diminished… I hope it makes me stronger. Gives me a deeper appreciation of what people are capable of – in the best and the worst senses."

Another pause, then I said, "We'll see."

Lucy let my observations claim their own space, as if out of respect for the analysis.

Eventually, she said, "Hearing you ask questions at Press conferences, I – we – can tell that it matters to you. There's an earnestness about you – and I don't say that in any pejorative sense of the word."

'Earnest' – it was a descriptor that I'd never had applied to me before but one which I instinctively liked.

Lucy went on. "Though I don't really know you, I reckon your indignation at the injustice of it all drives you on. Helps you deal with the fear. Maybe takes the edge off it. Not many journalists get as angry as you do. In a strange way, it might be a gift."

I'd been aware that my emotions bled into my questions at times – notably at Mayor Poljanić's Press conference when he revealed that he had faxed Prince Charles. But I was flattered to have been singled out in that way by Lucy. She was confirming what I had hoped: that I was neither jaundiced nor cynical.

I asked, "And what about you? Are you brave, Lucy?"

Although it might have felt a little intrusive as a question in normal circumstances, the atmosphere we had created so early in our road trip meant that I felt comfortable asking the question.

"It's not a question I've ever asked myself, Mick. I mean, what does 'brave' mean?" she asked rhetorically.

"Well, I think that in itself tells us something," I said. "I'd describe myself as fearful by instinct. You don't sound to me as if you're fearful."

"I suppose I don't break down into floods of tears when things go wrong," she said; then she paused, weighing the thought, weighing her answer, as if it mattered, as if it were a statement in a courtroom.

"I might be resilient… I hope I'm resilient," she said eventually.

"Resilient. That's a good word," I said.

It felt right for the conversation to halt for a while and for a period of silent reflection to follow. The exchanges had highlighted to me just how much I had internalised my Yugoslav experience so far. I told no one what I was thinking, how I was feeling – largely because no one asked. And here was Lucy, clambering in somehow, as if through a skylight, effortlessly sleuthing my anxieties and making it clear without words that, if I shared those anxieties with her, that very act might ease them.

My growing friendship with Saša was a source of great support to me, yet I had felt alone for much of my time in Yugoslavia. Of course, even pre-Yugoslavia I had tended towards introversion. Now here I was, just forty-five minutes out of Zagreb, feeling as if I was in a totally shared space. And I wanted to remain in that shared space for a long time. I wanted the journey and the flush that it was washing through me never to end. But, of course, it would end. This was too precious a commodity for longevity.

I would try to hold onto the memory of that sensation for as long as I could, but wouldn't it be life-enhancing to have a library of past sensations that could be taken down from the shelves and experienced afresh over and over again?

An hour out of Zagreb, our first port of call was Karlovac – famous as a southern outpost of the Habsburg Empire that the Ottomans failed repeatedly to overwhelm. Famous too for a brewery whose beer had become a household name.

I parked up in the centre of town and Lucy and I made our way to the Town Hall where a helpful official explained what he knew of the situation beyond Karlovac. I knew that we were heading into murky territory where, although this was Croatia, it wasn't clear which areas were held by the Croat authorities and which were run by Serbs. Known as the Krajina Serbs – frontier Serbs – many of them were the descendants of Serbs who had settled in these parts of Croatia over five hundred years earlier to escape the expansion of the Ottoman Empire.

In the autumn there had been a Croat swoop on JNA weaponry stored in Croatia, and the official explained to us that the JNA had evacuated Karlovac to avoid much of its best local kit being seized, relocating it to the south to one of its largest and best defended installations in Yugoslavia.

"There was a bit of a stand-off but the JNA didn't put up much of a fight. They'd obviously decided to cut their losses and consolidate their kit in a safer place. But I should warn you that, just a mile out of town, on the road south, we can't guarantee your safety. That's the Serb frontline and our writ doesn't run there at the moment," the official said.

"Slunj, fifty kilometres south, is in our hands but most of the road south is controlled by the JNA and the Krajina Serbs. We'll let you through but then you're on your own."

Under the terms of the Vance Plan, the Serbian militia should have surrendered their weaponry. It clearly hadn't happened yet. After a brief discussion, Lucy and I decided to press on with our plan regardless and get some sense of how the land lay with a view to reaching Slunj at least before nightfall.

Beyond the town, some large JNA military vehicles marked a frontline patrolled by JNA officers and members of the Krajina Serbs' self-appointed police force, the Martićevci. If the JNA officers were barely interested in our papers, one of the Martićevci waved the barrel of his rifle at the car, indicating that we should pull into the lay-by and get out. If I always felt a certain unease, I had passed through enough checkpoints and border patrols without mishap for me not to feel too jumpy.

As two policemen went through the car, the militia captain asked where we were going. I noticed that the badge on his cap bore the four Cs – two facing in the normal direction of Latin script, two reversed. *Samo Sloga Srbina Spasava: Only Unity Saves the Serbs.*

The symbols and the slogan had in recent years been invested with a deeper, nationalist menace. In the first months of the conflict in Croatia, there had been reports that, in the event of victim swaps, many of the Croatian corpses handed back to the authorities were found to have had the Serbian four Cs symbol carved into their flesh.

"We're heading for Knin. A Serbian friend of mine is an aide to General Mladić and he's fixed up an interview for us with him," I said.

On my way down to Dubrovnik, a young soldier in a café in Knin had talked to me about Mladić, the JNA's second in command in the area. A Bosnian Serb, he was a popular figure with his men and with Serbian paramilitaries and hence a likely name-drop with which to unlock a roadblock. I calculated that a militia captain on the fringes of the Krajina two hundred kilometres from Knin would be unlikely to radio in and debunk my little white lie.

"General Mladić? Great man, great man," the captain whispered, as if in awe. "Okay – on your way." And he tilted his head in the direction of the car. "And give the general our regards… And tell him the Krajina is safe in our hands."

As we headed away from Karlovac, there was a repeating and disturbing pattern to the settlements we passed through. Life went on as normal in the villages populated by Serbs, but these were interspersed with villages that had been emptied of their Croatian inhabitants. Had they fled or been driven out forcibly? If these villages lacked the devastation wreaked on the Croatian homes that I had witnessed in Konavle, south of Dubrovnik – a window broken here and there, a gate hanging on one hinge – they had been evacuated just as efficiently. This was a region through the forests of which Tito's Partisans had swarmed and Partisans and Croatian Ustaše had committed appalling atrocities on each other's forces during the Second World War. Lucy and I were now witness to the abrupt shattering of a trust slowly rebuilt over nearly fifty years.

Passing through one abandoned village, I pulled up in the market square next to a hairy pink and grey mound on the pavement. The pig lying dead had a bullet wound in the side of its head.

"Target practice, Lucy," I said. "That's been shot gratuitously. I mean… why would you do that?" I shook my head.

A few miles further down the road, the car crested an incline and, in the dip beyond, three hundred metres further on, we saw another Serb checkpoint, alongside a house that had clearly been commandeered for military purposes after hostilities broke out. I imagined that its owners would have been Croatian and forcibly evicted.

"Oh, shit! We could do without this," I said.

The checkpoint was manned by two policemen, half a dozen JNA reservists – no doubt Serbians – and two Chetniks, a near-ubiquitous presence in any gathering of this kind in the area.

I eased the car into the lay-by indicated and Lucy and I stepped out, trying to ooze sweet reasonableness underlaid with a firmness about our mission and the relative urgency of our need to proceed and fulfil our interview commitment.

The two policemen examined our Press credentials and passports. They were polite and workmanlike.

"We'll just check these out with the chief and we'll be right back," one said, and both headed into the house. The JNA reservists had lost interest and wandered across the road, chatting and smoking, but one of the Chetniks hovered uncomfortably close, his colleague keeping a more circumspect distance that didn't invade our personal space. The first held a Kalashnikov rifle at a forty-five-degree angle across his front. He had a Glock pistol in a holster on his right hip.

Saša had told me that JNA officers in charge of weaponry and ammunition sometimes made a tidy sideline by selling off guns, bullets, grenades and even shells to their preferred militias. The Chetnik was clearly very proud of his purchases. He was now circling Lucy and me with a smirk on his face.

"So, Englander? Your girl. She's got fantastic tits. How many times a day do you fuck her?"

"I don't. She's a colleague – not a partner." The words were out and instantly I regretted them. I shouldn't have deigned to respond to the skinny hooligan in front of me, with his long, unbrushed, light brown hair, his ridiculous black bandana and his skull and crossbones T-shirt, a box of cigarettes folded into its left sleeve.

"Come on, man! Do you expect me to believe that? A chick like that? How many times?"

Five paces away, his Chetnik pal wheezed with quiet mirth at his antics. I extended my palms on either side of my hips and raised my eyebrows to indicate that I was telling the truth and couldn't add anymore. I kept close to Lucy, sensing her growing unease. I wanted to reach out and put an arm around her shoulder, but I sensed that, at that moment, it would not be the right thing to do.

"Well, if you're not fucking her, then maybe I should." It wasn't quite a question.

I let the words evaporate without a response, then said, "General Mladić is expecting us in Knin in a couple of hours…"

"I didn't ask you about Mladić. I asked you if I should fuck your girl." His tone was rising menacingly. He looped his rifle over his right shoulder. I said nothing.

With one quick manoeuvre, the Chetnik was on Lucy, grabbing her right shoulder from behind with his left hand and slipping the barrel of his pistol into her mouth with his right, pinning her back against him. I froze. Any abrupt movement and Lucy could be dead. I had no alternative but to let the horror of the moment sink in.

"Now, Mr Englander. You get your motherfucker ass out of here. The girl's staying with me." Even the Chetnik colleague of the man in the skull and crossbones T-shirt was looking uneasy now.

After a few seconds, I lent gently and slowly in the direction of Lucy and the Chetnik.

"*Molim vas. To nije mudro,*" I said quietly. And I gently took the barrel of the pistol and eased it out of Lucy's mouth. "*Nije mudro,*" I said once again, with as much priestly calm and authority as I could muster. As the Chetnik let his gun be eased away from Lucy until it was pointing down to the ground, the policemen emerged from the house with our documents. I suspected they may have witnessed the moment of disarmament.

"Oi! You, you skinny bastard! Get off that girl and behave – or I'll kick your arse," the policeman at the front shouted.

The Chetnik took a step away from Lucy. He gave me a look of contempt. "English motherfucker. Go fuck your grandmother."

"Enough!" the policeman barked. "Get the hell out of here!"

The Chetnik backed off into the middle of the road, his colleague moving with him, no longer enjoying the spectacle.

The policeman handed the documents back to me. "Don't mind him. He's just a junkie hooligan with no brains. You're good to go now. And best wishes for your interview with Commander Mladić. I hope you find it useful."

I wasn't sure how my legs took me to the car and I suspected Lucy was experiencing a similar sensation. As I placed my hand on the gearstick, I couldn't prevent it from shaking uncontrollably – but I switched on the ignition and jammed the car into gear. The threat might have been lifted but I wanted to be away from there as quickly as possible. The car tyres crackled and skidded a little on the gravel of the lay-by and then they were away, the thrum of the rubber on the firmer tarmac instantly reassuring.

Neither of us punctured the verbal silence initially. There was no need to. Our shared horror at the episode outdid any descriptors. The logic of putting space between ourselves and the checkpoint was crashing.

Eventually, perhaps three minutes on, I asked gently, "You okay?"

"Yes... I think so," said Lucy. There was more silence. Then Lucy asked, "What did you say to him about my mother? What stopped him from shooting?"

"You mean, '*To nije mudro*'?"

"Yes."

"It means, 'That's not wise – not a clever thing to do.' I didn't know what to say. I didn't know what to do."

"Ah… I thought you were talking about a mother."

More silence. The VW Polo lapped up the miles and, as dusk deepened, I sensed Lucy beginning to shiver. I looked across to see that tears were streaming down her face – quiet tears that never risked tipping into sobbing. I stretched out my right hand and laid it gently on the back of her left hand.

"We'll be okay, Luce. We'll stay safe," I said. I knew my words were empty reassurances. They held little logic in our shared situation, but I didn't care. I knew it was right to say them. After a pause, Lucy replied, "Yes… We'll stay safe." It was a moment when mutual reassurance outbid literal truth. I needed to change gear. I took my hand away from hers.

It was dark as we approached Slunj. At the Croatian checkpoint, Lucy and I didn't even need to get out of the car.

"Our friends in Karlovac said we'd be safe here," I explained. And we were on our way.

The River Korana flows all the way south from Karlovac, now close to the road, now sketching out extravagant parabolas far to the west. It twinkled far below the carriageway as our car approached the north of Slunj. Before a bridge swung south across the river, I saw the neon lights of what I took to be a guest house on the other side of the riverbank. Having crossed the bridge and desperate now to end this journey, I took a gamble and pulled off right at a sign that said 'Rastoke, Entry 3'.

There was a steep descent, a tight further right turn and I feared I might have turned down a dead end from which it would be difficult to reverse. I couldn't get a strong sense of where I was, but I sensed I was close to the river that was gushing fast and strong. At the bottom of the ramp I had taken I was able to turn right and slip into a parking space precariously close to the river's edge. The entrance to the guest house I had spotted from above was a hundred metres away. I prayed that they might have vacancies.

When I opened the car door and stepped out, the background soundtrack of a steady wind whispering through the trees was all but drowned out by the rushing and plashing of water, coursing and, apparently, tumbling over rocks and stones. It was too dark to make out much detail.

At reception, a man with silver hair and a full, silver moustache welcomed us. He couldn't offer us two single rooms as they were all taken but he did have a double with an extra sofa bed.

"We'll take it," I said, dreading getting back into the car.

"Are you sure, Mick?" asked Lucy. "Shall we not find somewhere else?"

"Lucy, we're in the middle of nowhere. Let's stick with this."

I didn't relish the prospect of trying to reverse out of that space by the water's edge in the dark, find my way back up the ramp, and begin a fresh search for accommodation. This time Lucy didn't demur.

The man I took to be the owner took a set of keys with a torch attached to them and led us back out of the property, down a walkway and through a corridor of shoulder-high shrubs to a self-contained, converted barn with a sign above it that read *'Bungalow Vir'* – *Whirlpool Bungalow*.

Inside, a wooden staircase led up to the single stretch of accommodation: a sitting area featuring a small table, leading into a bedroom area. Wood panelling was the dominant theme. But it was not without its own charm, having the feel of a ship's cabin, albeit the captain's cabin and bigger and longer than most vessels could accommodate below deck.

All around came the sound of gushing water, even though the windows were closed. But I had no mental capacity to inspect the environment at this moment. Lucy was standing at the top of the staircase, her case in her hand, looking not just forlorn but in need of direction. I beckoned her to the middle of the room. She walked across, set down her case, and stood before me, looking vulnerable. I wrapped my arms around her and hugged her tight. She placed her hands and then her arms snugly round my waist. She laid her head against my chest and leaned in.

"Jesus, Mick! That was scary," she said, but the sigh that accompanied her words could have been interpreted as her moment of acceptance that the episode was over and none of its threat remained.

My reflection at that moment was that I had never before felt the kind of fear I had experienced at that checkpoint – a fear that had all but overwhelmed me. And if I wasn't one for 'what-ifs', the brutality of the image of Lucy with the barrel of a pistol in her mouth and the prospect of her head being blasted off before my eyes continued to send what felt like paroxysms through my brain. They came in pulses, each one moving uniformly like a ripple, then falling away, only to be followed by another, as if my senses couldn't compute the reckless enormity of the threat of that moment, now passed.

But this fear 'thing', I was now realising that it was insufficient to learn how to deal with a single sensation called 'fear', if in fact one could learn at all. The damn thing was nuanced. Whether it was in Malo Selo, or in the blasted house of Delila and Azra's parents, or in a lay-by just south of Karlovac, I had found myself at different distances from and angles to the real epicentre of a potentially fatal moment.

The fact that I hadn't witnessed the shell crash into the girls' parents' bedroom didn't mean that the realisation that I was now guardian to two orphaned children under the age of ten was other than terrifying. The relief that I had not been hit by the blast at Malo Selo didn't mean that the aftershock was anything other than paralysing. But, in this latest episode – though the pistol was in Lucy's mouth, not mine – I felt I had been closer to a fatal epicentre than ever before. What next? How would it feel when a gun was turned directly at me? And could I continue to handle these variations on a theme, particularly if the threat became starker and starker?

Already nine months into the conflict in Yugoslavia, twenty-two journalists had been killed, another four missing, presumed dead. Did I need simply to stay lucky? I had to face up to the fact that my instinct – *Well, it won't be me* – strong though it was, offered zero protection. At that moment, as I held Lucy tight, the pull between a desire to get the hell out and my personal mission to see through this war and make sure its details were telegraphed to the wider world was stretched to near breaking point. I realised again in that instant that I wouldn't walk away, but, please, was there a way of dialling down the danger? Was there some firmer ground I could occupy away from the seismic rumblings close to epicentres of risk?

Well, there was such ground, but wasn't that the Press pack, who hung around in hotels, took the lines from spokespeople and Press releases, ponced off others' stories, took no risk? I wasn't going to get what I needed to answer the exam question set by Paul on the foreign desk: where are the people and the stories? And I wasn't going to understand this war from the comfort of a hotel lobby.

Lucy and I tumbled onto the bed and clung to each other, in my case relief trying unsuccessfully to crowd out the aftershock. Lucy would tell me later that the sensations jamming her mind were the feel of the Chetnik's metal gun barrel against her teeth and an image of what the hole he risked blowing through the top of her head might look like. No matter how firmly she buried her eyes in my chest, she had struggled to blot out the Chetnik's face and the image of that fatal wound, she would tell me.

After ten minutes of being locked together on the bed, I kissed Lucy on the forehead, then lifted her chin and gently kissed her lips. She didn't resist and, if at first she didn't respond, she was soon nibbling my lower lip and we were kissing properly, meaningfully. I hadn't planned or even foreseen this, but I was soon slowly unbuttoning her blouse and laying my hand on smooth, warm flesh. She laid a hand on the zip of my jeans and I knew she felt my swell.

My mouth dry, the moment of penetration, though approached gradually with a rising sense of quiet excitement, was as shocking as ever and as replete with a million, thrilling, tingling sensations as the first time I had done it. A steepleful of bells ringing out in celebration. She gasped; I exhaled. And, if our lovemaking was not that of a seasoned couple totally attuned to one another's bodies, we went about it eagerly, perhaps greedily, before climaxing in impressive coordination. I issued a muted lion's roar and Lucy a sweet, rising crescendo of ecstasy.

And then we lay there, still coupled together, the chemical processes that work through the brain during the sex act providing us both with that heady, intoxicating, post-coital high that is without replica in any other situation.

We slipped under the covers. I laid gentle kisses on her cheek, her shoulder, her navel, subconsciously seeking to demonstrate that this was no one-off action. She tousled my hair and occasionally kissed me back.

The exertion and the shock of the day's encounter on the road to Slunj tipped us both into a deep, absorbing, satisfying sleep. After some hours, I surfaced occasionally and thrilled anew at each fresh realisation that I had begun the day alone and was now in the presence of an angel. But Lucy slept on, as women do, locked more deeply into their unconsciousness than any man can be, appearing to an observer as if they are concentrating hard on their sleep, resisting any attempt to lift them from this apparent, absolute relaxation. I envied her absorption.

And I wondered which Lucy would awake in a while. Might she be more traumatised the day after? Or relieved? And I reflected on her musing in the car out of Zagreb: "I might be resilient… I hope I'm resilient."

I got out of bed and opened a small side-curtain that let a shocking, intrusive shaft of late winter sunshine into the darkness of the room. As I pulled on some clothes, Lucy began to stir. I laid a hand on her head and whispered, "Luce, I'll get tea."

I made my way downstairs and out of the bungalow. The silver-haired man on reception was already installed.

"Could you do two teas?" I asked. "To take out to the bungalow?"

"Yes, yes. Of course."

As the owner of the guest house went off to boil water, I stepped out of the front door and wandered beyond the path to the bungalow, across the grass in the direction of the sound of rushing water.

If I had stepped out of this corner of Croatia into the pages of a lavishly illustrated book of fairy tales, the effect could not have been more breathtaking. The property seemed to be wedged onto a triangle of land bordered by rushing streams that descended in steps. Shimmering plates of water collided into turbulence, culminating in dramatic waterfalls that tumbled down fifty to a hundred metres into the River Korana. Rushing, cascading water on rock, stone, pebble and fallen branches combined in a mesmerising, musical composition. I stopped and stood stock still in awe. I swore I could hear harpsichord, triangle and harp notes set against a gentle violin wall of wind in the trees.

Reluctantly, I turned back so that our host's tea-making would not be a wasted effort, but I knew I would be back to explore further within the hour with Lucy.

"I didn't realise that Slunj was actually a corner of paradise," I said to the owner as I stepped back through the front door.

"It's very special, isn't it?" he replied. "But we think of this as Rastoke rather than Slunj. It's the historic, old part of the town – and, at least for those of us who've always lived here, it's the most beautiful and authentic district in the area."

The owner of the guest house went on to explain that the abundance and the fast-flowing nature of the water was because this was the confluence of the River Slunčica and the River Korana. The area used to have nearly two dozen watermills, where wheat was milled for bread and flax and hemp for clothing, before electric mills came along and made them uneconomic.

"South of here, the Slunčica keeps surfacing and disappearing along its route. I tell my grandchildren that it's a magic river. It's really the porous, karst limestone that its waters submerge beneath and then burst out of – but I don't spoil the story by telling them that."

And his eyes had lit up. He clearly never tired of telling visitors of his little fib to his grandkids.

"And that limestone – it chills the water. You'll see. It's the sweetest, cleanest, coolest drinking water you'll find anywhere.

"I think it's warm enough outside for me to set up breakfast for you and your lady friend on the table on the terrace with the best view. I'll pop a jug of fresh water on there for you," he said.

"Sorry – I didn't catch your name," I said.

"Ivo."

"Thanks, Ivo. I'm Mick and my friend is Lucy. We'll be down for breakfast shortly."

I bumped open the bungalow door with my hip without spilling any tea and scaled the staircase. Lucy was still lying in the bed, just her head and her bare shoulders showing above the sheet. She raised both eyebrows as we looked at each other for the first time in the light of a new day. It wasn't a smile or a censure. I took it to mean "How the hell did we end up here?!" And I took it to mean we both were to blame – if indeed 'blame' were the right word.

"Here you go, Lucy." She stretched out to take the mug, clasping the sheet to her with her other hand.

"Thanks, Mick. You're a star."

I smiled and sat on the bed. I told her that it was nearly ten o'clock and most of the other guests had gone. I wanted to ask her how she felt – after yesterday's trauma, after last night. But I thought it better to leave that till later.

"Lucy, you wouldn't believe what a glorious spot this is. Waterfalls, fast rivers, beautiful trees. It's like a corner of paradise."

And I gave Lucy Ivo's introduction to Rastoke, and I wasn't too concerned that I was ignoring the two big elephants in the room. In fact, I wasn't ignoring them; I was leaving them to be addressed a little later. That's all, I reasoned.

After drinking half of her tea, Lucy said she needed to shower and, with her side of the bed pushed against the wall, she handed me her cup, peeled back the covers, and slid across the bed. She put her feet on the floor, stood up and raised her arms ceilingwards, exhaling as she stretched.

Now that I could see her completely naked, I wondered how I hadn't noticed it before: she had the body of a runner. About five feet eight inches, she was lean but with strong legs. Her short brown hair was cut in a shake-dry style that was practical for a serious athlete. And, if the Chetnik had not quite used these words, he had at least been right about one thing: she had quite magnificent breasts, shapely and firm but not so big as to represent an impediment to serious middle- and long-distance running.

I tried not to ogle and handed Lucy the red-and-black checked shirt I'd been wearing the day before.

"Here. Put this on till you get under the shower." I wanted to hold it out, as a gentleman might hold out a lady's coat after a restaurant meal, inviting her to slip her arms into it. But I suspected that that would appear *faux-galant*, so instead I simply handed it to her.

"Thanks, Mick."

As I waited for Lucy to shower, there was a further surprise. Drawing back the curtains opposite the bed, I found the property's main picture window to be entirely filled with a view of the careering, tumbling, swirling waters of the River Slunčica. They came at me, as if they might engulf the whole room, dipping and slaloming just feet below the bungalow, then off to my right on their urgent, dramatic way down into the Korana.

Spellbound. The word formed in my mind. I could have gazed at the spectacle all day.

But Lucy was emerging from the shower in the bathroom at the bottom of the stairs, scaling the stairs in a towelling dressing gown and exclaiming, "Hell, Mick. I'm so stiff. All that sitting around. Sitting in the car. I'll die if I don't get out for a proper run sometime soon."

"Never mind that, Lucy. Just take a look at this."

I glowed with satisfaction when Lucy gave a second "Wow!" as Ivo led us to a table on the terrace, as if I were personally responsible for providing her with this view through trees to a waterfall that split its river into a dozen separate channels before each fell, frothing and steaming where it landed. I would learn later that this waterfall was called 'Angel's Hair'.

The breakfast of fresh local bread, jam, fresh fruit, and strong black coffee without a hint of bitterness was perfect for the setting. And Ivo was right: if water could be described as delicious, this was. Clean and with a delicate mineral edge. If it wasn't hot, there was enough sunshine to warm us. It was another moment, another environment, that I wanted to freeze and keep forever. But there were conversations to be had.

After a pause between us that I felt we both understood was avoiding the essential agenda, Lucy looked down into her coffee cup, then looked up at me, her brown eyes with a hint of green fixing me.

"Mick? You know... last night?" She paused. I didn't interrupt.

"After what had happened, it was so comforting. Being hugged like that... and then... Well it was lovely... but..." Lucy stopped and the silence began to expand.

"But," I said, helping her complete her sentence, "we shouldn't do it again. That's what you mean, isn't it?"

I hoped I had spoken neutrally. I felt no complaint and I took no offence at her drawing stumps so abruptly after the start of a physical relationship. I hoped Lucy recognised that in my tone.

"Yes. Yes... that's what I mean." She paused again but there was no extended silence this time. "Mick, you're a sweet, lovely man and I'm really relaxed in your company but... well, we fell into this, didn't we?"

"Yes, we absolutely did." I stretched out my hand and laid it gently on the back of Lucy's. "But it's okay, Lucy. It happened... Well, more than that: we chose to let it happen. But initially, all I wanted to do was hug you tight and make you feel safe again. I hope I did that."

Lucy smiled. She looped a forefinger round my little finger. "Yes, you did do that."

I went on. "We'll always have this between us but, if it helps, we don't need to talk about it again. And I'll never tell a soul… Ever."

I paused. I smiled. "Well… apart from Saša!"

Lucy grabbed a sugar cube and flicked it at me, then slapped the back of my hand affectionately. She smiled. "You dare!" She knew I was joking.

After a respectful pause, I addressed the second elephant. "And how are you feeling after our episode on the road? Does 'resilient' describe it?"

Lucy didn't answer straightaway. She looked out, as if gazing at the waterfall through the trees, but I knew she wasn't focusing on that.

"I think I'm feeling a little less resilient than I'd hoped I would. I feel frailer than I did this time yesterday," she said eventually.

I left Lucy space to frame her thoughts more precisely. The best tip in journalism I'd ever been given was not to fill someone's silence with a comment or a fresh question, tempting though it always was. Some of the best quotes, the most insightful comments I had harvested for stories, emerged from silence, from a vacuum I had actively chosen not to breach. But here, it wasn't just a tip for journalism; it was a tip for life, a tip for friendship – if that didn't sound too grand.

"I just keep thinking What if? What if he'd pulled the trigger? What if he'd made you drive off and leave me behind?" she said.

"I wouldn't have left you behind, Lucy. Not ever," I said. "He'd have had to have killed me."

I said those words not having framed the thought to myself previously – but I realised in that moment that it was true. I couldn't have left her with that hooligan, however many policemen were hovering in the area. It didn't mean I was brave; unusually, it would have been a dilemma with only one solution.

I went on. "And the thing is, Lucy, there are no 'what-ifs'. There are only things that happen and things that don't happen. We can learn from situations. Might we do something differently next time? But 'what-ifs' – they take us nowhere."

"Hmmm," said Lucy. I sensed that, if she agreed with my logic, she still couldn't stop herself from thinking about what might have happened, however much she wanted to move on.

"I don't know, Mick. At the moment I'm not going to give in, even if I do feel a little frail. I'm not going to go back to London – but I do know I never want to go through that, or anything like that again… Obviously."

There was more silence between us, just the sounds of rushing water. Then she said, "But, Mick, I might feel frailer… but I'm not going to be diminished by this."

I smiled. "That's my girl!"

And Lucy broke into a smile. "I'm not your girl. I'm my own girl." She was teasing, not chastising.

I know, I know," I said, raising my palms to indicate I'd misspoken. "It's a manner of speaking – not a statement of possession!"

We were both smiling, and the exchanges had done what I had hoped they would: popped a balloon of tension that would have continued to float above us, had we not pricked it.

"Come on, Lucy. Let's go a bit further towards the waterfalls before we decide what to do next."

We walked down some steps and were about to follow the path when I said, "Lucy, notwithstanding what we agreed before, will you do me just one more little favour?"

"What's that?"

"Will you hold my hand… one last time?"

She looked up at me. There was a softness in her gaze. "Yes, Mick. Of course."

And we held hands and headed off towards the waterfalls. And a passer-by on the road above would have seen us on the path by the river and thought that there was nothing unusual about this pair of lovers on a romantic walk in a magical corner of Croatia. The passer-by would have been oblivious to the circumstances that had brought us together, tested our strength of mind, and transformed each of us into a source of support for the other.

A little further beyond the waterfalls that I had seen earlier that morning, we turned a corner to be met with what could have been

Rastoke's pièce de resistance, had there not been so many candidates: an old mill some fifty feet above us, water sliding and spilling beneath its base, where once a waterwheel would have been driven. The water shivered there precariously like a spillage on an upturned tray, before tumbling in six separate strands down rocks striped ochre and moss green. The channels then slalomed together, twisting in one flow past thin, tall trees until they reached the riverbed proper.

We stood and watched the endless cascade in fascination and felt a film of spray on our faces. There was no need for words. We stood in silence for five minutes, in thrall.

A fatuous comparison popped into my head: the horror of the previous day set against this unimaginably beautiful, dreamlike experience. I brushed it away. It was an irrelevant and unhelpful contrast. And I gripped Lucy's hand a little tighter and said, "Come on. Best head back. Work to do."

Back in the guesthouse, I wrestled with my conscience as I tried to accommodate Lucy's strong disinclination to feature in a news story about our journey on the road to Slunj.

"Mick, I'd have to do an interview with *ITN* before it appeared in *The Times*. Or they'd fire me. I just don't want to be the story… I can just imagine some idiot in the newsroom in London sending a camera crew to my parents' house. I really, really don't want it, Mick.

"I'm sorry. Does that screw everything up for you? Could you perhaps pretend it was a guide – or a translator?"

Again, it was a dilemma with only one solution: there was no way I would name Lucy, if she was uncomfortable with what that might trigger. However, without being pompous, my own journalistic principles would not let me create an alternative, fictitious Lucy. The fact that other journalists might did not make it right.

It was frustrating; the episode filled Paul's 'people and stories' box with a great big, fat tick, but acknowledging Lucy's strongly held preference was more important to me than a single story, however powerful it might be. And no, I said, stilling at a stroke the cynical voice inside my head: I wasn't self-censoring because the night before we had made love.

In the end, I told the tale as though it had been recounted to me by a local. It meant I named no names. My only regret was that the power of the narrative and its immediacy were diminished – yes, that word again – by being told at one step removed.

"So, do you want me to drive you back to Zagreb or will you come with me to interview Begić? I'm easy either way," I said. My profound hope was that she wouldn't ask me to delay my drive to Velika Kladuša, where the leading Bosnian Muslim politician and CEO of Bosnian food conglomerate, Lanac Ishrane, which translated as 'Foodchain', was based.

"That's kind of you, Mick. Let's stick with Plan A and go and meet Begić."

After filing my story, I put a call through to Lanac Ishrane. Yes, Mr Begić would gladly see us later that afternoon, his secretary said.

10
FEBRUARY 1992

If the previous twenty-four hours had felt unreal, yoking the terrifying and the magical, Lucy and I sat that afternoon in another extraordinary location, different again from the spellbinding charms of Rastoke.

We were gazing out through an entire wall of plate-glass windows across rolling, fertile plains and woodland that stretched south-west as far as Bosnia's border with Croatia and beyond. What's more, we were sitting in a castle. Between us sat an achingly beautiful woman, who I'd later learn was called Petra. To my right was a small man, perhaps five feet six, five feet seven inches tall, in a navy suit with an open-neck white shirt, his dark brown hair beginning to silver at the edges. His hair waved abundantly out of a parting on the left that appeared to be designed to try to bring some order. It was unsuccessful.

When we had arrived at Velika Kladuša, just half an hour's drive from Slunj, we had been redirected by Tarik Begić's PA at his company's headquarters to his home – a castle in the Old Town. In so far as any castle is 'ordinary', this was no ordinary castle. Begić's, or a previous owner's, architect had redesigned it, using all the centuries-old stones, some dating back to the thirteenth century, but creating a modern design with four towers and a glass-fronted gallery. In its dominant position on a dome-shaped hill above the town, it was quirky but not without architectural attraction. Begić had clearly been keen to show off his five-star residence to a couple of members of the international media to mark him out as someone cut from special cloth.

As I had explained to Lucy in the Astoria and on the road, Begić was the leading light in an area known as the Bihać pocket – as far north-west in Bosnia as one could go without tipping into Croatia. He had topped the poll in elections for the seven-strong Bosnian Presidency in 1990 but, for some reason, had ceded the top job to Alija Izetbegović.

Another intriguing detail I had unearthed was that, as head of Lanac Ishrane, he had been jailed for around two years in the late '80s – allegedly for fraud.

"It sounds, Lucy, as if many people thought he was fitted up, because he was elected to the Presidency shortly after he was freed. It's all very strange," I said.

After parking up at the castle, we took a curved stone path that led to solid, wooden double doors. I rang an old-fashioned cowbell on a chain and a woman in her thirties, with eyes like Sophia Loren, opened the door and welcomed us. Her black hair had a natural blue sheen and it was tied back in a long plait. She was wearing a white silk blouse and navy pencil skirt.

I tried not to show it to her or to Lucy but I was almost overwhelmed by how beautiful she was. Annoyingly my mind set off on a trawl of when the last occasion was that I had come across any woman as attractive as her. I had drawn a blank by the time I realised I needed to sound coherent or there would be a real danger of my babbling uncontrollably as I drank her in.

"You must be the British journalists," she said in immaculate English.

"Yes, yes – we are," I said.

"I'll just go and see if Mr Begić is available to see you now."

I paced randomly and slightly nervously but I enjoyed the sound and the sensation of the clack of my heels on the stone floor.

"I bet he came back here especially this afternoon so that we'd get to see his castle," I whispered, as if the setting required the hushed tones appropriate for a sacred space.

"I'll show you up," Begić's assistant said, when she returned two minutes later. "I don't know if it's a problem, but Mr Begić doesn't speak English. Only Serbo-Croat. But, if necessary, I can sit in and translate."

"Well, I can speak to him in Serbo-Croat, but maybe you could keep Lucy up to speed with the conversation and translate, if she has any questions," I said.

"Yes, that would be great," said Lucy.

"Okay. I'll do that."

Once up in the gallery room, if I had expected the firm handshake he had offered and noticed the thinness of his lips, I hadn't quite been prepared for the way in which his eyes would fascinate me – in the original Latin meaning of the word: to bewitch or enchant. Deep set and rich brown, they gave me a feeling of Begić looking for a window into my soul. It was slightly unnerving. As the conversation progressed, his way of hooding his brows in concentration would add to the impression of a man who tended to control conversations, to manage situations rather than allow himself to be managed or manipulated. If he was physically unimpressive – as well as his modest stature, I could see over time he would tend towards the portly – his manner signalled to me, unmistakably and without fear of contradiction, that I was in the presence of an individual with special qualities.

I introduced Lucy and wondered whether the Begić eyes might have a similar effect on her.

"This is some place you've got, Mr Begić," I said.

"Yes, it's special. I'm very fortunate. This is where the Old Town was. There's been a settlement here since 1280 but the castle was completely renovated in the 1970s."

"Nice job," I said.

Begić's Girl Friday returned with tea on a tray and a plate of biscuits. Lucy looked at me and smiled.

"They're Jaffa Cakes, Mick!"

"What's she saying?" asked Begić.

"These biscuits. At home we call them Jaffa Cakes – from Jaffa oranges," I explained.

"These, my friends, are Bosnia's favourite biscuits. In Lanac Ishrane, we named them Pops biscuits. And you could almost say that the streets of Velika Kladuša were paved with the money they made. We make them by the million and we export them to twenty-two countries."

He paused. "Well, we did. Until they buggered up the business by putting me in jail… Still… Bumps in the road. We'll get it back on track."

After we all sat down on leather sofas and chairs that squeaked expensively, Begić told us how he had grown a business empire that had completely transformed not just Velika Kladuša but the entire surrounding area. In the late '60s, Velika Kladuša had barely fifty metres of asphalt road, and it had one TV set, kept under lock and key in the community centre. Endemic syphilis and infectious hepatitis were rife due to too many poverty-stricken people living on top of one another.

After the company's successful transformation from a small agricultural cooperative employing twenty-six people to a modern food-producing and processing conglomerate under Begić's management in the 1970s and 1980s, local labourers were able to quit their seasonal work in Croatia and Slovenia. More than thirteen thousand jobs were created in the area, every family benefiting from a Lanac Ishrane salary – some earning two – and the company paved the streets, laid tarmac roads, brought running water and a reliable electricity supply to the area, and spawned poultry farms and factories in abundance across the area.

"Mick, I'm not boasting but they call me 'Babo' round here," Begić said, having graduated from 'Mr Morrison' to 'Mick' at my request.

"Petra. Tell them what 'Babo' means."

"It's a Muslim word for Daddy' – but it's more than that. It means a respected figure of authority in the community. One whose word is rarely challenged," Petra said. Then she added with a smile, "There's a saying round here – '*Voda teče kud Babo reče.*'

"The water flows where Babo tells it to go," I translated for Lucy.

Begić smiled and wafted a hand before his face as if to dismiss the saying as nonsense. I suspected he had enjoyed Petra sharing it with us, nonetheless.

Begić went on to explain that, despite what he had done not just for Velika Kladuša but for Bosnia and Yugoslavia as a whole, 'the authorities' had nearly wrecked his business by arresting and incarcerating him.

What followed was a complex tale of how he was collateral damage in a Belgrade-driven plot to ensure that the Bosnian figure the Serbian establishment feared most, Hamdija Pozderac, was knocked out of the game.

Pozderac and his family hailed from Cazin in the Bihać pocket and he had been a resolute supporter of Lanac Ishrane and, therefore, of Begić.

"Mick, this was a giant of a politician. He was close to Tito. These guys today – they're minnows. Not fit to follow in his footsteps," said Begić. "He was professor of political science at the University of Sarajevo but he had years of experience of how you really get things done in the political world. And, in Tito's era, that wasn't always easy. He was in line to become President of Yugoslavia.

"The Serbs who planned to carve up Bosnia knew that they had to stop Hamdija. They knew he'd have found ways as Yugoslav President to halt their…" Begić hunted for the word. "Machinations."

Begić explained how, after Tito's death, with the Yugoslav economy in the second half of the 1980s in a terrible state and inflation rampant, he and Lanac Ishrane did what many businesses at the time did and issued promissory notes rather than paid with cash for their supplies. Wait for inflation to settle and then regularise. That was the logic, he said.

"They said my notes were fraudulent – but they were pegged against all the land and the real estate and the buildings that housed our animals. Worth millions! When the charges against us broke, inflation leapt further. And I got the blame. But it was bullshit."

But 'Belgrade' had used his relationship with Lanac Ishrane to draw Pozderac into the frame, Begić claimed. He must have known about the Lanac Ishrane activities, they reasoned. He must have been complicit in the so-called fraud. Shortly after the allegations surfaced, Pozderac resigned and stepped away from politics after decades of public service.

"And you know what, Mick? Within a year, he was dead. He had a stroke."

Begić looked down at the rug on the floor and shook his head. I wondered if those eyes might be filling up.

"They killed him, Mick. His heart was broken… He didn't deserve that."

I caught a glance of Lucy out of the corner of his eye. She was transfixed by Begić and this near-Shakespearean performance.

Begić regained his composure. "And you see, Mick, if there'd been any truth in this whole thing, they'd have banged me away for twenty years. Instead of which, I'm out in a couple of years. Four thousand people lost their jobs straightaway and thousands and thousands of our animals died because our food suppliers thought they weren't going to be paid and stopped deliveries. And a man – a big man – died. Tragic – really tragic."

"If you don't mind me asking, Mr Begić," I said, "how was prison?"

"Well, to be strictly accurate, I wasn't 'jailed'. I was held in 'interrogative detention'. Two years on, when they couldn't raise a meaningful indictment, they had to let me go. But to answer the question: prison was okay. To be honest, I used the time to recharge my batteries. I read a lot of stuff I wouldn't normally have found time to read. My fellow inmates treated me like royalty. I was Babo after all!" He laughed.

"And the guards made sure I was generously supplied with pear brandy so…" The sentence trailed away. "Of course, when I came out, after so many people had lost their jobs for what people felt was a fit-up, I was more popular than ever. I was always going to cruise the elections," he said.

"But what I don't understand, Mr Begić, is you won more votes than anyone. You could have been Bosnian President. Why did you stand aside for Izetbegović?" I asked.

"It's complicated, Mick, and I may have to take up the reins at some time in the future. I'm not ruling that out. But I'm busy here. My people here need their Babo. In the end, I did a deal where Alija took the top job but I got my people in key posts." He paused. "Mind you, I fear he's going to mess up."

"In what way?" Lucy joined the conversation.

"Miss Lucy, Izetbegović likes to discuss Kant's *Critique of Pure Reason* over a coffee. He can write elegantly about what the ideal Islamic state might look like, but I don't think he knows how to do deals. You *have* to do deals. I'm a businessman. And I might be from a Muslim family, but I'm working here, surrounded by Serbs and Croats – and, when I say 'surrounded', I mean many of them are my friends. And how do you think I've kept my business on the rails? Grown it? Exported internationally? I've done deals." He paused again, then said with emphasis: "You *have* to do deals."

And Begić told us of a famous Bosnian Muslim commander, Huska Miljković, who led a militia of several thousand armed men in the Bihać pocket during World War II. At different times in the war, he and his militia aligned with Germans, Croats, Partisans and Chetniks.

"One night, when he couldn't sleep and his comrade asked him what he was thinking, Huska admitted, 'I don't care about Nazism, or Communism. I don't care about Hitler, Stalin or Tito. I'm only interested in what will happen to me – to us, to this Muslim nation here,'" said Begić.

I kept to myself the reflection that this was hardly the stuff of heroic commitment but, over the next eighteen months or so, I would come to understand precisely why a story that jarred with me held such resonance for Begić.

Begić stretched his arm to look at his watch.

"Mick, Lucy, I've a call to make shortly. I hope I've given you enough material. Just put a call through, if you need anything more or you want to check a detail, Mick."

He turned to Lucy. "Petra, tell Miss Lucy that I'd be delighted to welcome her film crew at any time. I think the world needs to know the dangers we face here and how we might get out of them."

Begić stood up and shook hands with us.

"Petra, thank you for helping Miss Lucy," he added graciously.

"That's okay." Petra lowered her gaze and suppressed a smile, like a schoolgirl embarrassed by a teacher's praise in front of the rest of the class.

I was aware of Begić picking up the receiver of a chunky cream Bakelite telephone as the three of us headed through the doors to the staircase.

As I stood on the cobbles outside the castle, the elements of the story swirled around me. I knew that there was rich colour in describing this minute man with a piercing gaze, living in a crazy castle on a Bosnian hilltop – fresh from prison yet fêted by the local population. But how to explain who Hamdija was and where he fitted into the Yugoslav and Bosnian mosaic? And when we talked about 'Belgrade' trying to bring down Begić to get at Hamdija, who was Belgrade? Was it Yugoslavia's government, or Serbia's – or was it just Serbian President, Slobodan Milošević?

It was another example of the complexity of causes of conflict that made the seemingly unstoppable collapse of Yugoslavia almost impossible to explain within the scope of a news story, even to an intelligent, well-informed reader. And Lucy and I would discover over the next couple of hours a further twist to the tale that would make our task yet more challenging.

Well – what did you make of him, Lucy?" I asked.

"I warmed to him, Mick. He's terribly engaging – but I suspect he's quite artful. I'm not sure everything he said will turn out to be true. But – hell! Interesting guy."

Back in the car, we decided to scout a local café – any café – to check how deeply the Babo narrative ran. Was it real, or were he and his entourage spinning a line?

The man behind the counter in the Toscana Caffe Slastičarna was positive without being fawning.

"There's no doubt this place wouldn't have been here and I wouldn't be making the decent living I am, if it hadn't been for him. It wasn't just him. Lanac Ishrane changed everything."

He paused. "But, as for Babo – well, you know, these guys smell success and they do get a bit above themselves. We see him being whisked up to his castle in his chauffeur-driven Merc with the blacked-out windows and you do think maybe he's got ideas above his station."

An elder man sitting on a table a little further away from the counter chipped in, having earwigged the conversation.

"I don't think he's a bad person but, you know, he was once a little runt like the rest of us. Third of thirteen kids, he was. With that size of family, he'll have had holes in his pants and the soles of his shoes once. I think he just got greedy. That's it, you see. You get money and then you can't get enough. Yes – he went down. But thousands lost their jobs."

Twenty minutes later we were at the council offices, having been advised to look up a local councillor who we had been told had a story to tell about Begić.

Councillor Harun turned out to be a small man, wearing a brown taqiyah cap and a pale brown loose jacket over a blue and white open-neck shirt. Aged about sixty, he had a grey toothbrush moustache and the slightly pained expression of a man who was either suppressing an ailment or had been worn down by the cares of years of toil and imperfect health.

"So, you want to know about Tarik, then?" asked Harun.

"Yeah – we met him earlier, up at the castle, and heard his story."

"The castle?" Harun raised his eyebrows in evident distaste. The councillor then tipped into a complicated tale of how his own influence on the council had been checked and thwarted. And his claim was that Begić was the figure behind this, without offering up any hard facts to support this thesis.

"Fact is his and my family fell out years ago. Over a girl, I think. And that hostility has been passed down. He's always had it in for me. I could've done so much… but." The sentence trailed away.

"But they do call him 'Babo' round here, don't they?" I asked.

"Yes, they do," said Harun. "But he's got too big for his boots."

I smiled. "But he created – his company created – thousands of jobs."

"Yes, but why get so greedy? He's risked wrecking the company. People were thrown out of work through his greed."

"He said it was a fit-up and that his promissory notes were sound," I said.

Harun chuckled. "Sir! There was a three-hundred-million-dollar hole in the company's finances. And he claims that his paper was real because it was backed by a bunch of chicken shacks! Come on! Really!"

And Harun raised his right forearm, as if to say that he could take no more of these claims.

Then he was bending over the table towards us, as if he had a killer blow to deliver to Begić.

"And I'll bet he didn't tell you about how he sent Hamdija Pozderac to an early grave?" Harun asked.

"No. He told us it was Belgrade that squeezed out Hamdija. Linked him with Lanac Ishrane to force him out of public life," I said.

"Pah! That's disgusting!" There was a full snarl of contempt on Harun's face now.

"When the police came for Tarik, he told them that he had tapes of conversations that proved Pozderac knew about the promissory notes. I think he thought that, if he mentioned Hamdija, he'd somehow be protected because he was such a huge political figure. He betrayed a man who'd helped him create his millions. And when Hamdija learned what Tarik had said, *that's* when he quit politics completely. Walked away."

Harun paused, shaking his head in anger, before resuming.

"And did he tell you that Hamdija is now dead? Died within months?"

Now Harun was shouting. "*He* did it! That fat midget brought about the death of a great man. You ask him about *that*!"

The tension had risen to a point at which a slice of silence seemed appropriate. After a moment, I said, "That's quite some claim. Are you sure about the tapes, Councillor?"

"Sir, sure as you're sitting before me. Chief of Police told me himself. He told me he didn't even know whether any tapes existed. He didn't need to. Because Hamdija stood down as soon as that story broke. Disgusting! Disgusting, I tell you."

After Harun attempted to settle a few more, less dramatic scores, I sensed it was time to wind down the meeting. We shook hands and left.

In the street outside, Lucy and I looked at one another in bewilderment. There was barely a need to comment.

Eventually, Lucy said, "Well… which crazy guy is telling the truth and which is lying?"

We overnighted in Velika Kladuša – a simple, delicious dinner, two single rooms in a cheap motel – and the next morning we were on our way back to Zagreb. The trip was uneventful, checkpoints passed without drama, though Lucy did ask me how much of Croatia I had known from trips as a child with my mother.

"I never once came with her, Lucy," I said.

"Really?"

"No. It didn't cross my mind as strange before I reached fourteen and she died."

"So you never even met your grandparents on your mother's side?"

"No, I didn't. My dad told me they both died within the space of a couple of years, when I was little. After that she showed no interest in coming back, he said."

"I'm still surprised she never brought you."

"Dad said her family had a pretty miserable life. Her dad wouldn't join the Communist Party so they got no privileges or cushy jobs. But I agree; in hindsight it seems strange she never brought us to learn something of our ancestors. Even if it was just her home village and surroundings."

The closer we got to the Astoria, the sadder I felt about my road trip with Lucy coming to an end. Her company was so relaxing. But, of course, I didn't let on.

On the outskirts of Zagreb, I had one final question.

"Lucy?"

"Yes?"

"Do you think Begić is screwing Petra?"

"Mick! Don't even ask that! That's so bad!"

"I bet he is." I chuckled mischievously.

"Mick, you're presuming Petra would let him anywhere near her. A classy woman like that. Really!" I couldn't tell whether her outrage was mock or real.

"Ooogh, those Sophia Loren eyes! A man could drown in them," I said.

"She'd eat you alive, young Michael."

I flushed inwardly. I loved that 'young Michael' bit.

Back in my room, I put a call through to Lanac Ishrane and spoke to Begić's office. Thirty minutes later his PA called me back.

"Mr Morrison. Mr Begić says the story about the tapes just isn't true. He suggests you shouldn't put it in your story. He might have to contact his solicitor. But he's busy now. He can't speak."

When I sat down to write, as often was the case, the clouds of confusion parted and shafts of sunlit clarity shone through. The story became clear. Forget about the deep background and the machinations that were impossible to prove or disprove. Having been warned off suggesting that Begić had fitted up his own biggest political supporter by legal threats that I had insufficient proof to collapse, the story was simple.

I wasn't terribly pleased with the headline – *Pocket-sized 'General' says, "I can save Bosnia from war"* – but I was pleased with the way in which I had pared the story right down to its bare bones.

The sub-editor who had fixed the headline had translated my adjective 'minute' into 'pocket-sized' – words I felt trivialised Begić unnecessarily. And he had labelled him a 'general', the quote marks suggesting correctly that he was not a real military general. I couldn't kick up a fuss about either piece of finessing – this was typical of the trade between reporter and sub-editor and it was an arena in which not much love was lost – but I felt that, despite the headline, I had captured the essence of this apparently shrewd operator.

I had made not just a mental note but also a diarised written note to myself to check up regularly on whether further evidence emerged, suggesting that the claim had substance that it was Begić himself who had stitched up Hamdija. But the story I'd written was still strong and the colour was rich: a man who had tried to look into my soul and had told me with considerable conviction that he could prevent bloodshed almost single-handedly.

I had asked my father every time he saw a news bulletin about Yugoslavia on the news to press 'record' on the video player and, some weeks later at home, I had caught up on an ITN interview with Begić. Lucy had been offered the perfect invitation: camera shots of this small but charismatic man on the battlements of his castle, fields and forests stretching out over his shoulder as far as the eye could see, explaining calmly and intelligently how to extinguish this potentially fatal inflagration before it took hold and ravaged his native land.

Over the next year, I would see Lucy at various events, usually from afar. She'd be manhandling items of broadcasting equipment and looking serious. But we had no further in-depth conversations. Then she was gone – off to other locations. And, though I would go some years before meeting her again, for the first three years till the end of the war I never went more than a couple of days without recalling her to mind.

What was she, I'd ask myself? Uncomplicated. Interested. Empathetic. Kind. Lovely smile. That's what she was. And what would her adjectives have been for me? Yes, she'd said at Rastoke that I was 'a sweet, lovely man', that she felt relaxed in my company, but I suppose I was looking for something more profound. I had repeatedly to brush away the thought because I couldn't know.

When I got back to Zagreb, Saša was rattling at the keyboard of his word processor in the space that we journalists had made our own in the Hotel Astoria. Without looking up, he called across to me.

"So, how was your trip? How was Begić – and did you give him my love?" he asked.

"Interesting," I said. "And Begić – well, he's some character." I paused. I was puzzled. "As for giving him your love, you didn't say you knew him, Saša," I said.

"Oh, the old rogue. Yes, I've known him for years. Everybody knows him."

"So why didn't you say… before I set off?"

"Better for you to reach your own conclusions about him, Mick. I didn't want to colour your judgement of him."

"Oh… I see." I weighed up the comment and I was just coming round to the view that Saša's approach might have been sound, one for which I should be grateful, when Saša said, "He's got a gorgeous assistant, mind you…"

He wasn't looking at me. He kept on typing.

"You mean Petra?"

"Yes, that's her. Petra. Did you meet her?"

I didn't answer straightaway. It took just a few moments for a great big penny to drop with a clunk. I tried to stop my jaw from dropping too.

"Saša." My voice fell to a whisper. "You didn't, did you?"

Saša finally looked up and across at me.

"Me?! Really! Mick?!" If it was an attempt to ooze innocence, I wasn't convinced.

"Yer little…" I didn't know which noun or adjective to use and I was havering between shock and admiration. I shook my head in bewilderment at his chutzpah.

11

FEBRUARY 1992

I didn't much like the idea of returning to Britain while the wars were still raging. Even at times when the conflicts felt more like a slow burn than a conflagration, I suspect I was concerned subconsciously that something big might blow up and I might miss out on the story or, worse still, be edged out as lead reporter. But Paul would winkle me out of Yugoslavia now and then, aware from personal experience of the cumulative impact frequent gunshots, explosions and exposure to carnage could inflict upon a reporter. However, on this occasion I had something of a mission: visiting my father in the north-east on something of a fact-finding mission.

On one of our road trips in Croatia and Bosnia, Saša had asked me about my mother. What was her maiden name and where was she from? I recalled that she had been Nada Pavlović before she married but I was slightly embarrassed to admit that I wasn't sure where she had been born.

"I know she met my dad in Split, so I've always presumed that she was from near there. The sense I have from the stories she told is that she was brought up in a small village," I told Saša.

"Well – if she was called Pavlović, that's not much of a steer. It's one of the most common family names that there is in Croatia. You can find a Pavlović just about anywhere. But do find out where she was brought up, Mick. I'd be interested to know," Saša said.

"Now you mention it, so would I," I said, and I laughed to conceal my embarrassment at my ignorance.

If it felt somewhat remiss of me never to have asked the question before, I reasoned with myself that a child at fourteen is so self-absorbed that it wasn't so surprising that I had failed to ask the question before she died. I suppose I had carried with me my own myth that she was raised in a village near Split, without knowing whether it was true or false.

My visit to the north-east wasn't a total success. I pottered around the house, finding it hard to settle or relax. Downtime felt trivial at moments when people I knew and increasingly cared for were under fire. War had created in me obligation. Somehow I appeared to have made it my duty to remain there till hostilities ceased and to try to draw the attention of decision makers outside Yugoslavia to the injustices being done within. At Press briefings with representatives of the United Nations and the European Community Monitor Mission, visiting political leaders from Europe, Russia and the US, I would push them as vigorously as I could, arguing that their current policies of either refusing to intervene or intervening limply and ineffectively meant hundreds of people were dying unnecessarily. That needed to change.

If Saša and many other of the journalists on the story seemed to be less emotionally engaged, Saša never scorned my approach nor described it as idealistic. I might have imagined it but I think I heard the word 'altruism' fall from his lips during one precarious mountain road trip.

"I mean, Sash – it's not as if Dubrovnik or Vukovar are Badlands somewhere in the wilderness. They're distinguished *European* cities with educated citizens. Where do they draw the line? Is it okay to trash Dubrovnik or Vukovar but west of the border with Italy everything is sacrosanct? It doesn't make sense, Sash – it really doesn't." I was aware I was sounding aerated.

"So what you mean is you want to shame Europe's leaders and President Bush into action?" Saša asked.

I thought for a moment. "Yes – precisely."

"Well, that's bold, Mick… But noble," Saša said.

And, on a sofa in the lounge at my father's house, I realised there had been two important developments over the preceding months. I had acquired a second ambition to add to my original reputational aim of becoming renowned as an analyst of conflicts and international politics – a Ray Massingham-Byrd Mk II. With my columns in *The Times*, I also genuinely aspired to influence the course of the wars. I might have been wielding a pea-shooter, but my ambition had been labelled noble by the man whose experience I most valued.

The second development was something I had not anticipated and had not thought likely: namely, far from Saša showing me the ropes and then making me stand on my own feet, over time we had become closer and our working together had become our default position rather than the exception. I didn't understand what it was I offered a man of his range and ability. There were far more experienced sidekicks he could have recruited. But the truth was we were undeniably closer and I suspected that, before long, I would need to ask him directly what precisely it was that I brought to his table. What I was clear about was the fact that he could not possibly imagine the degree to which I cherished his friendship, his advice – and his teasing.

Back in the here and now, my father's short attention span for the fine details of the collapse of Yugoslavia was something of an irritation to add to my restlessness. I couldn't tell whether I had failed to engage him – and, therefore, other target readers – in a story I found absorbing, or whether he was consciously feigning disinterest because he wanted me out of harm's way and, consequently, out of Yugoslavia. My note to self was to try still harder to make mine compelling accounts of the human resilience and damage playing out among the politics.

"Dad – Mum was called Pavlović, wasn't she?" I asked.

"Yes – Pavelić," he replied.

"And where was she brought up? Was it in a village near Split? That's where you met her, wasn't it?"

"No – she was from further north. From a one-horse town outside Senj. On the north coast of Croatia. Blink and you'd miss it, as you drive through," he said.

"Did you ever go?"

"No. Her mother made it to our wedding but I got the impression they didn't have enough money for her father to travel as well. And I never really got an invitation to the family home. I think they thought I might look down on their humble home – which, of course, I wouldn't have."

"I feel bad now that I never asked her more about her home and her childhood…" I left the comment hanging.

After a silence, my father picked up the thread.

"You were young, Michael. Why would you have asked? Maybe if she'd been around when you were older, you'd have got round to it. Not that I think she'd have had much to say."

"Someone's past, the place they were brought up – that's always interesting, isn't it?" I said.

He shrugged. Perhaps it was just the journalist in me, I reflected; but then I swatted away my doubt. Of course it was interesting.

"Did she talk much to you about her upbringing?"

"No – not much. As I've said before, I think it was quite grim for a family beyond the party."

But just as I sensed that either he simply had no more details or was keen to shut down the subject, he stood up and said, "If you're interested, I did keep a box of documents and pictures that she left. Not sure there's anything of interest in there – just certificates and a few photos. But you can have it if you want."

Minutes later he came down from his bedroom with a frayed Clark's shoebox, its lid held on by a couple of thick brown rubber bands.

"Take it with you, if you want. I've got all the memories of her here that I need," he said.

A black and white photograph of her in a dark brown antique frame looked out at him from the mantelpiece. She would have been in her late twenties. Kindness shone from her.

I flipped off the rubber bands and took a look inside the box. It felt like a special gift, one whose potential magic I didn't want to open to the elements straightaway. I wanted to dig through the contents on my own and in my own time when I got back to London, so I flicked through a couple of documents, glanced at one picture of her as a youth with a girlfriend but then shut it up again.

"I'll take a good look when I'm back in London," I said. "Let you know if there's anything interesting – anything you should have back."

When it came to the time for me to head south, he saw me off with a formal handshake. He wasn't one for being demonstrative so that wasn't anything unusual. What was different was the sense of remoteness I felt towards him at that moment. I wondered whether it was generational.

I felt he had a tendency to think that keeping your head down was the right approach and that, if you raised your head above the parapet – as I had been doing in Croatia, in Bosnia and in *The Times* – someone might be tempted to knock it off. I hoped that my idealism wouldn't dim and I didn't believe that a campaigning spirit would inevitably dilute as I grew older. However, although I didn't expect the remoteness to last, the distance between us saddened me. So I tried to snuff out the thought and headed off.

Back in London I had a relatively tight turnaround before I took a flight back to Zagreb, but I made the time before I left to look through the contents of the shoebox. There were photographs of my mother as a child, one featuring a couple I presumed to be her parents. Her mother had clearly passed on her fair complexion and kind expression to my mother. Her father's face was expressionless but, in an identity parade, his distinguishing features would have been slicked-back black hair with a side parting, a wide mouth with thin lips, and ears slightly larger than scale.

Another photo featured what appeared from their demeanour to be a family: a couple with two grown-up children captured on a palm-fringed beach. The father was wearing a rakish Panama hat. On the back of the photo there were some words I couldn't make out, the ink having faded. More legibly was written in my mother's hand 'Santa Pola, Alicante – 1958'.

I could have presumed that this family was related to my mother but I knew she had moved to England in 1963. What might the connection be to a family in Spain five years earlier? From past experience, I was loath to make any assumptions.

Then, amongst Baptism and First Holy Communion certificates, I found my mother's birth certificate. Her father's profession was Shipping Maintenance Supervisor and his full name was Želko Stevnić Pavelić. Her mother was Marina (née Božić). My mother had been born Nada Pavelić on 3rd August 1941. Her birthplace wasn't Senj, as my father had suggested, but Krivi Put. It was a village I couldn't even find in my basic atlas, though subsequently I would establish that it was a tiny hamlet just outside Senj.

My first instinct was that the village was called 'Bloody Road' and I wondered what gruesome history might have lain behind it; but a quick dictionary check reminded me that, while 'krv' meant blood, 'kriv' meant sloping or bendy, so its name was simply a description of the steep mountain roads leading to it.

What slightly jarred, though, was the detail that her family name was Pavelić and not, as I thought I had been led to believe, Pavlović. In our conversation the day before, when I'd asked my father whether my mother was a Pavlović, he had said yes but had then repeated the name back to me in a way that, in hindsight, sounded more like Pavelić than Pavlović. Perhaps years earlier I'd simply latched onto Pavlović and he'd never pulled me up on it or felt he needed to pull me up on it.

I flicked through the rest of the contents of the box and then tucked it away in a wardrobe. For a moment my hand hovered over the photograph of the family in Alicante – the most intriguing item in the collection – and I wondered whether I should slip it into my inside jacket pocket. But I was afraid I might lose it on my travels, its potential significance disappearing along with the picture itself. So I left it with the rest of the documents and made a mental note to show it to my father at a later date and ask him if he knew who they were.

12
APRIL 1992

The Renault 5 in which we had made the two-hundred-kilometre drive through the night, along back roads from Banja Luka in northern Bosnia to Jablanica south-west of Sarajevo, felt as if it had offered me scant protection. In fact, I had been left feeling like a bag of nerves. Saša's aggressive approach to the speedometer and his combative cornering had seen me clinging onto the sides of the passenger seat in the vain hope that that might somehow slow the car.

He was a confident driver; it just wasn't my style of driving. I preferred to deliver my passengers to their destination in a state of calm rather than wrung out and somewhat surprised at having arrived safely. Saša drove as though travelling between A and B was precious time wasted in a life that needed to be crammed with activity. For me the journey was itself activity.

But now we were pulling up in the main square at Jablanica and the headlights of a builder's van flashed across the way. We fished our bags out of the boot of the Renault 5 and approached the van.

"Ševa?" Saša asked through the driver's window.

"Yes, that's me."

A man with a huge frame, dark hair and an impressive, shovel-shaped beard stepped down and gave each of us a firm handshake. Notwithstanding the beard and the frame, even in the half-light it was clear that Ševa was a young man. His demeanour spoke of self-confidence and a generous spirit. There was a brightness to his eyes.

"Ševa, we're really grateful for your putting yourself at risk like this. We appreciate it," said Saša.

"Don't mention it, Saša. It's usually not too hairy, this route – though the situation is changing all the time. So, we'll go carefully. It'll be good to have you guys in the city. We're hoping this crazy stuff just fizzles out but we're not banking on it. We might just need the likes of you to tell the world what's going on."

Frankfurter Allgemeine's Sarajevo correspondent had put Saša in touch with a leading figure in Izetbegović's political party, the SDA, Ismail Ljevaković, and his son, Ševa, had volunteered to pick us up from Jablanica when he heard the nature of our mission.

Saša crossed the square and dropped the keys to the Renault into the letterbox of the car-hire company. Then we were off. I was wedged on the front banquette between Ševa and Saša, like a trio of builders off to work. I felt safer with Ševa behind the wheel than I had in the Renault 5, though I knew that Ševa's attempt to smuggle us into the now besieged Sarajevo through districts still controlled by Bosnian Muslims would be fraught with danger.

It wasn't that Bosnia's leaders had fallen into a trap in the weeks that preceded our attempt to add ourselves to the numbers of the besieged in the country's capital city. They had had a choice from two options: one bad and the other worse.

Like Croatia and Slovenia, they could seek to peel off into a state of independence, risking a backlash from Belgrade and Bosnian Serbs, or they could be a weak force left in a broken Yugoslav Federation and most likely find themselves in thrall to the Serbs.

Bosnia's Serbian population had boycotted its independence referendum, but more than ninety-nine per cent of the two-thirds of the population who did vote backed an independent Bosnia. It allowed Belgrade and Pale, where the Bosnian Serbs' headquarters were located, to claim that it was the Bosnian Serbs who were now in need of protection.

Immediately one of the concerns that I had aired to Lucy on the road proved to have been insightful: mini-wars, unscrutinised by journalists, began breaking out across the state – largely initiated by Serbs or Bosnian Serbs looking to stake claims to swathes of land in Bosnia.

Bijeljina, one of the most north-easterly towns in Bosnia just miles from the Serbian border, was one example.

After tension had risen there, Bosnian President Izetbegović had asked the JNA to protect the Muslim population of the town, who made up one-third of the population of about a hundred thousand. But, according to reports, instead of intervening the Yugoslav National Army were facilitating the harassment, murder, and expulsion of the majority of the Muslim community by the notorious Serb paramilitary group, the Tigers.

The Tigers were led by 'Arkan' – the nickname of Željko Ražnatović. To call him a ruthless thug would be to understate his capabilities: he had a record across Western Europe of armed robberies, bank robberies and murder. Rumour had it that the Yugoslav Secret Services subsequently offered him protection in exchange for his carrying out missions for them abroad, including political assassinations. As a sideline, he led the nationalist hooligans associated with Red Star Belgrade Football Club, the 'Delije' or 'hard men'. They provided him with a conveyor belt of recruits for his Tiger paramilitaries. With them, he had cut his ethnic cleansing teeth the previous year in and around Vukovar and other parts of Eastern Slavonia in the north-east corner of Croatia.

Monitors sent out by the Bosnian President reported back that the Tigers first surrounded the town, sniping into Muslim areas, then they patrolled the streets, then hunted down Muslim leaders in the community and executed them summarily. Non-Serb citizens did not need further encouragement and virtually all fled. The pictures that reached Sarajevo from an intrepid photographer showed dead bodies, including women, lying abandoned in the streets.

Whole districts of the town were practically empty and, though local authority officials gave an account of what happened to the Presidency team, there wasn't a single Muslim there to give their version. Those who hadn't already fled were too scared to come out and talk about their ordeal.

I was already rueing the fact that, increasingly, journalists were having to rely on second-hand reports and, therefore, making subjective judgements as to their veracity without all the necessary background information and context.

The Bijeljina atrocities finally persuaded President Izetbegović that he could no longer trust the JNA to defend his people. Before long he had merged and mobilised his Territorial Defence units and his paramilitary 'Green Beret' volunteers into a force that would become the ARBiH, the Army of the Republic of Bosnia and Hercegovina, 'to enable people to defend themselves from future Bijeljinas'.

Although this could have been seen to be a logical move deemed long overdue by some of Izetbegović's colleagues, Saša pointed out how it would trigger still further aggression towards the non-Serb Bosnian population.

"It lets the Serb leadership ask the question: 'Who are these forces being set up to fight?' The obvious answer is them, their people. Another justification for them aggressively 'protecting' Bosnian Serb communities," said Saša.

"So Izetbegović is damned if he does and damned if he doesn't," I said.

"Precisely," said Saša.

Shortly after the Bijeljina reports, a member of the European Community Monitoring Mission, who I had met in Zagreb, told me of disturbing developments on the opposite side of Bosnia – ironically in Begić's patch, the Bihać pocket. Hugh, a Falklands veteran, whose credentials and credibility outstripped those of the pliant colleagues of his I had come across in the Hotel Argentina in Dubrovnik, had had to evacuate the town of Bosanska Krupa with his fellow monitors as machine-gun fire and later shells were targeted at the area round the Town Hall from the hills overlooking the town.

Some of the Muslim community in the area said that Belgrade had been making sure over the past nine months or so that a steady stream of weaponry was channelled to the Bosnian Serb community via the JNA. Hugh had been told that the JNA had even helicoptered in mortars and anti-tank weapons to some parts of the pocket. They said Serb women and children had been evacuated from Bosanska Krupa, and their networks were telling them that this was exactly the pattern of behaviour that had preceded attacks on Muslim communities in Eastern Bosnia in previous days and weeks.

After the ECMM's flight from Bosanska Krupa's town square, Hugh had learned that many of the Muslim population had fled but around one thousand of them were trapped in the town and, around one hundred kilometres from where Lucy and I had been held up by the Chetnik, fellow Chetniks began an ethnic cleansing of Bosanska Krupa. Bosnian Serbs from the town, who were in league with the Chetniks, wandered through the houses on the right bank, identifying with a white chalk cross the houses of Muslims. The Chetniks followed hard on their heels and did the dirty work. Those of the one thousand or so Muslims left in Bosanska Krupa who resisted were killed on the spot. The rest were rounded up and, with Muslim residents of nearby villages, shipped off to camps.

"We think around forty were murdered in those few days. To be honest, I'm surprised it wasn't more," said Hugh.

From events in Bijeljina and in Bosanska Krupa, it appeared increasingly that the conflicts were broadening out from artillery and shell bombardments and featuring increasing examples of brutal hand-to-hand combat, torture, rape and murder.

"Hugh, do you understand how people, who have lived side by side with neighbours of different ethnicity for decades, can flip and either go round chalking crosses on the homes of families to be driven out or actually indulge in the throat-slitting itself?" I asked.

"I think we'd need a couple of hours to put even a dent into that conversation but…" Hugh thought for a while. "You do have to lay some of the blame at what's coming out of TV studios in Belgrade and Zagreb. They're both trying to make safe people feel in danger. And, of course, it's come from the very top. These TV stations are completely in the control of political leaders in both Croatia and Serbia."

"Absolutely," I said. I had watched in horror and near disbelief at the images pumped out to maximise fear and distrust. Plucky Serbian frontiersmen terrorised by Croatians. Croatian villagers fleeing Serb militias. Trumped up 'historical' documentaries designed to reignite ethnic hatred. And, of course, the propaganda had a multiplier effect. The fear engendered in turn bred its own cruel backlash. Soon the leadership didn't need to persuade broadcasters to trick up any pictures or misrepresent, because those convinced they were under threat took their own initiative and got their retaliation in first.

Now, in the first half of 1992, the propaganda machines were being turned on Bosnia's Muslims: according to Croatian TV, the Bosnian

President wanted to create a Muslim landmass from Bosnia through Kosovo to the Montenegrin border and all the way to Turkey. And to achieve this ambition of a Greater Bosnia, President Izetbegović allegedly had secret plans to flood the country with five hundred thousand Turks and to reward families who produced multiple Muslim offspring in order to entrench Muslim dominance.

In tandem, Bosnian Serb leader Radovan Karadžić was repeating to anyone who would listen a menacing threat he had first made in Bosnia's Parliament the previous year: if the Bosnian Government continued its efforts to gain independence, "one nation will disappear".

For Hugh, the febrile atmosphere created and the levels of cruelty employed, which bore no relation to anything resembling self-defence, were not special Balkan features.

"Some people will say to you 'These people have always hated each other; you can't stop them from turning on each other.' But, although there's undoubtedly a legacy from World War II, these people have more often lived and worked side by side. Even in this region, right on the frontlines of the Fascist-Partisan conflict in the Second World War, the hatred and distrust had eased. And, historically, as you know, over the centuries the Balkans have been more invaded than invading."

And he spoke of his experience as a soldier on the streets of Northern Ireland during the Troubles. "I saw exactly the same phenomena there. A window gets put in, someone is shot, and, within ten minutes, there are ten different versions of what happened spreading across the community. The rumours are unstoppable. They create fear. That fear fuels fear. It breeds the distrust that turns neighbour on neighbour."

"Without wanting to sound ghoulish," I said, "it's the psychology that fascinates me. And appals me. I mean, I'm someone who tries not to hurt a fly. I try not to cut a worm in two when I'm digging. How do you get to the point where you're not only capable of slitting someone's throat but you feel the need to carve initials into a victim's flesh – before or after you've killed them?"

"Well, there are out-and-out psychopaths and sociopaths – people capable of committing any action without feeling any sense of remorse," said Hugh. "Self-gratification is their only emotion. Then there are career criminals. War is an opportunity for them to pursue their criminal instincts but dressed up in the ribbons of a so-called cause. I suspect our friend Arkan is both. Part-psychopath, part out-and-out criminal.

"But then these guys recruit whole bands of the easily led. You take some no-hope kid with a low IQ, you show him how to kill a cat, then you show him how to slit a throat. And you convince him that, in a theatre of war, there is no punishment for that killing. He can kill with impunity. It's a perverse kind of empowerment – but that hopeless kid, who had been a loser all his short life, can now kill and rape and steal from his victims.

"We build strong walls that protect what we call civilised behaviour. The tragedy of the situation here and now – and it's a tragedy the Milosevićs and Tuđmans should be eternally ashamed of – is that it allows the ringleaders to take down those walls. There are no boundaries of respect, of decent behaviour."

I told Hugh of my experience south of Dubrovnik.

"From what I could see, Hugh, those Montenegrin men of the mountains had pretty much been given permission to loot and persecute," I said.

Hugh paused. "But you know what, Mick? Those walls are only deconstructed temporarily. There is no impunity, no punishment-free killing. Or, at least, that's what I have to believe. I have to believe that these people's past deeds will catch up with them."

He paused again. "But then I suppose that's how I justify my life. I've spent my whole career trying to defend civilised behaviour."

As we headed east towards Sarajevo with Ševa at the wheel, it emerged that, despite his impressive beard, he was just seventeen years of age.

"I should have been starting my last year of high school in a few months," he explained. "I'm all teed up to study chemical engineering – maybe at one of the universities in Vienna or Munich. Dad says, if it comes to war, I'll have to think about putting it all on hold and volunteering for the Patriotic Defence Force."

Ševa paused. "And he's right," he added, without apparent regret or rancour. "Thing is, I've got that" – Ševa pointed over his shoulder at a hunting rifle lying in the back of the van. – "and they've got the weaponry of one of the biggest armies in Europe." Ševa shrugged.

He explained that we were going to take a route over Mount Igman, the peak that had hosted many of the activities during the 1984 Winter Olympics that Yugoslavia and Bosnia had been so proud to clinch. It would be part dirt track, old logging routes through the woods, and part tarmac. That would get us into the city through districts still largely in the hands of Muslim communities.

Coming off the main road, Ševa picked a careful path through the dirt tracks. Some crackled with loose gravel but, at times, these appeared to be just mud strips where a vehicle could get stuck when rain fell.

As the van appeared to begin heading down, after ascending the south side of the mountain, there was a crack and the vehicle tipped slightly to its right side.

"Hell! Flat tyre," said Ševa. "That's all we need."

The plan had been to get down the mountain before daylight to minimise the risk of shelling.

"We'll need to get the spare on quickly," said Ševa.

Between them, Ševa and Saša, with a little feeble help from me, managed to jack up the passenger side of the van. The nuts on the wheel with the puncture were rusted in place so loosening them took more time than any of us would have liked and dawn was just beginning to break as Ševa and Saša secured the spare wheel in place and pumped up its tyre.

"Are you okay to go for it, Saša? Mick?" asked Ševa. "If we go now, those dozy Serbs may not be up yet – or we can go back to Jablanica and try again tonight."

I heard myself reply, "No – let's go for it, Ševa."

"Okay. Hold on tight, boys."

A few hundred yards further on, Ševa eased the van onto a surface that at last bore some resemblance to tarmac and, as the tyres gripped the ground, he put down his right foot and gunned the van down the winding road. Sarajevo was laid out below us like a map spread across the bonnet. Despite finding myself gripping the edge of the banquette seat, as I'd done in Saša's Renault, I was still able to admire the sight of this splendid city zooming in ever closer, its outskirts stretching right out into the foothills of the mountains north of the city. Ševa, Saša and I tipped and swayed and bumped biceps, like skittles with no room to fall over. We were close to the outskirts of the city when the whistle came.

The missile zipped above and in front of us – fifty yards or so, I estimated. It thudded into the earth bank to the left of us, throwing up a cloud of soil and shrubbery, but its blast was limited by the give of the soil. Ševa slammed his foot down as branches and twigs and mud rattled off the windscreen. He swerved expertly, just keeping the van from the brink of the mountainside to the right. Then we were down and round a bend to apparent safety. My heart was thumping in my chest. I was shocked but, having seen the shell hit the earth bank ahead of us, I hadn't really felt in mortal peril this time round.

As we slipped into the relative shelter of the streets on the outskirts, I said, "Forty mill anti-aircraft shell, I'd guess…"

Saša looked at me quizzically. "Since when did you become an expert in military hardware, Mr Morrison?"

"Hugh told me. They use anti-aircraft fire for most targets: blocks of flats, cars, people. It's the 120 mm mortars you don't want. Size of a golf bag: a chunk of hot metal that splinters into thousands of shards. If you're within seventy-five yards, it'll shred your organs."

"Charming!" said Saša.

Ševa wiggled the van through the back streets south of the river. As he reached the end of a street leading to a bridge, two men in black woollen hats, carrying rifles only slightly more modern than Ševa's hunting rifle, beckoned the van to a halt. One peered out into the crossroads, then waved fast.

"Go! Go! Go!" he shouted.

Ševa sped over the bridge and pulled into a narrow street just east of Baščaršija, the city's main Muslim district. He installed us in a neat flat above a courtyard behind the City Hall, his uncle having been moved out temporarily and rehoused in the family home, till we found hotel rooms.

I quickly fell fast asleep on a mezzanine bed above the main living area. Despite driving through the night, Saša wasn't sure he'd sleep. I had him down as a four-hours-a-night man and made a mental note that this was perhaps another sign of a restless spirit concealed beneath an apparently imperturbable surface.

The most disturbed I had seen him had been some days earlier when we had watched from Zagreb the scenes on TV that heralded the descent of Sarajevo into violence, segregation and siege. Saša had called up to my room and told me to get downstairs to watch as barricades went up across the city after a small-time crook, a Muslim, had shot at a Serb wedding party, killing the groom's father and injuring the priest.

Saša said that, in a city renowned for its cosmopolitan mix of people, it would be hard to establish where Serb and Bosnian Muslim paramilitaries could set up barricades. But set them up they did. Over the next few days city police reasserted some control, but turmoil would quickly turn into tragedy.

From the west of the city, in Dobrinja district, a protest march which had started small began to swell. It acquired what seemed to be a spontaneous, unstoppable momentum, hoovering up supporters by the thousands, Sarajevo citizens of a wide range of nationalities.

A bespectacled, serious TV reporter peeled one marcher from the moving column.

"We're marching against those who try to divide us. This tolerant city won't accept Serb and Croat and Muslim and Roma and Turk being set against one another," said the bearded man in his thirties, wearing a fashionable, knitted, woollen hat despite the spring sunshine. "People of all races and religions have lived here in peace for five hundred years. We're here to tell our leaders that the people won't stand for their words of hatred and division. We're here to show that this city is a global city. And this city belongs to the people – all of the people."

"Saša, do you think this is like Dubrovnik? Its citizens just can't believe their special place can be dragged into a war?" I asked.

"It may well be. It may well be, Mick," said Saša.

The march reached the Parliament building but part of the march continued its momentum and swung right, heading for the Grbavica district on the south bank where there had been reports of Serb paramilitaries seizing a police station. The column started to file across the Vrbanja Bridge. Half a dozen shots rang out, what sounded like a grenade exploded, and the crowd panicked and began to split in different directions. A body lay prone on the bridge, immobile, stranded. Then one of the marchers, then another, then a few more ran back onto the bridge and surrounded the body on the ground.

Later that day, it emerged that a twenty-one-year-old medical student, Suada Dilberović, had died from a gunshot to the chest – most likely from the barrel of a Serb paramilitary's gun. The final irony, if irony had anything to do with the situation, was that Suada was not from Sarajevo, or even Bosnia, but was a Muslim from Dubrovnik. Her parents had been holed up in the siege that I had lived through. She was to have graduated from medical school the following month.

A crowd of around two thousand stayed overnight, some having stormed the Parliament building, others staying outside in its forecourt. They were joined the following morning by many more protestors. Overnight, the JNA had seized Sarajevo airport, placing tanks and armoured vehicles by the terminal and on the approach roads.

Just after 1pm, inexplicably, shots were fired at the crowd outside the Parliament building from the roof and the upper floors of the Holiday Inn across the way, killing six people and injuring dozens more. The hotel had housed Radovan Karadžić and other leading members of his SDS party just two days earlier but, when Bosnian militiamen stormed the hotel and seized six Serb gunmen, Karadžić and his entourage were long gone.

As we watched the chaos onscreen, Saša said, "And you know, Mick, Sarajevans were liberated from occupation by the Nazis forty-seven years ago to this very day."

He shook his head despairingly. "You might have fallen in love with Dubrovnik, Mick – but Sarajevo is something else. What was it Ivo Andrić said? 'It is the city of the most beautiful longings and endeavours and bravest desires and hopes.' It's heartbreaking to see it descend into anarchy. And I say that as someone brought up across the Serbian border in Užice. Sarajevo belongs to us all, Michael. Even you, all the way from England."

It was the first time Saša had called me Michael – as if this were a moment for formality, for veneration. It was the first time I had seen Saša emotional to the point of a profound sadness.

I could only have slept for half an hour or so in our Sarajevo flat when I was awoken by the sound of machine-gun fire, probably somewhere in the centre of the town half a mile away. Then there was a huge explosion

– about four hundred yards away, I guessed – as the Serb paramilitaries began a bombardment.

We would only realise later in the day that Saša and I had snuck into the city on what an anchorman on Sarajevo radio would describe as 'the most difficult and dramatic day in Sarajevo's long history'. But, if it was the heaviest bombardment of the city so far, it would be outstripped in its ferocity time and time again in the days, weeks and months to come.

I had seen fear, misery and anguish among Dubrovnik's besieged. I had first-hand experience of victims of JNA and Serb paramilitary bombing there, but the scale of this assault on Sarajevo, with no supposedly sacrosanct areas like Dubrovnik's Old Town, would take me aback.

Saša switched on the TV and we sat at the table, watching the shooting and bombing and killing unfold. A sniper had pinned down the railway station and had been picking off passengers emerging from it until ten people lay dead in the street. One man lay flat on his back. There was no indication as to where his fatal bullet had penetrated. Another man lay on his right side, blood pooling from his head. A small elderly lady in a headscarf lay face down, an old-fashioned raffia shopping bag about twelve feet from her.

Hugh had told me that a sniper with a clear view and the right rifle could target a position from between three-quarters to one-and-a-half miles distance – so a single gunman on the south side of the of the river in the district where the Serbs had dug in could be sitting patiently, picking off his victims so remotely that he might have been able to pretend that this was some kind of harmless video game.

"Saša. These people coming out of the station – they could be Muslims, they could be Serbs, they could be Croats. What's the sense in this?" It was a rhetorical question.

"It's a grab, Mick. The Serbs are trying to grab as much as they can. So, when – if – someone steps in to put a stop to this, impose a ceasefire, they have as much territory within the city, within an independent Bosnia as they possibly can to negotiate from.

"We've seen him say it on air. Karadžić is openly talking about his plan to divide Sarajevo into Serb and Muslim areas. He's explicit about it.

I mean, Jesus! This is one of the coolest, most mixed cities in the world. It's exemplary. It's cosmopolitan. Fuck them!"

I was struck again by how deeply the plight of Sarajevo was touching Saša, a Serb brought up over Bosnia's eastern border. But I knew too, from the limited time I had spent with him, that he abhorred nationalism, badges, flags.

Over the past months, I had had a repeating train of thought that had ticker-taped beneath the surface of full articulation, questioning why Saša had befriended me, shared so much with me and, apparently, trusted me. In this moment, the thought surfaced and crystallised. Yes, Saša and I were very different characters, but we shared so many convictions about what was right and what was wrong. I felt a warm squeeze of bonding for an instant and revelled in it.

My reflections were interrupted by the Sarajevo TV reporter switching from footage of the railway station shootings to clips of explosions and fires breaking out across the city. This was not a softening up of Sarajevo. It was a bombardment.

"Might sound crazy, Mick, but we need to go out and get a sense of the scale of it," said Saša.

He explained that, in a bombardment like this, the key was to shuttle from doorway to doorway, always looking out for the source of the gunfire and missiles and their likely targets.

"We don't wander over open boulevards and squares or crossroads. We inch our way towards the eye of the storm – if there is just one storm," he said.

We slipped out of the gate to our courtyard and moved gingerly towards the market at Baščaršija. I found myself walking on tiptoes, as if that might somehow help me avoid detection or protect against gunfire. The streets beyond our street were largely abandoned, only the odd individual, who'd found themselves out of place when the shooting started, scurrying in bursts to try to return to loved ones and some kind of personal safety.

We passed on the other side of the street to the Church of the Holy Archangels, where the shots fired at the wedding party had prompted this violence some three weeks earlier. We ducked down a side street and were cutting in front of the courtyard of the Gazi Husrev-Beg mosque when a trio of missiles zipped overhead, producing explosions that seemed to be about half a mile north.

"That's a residential area. I'd be surprised if there are no casualties from that," said Saša.

We edged west surreptitiously, taking backstreets where we could, aiming to get as close as we could to the railway station, where much of the action seemed to be focused.

"Look! There's Jonny!" Saša had spotted a colleague tucked into a shop doorway. Jonny was Jonathan Lomax of the international news agency *UPI*.

Saša scurried across to him. I followed. Saša and Jonny slapped palms.

"Jonny, this is Mick from *The Times – of London*."

"Hi, Mick."

Jonny was a young, lean American with neatly cut dark brown hair and perfectly shaped and proportioned ears. He showed a facility in mixing geniality with concentration on the threat in hand. He was gazing in the direction of the Serbs' target area.

"Have you seen much, Jonny?" asked Saša.

Jonny said that the Serbs were controlling the hillside Grbavica district just south of the river and were targeting the Marijindvor area that Radovan Karadžić had identified as the eastern border of the slice of the city that he wanted to declare Serbian.

"If they can hold Marijindvor, they could have as much as half of the city in time. But it's not yet a clean, strategic push. It's pretty random. There's offices and flats here and there that have been hit. Some of them are on fire. And there are fucking snipers, just picking people off."

I loved the way he said 'fucking' in an emphatic, American way.

"A shell's hit the radio and TV station a good way west in Alipašino polje, but, as far as I can tell, they're still managing to broadcast. The UN Protection Force – it's a Swedish unit – is floating around outside the TV station, claiming to be making a difference, but I can't see it myself," said Jonny.

"You been in the city long, Saša?"

"Me and Mick just landed this morning. Came over Mount Igman."

Saša paused. "Nearly got our heads blown off by a forty-mill missile on the way – but we made it in one piece… as you can see."

I smiled inwardly at Saša's seamless appropriation of my piece of knowledge about military hardware – the knowledge about which he had teased me earlier that morning.

"This is the worst it's been," said Jonny. "Apparently, a guy from the US State Department was in Belgrade yesterday to tell Milošević they wouldn't tolerate him gobbling up as much territory as he can across Yugoslavia, while we're in turmoil. Six hours of talks that got nowhere. Then this bombardment started."

Jonny went off to file, having revealed that most of the international journalists were staying in the Holiday Inn – ironically, the building from which Serb gunmen had shot at peace protestors just over a fortnight earlier.

"We'd better move over there soon, Mick. Easier to plug into the gossip and know where the briefings are happening," said Saša.

I would rather have stayed in Ševa's uncle's flat. It felt safely tucked away. But I knew Saša was right.

We continued edging in the direction of the railway station, the frequent rattle of automatic weapons, machine-gun fire and a steady stream of shells growing louder, a smell of smoke and burning growing stronger and stronger. In a narrow street not far from the Parliament building, two men with rifles beckoned us to a halt, their eyes still focusing principally on plumes of smoke thinning and dissipating north-west of where they were standing, in the direction of the railway station.

"Hi, guys. We're Press. *AP* and *The Times of London*. We know Ismail Ljevaković. His lad, Ševa, brought us into the city early this morning," said Saša.

"Welcome," said one of the men. "Any friends of Ismail and Ševa are friends of ours. I just wish we could have given you a proper welcome."

He paused. "I wouldn't advise you to go much further than here. If you stick your heads beyond the end of this street, you can see burned-out floors of office blocks, apartments on fire. There must be quite a few casualties."

He turned and raised an arm north-eastwards. "But there's also a steady stream of missiles going over that way. We're afraid they're targeting the hospital and one of the main Muslim residential areas."

"We'll just go to the end and take a look," said Saša.

"Okay, boys, but go gently. Keep as safe as you can."

Saša led the way and I tucked in behind. We slid along walls, looked around constantly, aware that a single bullet could spell the end of either of us, were we to expose ourselves.

Saša peered round the corner where the road opened out and I hunkered down beneath him. There were two blocks within view with flames licking from their upper floors. Others were blackened with scorch marks or just blasted open gapingly.

All of a sudden a man in his fifties, his open raincoat flapping, was running across the main carriageway, a young girl and a boy sprinting ahead of him. He was trying to shepherd them with his arms out at forty-five degrees on either side of his body, as if his arm span could somehow protect them. There was gunfire as they ran, but I couldn't sense how close it was to them. After their dash, which lasted just seconds, the trio managed to reach the corner where we were tucked in and the man placed his hands on the wall either side of the children, effectively pinning them, as he sought to establish whether this was safe ground. It was – relatively.

At that moment, there was a fresh whistle and, this time, I turned to see a direct hit on a shopping centre three hundred yards away, a shell ripping a chunk of masonry from the top corner, as if a monster had taken a bite out of the building.

"Are you okay?" Saša had turned to the man with the children. He was gasping for breath, an unfit man who had probably not had to break into a sweat for some twenty years. The children, a girl probably aged around thirteen and a boy aged ten or eleven, breathed fast but without having to gasp for breath. The boy, crudely barbered, looked up at us, moon-eyed. The girl had managed to retain an element of composure. She had kind, intelligent eyes. She wore a checked headscarf.

"Holy *shit*, that was close!" the man exclaimed, his relief eliciting a profanity he might not normally have uttered in front of children.

I sensed from the dynamic of the three that he was not the father of the children. He was a little too old and the children did not relax into his enfolding in the way that they would have done with a parent.

"They're my brother's children," he explained. They were living in Derventa near the border with Croatia. Chetniks and Serb paramilitaries were trying to drive out the Muslims and Croats from the area. A couple of shells came close to hitting their home."

The man explained how the children's parents had bundled them into a truck along with other local children and they had been taken to Doboj, where they stayed overnight with cousins.

"Their dad told them to get the train from Doboj early this morning and come to Sarajevo. We figured that when Croatia and Slovenia declared independence, Zagreb and Ljubljana didn't see heavy fighting. We thought it would be the same for Sarajevo. And then they land here – just as mayhem breaks out."

The man explained that the train had been stopped an hour outside Sarajevo. There had been an announcement over the tannoy of ten dead at Sarajevo station and a lot of passengers got off. But the children stayed on.

"Their dad had told them to go to Sarajevo and they did what they'd been told to do. I had to bob and weave and dodge the bullets because I knew I had to be there for them," he said.

"It looks like carnage up there," I said. "We saw the bodies in the street on the TV."

"It's grim. Just random victims lying there. We hunkered down for an hour or so but, in the end, I thought we just had to get out of there. Make a run for it."

I looked the boy in the eyes. "You okay, do you think?" I hoped I'd managed a tone that might prompt a positive response and rally his spirits.

"Yeah, yeah. It was scary – but I'm okay."

"So, where do you need to get to?" Saša asked of the children's uncle.

"We live up north of the Baščaršija."

"We've just come out that way. If you go through the backstreets, you should be okay. But be careful north of the market. The Serbs have been shelling that district quite extensively, I sense. From the direction of some of the missiles."

We wished the uncle and his two refugees well and they slipped off back in the direction we had come from. We manoeuvred a little to try to get a better sense of the impact of the bombardment but, beyond a certain point, the automatic rifle fire and the shelling just became too dense and repetitive. There were only so many direct hits, fires and pieces of crashing masonry that you could take in. We turned back and headed for the flat to file our stories, trying not to let our guard down the nearer we got to home base.

Saša was preparing coffee and sandwiches as, on TV, a Croatian member of Bosnia's Presidency, Stjepan Kljuić, called on all the city's inhabitants 'to mobilise to defend our city'.

He said, "This is a clear attempt to divide the city. This is terrorism. They're trying to seize all vital installations. We must stop them from trying to cut our city in half."

It would be a rallying cry that would chime with many Sarajevans, including those Bosnian Serbs who cherished their city as a special place, as a cradle of tolerance.

The buzzer went and Ševa announced over the intercom that he was coming up to the flat. As his huge frame edged through the doorway, I realised I was already extremely fond of this bear of a young man. His whole demeanour spoke of selflessness, of concern and support for others, his maturity way, way beyond his years.

"Everything okay?" asked Ševa. His focus was on his guests, initially concealing a trauma he had just been through.

"Yes, yes," said Saša. "We went downtown as far as we could – but the shelling's pretty intense and we got the sense that the snipers were pretty accurate, so we didn't push our luck."

Reinforcing Jonny's assessment, Ševa remarked that the day's bombardment was by far the worst it had been.

"We've already had a couple of shells hit our street today," he said. "It's largely Muslim, our area. There aren't any military bases or government buildings, so it must be deliberate targeting."

And Ševa told us about an elderly couple that a neighbour had had to drive to hospital in the back of his estate car after a shell hit their house and shrapnel smashed through their kitchen window. All the city's ambulances were busy elsewhere.

"Their home had been hit five days earlier – a shell knocked a hole in the roof. But we patched that up. No one was hurt. This time, they were drinking morning coffee in the kitchen and the shell hits the outside wall and shrapnel tears through the window.

"The neighbours – we all piled over their front gate, though there were still bullets flying and shells exploding in and around. Inside, the old lady was unconscious, lying face down. The old boy was just clinging onto her, trembling and dazed but conscious. They're both alive but…"

Ševa looked up at the ceiling and took a few random steps in no particular direction, trying to deep-breathe his way out of his distress. He recovered most of his composure.

"Why are they doing this to us?!" he asked plaintively. Then he answered his own question. "I *know* why they're doing this to us – but it's wicked." He paused. "I just hope this doesn't get a whole lot worse before it gets better."

He thrust his hands into the pockets of his long coat. His pain was palpable. In the face of his evident distress, my reflection bizarrely was further admiration of the thickness and weave of his beard.

"The only good fortune we've got is that we have one of the few houses in our district built with a cellar. We'll have to live like cavemen!" And he laughed without mirth.

Saša told Ševa about the uncle with his brother's children and their ordeal at the railway station.

"I saw those kids!" said Ševa, excitedly. "Their uncle – he lives near us. Ekrem Kapić. He was walking up the hill just as I was coming down. Did he tell you the parents of those poor kids sent them here to escape the Chetniks in the north?"

"Yes, yes. He did," said Saša.

The three of us fell silent for a while, leaving only the earnest words of the TV anchorman, summarising events in Sarajevo so far that day.

"Look, Ševa. We'll try to get into the Holiday Inn tomorrow. You'll maybe want your uncle back in here. It feels safe here. And we should be with the Press pack anyway," Saša said.

"Whenever, Saša. We're just behind the City Hall, here. We may not be that safe. If you get fixed, fine – but it's pretty hairy up there round the Holiday Inn, so there's no rush."

"Go carefully," Saša called down the stairwell.

"I will, I will."

Saša and I drank coffee and snacked and took it in turns to file our copy from the phone in the flat.

As we lazed as best we could on the sofa an hour later, the fusillade of missiles having finally ebbed if not ended, Saša cut across the voices of the TV reporters.

"Mick?" He was looking at the screen, not at me.

"Yeah?"

"How do you do that stuff?"

"What stuff?"

"That writing."

"What writing?"

"Well – your stories. I mean, I whack over the facts, as best I can but you – well, it's like you paint pictures with your words."

I didn't instantly have any response.

"I'm sitting here listening to you file, and you've just captured it. The trip over Mount Igman. That feeling in the streets. The atmosphere. The kids and their uncle. Ševa talking about the couple drinking coffee when shrapnel comes through the window. It's like I was seeing it, feeling it all over again."

I paused and reflected before responding.

"Well, I just try to think myself back into what it felt like. The trip over the mountain. Those kids and how they looked. About how it felt on the streets. If I labour over anything, it's the precise word – the verb, the adjective."

I was wary of coupling nouns to the adjectives they were most frequently yoked to, and I resisted obvious combinations because they often came across as glib. My image of myself was of my picking up my verb, noun and adjective and, on each occasion, inspecting it in the round, as if looking at an object from a three-hundred-and-sixty-degree perspective until I was sure each element did the job it was meant to do.

I paused, then added, "But it's not hard…" It was a comment designed to sound modest rather than arrogant. I hoped it landed correctly.

Having kept his gaze on the TV screen while he framed his tribute,

Saša finally looked across at me. "That bit about the way the guy ran across the main road with 'his arms out like the wingspan of an improbable guardian angel'. I remember how he looked with those kids with his arms outstretched. I mean, I couldn't write that. To be honest, I didn't even see that… until you wrote it…" Saša paused. "But it's lovely. It captures it perfectly. Why can't I see that? Do that?"

"To be fair, Saša, you're a wire agency guy. Your customers want quick facts. You're delivering what your editor wants. My man wants to know what the war means for ordinary people. What are their stories? A guy in his fifties, probably living a dull life, having to dodge bullets trying to save his brother's kids. Well, as a scene, it's a gift to a journalist looking to capture the madness of the situation we've landed in. Capturing that kind of moment – well it's way, way what I love the most."

Saša looked back at the TV screen. "Well, Mick, nurture it – because it's a remarkable gift."

"Thanks, Saša… That's kind of you to say that."

"Well, it might be, Mick. I don't mind 'kind' – but I'm not saying it to be kind. I hear what you write and I'm swept away. You've captured what we've been through… beautifully, tragically."

"Thanks, Saša," I said again.

Then, after a moment, I added, "But, Saša – you're way braver than me. You go places, you talk to people in a way I wouldn't do, if you weren't leading."

I paused for a moment for effect: "We may just be the dream team."

Saša laughed. "Get away with you!"

The following day, Saša and I made it across to the Holiday Inn, where a serene, apparently unflappable receptionist, Amira, found us rooms and wished us a pleasant stay, however long that might be.

"Always come into the hotel through entrances other than the main door. It's already been hit and it's in direct line of fire from Grbavica where the Serbs are encamped. And, when you get to your floor, always go to your room in a clockwise direction from the lift. If you go anticlockwise, it may be quicker but it puts you in the line of fire," said Amira calmly, as if her instructions were as banal as how to work the in-room safe or switch on the television.

The Holiday Inn was to prove a strange haven. There was something of the Hotel Argentina in Dubrovnik about it, with the staff dressed always in jackets, white shirts and bow ties. But I was relieved to find that it lacked the Vaudeville kitsch of the Hotel Argentina and the exuberance that some guests claimed to be a strong, never-say-die spirit but which I had found showy and distasteful.

Staff admitted privately that they were able to keep up a tolerable level of service by buying oil for the generator on the black market, using the international currency they obtained from their journalist clientele.

Inside, the rooms were comfortable enough, and mine, north-facing, gave me some sense of protection, given that most of the shelling was coming from the south – if not from Grbavica district, then from Mount Trebević, another of the mountains south of the river used for the Olympics.

The hotel had been and continued for some time to be hit by missiles but, after a while, although it was located on what became known as 'Sniper Alley' right at the heart of the siege, an unspoken truce did seem to emerge, whereby the Serbs besieging the city did not target it routinely. This was likely to have been an awareness that the international backlash from multiple deaths of international journalists would be more severe than if they simply lobbed missiles into largely Muslim and Croat districts.

After a few days of merely moderate bombardments and random fatalities, the assault on the city ratcheted up several notches as Serbs tried to cross the River Miljacka and grab a slice of the city. Bosnian paramilitaries had been able to hold off the attacks using shoulder-held anti-aircraft missiles. So, abandoning any prospect of hand-to-hand combat, Serbian paramilitaries dipped into the JNA's deep reserves of rockets and shells and poured fire on the city in attacks still more sustained and damaging than on the day Saša and I had arrived.

With the bombardment paused, Saša and I and the rest of the Press pack were out on the streets of the city centre the following morning after a bizarre late twist to events the previous night.

After Serbian paramilitaries had seized a key police station south of the river, Bosnian paramilitaries retaliated by surrounding the barracks at Bistrik – also to the south of the river – trapping inside four hundred JNA soldiers. In an attempt to trade their way out of the situation, the JNA had seized President Izetbegović at the airport after he had flown in from an unsuccessful European Community-led set of peace talks in Lisbon. 'Free our soldiers and you can have your President back' was the offer.

So, the following morning we were in a Press pack heading out to witness what could be the most dramatic of prisoner-swaps: Bosnia's President for the head of the JNA in Sarajevo. But would the swap include the other four hundred JNA troops? No one could know.

We had stepped out into the streets once we'd seen on TV a UN convoy followed by a clutch of JNA military vehicles leaving the JNA base near the airport. We presumed one of the vehicles contained the President and his daughter, who had travelled with him to Lisbon as his interpreter. Our plan was to slip into the streets near the Bistrik barracks and, between us, cobble together the story of the prisoner swap.

The devastation of the previous day's Serbian bombardment and Bosnian forces' fightback was everywhere in evidence, as we made our way in the direction of the brewery on the road up to the barracks. Cars, buses and armoured vehicles were in various stages of destruction by the side of the roads. A smell of burned fuel oil lingered. Electricity cables that had been slashed sparked like intermittent Christmas lights. More disturbingly, burned corpses lay scattered through the streets, some partially dismembered, some charred to varying degrees of incineration. Some were just dusted in ash, others' scorched skin had begun the process of perishing before cool air had halted the process, wrinkling it like wax that had melted then solidified. I struggled to stop myself from trying to make out what was missing and what was left of each individual body.

If I felt horror at the spectacle, the combustion of these corpses did make remote objects of them. These couldn't be real people who yesterday had had personalities and individual behavioural characteristics, could they? And though I was in touching distance of these deaths, I still felt as if I was someone from a different place, someone to whom this kind of thing could never happen. Never mind that I could have been a victim of an instantaneous cremation myself, had I been in that street eighteen hours earlier. This was something that happened to other people, of other races, from other places, I felt illogically.

I knew I could touch hearts with the story of Delila and Azra and their blasted parents, but these blackened, unidentifiable individuals told no stories. Not yet. Not until the rings had been prised off their fingers, dental records checked, relatives finally, reluctantly, corroborating the reality of their brutal ending. Perhaps that was my story: how charred corpses only tardily give up their truth. I shuddered as I walked by another body lying in the gutter and I had to resist an inexplicable urge to stretch out a leg and prod its thigh with the toe of my shoe.

In the streets and alleys around the barracks, Patriotic Defence Force 'Green Berets', Bosnian military police and other armed men in civilian clothes were gathered in small, mixed groups. The mood was ugly. There was anger in the air at the devastation that had been wreaked upon their city over the past twenty-four hours. Occasionally, chanting, football terrace-style, would break out.

"Come on! Let's go!" groups sang. A clash of sorts looked and felt inevitable. On the roofs of the houses overlooking the barracks, marksmen were positioned, ready for action. Everyone held back and allowed the convoy of UN and JNA vehicles to snake their way up to and into the barracks' courtyard.

Saša and I had tucked into a side street down the hill, north of the barracks. Other journalists were with us or scattered across other side streets. There was a lull as, no doubt, final negotiations were taking place about the nature of the swap. When the gates to the barracks reopened and the original convoy re-emerged, it became clear that a crocodile of additional JNA trucks was tagging along. There was a commotion as the Bosnian Muslim groups outside realised that all four hundred of the JNA troops felt that a safe passage out of town had been negotiated for them.

The front of the convoy had progressed slowly just five hundred metres down the hill and was in Dobrovoljačka Street when, suddenly, out of sight, there was the screech of the tyres of a car being driven in a short, sharp burst. Gunshots rang out. There were shouts and screams. They lasted just minutes.

Piecing together the events later by pooling our experiences, the Press pack established that a red VW Golf had shot out of a side road and cut the convoy in two. Bosnian Muslim forces then swooped. Trucks in the back half of the convoy were seized, JNA troops were shot at or pinned down, weapons were hauled out of the JNA trucks and piled into Bosnian Muslims' vehicles.

Saša and I witnessed a handful of marksmen spraying rifle bullets into the convoy but we had no sense of the level of casualties. After the shooting stopped, some vehicles reversed back up and into the barracks while the front of the convoy went on its way. When eventually we were able to pick our way safely back towards the city centre, one military truck was parked by the side of the road, its driver's door open. There was a blaze of blood splashed across the inside of the windscreen. The corpse of a victim of a bullet from a high-powered rifle had been whisked away. This time, instead of a Bosnian casualty, it looked as though a member of the JNA had died from a shot from a Bosnian Muslim rifle.

Saša's words 'There are no good guys in the Middle East' reverberated in my head. As he had forecast, perhaps the same applied now to the Balkans.

Sarajevo TV would report later that there had been seven fatalities, all JNA officers and soldiers, four injured and one hundred and sixty JNA men taken prisoner in the barracks. Some of our Press colleagues had witnessed President Izetbegović popping his head out of the lid of an armoured car at the pleading of a senior United Nations Protection Force officer, risking his life to call off the gunmen and calm the situation.

The President would eventually reach the Presidency building safely and the head of the JNA, General Kukanjac, made it with the front half of the convoy to the JNA barracks by the airport.

Saša had a good relationship with Izetbegović's son, who explained later that the confusion in the streets had come from his father – incarcerated and concerned for the safety of his daughter – agreeing safe passage for all JNA forces, while his deputy, unaware of what the President had agreed, had insisted that the deal consist only of an Izetbegović-Kukanjac swap with the fate of the remaining four hundred a topic for negotiation.

Within hours the Serbian propaganda machine was whirring. The seven dead became forty-two, the exchanges rather than a few fatal minutes became 'the massacre of Dobrovoljačka Street'. Dobrovoljačka Street would become shorthand in Serb nationalist minds for the scene of another tragic Serb massacre. And this ambush would be cited again and again as justification for Serb bombardment of the city, yet another example of their behaving selflessly over the centuries only to become the victims.

Meanwhile I took a call from the young officer I'd met in Knin working for the JNA's second in command in the Krajina, General Ratko Mladić. The JNA was seen as having mishandled the situation in Sarajevo, it was being pulled out of Bosnia and a new Bosnian Serb Army was being set up. General Mladić was to lead this new army and we would soon see that this meant not relief for Sarajevans but further years of sustained misery.

13
APRIL–JUNE 1992

I was far from cavalier in my trips out of the Holiday Inn but, try as I might to convince myself that sheer statistical probability meant I was as vulnerable as any other resident of the capital, nonetheless I never expected to be killed or injured.

I mentioned it once to Saša and he snapped at me uncharacteristically.

"Try telling that to the widow of my mate, Steveo. Took a sniper's bullet in the head in Beirut and I lost my best buddy…"

His voice tailed away. He looked chastened at having slapped me down, but I sensed I shouldn't dig for more detail.

Nevertheless, I found it hard to shake off a determinism that I had neither nurtured nor encouraged but which was lodged stubbornly among my preconceptions. I didn't dress it up as any romantic or divine concept, some protective cloak that would enable me to continue reporting this war to the world; I just felt I wasn't about to die. But this mindset brought with it no bravery and it banished no fear. And, as I turned a corner near the Drvenja Bridge and a shell whistled above me, crunching into masonry somewhere near the Baščaršija market, I tried to ignore a tic that was becoming too regular – a twitch of my lower left eyelid.

"I'm going to end up like one of those crazy blokes, twitching and mumbling to myself in the street," I said to myself, and I laughed, though, admittedly, it wasn't particularly funny.

The shell into the Baščaršija area was somewhat alarming because Saša and I were making our way north of that district at Ševa's invitation. The automatic fire and the shelling of the area near his family home had continued with little respite. Our trip to get a sense of the human face of coping Sarajevo-style represented a sound journalistic exercise but one that might challenge my concept of being untouchable.

The street where Ševa and his family lived, Longavina Street, was a long road, rising steadily above Baščaršija in the direction of the mountains to the north of the city. It was a mix of ageing blocks of flats and some ramshackle homes set among grander, detached homes with walled courtyards and gardens; but for a main road leading towards the city outskirts, it was narrow and, I suspected, it might be difficult to arc a missile into it with any precision.

Yet Ševa would make clear that still the bombs fell on it, the shrapnel ricocheted, and hot metal flew into people's parlours and sitting rooms in shocking, split-second invasions, deadly at worst, merely demoralising at best.

Ševa was of the view that it and the surrounding area were being particularly heavily targeted because this was the closest Sarajevo had to an exclusively Muslim area. It wasn't exclusively Muslim, and Ševa would later introduce Saša and me to Serb neighbours as determined as any Bosnian Muslim to sit tight, to see out the siege and get on with the lifestyle that had prevailed before anyone felt a need to label themselves according to ethnic background.

Just one young man had recently left the street to join Ratko Mladić's new Bosnian Serb Army and, Ševa insisted, his parents were treated with as much affection as ever – as if they had suffered a death in the family rather than shared the guilt of an act of treachery towards the citizens of Sarajevo.

Ševa's family home was a substantial two-storey detached house with basement, accessed from the street through a snug-fitting gate fitted with a black japanned Norfolk latch, the thumb plate of which clunked satisfyingly as I let myself and Saša into the courtyard.

No doubt to make his guests feel safer than we might at ground level, Ševa led us down into the basement of the family home. Ševa's parents were sitting ten feet apart from one another on wooden chairs, clearly alert to the arrival of guests. They appeared meek, as though awaiting inspection. I detected a sense of expectation in the air so ephemeral that any articulation of it risked gusting it away. Yet I felt a thought-bubble above Ševa's father's head might have been asking whether Saša and I could conjure up words to the outside world that might cause the siege to be lifted? After what I had witnessed so far, I doubted it – despite my ambitions, admitted to Saša, of shaming decision makers into intervention.

Ševa's mother, in a green headscarf, a black cardigan, and an ankle-length green-and-black-striped print skirt, greeted us quietly and went off to prepare coffee and baklava. Ševa's father shook our hands firmly. He was a small man, in his early fifties I guessed, with a calm, thoughtful air about him. He was wearing a pale brown suit and a shirt and tie, as if guests required such formality. He had a small grey moustache and neat dark grey hair brushed back and shaped with scrupulous neatness. When I learned later that he was a university lecturer in chemistry, I could easily imagine him carrying out experiments with meticulous precision and unstinting patience as he explained processes to students with less intuitive understanding than him. I warmed to him immediately.

As Ševa towered over his seated father, I felt comfortable enough to say with a smile, "Well, sir, you've produced a fine specimen there!" I pointed at Ševa, highlighting their contrasting heights. I felt there was no risk of my remark being interpreted as impertinent.

"Please – no need for 'sir'. Call me Ismail," Ševa's father said. "My father was a big man – like Ševa," he explained. "But my mother was minute, like a baby bird. And it was just my luck to take after her! The runt of the litter! The kid who was bullied in the playground."

He smiled and patted Ševa on the hip. "No one bullied my Ševa in the playground," he said. And he laughed, and we laughed too.

After coffee and baklava were served and Ševa's mother spirited herself away, no doubt suspecting that the conversation would be men's business, Saša asked how it had been.

"It looks from where we're based as if your district has taken a bit of a pounding," he said.

"Yes," said Ševa. "It's been grim. I told you about the couple hit by shrapnel the other day. Well, they're still in Koševo Hospital. It's on a hill over there."

Ševa pointed in a north-westerly direction.

"But, because it's exposed, the Serbs are taking potshots at it. Just after our neighbours were admitted, a man in the cardiac care unit was shot through the heart as he looked out of the window. Then, a couple of days later, a retired man in his late sixties, who lives a little further up our street, was in the ground floor of his house with his son-in-law. They thought they were safe because any shell would come through the roof, two floors up, but a shell hit a gate across the road and shrapnel from it bounced back into their sitting room and sliced through the old man's back, piercing his heart. All you can say is that at least he died instantly."

I guessed that that would have been one of the missiles the size of a golf bag that Hugh had told me about.

"This may not be an easy question to answer, Ismail," said Saša, "but do you think there's any way the Bosnian forces can halt the bombardment? End the siege? Or will it need outside intervention?"

Ismail explained that though the Bosnian forces were defending bravely, they weren't yet properly organised.

"You've got the Patriotic Defence Force, you've got the Territorials, you've got the police – but there's a criminal element about as well. I think what happened in Dobrovoljačka Street the other day, from what I've heard, was just a coming together of disparate groups. No wonder there was chaos. Our boys are brave but sometimes they're still operating randomly. Alija and his people need to get a grip on it. Get things organised."

Ismail went on to explain that perhaps the President and his people had been a bit slow to read the warning signs.

"By the time the arms embargo was imposed, we really should have been better prepared."

The UN Security Council had imposed an arms embargo across the whole of Yugoslavia in September of the previous year, just around ten days before the siege of Dubrovnik, freezing in place the massive superiority in weapons and equipment enjoyed by those who inherited the JNA's capability – largely the Serbs. Now Bosnians trying to defend Sarajevo were scrabbling around for arms.

Ismail went on. "I'm a man of peace, gentlemen, as Ševa will tell you

– but I just wonder if the President believed a little too much that some unreasonable people in places like Belgrade and Zagreb could be made to behave reasonably by the force of rhetoric.

"I know Alija. I'm a party member. I know he'd rather be sitting having a coffee with intellectuals and discussing philosophy than dealing with the gritty stuff. Negotiating with frauds like Karadžić or clever, devious men like Milošević. But he's got to step up. I don't think we have anyone better – but I'm not sure he's ideally suited to this."

But Ismail?' I said. "If Alija can't do it, where is Bosnia? I met Tarik Begić. He said the Bosnian Government needed to do deals with the Serbs and the Croats."

Ismail waved his hand in front of him, left to right, right to left.

"Michael, Michael. No – not Begić. He'd sell Bosnia down the line. He's only interested in money and power. He has no principles. What I'm saying to you is Alija Izetbegović is a deep, thoughtful, committed man. In a way, he's too cerebral to lead this country to our sunlit uplands."

Ismail paused, as if he had misspoken. "Sunlit uplands?" He was querying his own projection and suddenly looking glum. "When did we last have 'sunlit uplands'?"

Frustration bordering on anger was seeping through. He delivered his next words in staccato fashion: "This-is-a-mag-nif-i-cent-country." Then, more quietly: "If it was allowed to thrive without external parties trying to define it and shape it, it would be seen rightly, fairly, as one of the finest physical, topographical and cultural countries in Europe. People would flock here. But, year after year, decade after decade, century after century, others trample across our land. They dilute its intrinsic character. They reduce our Bosnian spirit. Or try to."

He paused. There weren't tears in Ismail's eyes but there was emotion.

"For the love of God, let us Bosnians get on and live our lives. Without outside interference."

He looked down at the floor.

"Michael, Saša – I'm not sure Alija is the man to take us there but, as I've said, now, here, at this moment, I think he's the best we've got. God help us. God make him the man to lead us to where we deserve to get to. Even if they're not sunlit uplands."

The room fell silent, as was only correct. At that moment, my heart ached for this wise, gentle man, marooned in his sorrow, and at a loss to make sense of the wanton cruelty inflicted on his city and his people.

One of Ševa's personal survival mechanisms seemed to be a need almost always to remain on his feet. He rarely sat down, as if he might literally be a sitting duck, should he take a seat. He padded around in a small half-circle before speaking again, shifting the conversation back to the chasm between the firepower of the besieged and the besieging.

"We have neighbours – a lovely couple, Vera and Jovan Divyak. Live a couple of doors away. He's a deputy commander of the Patriotic Defence Force. He's a Serb but he loathes the Serb nationalists, so he came across to our side from the JNA. He told me that their calculation is that there is just one rifle for five of our men at the moment. I hate to say it but sometimes I'm grateful for those low-life criminals, with their caches of illegal weapons, who are fighting to protect the city. Mind you, as Dad says, whether they're controllable is another matter. The danger is they're a law unto themselves."

Ševa forecast that Muslim countries would soon come to the aid of Bosnia and would supply arms clandestinely over time.

"Alija was in Iran and Turkey last year. He's got good connections into the Organisation of Islamic Conference. These guys won't stand by and see us shredded to bits."

There was another pause in the conversation, then Ševa said that, if Saša and I were happy to venture out again, he would introduce us to some of the other people in the street so that we could gain a sense of how people with different challenges were coping or not coping.

We picked our way from home to home. At this time of the day only occasional explosions were happening somewhere in the distance. There was the couple who had been affluent but whose savings were all but wiped out by inflation rates of around one thousand per cent at the end of the '80s. Their family had links with that of Radovan Karadžić back in Montenegro.

"He came to our old house in the late 1970s," said the husband, a frail man in his seventies, "spouting all of this crap about Greater Serbia. Told us how we Serbs needed to 'guard our interests'. I didn't want our grandkids hearing that sort of stuff, so we got rid of him. He was a psychiatrist then, though I think he's the one who needed therapy."

Then there was the young mother whose daughter was just shy of two years of age when the bombs began to drop. The child developed diarrhoea, whenever the explosions were at their loudest. Her mother, a delicate, beautiful, fashion-conscious woman in her early twenties, washed out nappies till the early hours because there were no disposable nappies left in the shops, she explained.

On the way down from the flat, Ševa explained how she had had pretensions to be an actress and was beginning to get some film roles, when her husband was killed in a motorbike accident.

"They were a beautiful couple – he was big and strong and handsome and you can see what a looker she is. They looked great together. And now, instead of all those hopes and dreams, she's having to cope on her own in a dingy flat with a young kid and little support. It breaks your heart. We all do what we can to help, but…" Ševa's voice trailed away.

There was a Bosnian Army officer in his thirties, softly spoken with volumes of Romantic poetry on his shelves, quietly pining for his wife, whom he had reluctantly sent out of the city just before the siege gripped tightly.

There was Vera, the wife of General Divjak. He was out 'soldiering', of course, but she explained proudly how her husband, a lifelong military man, had been appalled at how the JNA he had served all his career had intervened bloodily in Croatia on behalf of Serbs a year earlier. He despised President Milošević's claim that all Serbs needed to live together within a single Greater Serbia across Yugoslavia.

Vera said, "He would say, 'In my family, there was never any talk of that kind. I found it insulting to suggest that we Serbs wouldn't want to live with other peoples.' And then, when in early April the attack on Sarajevo began, he walked out of this flat to the new headquarters of the Bosnian Army and volunteered. They instantly made him second in command – and he would say, 'This shows this is not a Bosnian Muslim Army. It's a Bosnian Army.'"

We popped into the home of the uncle of the refugee children from Derventa, who'd scuttled across the street almost into our arms a few weeks' earlier. The children were quiet and uncomfortable and dealing with their switch from hell to Hades simply by internalising everything. If they were supporting one another psychologically – and I had a hunch that they were – they did so wordlessly, telepathically. The younger boy liked to sit on the floor with his back flush to the wall, as if he felt that that might reduce the chance of his being hit by a missile. He liked to keep his outdoor jacket on indoors, perhaps to suggest that he wasn't planning on staying. He had a way of shrinking his neck so that the collar of his jacket swallowed up his chin, like a tortoise retracting its head for protection.

"They're fine. I think they're fine," said their uncle, as if it were his fault that they had landed in this prime target for Serb bombardments. I recognised the male inclination to say that things were fine, even when, clearly, they were not. Why did men think that that might make things better? His wife scurried around in the background, as if busyness might provide some succour.

Then Ševa introduced us to his friend Dervo. Dervo had been working on utility installation contracts when he noticed some of his Serb colleagues absenting themselves for a range of increasingly bizarre reasons. One was going to pick up a new car in Belgrade. Didn't they sell cars in Sarajevo? Another's holiday home needed urgent DIY. A third said he was taking a month out to go on a hunting course. Dervo would later learn that the 'hunter' had in fact transitioned to sniping at his former fellow citizens from the mountains south of the city.

Dervo and Ševa and some of the other youthful, able-bodied men had managed to set up two refuges for the times when the bombardment meant it was too dangerous for families and children without basements to stay in their homes. They requisitioned seventy camp beds from the Boy Scouts and set them up in the basement of a school on the street.

Ševa and Dervo led Saša and me into the unlocked building and I recognised instantly that stale smell of school that the disinfectant of no cleaner seemed able to shift. Here, at the Razija Omanović School, the standard staleness was multiplied by three, the school no doubt having been abandoned by its cleaning staff some weeks earlier.

Ševa led the way down to the basement, a few naked light bulbs casting a little light across a landscape of camp beds, squeezed together in what had been the school kitchen. There were just five people lying on beds.

"Most people get out of here as soon as they dare, as soon as there's a proper lull in the shelling, but a handful just can't be bothered to keep to-ing and fro-ing," said Ševa.

An elderly man in the far corner was twiddling with a transistor radio, trying to get the news, creating irritating bursts of tinny voices amongst blizzards of untuned crackling.

"Tune that thing or fucking well turn it off! You're driving everyone mad," shouted a woman in her sixties, thirty feet away from the man with the radio. From the back, most of what I could see of her was her hair, tumbling chaotically out of a hair tie at her crown as if she'd given up trying to tame its gold and grey meanderings.

A bored young man in his twenties, in a white vest and black tracksuit trousers, his hair shaved short, lay on another bed, nibbling his nails and looking vacant.

At the top of the street, the second refuge was a grim, rambling building, which screamed the word 'institution'. During its century of existence, housing thousands of orphans over the decades and, for a period, convicted criminals, it seemed to have absorbed into its walls so much of the misery and sorrow it had played host to that a sense of the malign appeared to be simultaneously locked into the masonry and oozing out of its walls.

The limited square footage of window and the depth of the halls meant Dervo had to click on a torchlight occasionally to probe its recesses even in the middle of the day. The building at least had some refuges that children could claim as their own spaces. Crudely written signs were stuck to the doors, warning adults to keep out of these makeshift dens and playrooms. Again, the basement was the safest place, but the orphanage's location at the top of a ridge meant it was still targeted.

"A grenade came through one of the windows, blew a hole in a staircase and sent bricks crashing into the basement. One of the kids was hit but she was okay. Just a cut to her head that we were able to patch up," said Dervo.

As our group picked its way down to the basement where a dozen people sat in groups or pools of isolation and a flickering TV chatted across a sea of mattresses and sleeping bags, Ševa said that some local people, particularly superstitious elderly women, believed the building to be at worst haunted, at best just cursed.

"They say there are bad spirits here – but, when you've got a house made of wood and plaster walls, you put up with the bad vibes and you tuck yourself away here in the hope that its solid stone and its basement can keep you safe. Everyone's miserable – but everyone wants to stay alive," Ševa said.

"You don't seem miserable, Ševa. You seem to be toughing it out… so far," I said.

"I'm doing my best. It's up to people like me and Dervo to do all we can, make things safer and give people some hope that we'll all emerge from this sooner rather than later. And then it might all seem like a bad dream."

The sound of shells landing within a range of around half a mile began at the back end of the afternoon, sporadic and unnerving but a little too distant to trigger jolts of fear. People began drifting into the orphanage in dribs and drabs: an elderly man, his hair streaked light and dark grey and combed flat away from a parting on the left, walking with a limited, shuffling step, still in his carpet slippers; a young family, parents in their late twenties or early thirties and three young girls – girls that a photographer could have captured in perfect uniformity, side by side, the same, wiry, straw-coloured hair, youngest to eldest from left to right, each elder sister three inches taller than her closest younger sister; then a couple in their fifties, their bodies thickened over the years, with the demeanour of those whose children had long since flown the nest, experienced with youngsters but no longer hands-on.

Most of the elderly had a vexed air, many displaying a fatigue that had no doubt crept upon them invisibly, gradually over the years but was now exacerbated by the effort and the stress of having to make it up the steep hill to the orphanage before any serious bombing began.

By seven o'clock, had a stranger from a far-off land with no knowledge of what was happening in the Balkans walked through the door, he could never have divined why this cross section of people had come together.

The spread of ages might have spoken of a wedding party, but without a bride and a groom, without joy, without tables groaning under plates of food and bottles of alcohol, without strings of cheap pink-and-white bunting adorning the walls.

The chatter ticked up to a babble, and only the occasional phrase or snatch of conversation made it intact out of the increasingly populated scatter of mattresses, sleeping bags and blankets as far as Saša and me, sitting on uncomfortable wooden chairs at the side of the room. If the aim of our journalism might have been noble, I felt that we were both uninvited guests at a party devoid of celebration. We could justify our presence rationally, but this didn't feel like a place where rationality would necessarily hold sway.

A man in his seventies picked his way out of the ocean of bedding and made a beeline for Ševa. He had weather-beaten skin, the flat smudge of a moustache that so many men of his age wore, and a slight tremble, barely visible, but which spoke of a stroke or some other life-threatening ailment in the recent past.

"So, Ševa? I hope your father and mother are well. Do give them my regards," he said.

"Thanks, Vedad. They're both staying at home. They feel they should be safe there." He shrugged. "But who knows?"

The familial greeting was not this man's purpose, though.

"I hope you don't mind me asking you but…" He jolted a thumb. "Who are they? Are they journalists?"

"Yes, they are, Vedad. They're our guests. They're here to see how the people of Sarajevo are coping. This is Saša from the *Associated Press*. And this is Mick from *The Times of London*."

The man turned to Saša. "Sir? May I ask you? Are you a southern Slav?"

"I am, sir. I am from Užice just over the border. Though it's a long time since I've lived there permanently."

The man was clearly reining in a belligerence with only a limited degree of success.

"And are you not ashamed of what your fellow countrymen are doing to this city and its people," he asked, fixing Saša with a look that didn't deviate.

"None of what is being done is being done in my name, sir," Saša replied calmly. "I hope you'll be aware also that millions of Serbs are opposed to what happened in Croatia and what's happening now in Bosnia. We don't support the leadership in Belgrade. In fact, I would go as far as to say, sir, that I regard Sarajevo as as much my city as yours. It's always been a symbol of peaceful coexistence. Of tolerance. No. More than that. Of cooperation and respect between people of all types."

"Well, that's as maybe – but you Serbs need to let your leadership know that you won't put up with this."

Without letting Saša come back, he turned to me. He raised a forefinger. I noticed again his gentle tremble.

"And you, sir? Where are you from? From England?"

"Yes, yes. I'm from England."

"Well, we're grateful for what you did in the war. Helped us get rid of the Nazi Ustaše – but really? Now?" He shook his head with an air of deep regret. I thought it best not to engage further until he had fleshed out his criticism.

"Your man – what's his name? Major. If he hadn't caved in to the Germans, we could have found a way of holding Yugoslavia together. A looser arrangement maybe, more autonomy for the individual states. But he caved in. Let go of Croatia and Slovenia – and now look at the consequences."

I was searching for the right tone of response, when Ševa intervened. "Mick, you should know that Vedad was one of the Partisans who fought the Fascists in the war. He risked his life."

"Multiple times, multiple times," Vedad interjected, with a stern look on his face.

"He believed in Tito's vision of Yugoslavia." Ševa turned to Vedad. "And I think you still do, don't you, Vedad?"

"Who wouldn't, when you see the situation we're in now," Vedad said grumpily.

I pushed back gently. "But, sir, with the best will in the world, I'm not sure that anyone could have prevented Croatia and Slovenia from going their own way. The timing wasn't good, and we should have had in place a solution for the whole of the rest of Yugoslavia before their independence was blessed, but…" I let my comment hang in the air. Vedad didn't respond instantly.

I went on. "I'm not defending John Major. But, with the Berlin Wall down, the Soviet Union breaking up – I'm not sure this is a time when you can hold reluctant states together."

Vedad jabbed his finger in my direction again, pulling the rank that his personal experiences endowed, despite that experience being framed in very different times.

"If you'd seen what I've seen, you wouldn't speak like that. Nobody believed a strong Yugoslavia could stand up to Stalin after the war. Nobody believed we could thrive independently without being swallowed up by the West. But we did. Tito called it perfectly, positioned us brilliantly. The man was brave. Laid his life on the line time and again. A tactical and political genius."

All of a sudden Vedad looked wistful, as though memories of his leader had temporarily diluted his anger towards Saša, me, Belgrade and the West.

"Aaagh, if only he was still around today."

"Sir, with respect," said Saša, "these are not the times for a new Tito. People want freedom. Not another dictator."

Vedad turned to Saša, the wistful eclipsed by the angry. This time, his accusing forefinger swayed from Saša to me to make clear we were both to blame, little cables of spittle connecting his upper and lower lips as he made to reply.

"Gentlemen, I don't agree with that. Tito was a real leader. Not a dictator. But what about *your* so-called leaders? It's a disgrace that Western leaders are doing *nothing*! *Nothing*! Nothing to stop the bloodshed and misery here."

He cranked up his indignation a notch. "What is it? Are we one war too many for you? Or are we just unlucky we don't have Kuwait's oil?" He paused. "That's it! That's it! All you people care about is your own wealth and lifestyles. We fought alongside you for freedom. And now…" His voice dropped in sadness. "You let us down."

He turned, as if to go, then turned back. He said quietly, "I've had it. I've had it with the West."

Before he could turn away again, Ševa spread out his arms in front of him. "Vedad! Come on! These guys are here to tell people what's happening. If people can read about what's happening, see on TV the devastation, we'll have a chance of getting all of this stopped.

"Mick's not John Major. Saša's not Milošević. These are independent journalists. We need them."

The conversation stopped for a moment. Vedad looked at the floor, then brushed a hand over his thinning hair from forehead to crown. He looked back at Saša and me.

"Gentlemen, I hope I haven't offended you. I hope you can do some good. But…"

We were straining to hear his words, now a near whisper against the hubbub in the background.

"I'm just too tired to take much more. I've toiled all my life, tried to do the right thing – not for me, but for everyone. And it's disintegrating before my eyes… and I haven't the strength to do anything about it."

He looked down at the floor, before looking back up at us.

"Can you imagine how that feels? To be powerless."

His gaze then seemed to lose its focus on us but to fix onto some other image that no one else could see. Perhaps an image from his past.

"We were out in the hills and the forest, prepared to die for one another. We thought we were unbeatable. We felt *we* had the true cause." He paused again. He stretched out his arms, his hands pushing out beyond the over-long sleeves of his jacket.

"But look at me now. Just a husk of a man. Powerless." His anger had ebbed away. Regret and vulnerability had taken its place.

Ševa took a step towards Vedad and gently wrapped his bear-like arms round both of his shoulders from behind. He said in a hushed tone, "Vedad – don't speak like that. You're a hero in this community. You've given your life for others. No one has given more public service than you."

He gave Vedad a squeeze. "It's for people like me and Dervo to pick up the baton now. It's for people like us to make sure that you and your generation are cherished, respected."

I felt a warm flush of admiration at this earnest seventeen-year-old automatically assuming a role as one of the community leaders, but my sense was that any son of Ismail would have conducted himself that way – instinctively and certainly not under instruction.

I sensed that this was an important moment for Ševa, but it would be some time before I learned that this was the moment that convinced Ševa that he needed to shelve, for a while at least, his academic ambitions and volunteer for the Bosnian Army. The elderly man who had given so much selflessly now needed others to make sacrifices for him.

Vedad shook our hands as firmly as he could. He dipped two fingers into his breast pocket and fished out two business cards, a little battered – the kind that a print shop would lay out and produce cheaply for an individual. 'Vedad Mirković – former Sarajevo City Councillor, 72 Longavina Street, Sarajevo' it read, with a phone number in the corner. He separated them carefully and gave one to each of us. I dug out a card of my own and gave it to Vedad. Saša apologised for not having his with him. I recognised the phenomenon and was touched by it: a former man of influence seeking to cling onto his status via a set of business cards.

"Now, I must try to sleep," he said. And, for the first time, he gave a weak smile. "If I can, in this madhouse." And he turned and headed off into the gaggle.

"He's still an out-and-out communist, guys," Ševa explained. "But, as well as fighting for the Partisans, he's been a local councillor for decades. But not one of the pompous, useless types. The type who got things done. Made sure the weak were protected. Had roofs over their heads, food on their tables. Politically, I can't remember agreeing with much of what he said over the years. But he's an example of what public service really should look like."

With Vedad having been swallowed up in the sea of bedding, I looked across the jumble of humanity before my eyes: families grouped together, the parents trying to prevent their youngest from trampling onto the space of adjacent, unrelated elderly; some groups of men in card schools, betting for matches, yawning in sequence but incapable of rest; older children occasionally jumping and racing into what narrow corridors of space there were, pretending they needed the loo but seeking mainly to be up and active, to muck about with their friends. It was a kind of chaos streaked through with a tension from which only the young teenagers seemed immune.

The shelling had moved closer, as if the rangefinders were narrowing in on the orphanage. But no one could know if there was a target at all. A blast a few hundred yards away temporarily turned down the volume of the people in the orphanage basement. There was total silence followed by gasps of shock and relief after a shell hit the area of weedy concrete scrub that divided the orphanage from the road. Pieces of shrapnel crashed against the outside walls but, this time, caused no casualties. I winced and felt the tic below my left eyelid activate.

The hours dribbled by, most of the basement lights were extinguished, a child cried, an elderly lady tutted, a man reprimanded giggling teenagers. And the air grew staler and only exhaustion dimmed the tension and fear – until the next blast nearby reactivated it. Then it dialled down again.

Saša and I had been allocated blankets and thin mattresses, but we stayed on the fringes of this mass of Sarajevan humanity. I would drift off occasionally, only to snap back awake abruptly, sometimes at the sound of an explosion, sometimes simply to drink in the experience, bizarre and depressing though it was, anxious to record and remember and, I hoped, capture every key detail and sensation.

The guns fell silent at around 3am and, after twenty minutes or so, individuals and groups and families began to get up and drift slowly away, taking their chance that this was 'safe' time. When more people had left than remained, Ševa suggested that we head back to his parents' home. Dervo slipped away into his own flat on the way down the hill. Ismail was sitting in the basement, holding a cup of something that looked like green tea.

"Was it okay, Dad?" Ševa asked.

"Yes, it was okay. One shell landed a bit close for comfort but it wasn't our worst night. I think your mum managed to get some sleep. She's still in bed now. I couldn't stay there," he said.

"You'll laugh, Dad, but Saša and Mick were monstered by Vedad." Ševa chuckled.

"No-o-o? He didn't, did he?"

"Yes. Usual thing. You know, Tito and all that."

"I must apologise, gentlemen, for my fellow citizen," said Ismail with a smile, turning to us.

"He was fine. Fine," said Saša.

"Dad, they handled him really well. Listened to him, didn't give him grief but a bit of pushback, y'know. Saša told him the last thing we needed was another Tito!"

"And did he take it?"

"Kind of… Well, he changed the subject."

Ševa paused. "Mind you, Dad. I have to say I felt sorry for him tonight. You know he's always pegged on. Never given up. But he looked frail tonight. Said he was tired. 'A husk of a man' he called himself."

"Well, he did have that minor stroke four months ago," said Ismail.

"Yes, I know… but it's just… well, he sounded as if he was close to giving up. Whatever 'giving up' means…"

Saša cut in. "Ismail, your boy was brilliant. Put an arm around him just as he looked as if he might crack. You can be proud of him."

Back at the hotel, I knocked out the opening paragraph of the piece I had been honing all the way back from Ševa and Ismail's street: "In a century-old orphanage on a hill above Sarajevo, decades of misery, alienation and repressed anguish seem to seep from the walls. Now, this grim, daunting institution plays host to a new kind of despair."

Later that day, Paul gave me feedback on my article.

"It's nicely done, Mick. I've negotiated a nice bit of space for it. And I think your people come alive. It's a strong set of cameos and they hold together. I particularly liked the chemistry lecturer. I know he's not the most tragic figure, but he leaps off the page. You can feel his pain for Bosnia… and the Bosnians."

Paul paused. "Mind you, if the siege spins on, we'll be hard-pressed to keep our readers engaged. I mean I don't want to sound callous – but it's like suicide bombings in Tel Aviv and Jerusalem when I was in the Middle East. The first one is huge news – appalling in its brutality and impact. The second and the third still prompt a reaction. By the tenth, we stop covering them. I mean, I'm not proud of that. It's just the way it is."

"I know what you're saying, Paul. And I understand. You're not being callous," I said.

And then I heard a proposal emerge from my mouth that I had not been aware was baked sufficiently for it to be aired.

"I've always said to you that my fear was that this was a war largely going on out of sight of the Press, the media, the wider world. I'm just thinking of when and how to break out of here and try to prove my theory" – and I repeated a refrain often shared by me and Saša – "without getting my head blown off."

I didn't know to what degree that sounded like a promise, and I had no idea how I could get out of the besieged city – I could ask Ševa or UNPROFOR, I supposed – but Paul appeared to warm to the idea without asking me specifically to put my neck on the line.

"Well, let's think about it," he said. "But lockdown in Sarajevo, day seventy-five probably isn't going to make much of a splash. Have a think about it and we can talk some more."

14
JUNE 1992

"So the younger sister took her place? Wow!" Saša appreciated the twist at the end of the story as much as I had.

I was just back from witnessing a dramatic child swap in a Sarajevo park to which I'd been given exclusive access by a UN Peacekeeping Force officer who Saša had deemed too dull to cultivate.

"Never given me a helpful steer and he's just so borr-ring!" he had said.

It was a lesson I'd learned long ago: be nice even to boring people because one day they might just bring you a scoop.

UNPROFOR had negotiated a deal between the Bosnian Army and the Serbs that wouldn't allow a couple from a mixed marriage, separated during the chaos of an early bombardment, to be reunited, but it would allow them to swap children. He was Muslim, she was a Bosnian Serb and, as they had fled a bomb blast, the husband had found himself with a baby just weeks old on the Bosnian Muslim side of the barricades, while his wife was with their eight and ten-year-old daughters on the Serb side. The Serbs did not want to help someone of their ethnicity reconnect with a Muslim; their compassion stretched only as far as a deal whereby the baby was handed back to the mother and the ten-year-old would leave her mother to go with her father.

The swap was to be administered by an intermediary in the open spaces of Heroes' Square. My UNPROFOR man told me that, though we couldn't see them, Bosnian Army and Bosnian Serb guns, located at either side of the park, were trained on the spot where the handover would take place. The intermediary would swap ten-year-old for baby, but the parents would be kept apart.

In the event, the deal, the terms of which were explained in detail to both parents in advance, all but collapsed. As the baby was handed to the intermediary, the ten-year-old refused to go with her father. When it came to the crunch, she wasn't prepared to leave her mum. In the panic and confusion that followed, the family had ended up ignoring the conditions of the agreement and had sprinted together from either side of the square to the centre to participate in a mass hug.

"You know, Sash, I thought one of the armed men round the square would think there had been a double-cross, and any second I was expecting an itchy trigger finger to squeeze, a single shot, and then maybe a hail of bullets. I thought for a horrible moment that I might watch the whole family being wiped out. It was terrifying… but, amazingly, not a single shot was fired."

I told Saša how I'd watched in awe as the ten-year-old then turned and headed south with her mother but her little sister elected to go with her father.

"When I realised the ten-year-old was refusing to go with her dad, I swear I could sense, even from fifty metres or so, that it was dawning on him that he'd be going from separation to total isolation," I said.

I hoped that this was a precocious act of compassion and empathy. I couldn't conceive that there might have been sufficient time coolly to persuade the eight-year-old to swap places with her big sister. She must have sensed and abhorred her father's imminent isolation and acted selflessly to prevent it, I concluded. That night she might lie in her bed and weep for her lost mother. I hoped that, if she did, she might still consider that she had made the right choice.

'Eight-year-old Eva's brave walk to a new kind of purgatory.'

I had suggested the headline after I had filed my story, even though it wasn't my job to do so. I didn't know whether that was how the sub-editor would entitle the piece – it would depend on how much space he was allocated for the headline – but that remained for me the best way to encapsulate the episode.

Saša looked up, recalling something he'd forgotten. "Oh, by the way, Mick. Forgot to tell you – that Dutch guy from Sky was asking for you this morning. You know, Bart van Leeuwen."

"Bart? Really? What did he want?" I was aware of him but I didn't really know him at all.

"Dunno," said Saša. "Said he just wanted a chat."

Bart's recent arrival in Sarajevo had caused something of a stir because of his background in the Dutch Marines, where he had served as an infantry officer with special training as a mortar platoon commander. To journalists who barely knew one end of a gun from the other, this was impressive enough; but he had then become a war correspondent, covering conflicts that represented a potted history of global strife over the last dozen years.

He had been one of the few journalists to witness at first hand Saddam Hussein's attack on Iran and the implausible way in which an outgunned Iran had fought Iraq to a standstill. He had trekked into Soviet-occupied Afghanistan on four three-month missions alongside the Afghan resistance, then lived in Beirut as Lebanon was wracked by war. He had witnessed the fall of the Ceaușescus in Romania and been present at the liberation of Kuwait. In the last four years, after working for newspapers and radio stations, he had been heavily involved in the establishment of Sky News, helping it launch, anchoring news bulletins, and then reporting from overseas.

Saša had told me there was a rumour that Bart was descended from Dutch aristocracy, that he was loaded, and that he had no material need to tear around the world, moving from trouble spot to trouble spot. I couldn't know if it was true and I wasn't about to ask him but, when I found myself sitting with Bart in an empty lounge in the hotel later that day, I divined no aristocratic antecedence.

Bart, like so many Dutch men, was tall and broad but lean. He had a long, oval face, with something of the equine about it. He had thick chestnut hair, parted on the left and swept generously across his forehead, and rich brown eyes that locked onto their interlocutor. The only characteristic that might remotely have spoken of entitlement was that sense of assurance that I had come across in some colleagues I had met at Oxford University.

It was as if these people moved through their lives achieving their goals almost effortlessly. Smooth gear changes. No bumps in the road. If their career paths and relationships were considered, they never appeared so. They appeared instinctive, automatic. In contrast to my own constant self-questioning, my jumpiness, my nervy demeanour, Bart transmitted apparently unshakeable composure.

I had heard that, a few months earlier, in a misunderstanding about paperwork in the small Croatian town of Dvor Na Uni, just over the north-western border with Bosnia, Bart and his producer had been put up against a wall by Serbian paramilitaries and told they were going to be shot. Their captors had second thoughts, but the episode appeared to have left not so much as a dent in the Dutchman's self-assurance.

What I particularly liked – and I hoped that Bart recognised in me a kindred spirit – was that, beneath a gentle manner, it was clear that he was driven by a twin desire: first, to understand why people made the decisions they did; and second, to communicate to the rest of the world the effects that those decisions had on others. His war journalism was not a jaunt or an attempt to show how brave he was by risking his life on as many continents as he could. It was about informing the uninformed or ill-informed about what was really going on and prompting decent people to join forces and put a stop to injustice and cruelty. I hoped that this summary of our shared philosophy didn't sound pompous; I was convinced it was the correct track to pursue.

I had expected Bart to speak with a Dutch sing-song ring, but from his mouth came immaculate, accentless English, distinguished but not 'posh', delivered in a rich bass tone, the product of an English mother and a British secondary and higher education. I found it simultaneously authoritative and beguiling.

And I was flattered to learn that, having stumbled across a couple of my pieces, Bart now sought them out.

"Congratulations on how you've made this conflict come alive," he had said.

I flushed inwardly and hoped I hadn't blushed outwardly.

The proposition Bart had for me was interesting. He had found a vantage point in the heart of Sarajevo near the top floor of a former military hospital. If it was where I recollected it to be, I could see how it might afford him an unrivalled view of the bombardment of Sarajevo. I could also see why no other reporter had previously thought of climbing up there, given its central location and, therefore, exposure to fire.

"You and me witness the bombing and the shelling on the ground and we can appreciate its scale but it's way harder to capture on film. We've failed so far but I think we might just be able to do it from there," said Bart.

He wanted to offer me the chance to accompany him so that, while he delivered crisp commentary alongside what he hoped would be powerful footage, I would have the opportunity to capture the scene more expansively on the printed page.

"I can't promise you it's one hundred per cent safe." Bart paused. "Well, to be honest, it's not safe – but, if there's a fire-show tomorrow, I think you'll have some first-class material to capture."

Later that night, as I pulled the fringe of my grey blanket with its blue thread edging up to my chin, my last thought of the day was a hope that I wasn't being brutalised into a kind of torpor. There were dull days when the bombardments seemed cruel and repetitive, yet indistinguishable from the previous day's. Only the roll call of victims would be different. Was that what war did to one? Flattening out episodes of brutality into a new kind of normality? And might tomorrow be different?

In the late afternoon of the following day, just before dusk, Bart and I made the short journey from the Holiday Inn to the City Hospital, sometimes known as the Military Hospital. For the first time, I put on a bullet-proof vest. Bart offered it to me with the advice that I put it on. I sensed that it was more instruction than advice and that Bart couched it as advice only because we were in the foothills of our relationship. I had no inclination to ignore the guidance anyway, given the steadily rising number of journalist casualties from this conflict and the exposed vantage point I was about to access.

When Bart, his cameraman and his producer arrived in Sarajevo, the Holiday Inn had been full, most other hotels were shut, and the accommodation offered by the Bosnian Presidency had been near ground level and inadequate for filming. Searching for suitable locations from which to film, Bart had identified the potential of the City Hospital.

Around a dozen storeys high, with an ugly, concrete façade, it had a Soviet-style robustness that might lend it some resilience in the face of bombardment. Its architects had exhibited the same lack of concern for design that characterised many Cold War cities, contrasting it starkly with those Sarajevan buildings that spoke so eloquently of the Habsburg and Ottoman eras.

The exterior of the building was not just pitted with bullet holes; there was evidence too of some hits from shelling. Bart told me that some of the damage had been inflicted by heavy artillery.

"There's one lift shaft in there that's been knocked out by a shell and there are some big holes knocked in the exterior... but I still think this is a solid building. I still think it offers some protection."

I noted Bart's qualification: 'some' protection.

"As the lead journalist, the safety of our cameraman and producer is my responsibility. But we asked the hospital director if we could take a look around, and he was a bit surprised when we asked him if we could use one of the top floors as our vantage point and as somewhere to stay at night. His brother is chief surgeon here and he and his team had abandoned the upper floors very early in the siege. They now operate largely in the basement and, if necessary, on the lower floors that are less vulnerable to shelling."

Bart led me up the staircase to the tenth floor where I was introduced to a Bosnian cameraman and a British producer. Bart gave me a quick tour of the vantage points: a balcony facing east over the Old Town, another facing west to the newer part of the city, and a more vulnerable vantage point to the south that looked out at the mountains from where most of the gunfire and shelling issued. We'd be sticking to the east and west balconies, he assured me. All the city's main landmarks were visible from them but Bart's cameraman explained that it still wasn't easy to capture the essence of a bombardment, even from these locations. A burst of fire might target the Old Town but, by the time the camera had been set up on the balcony to the east, the target might switch to the west.

"You'd think it would be easy, given – as you've witnessed – the scale of some of the bombardments, but there are times when you look at your clips and there's just not enough there to get across to the viewer the full intensity and brutality of it all. Our editors in head office think it should be easy. I can tell you, it's not," he said.

In the quiet ahead of the evening's outbreak of fire, Bart and I sat on the ground, our backs against the west balcony, our legs outstretched, Bart's a good three inches longer than mine. We were like two boys tucked behind the school playground wall, swapping stories and confidences, friendship growing like an invisible but irreversible chemical process. And I recalled those days in the schoolyard when you were thrown in with another and, by the time the school bell rang, a bond had been tied, an unforeseen friendship hatched through the sharing of dreams and vulnerabilities. You had to reveal some of your fears or regrets if you were to savour the rich taste of friendship.

Bart was telling me that he had never witnessed anything quite like the siege of Sarajevo.

"I've never been anywhere before where the streets are virtually empty of traffic and where everyone has to run across the main streets. Even in Beirut, during the war in Lebanon, people didn't need to run across the streets."

And Bart recalled an incident just a couple of days earlier in broad daylight, on Marshal Tito Boulevard, where he and his crew had come across three people lying in the road. Onlookers hiding in the shadows told how one person crossing the road had been felled by a sniper, a second had gone to help and had been hit too, only for the pattern to repeat itself with a third person. Even as a police armoured vehicle zoomed into place to try to shield the three prone victims, snipers had managed to hit two of them a second time.

"We followed the armoured vehicle to Koševo Hospital. All three of them were dead by the time they got there. The man in the mortuary put his finger into the hole in the head of one of the victims – to show the trajectory of the fatal bullet. I'm not sure I needed that degree of detail." Bart winced at the memory and paused.

"These weren't military people or police, Mick. The woman had a shopping bag. She was middle-aged. These were civilians, shot in cold blood."

I told him of my experience of the corpses in the road on the day of the Dobrovoljačka Street episode; of how those corpses had given up no stories; of the sight of the blood-smeared inner windscreen of the JNA truck.

And then the fire-show began. Just as Saša and I had landed in Sarajevo on a day of previously unprecedented assault as the Bosnian Serbs had tried to soften up the city, so, that night, I had the best seat in the house to witness the heaviest pounding that Sarajevo had taken to date.

There were seconds when I was lulled unwittingly into viewing this as a light show without victims. Beautiful, identical streams of white globes, often in threes, sometimes as many as six, tracked across the skyline, equidistant, culminating in soft, firework crunches. Then bigger, single spheres would flash abruptly without tracking, prompting more violent explosions, their power jolting me out of any firework reverie. Sometimes those explosions would light a fire and leave a flaming target. Other times, there would be a debris-thump but no combustion. There were moments when these were other-worldly spectacles: astrological aspects featuring meteorites and burning stars. Then a big explosion would light up every detail of a city of brick and concrete for a second or so, bringing the observer abruptly back down to earth.

The hospital building took one hit, sending tremors throughout, but this time it was not the focus of sustained shelling. As it became clear that our vantage point was unlikely to be a principal target, my fear level eased. Early in the bombardment, it had jagged up and down with the tight angles of a seismograph's needle. I took deep breaths and tried to take in the detail. Only the odd, loud blast nearby sent my heart rate ticking up – briefly. Ironically, the incessant nature of the night's explosions over time risked normalising them. I repeatedly reminded myself that this would not be a soundtrack without casualties.

I watched Bart and his team drift from balcony to balcony, trying to make calm judgements, as they came to realise that there was an intensity to this night's bombardment that might just allow them to capture on film the scale of the assaults on the city – to make up for their previous 'failures'. As dusk turned to darkness, Bart's cameraman and producer also tried to capture his commentary in snatches between the shots that they had canned so that the light matched and it was clear his words were delivered in the middle of the barrage, not added afterwards.

It was a format that I had never had to consider or attempt. Despite having seen thousands and thousands of TV news clips since I had become a journalist and had begun considering how to convey news, it was like being shown a method of answering an exam question in a way that I had never previously contemplated. Watching and listening to Bart's delivery, I was struck by how this was almost a different métier to my own.

The speed at which Bart had to craft simple but telling sentences and phrases as the inky-blue sky lit up with explosions made me understand the stark nature of a broadcaster's challenge and appreciate the skill required in a way I never had before. It struck me as being simultaneously simpler yet somehow more demanding than my own more leisurely reporting in print.

"Dusk in Sarajevo. Amongst the city's ancient minarets, the rockets fall, heralding another night of heavy shelling," Bart said sombrely to camera, early in the bombardment.

After night had fallen, Bart was describing the fire on the city, the neat globes that I had witnessed drifting across the skyline, as if on ice.

"They come in ones, in twos and threes – and it sounds as if the city is crying."

He went on. "Eerily lit up by flames, the city is hit from every side by practically every imaginable projectile. Long lines of machine-gun fire gliding across the roofs, exploding against their targets. Heavy shelling slamming into the buildings, within seconds engulfing them in flames. A mass of crazy sparks lighting the brow of one hill from a quickfire volley of mortar bombs. For six hours, there is no let-up. Every night in Sarajevo, you think that it can't get worse." Bart paused. "But it does."

And then Bart's parting shot to his viewers in private parlours, in institutions, in governments and across international alliances: "This is a scene of wholesale devastation, of a city being obliterated, while the world watches – but does nothing."

It was simple. It lacked any of the hysteria that the situation might have been expected to have prompted, but it was more powerful for that understatement. And Bart had wrapped it up with a neat polemic. I loved it.

As the shooting and the shelling ebbed, I was aware of a quiet exhilaration among the Sky team. They knew they had in the can probably the best footage taken to date of the extent of the siege of Sarajevo; yet given the devastation and no doubt the victims and casualties of the night's violence, as yet unseen, neither Bart nor his cameraman nor producer wanted to make any public display of delight at their professional achievement.

It was left to Bart to lay his hand on the shoulder of his cameraman and say, "Thanks, guys. I think we've done a good job of work there."

As the day began to dawn, I looked west across the city. Smoke still hung in the air, fires burned in buildings in the commercial centre. Who knew what physical and human damage would be found when we were back at ground level?

And I reflected that a simple change of vantage point had given me a whole different perspective on the siege and the assault on the largely innocent citizens of Sarajevo. I had considered before, at the ground level to which I was accustomed, the scale of the stockpiles of ammunition and weaponry implicit in bombardments, but that night I had continuously expected the guns to fall silent. They never did. My UNPROFOR contacts had told me that 'a bad day' meant 3,500 shells falling on the city. It was a number I couldn't get my brain around. The Bosnian Serb Army and paramilitaries had inherited much of the hardware held by Europe's fourth largest army, the JNA, and they were behaving as if there was an urgent need to exhaust their bullets and bombs in the shortest conceivable time.

"Normally, this kind of bombardment is the prelude to infantry moving into a town or a city. It's a softening up ahead of the armoured vehicles and the tanks rolling in. That's what I witnessed in the Gulf War. But here – well, it's just a barrage, isn't it? There's no evidence of the Bosnian Serbs trying to carve out a bigger share of the city. I keep using this word, but it's just gratuitous from where I'm sitting," Bart said.

I asked him, "Did you have any second thoughts about that pay-off line, Bart? You know: 'The whole world watches – but does nothing.' Did you think of perhaps turning it into a question? Maybe "but will anyone do anything?" It's quite stark. It's a big charge to level."

Bart paused. There was no flash of irritation at an implied criticism. He was weighing the question seriously.

"Mick," he said, "as a European, I find what we're watching to be unacceptable. And I – you, all of us – are taking vast amounts of risk to show the world what's actually happening. Has it helped so far? No. Might it? I don't know. But, when this thing is all over, nobody can say 'We didn't know.' Nobody. And, if I have to be a little forceful in putting across my message, then so be it."

I nodded. I didn't disagree with any of that. I was ever wary of exaggeration in journalism. And there was much exaggerated journalism out there to be wary of. But this was not an example. Bart had captured the episode sombrely but accurately, even if he couldn't resist levelling his concluding accusation. We fell silent.

The exhaustion of six hours of exposure to relentless explosions was making itself felt visibly in the return of my eye tic. I relished the thought of climbing into my bed and sleeping without the sound of gunfire. But it wasn't to be.

"Right, boys," said Bart. "That's only half the job done. Now we need to get some sense of the human cost of last night. We'll check out what's happening downstairs and then go to casualty at the Koševo Hospital as well."

I felt a sense of dread. Part of me wanted to peel off. But I knew Bart was right.

I followed the Sky crew down, our footsteps clacking with a funereal gloom around the concrete stairwell. The sense of dread at the scenes we were likely to find on the ground floor and in the basement of the hospital deepened as we descended.

For me, this was the worst part of journalism: witnessing up close the atrocities that man can wreak upon man. I was convinced that I had seen TV journalists quietly thrill as they stood alongside scenes of carnage. I would never be one of those. Bart was not like that either.

I thought of one broadcast journalist who appeared to be fulfilled only if she was in the worst, most godforsaken parts of the globe. She was brave, yes – but how much were these broadcasts empathy with the world's most downtrodden and miserable and how much were they displays of bravado, designed to outdo her peers? And then I thought of another international correspondent who picked her way around the flashpoints of the Middle East, speaking gently and warmly to women and children in Arabic, as if dispensing kindness and succour, at the same time as capturing the essence of her story for her viewers calmly and without swagger. I knew which approach I preferred.

Once, when I had vented my frustration at the first reporter by shouting at the TV while her bulletin was being screened, Saša told me that she had gone to mainland Britain to university but, once she had graduated, her mother in Ireland had said to her "Well, you've got your degree, so now you can come home and, if not join the convent, at least teach in the convent school."

"So, Mick, each broadcast is a defiant rebuke to her mother. She's saying 'Not only am I not coming back to that claustrophobic, judgemental environment, I'm also going to go to the riskiest places on the planet just to annoy you,'" said Saša.

"Good story, Sash – but I still think those bulletins are all about her. In her mind, at least. And that doom-laden delivery. Christ, she irritates me."

I did wonder whether Saša's partial defence of her was because he'd slept with her at some point, but I didn't ask the question.

As for the second reporter, though it sounded like exaggeration, I couldn't help feeling that there was something of the Mother Teresa about her. She didn't ooze piety, but I felt she all but glowed with an aura of decency and kindness. It was exceptional for a journalist to leave those she interviewed feeling enhanced but I believed that that was what she did. It was a gift.

In the street outside the entrance to the hospital, the ambulances, private cars and vans bearing the dead, the dying and the wounded were already snaking back out of sight, as the city, briefly becalmed, began to give up the victims of a night that would stay in the memory of the Sarajevan people – until the next mother of all bombardments. I wondered whether it would be possible to hurl more missiles in one night than I had witnessed over the previous six hours.

Bart was in conversation with a man who turned out to be Bakir Nakaš, the hospital director.

"Yes, Bart. Of course. Usual rules. Discreet – and back off if a family or individual is uncomfortable. And just enough filming to capture the human impact. Okay?"

"Yes, of course, Bakir," said Bart.

I stuck close to the Sky team as they picked their way through the ground floor, where hallways and inner rooms had been transformed into casualty wards. Then they made their way down to the basement where the most seriously injured were being treated. The smell of disinfectant was failing to overpower a warm, fetid staleness in the air – a staleness that spoke of wards uncleaned and a breeding ground for bugs and infections.

Every bed was occupied. How would this casualty department deal with what was certain to be an influx of multiple new patients? What kind of stark choices would fully occupied nurses and doctors and surgeons have to make as they juggled existing patients with new arrivals, many of them needing urgent attention? As I would witness, they did precisely that: they made those choices and they made value judgements about who needed the most urgent attention and, worst of all, decided coolly who they could save and who they could not. I'd learn later that this was called 'triage'. In this environment, these were decisions required not just daily but hourly.

Before the steady flow of new casualties landed, as vehicles scooped up the injured and the dying from the four corners of the city, my attention was grabbed by the sight of patients patched up and clinging on and some whose lives seemed to be ebbing away from them. Two in particular stuck in my mind and wouldn't leave me for days, weeks. A young man, probably between nineteen and twenty-one. His head was swathed in cream gauze bandages, one eye was patched but, most shockingly, his arm, just two-thirds the length that it should have been, ended in a bandaged stump. I could read the pain wracking him in waves but, with that dignity that we learn as we enter adulthood, he was fighting to suppress it. Fighting to suppress it so that he didn't burden anyone else with a pain that those tending him had done all they could to ease.

The second image was of a young girl, perhaps nine years old, lying still, on a bed, on her back, in a shabby navy blue calf-length dress that looked as if it hadn't been washed for some weeks. Her eyelids were closed. Her breath was only just discernible. She had pale skin and straw-coloured hair in plaits.

"*Oh, that sweet, sweet girl!*" I thought.

I touched the shoulder of the nurse at her side.

"Will she make it? Will she make it through?" I hadn't framed the questions. They framed themselves.

"Sir, I'm afraid she won't. She's drifting away. She's got a piece of shrapnel lodged in her pancreas. I don't think even a miracle can save her."

The nurse spoke calmly and, in that moment, my insight was simultaneously banal and profound. Here was a young woman who had to deal daily with life as it was, events and their consequences – not life as we hoped it might be as we set off on our personal journey full of dreams and ambitions.

I felt a burst of fury. So Bosnia declaring independence represented such a threat to Bosnian Serbs that it justified this, did it? I felt that blockage at the back of the throat that preceded tears. I managed to hold them back. I succeeded in not shedding tears. It wasn't even a hollow victory, though, I thought.

And then the fresh stream of victims began to trickle in and flood down into the wards. And the answer to the question of how this casualty department could accommodate more of the wounded became clear: those who could walk or limp would find a space somewhere, anywhere, to squat down; those on stretchers were simply placed on those stretchers on the floor. As ambulance staff or just friends of victims deposited their patients and loved ones on the ground, I noticed maggots wriggling across the tiled floors, no doubt waxing fat in these warm, largely unsterilised conditions.

An elderly man in his eighties, I guessed, was helped down, his left leg below the knee shattered, probably irreparably. A young man in his mid twenties was carried in on a stretcher, trying to staunch a wound just above his navel that risked gushing blood. Both sought to dial down their outward expressions of distress as best they could, the old man out of a sense of dignity, I suspected, the younger man out of a sense of stoicism and resilience.

But, of course, young children lack that ability to rein in their spontaneous response to trauma and pain and, as I followed the Sky cameraman capturing the images he could to encapsulate these scenes of suffering, I heard the most baleful cry of pain issuing from the staircase leading from the ground floor to the basement. As the child was carried closer, the volume of the screaming increased to a level and a tone which I found unbearable. It tore into me. I quietly begged for it to end. But it wouldn't end.

It was a girl, probably seven years old, with beautiful black shoulder-length hair, brown eyes and coffee-coloured skin, in yellow pyjamas, crooked in the arm of her father. She would rip out three heart-rending screams and then gasp for breath before starting again.

Bart's cameraman did not point his camera at her out of respect for her family's distress. Perhaps he would later, once her hysteria had ebbed and he had established with her father what had happened.

A doctor and a nurse led the father and daughter through the ward and into an administrator's office alongside the main room. The jabs of screaming kept repeating as I saw the father lay his child on top of a desk, as the doctor prepared to sedate her. The nurse emerged from the office.

"Her father says she had been woken up by the bombing and let herself out into the back yard to see what was happening. We're pretty sure she's taken several slivers of shrapnel internally, but we can't tell yet where they've lodged and she's too distressed to let us examine her."

The volume reduced as the doctor shut the office door. I was now trembling from the shock of the volley of screaming. After several minutes the little girl fell silent, either sedated or having passed out naturally. The trail of the wounded and mutilated continued. Might the staff have to open up the first floor? The basement was crowded and the ground floor had been near to full when I had come downstairs. I concentrated as fiercely as I could and tried to find the words I might use in my reports to capture the atmosphere in that basement. Groaning, gasping, sobbing and quiet tears. Bewilderment appearing to trump anger. I almost wished that I hadn't been there to witness the victims of the night's firestorm. But Bart had been right. The lightshow was only half of the story. I stood to the side as Bart finally did his piece to camera, an hour after they had first descended to the basement.

"The intensive care wards of the city's Central Hospital are packed with amputees."

The cameraman had panned in on the young man in the gauze bandages. He swung to the girl in the grubby navy dress and plaits. She had passed away.

"Some of the victims of last night's bombing are covered, some are not – in a ward where maggots crawl the floors. This is a little house of Bosnian horrors," whispered Bart.

I decided against going with Bart and the crew to the Koševo Hospital. I felt I had seen enough. I didn't think I needed another gruesome exhibition of wounds and death to help me convey what had happened. I hoped I wasn't being remiss or cowardly.

"I'm off, Bart. Thanks for letting me join you. I'll catch up with you soon."

I slipped out into the streets where daylight was beginning to take a proper hold. I wanted to cry but I couldn't. I was empty. I felt hollowed out by emotion. I wandered back through the side streets. There was no comfort through numbness. The images and memories of the sights and noises I had experienced kept returning with a chilling persistence. Had I ever felt so low? I wasn't sure that I had.

Bart would tell me the following day that the little girl in the yellow pyjamas was dead. She had died within two hours of landing at the hospital, her body riddled with shrapnel shards so minute that their entry points were invisible. Her spleen had been ruptured.

15
JUNE 1992

"I pray that, by the mercy of Allah, this bridge will be firm
And its existence will be passed in happiness
And that it will never know sorrow."
Badi's 'tarih' – inscription on the bridge over the Drina in Višegrad

A few days after we had witnessed the fire-show from the hospital balcony and the little girl in the yellow pyjamas had died from her wounds in the basement, Bart was broadcasting live from a television screen that the staff had fixed to a bracket on the wall in the Press room at the Holiday Inn. I recognised the west balcony of the hospital as his vantage point.

Behind him, the nearer of the two identical UNIS towers, tall rectangular business blocks recognised as the most prestigious city addresses for an ambitious company, was ablaze.

"It was the symbol of modern Sarajevo," Bart commented, apparently dispassionately. "Now of its destruction. Flames tear across the floors and up into the higher storeys, showering debris into the streets of the Bosnian capital – its disintegration reflected in the broken windows of its twin.

"The Parliament building below is also struck – but it doesn't burn. This latest bombardment makes a mockery of the attempts by mediators to bring peace to this city, which is enfolded in war.

"Less than twenty-four hours earlier, the Serb commanders had put their signatures to a truce never adhered to. Now the gunmen in the hills show where their commitment lies. Under a sickle moon, the city rocks to their explosions."

His cameraman framed Bart in the shot with one of those rare but thrilling daylight crescent moons over his left shoulder.

Saša emerged at a brisk pace from the hallway.

"It looks like this new guy at the top of the Bosnian Serb Army has got a ruthless streak to him, Mick," he said.

"Mladić?"

"Yes – him. In fact, when I say 'a ruthless streak', it's maybe not even just a streak. I think he's just ruthless. I fear there's a lot more blood to be shed before we're out of this." Saša drew his lips back, revealing clenched teeth. It was a look I recognised: one he assumed only when profoundly distressed.

Saša explained that he'd had an update from the President's son, Bakir. During the night of the bombardment that I had watched from the hospital balcony, Bosnian intelligence had intercepted some of the Serb radio transmissions. It had been clear from them that it was Mladić himself who was directing much of the bombardment. He had ordered missiles to be fired at the Parliament and the Presidency buildings.

"They heard him order attacks on the Velešići residential areas as well. Mick, they actually heard him say 'Shell Velešići – there aren't many Serbs living there. Shell them until they are on the edge of madness.' So, what he's saying, Mick, is it's okay to kill some fellow Serbs, provided you kill a whole lot more Muslims." Saša shook his head.

"Kukanjac before him. The JNA man. He may have been a hapless bugger, but at least he thought his army should provide a buffer between Muslim and Serb. Clearly, Mladić doesn't see it like that."

Saša picked at the keyboard of his word processor without creating anything legible and without sitting down.

"Anyway. It's beer time. I've got an idea to run past you."

In the hotel bar, Saša suggested we break out of the city and head east, where he had heard there were some grim developments.

"I think there's stuff happening in Višegrad that will get us back on the front page. You've said it yourself. Paul has said it. I'm not being glib about people's suffering, but we can't just keep on writing about another day and another day of siege."

Saša explained that a Serbian friend of his from his home town, Užice, had moved over the border into Bosnia and settled in Višegrad for work.

"She says there are terrible things going on there. Though she's a Serb, she's appalled at what's happening to the Muslims there. She thinks we should see it. It's a secret that needs to get out." Saša paused.

"Thing is – I'll be okay. I'm a Serb. But it might be dangerous for you. If they found out that you were a British journalist. From what my friend Nevena has said, there are unspeakable acts being perpetrated. By people who wouldn't be relaxed about their details being broadcast. You know what I'm saying, Mick."

Once again, I heard the words emerge from my mouth before I had fully processed the implications.

"I'm coming, Saša. I've been saying to you for a while that there's a war going on beyond Sarajevo that we'd be negligent not to try to cover."

I knew that there would be plenty of time for fear, but I knew too that if I was true to my journalistic instincts, I had to make the trip.

For the first time, I wondered also whether Saša was trying to help me become braver. Not recklessly or irresponsibly. Just offering me the benefits of his experience of what was and what was not tolerable risk. Was he trying, in an unspoken way, to bump my risk needle up the dial? I couldn't know and I didn't want to ask Saša whether that was what he was doing. Not yet anyway. I did know that, ultimately, the risk assessment was mine.

Yet those words had popped out of my mouth – "I'm coming, Saša" – before I had weighed the risk in any reflective or meaningful way. Perhaps, deep down, I felt Saša would not expose me to any unacceptable risk.

"So, when do we go?" I asked.

"Soon as. As for logistics, we're going to need your UNPROFOR mate to magic us out of the city. Then Ševa says he's got friends in Olovo, north-east of here. They're car dealers and they can provide us with wheels. I've described you to Nevena. There are fake ID cards floating around Višegrad and she can mail out one for you that we can pick up from the people in Olovo. Then we'll take the mountain roads into the back of Višegrad. It's a bit of a circuitous route but it's safer than going in on the main M5 road."

Saša had folded out a map and was pointing to a road picked out in yellow. I noted how tightly it twisted and zagged down from the mountains into the town.

"You'll need your best Serbo-Croat, of course," Saša said, and he smiled. "You might have to pretend you've spent your teenage years in the USA and you're a bit rusty, but you've come back home to help create…" Saša paused again. "A Greater Serbia!" And he laughed. And I laughed.

"What would I not give for that cause?!" I said.

It was hardly surprising that I felt for the Bosnian people after I'd seen them bombarded recklessly in Sarajevo and heard of their plight in towns like Bijeljina and Bosanska Krupa, but it was on the road up into the mountains north-east of Sarajevo and then south-east down to Višegrad that I fell properly head over heels in love with Bosnia. How was it that no one had told me before of its almost British lushness set amongst mountains that appeared to tower three times higher than any peak in England? In the valleys, rivers glistened with a glorious hue somewhere between turquoise and emerald.

In the central belt, narrow roads wound and twisted between hectare after hectare of forested hillsides. From a car, one had to duck down to see where the trees met the sky. Shafts of sunlight frequently shot through them. There was a spectacular new valley view round virtually every corner. And it was a landscape with occasional walk-on parts for individuals and livestock that appeared to hail from a long-forgotten age. It was as if altitude had halted time and they had been frozen in the '50s or '60s: shepherds surrounded by goats; cattle ambling in the middle of the road, apparently unruffled by the rare motor vehicles they encountered. I was entranced. And, because of the frequency of hairpin bends, not even Saša could tear it up and spoil it for me.

To say that the route Saša took was circuitous was an understatement. We passed through small settlements with names I'd never heard of before and never would again: Kladanj, Živinice, Kalesija. Vlasenica was the last sizeable town, but after heading south-east from Han Pijeskat, the route became sheer wilderness. I would have been able to enjoy without qualification the beautiful vistas, the remote forest tracks from which emerged dramatic, heart-lifting views, had it not been for a niggle that perhaps we were lost in the middle of nowhere.

On that last stretch of the journey, there were times when Saša wondered out loud whether he'd taken a wrong turn. Just as during our trip over Mount Igman into Sarajevo, the road changed from asphalt to gravel as we passed through tall, dense trees, then it was just a mud surface. Though I tried to revel in the scenery and the isolation, I had to admit to a sense of relief when, eventually, the vehicle found tarmac again. Perhaps we weren't lost on the hills after all, just hours before sundown. Saša took the car down a final series of tight bends and then Višegrad appeared beneath us.

"Mick," said Saša, "at checkpoints, we just busk it. If necessary, I'll do the Greater Serbia thing and you've just come back from the US… to help the cause."

"Where from?" I asked. "Give me a place."

"Just say Connecticut, Mick. I've never been there – but neither will the monkey on the checkpoint either."

"Okay, okay."

I couldn't help thinking that our first checkpoint interrogation at the northern entry to Višegrad was lazy. My ID said I was Marko from Novi Sad yet, though I bore little resemblance to the man in the picture, we were waved through. Note to self: get better ID while you're in Višegrad. However, this was my introduction to a group of paramilitaries, the *'Beli Orlovi'* – the White Eagles – whose notoriety I would soon be sharing with the readers of *The Times*.

Dressed either in civilian clothes or black uniforms, each wore a badge either on an armband or on their hats, depicting a double-headed white eagle with four Cs inset. I was conscious of the nationalist connotations of the four Cs. Saša told me that the white eagle had featured in the Serbian national flag since the late nineteenth century and was also a symbol replete with nationalist significance. Saša's friend would tell us that the White Eagles had effectively been left in charge of Višegrad after the JNA had pulled out of the town a couple of months earlier.

Nevena buzzed us in through the entrance to her block of flats and we went up one floor. A raven-haired lady in her early forties had opened the door to her apartment before we had reached the top of the stairs. Saša wrapped his right arm around the back of her waist in a manner that spoke of familiarity. He hugged her.

"Nevena. This is my very good friend, Mick."

"Mick. This is Nevena."

I shook her hand, having logged Saša's upgrading of me to 'my very good friend'. I didn't think that this was a casual use of language.

Nevena wasn't a classic beauty. Her nose was a touch too Roman and her face had a hint of parchment to it, due, I suspected, to exposure to the smoke from too many Camel cigarettes over the years. Yet she was striking and sensual and her make-up and outfit suggested significant preparation for the arrival of Saša. Her thick, naturally wavy, shoulder-length hair had the blue shimmer to its blackness of a corvid. Was she a variation on the Petra theme? Had I identified Saša's 'type'? No. I swatted away the thought. Saša probably had many 'types'.

The contents of Nevena's living room were as eloquent a commentary upon her as anything I could divine from her appearance. The room contained only tasteful, quality items. From the carved wooden frame of the firm blue velvet sofa and matching chairs to the Blue Period Picasso prints on the wall, the design was harmonious. No clutter. A pair of replica Greek vases here, a colourful icon there, it was the flat of a woman who knew what she liked. Did she not share it with a partner because a man was almost certain to flaw its perfection? Or might she have compromised had that man been Saša? I sensed in the air past intimacy but no long-term relationship between them.

The sound of a wine bottle being uncorked echoed enticingly from the kitchen space and Nevena placed two generously filled glasses of deep red wine on the coffee table in front of us.

"From the vineyards between Dubrovnik and Mostar. Proper Bosnian red," she said.

The first sip was every bit as good as it looked.

"Heavens, this is good," I said. Nevena smiled.

"You've timed it well, guys. There's a curfew at around 8pm. After that is when most of the rounding up and the killing goes on," Nevena said, as if imparting a banality or an aside.

"The killing?!" Saša looked up at her.

"Yes. Not that they're averse to assassinations in broad daylight as well, mind you. Since the JNA moved out of town, the White Eagles have just got more and more brazen. There are some good guys in the police force but they know the paramilitaries are out of control." She paused. "Well – in control and out of control. Already some of the 'good Serbs', if I can put it like that – policemen, politicians – have been at best driven out, at worst murdered, just for threatening to get in the way of the thugs."

Nevena worked in the finance department of one of the biggest firms in Višegrad, having moved to the town from Saša's home town in Serbia three years earlier.

"I was quite happy here. It's a small town, yes – but it's a lovely spot and the walking in the mountains and along the river is spectacular. Nice people too. Everyone got on fine. Nobody gave a thought as to your background."

She explained that, as violence broke out in Croatia, some nervousness set in but, overall, the prevailing goodwill reassured the majority of the population that the contagion of war would not spread to this south-east corner of Bosnia.

As she spoke, I asked myself how many times I had heard that calculation. Each time the calculation had been proved wrong: in Zagreb, in Dubrovnik, in Sarajevo and now in Višegrad. As each set of citizens had asserted 'It'll never happen *here*', had they really believed it or had they been whistling to keep spirits up? Clearly, something in the mix of the crumbling absolutes of Tito's Yugoslavia, economic decline, the emergence of strains of nationalism, and individuals' fears for the safety of their families was creating fertile soil in which the worst of human instincts were able to flourish. The mix was also pulling away brick by brick the foundations of the protective structures that in normal times kept each citizen safe.

The story was that the White Eagles had descended upon Višegrad in April, about a month after the Bosnian referendum. Nevena said that most of them were paramilitaries and Chetniks from Belgrade, unknown to the townsfolk, but the ringleader was a young man called Milan Lukić. He had been brought up in Višegrad but had drifted off to Belgrade.

Then there were rumours of bar jobs in Offenbach, in Germany, and in Zurich, but his evident experience of methods of intimidation, brutality and, ultimately, extermination suggested the jobs were likely to have been cover for an apprenticeship within organised criminal networks.

Still just twenty-five years old, his swagger and arrogance – and perhaps some local knowledge that his colleagues from Belgrade lacked – seemed to have earned him a leadership role, said Nevena.

"He's certainly top dog round here," she added.

She explained that a unit of the JNA had had to cross the border from Užice to restore some order after barricades had gone up across the district, setting out demarcation lines between Muslim and Serb areas. There had been shelling of Muslim areas and a Muslim backlash. A former JNA officer, a Muslim appalled by the White Eagles' behaviour, led a swoop on the hydroelectric dam, took control of its engine room, and threatened to flood the whole town, if the killing and removal of Muslim men did not stop.

Nevena said that, at that point, a large percentage of the Muslim population and a not insignificant number of Serbs sought refuge with relatives, friends, or general benefactors beyond the municipality, fearful of apocalyptic developments.

"I went back home for a couple of weeks, hoping the temperature would cool," she said. "The atmosphere here was poisonous. The Serb hardliners were trying to spread rumours in the factories and the workplaces in the town of Muslim forces kidnapping Serb children and roasting them on spits. They said women were being shod like horses. It was ridiculous but, if you spread enough propaganda, people's certainties begin to be eroded."

She explained that, as the JNA took over not just the dam but the whole town, it wasn't quite a semblance of normality that returned to Višegrad, but it was the most tranquil few weeks that its citizens had experienced between the start of the year and mid June.

"They put out broadcasts, saying that all Muslims could come back to their homes safely. There would be no more purges. And the people – lots of them – came back.

"It wasn't like peacetime. There were still sweeps of what the JNA called 'reactionaries' in Muslim villages. One day, for example, four thousand Bosnian Muslim men were taken to the Višegrad football stadium. They were searched for weapons and held for a couple of days. When they went back to their villages, many of their homes had been damaged or burned out."

She said that, in town, the JNA manned checkpoints – sometimes on their own, sometimes accompanied by paramilitaries – checking Muslims against their lists, and they were stopped from leaving town or going to their jobs if they didn't have a certificate supplied by the local police stations, which were now no longer multi-ethnic.

"But relatively, it was an improvement. The removal and killing of Muslim men halted. It felt a little less anarchic – though a male friend of mine, a Muslim, did tell me that a friendly JNA soldier told him privately in the street 'Get out of Višegrad while we're still here, because woe betide you when we leave.' He clearly knew the JNA wouldn't be staying in Višegrad and he knew who would take over when they went."

Nevena said that before the JNA withdrew, all key police and political roles were stripped from Muslims and given to Serbs; but, after the army's withdrawal in mid May, all hell was let loose.

"Saša, Mick – over the next couple of days I'm going to take you to people who can give you first-hand accounts of what's been going on. I know you trust my word, Saša, but I can't tell you half of it. It's important that you hear the unvarnished truth – and that you tell the world what's happening."

Nevena, who was now sitting on the edge of the sofa, clasped her hands in her lap and, for the first time, began to look tearful.

"Why don't you get out of here, Nevena?" asked Saša. "You don't need this."

"Well, I've not been threatened but it's just been made clear to me that I'm expected to stick around, behave normally in the workplace, help keep the company ticking over. It's been intimated that it would be 'bad form' to quit," she said. "And this flat – I love it. I've worked hard to make it as perfect as I can. Lovely views over the river and out to the mountains. And I'm well paid but…"

She was on the brink of emotion again. She gulped and gathered herself. Saša stretched out a hand and laid it on her shoulder. She looked up and across at Saša and me.

"But how can I stay here? Every night Lukić and his men go round herding up Muslims. They take them to the bridges. They shoot them or decapitate them and they throw them in the water. God knows how many corpses there are floating down the river."

If Nevena was right, this was precisely the kind of activity that I had feared the international Press pack was missing – tucked out of sight, a clear 'progression' in the conflicts from sniper fire and shelling at indiscriminate targets to one-on-one brutality and summary executions. Saša and I had been offered front-row tickets to observe this next phase but, by taking our seats, we would be exposing ourselves to risk on an exponential scale.

There was an uncomfortable silence. Nevena leaned down and picked up her handbag. She opened it and took out a pack of Drina Gold cigarettes.

"Do you still, Saša? Mick?"

"Yeah, okay. I'll have one," said Saša. I had never seen Saša with a cigarette before.

"No, I don't – but thanks," I said.

"Let's go on the balcony, Saša."

Nevena stood up and opened French windows at the far end of the sitting room. She and Saša stepped out onto the balcony and the door was pulled shut from the outside. I knew that Nevena was ensuring that the smell of tobacco didn't pollute her perfect flat.

I took the time, while they were smoking, to examine up close Nevena's Picasso prints and to feel the impressive weight of her pair of replica Greek vases – clay-orange with black and white neo-classical images of female figures complete with extravagant angels' wings, some holding pan pipes. And an image flashed into my mind of Nevena alone in junk shops and in galleries, inspecting items with an air of seriousness, considering whether any might be suitable for her home. And I sensed a lonely woman, craving affection, focusing on her art when perhaps she would rather have focused on Saša or someone of his ilk – if such a person existed.

When Saša and Nevena returned, Nevena was in full flow.

"Not tonight, Saša – but many's the time I've stood on that balcony and seen them on the new bridge. They drive up, get out of their cars with a few terrified victims. They switch off the headlights so that no one can see. And then 'bang-bang'. And then the sound of something hitting the water. And then they're back in their cars, lights on and they're off. We know their cars. We know who they are. But the real police – well, they do nothing. They can't. When the JNA walked away, they were as good as saying the White Eagles are in charge."

It wasn't until the following morning that I registered the fact that Višegrad wasn't a town with a magnificent bridge; it was a world heritage-status bridge with an otherwise unremarkable town tagged onto it.

We had walked into the town centre, ostensibly for a coffee but principally to enable Nevena and Saša to show me Višegrad's sixteenth-century bridge – a construction that had helped Ivo Andrić to the 1961 Nobel Prize for Literature with his novel *The Bridge Over the Drina*.

The central 'character' in the novel, the bridge appears before the traveller unexpectedly at the top of the town's unprepossessing main street and ordinary town square. It seemed to me to be a construction of such scale, ambition and magnificence that it was as if it had been transported either magically or meticulously, stone by stone, to the south-west edge of this unremarkable settlement from one of the grandest cities in the world.

The key to its scale lies not just in the fact that the broad span of the River Drina demands a substantial structure as it skirts west of Višegrad; it lies also in the strategic importance of this crossing to the Ottoman Empire. As much as any landmark does, it marks the cultural grid reference of where East meets West.

As we walked towards the bridge, Saša explained that Višegrad was a majority Muslim settlement. They made up nearly two-thirds of the nine thousand population. But, being so close to the Serbian border, this was part of a boomerang of land that the Serbs would try to seize along the east and north of Bosnia. In the event of an externally imposed peace deal, they would then argue that this was their territory. This and many other towns like it were historically Serbian, they would claim – even if the historical demographics suggested otherwise.

Saša suspected what was going on was part of a plan in Belgrade to grab as much land as possible in Bosnia and Croatia and dig in and hold onto as much of it as it could ring-fence. If Milošević couldn't achieve a Greater Serbia in a neat, clean way, he might just bring it about using dubious methods and flawed historical claims.

As Saša had forecast, when the Old Bridge, the Mehmed Paša Sokolović Bridge, came into view, it took my breath away. It wasn't elaborate but there was something majestic about the perfect construction of its eleven arches.

Nevena and Saša let me view the bridge from every angle, as if I were a photojournalist looking for the optimal shot. From beneath the bridge, standing on the riverbank on the east side, I could see how each stone had been shaped and cut to create perfectly proportioned arches. At first sight the arches were identical; on closer inspection, on either side of the central plaque of white marble there were two arches of exactly the same proportions and then arches stepping away on either side, each almost imperceptibly smaller than the next. The bridge had a perfect symmetry.

The colour of the stones modulated according to light and angle, from pale brown to starchy white to pinkish grey – shades set against a backdrop of the gently churning green waters of the Drina, nearly two hundred metres wide where the bridge crossed it.

It represented a leisure spot that was as relaxing as it was uplifting in times devoid of strife: a playground for children's games, a photographic backdrop to christening and wedding parties, a tranquil place for the young and the old. Often elderly couples would sit quietly on the terraces known as the bridge's 'kapia' and gaze out at the rich green waters of the Drina, the mountains and the meadows, the pastures and orchards by its river banks. There was perhaps no finer spot between Sarajevo and Serbia, Saša suggested.

Yet Nevena was inviting me to dwell on the details and the spirit of the bridge because its history of having played host to some of the darkest deeds ever to have afflicted the area was being relived. She wasn't being ghoulish in wanting us to witness some of those dark deeds; she wanted us to relay their occurrence to the outside world.

In her car on our way to the Dušče district of town, halfway between the Old Bridge and the region's hydroelectric dam, Nevena warned us that her friend, Madiha, was grieving. She said she had good reason to believe that her husband had been shot by a sniper a few days earlier in a village nearby called Osojnica. She had been trying to get his body back so that he could be buried properly – but without success so far.

"Perhaps a sliver of her heart is hoping it's a case of mistaken identity but… this is just the latest of her traumas. Anyway, despite everything, she wants to tell you her story – get it out beyond Višegrad, beyond Bosnia."

The face of the woman who opened the door to Nevena bore a sadness and perhaps some fear, but there was a kindness too that was unmistakable. She was an ample woman with large eyes of a shade of grey that I couldn't recall ever seeing in anyone else. I noticed too her long filigreed silver earrings and her soft, peach-coloured chiffon neck-scarf.

After Nevena had located Saša and myself in the international journalistic firmament and made it clear that she trusted us implicitly to tell Višegrad's story to the outside world, Madiha said, "Gentlemen, I just hope you can warn people that if a quiet little backwater like this, where everyone pulled together, everyone got on more or less, can be transformed into hell on earth in a matter of months, then it can happen anywhere. We weren't bad people before and we're not now. But a minority have bred evil. Some came from outside but some were part of this town's daily life. I don't understand how they've turned. I really don't. It's become a contagion I would never have believed possible."

She admitted that the male side of her family had not been passive, as the JNA and the paramilitaries had begun to tighten their grip on Višegrad. Her husband had helped set up barricades and defend the districts of Višegrad's municipality that the Muslims had continued to hold outside Višegrad town. Her brother, Mujo, had been one of the group that had seized control of the dam and threatened to inundate the town. These were actions that had made both her husband and brother marked men. No police certificates for them, allowing them to work, travel freely, or leave town.

Madiha explained that she had not known Milan Lukić from his time as a schoolboy in Višegrad but she had first met him earlier this year, after he had re-emerged in the town, she believed, from Belgrade.

"I came across him at the Old Bridge. It was the middle of March. He asked me my name. I think I knew he was trying to find out whether

I was a Muslim – but I was so shocked by the directness of his question that I answered him.

"That's when he said to me that he was Milan Lukić, that he was twenty-five, and that he was there to 'cut some Muslim throats'. He would have worked it out over time anyway, but I was effectively telling him I was my husband's wife and my brother's sister – and both of them were bound to end up on his hit list."

If her current concerns were the whereabouts of her brother and her husband, dead or alive, her story for us was about her next-door neighbour and best friend, Behija Zukić.

"Behka was a real character. Everyone in Višegrad knew her. She owned a fruit and veg store in the middle of town. It was a real money-spinner. And being a flamboyant woman – she was beautiful, tall, with striking black braided hair – she splashed out on a top-of-the-range cherry-red VW Passat. It was always parked outside her shop. When people thought of Behka, they thought of that car."

Madiha shrugged but looked more sad than angry. "And now that asshole, Lukić, is driving it around town… with a black flag with a skull and crossbones on it fluttering from the backseat window with the words 'The Avengers' on it."

"Behka was Muslim, yes. But, do you know, I think he just saw himself cruising around town in that red Passat car. I think he felt he deserved to be the guy driving around in the best-looking car in town."

Her face crumpled, as if she was about to weep, but she kept her tears at bay.

"I mean, who is he avenging? It's a sick, sick joke. I'd say it was boys dressing up in paramilitary uniform and posing as big shots. But that kind don't leave a trail of corpses in their wake. That kind are all talk and no action."

She paused, as if to deliver a weighty assessment. "That man, his cousin and their gang are responsible for dozens of deaths. And I've personally witnessed several of them. In broad daylight. How can that be? In a place like this?"

I noted that phrase again – 'in a place like this'. Everyone seemed to feel that their home town was special. It could not be consumed by the flames of hatred that had caught light elsewhere. And in so many cases now, they were clearly wrong.

Madiha said Behka's house was just a few paces away from her boundary and their homes were shared spaces.

"We would flit in and out of each other's places. We had no secrets from each other. We were like sisters."

On the day in May before the JNA had left town, rumours were rife that they were about to pull out and Behka tried to flee Višegrad with her family. Lukić and his cousin and their White Eagle sidekicks came three times to Behka's house on that day.

On the first occasion it was forcibly to drag Bekha and her family back. The second time they came, Milan Lukić took Behka's car, his cousin took the family truck and their gang took the menfolk of the household away.

"When they came back a third time, just before midnight, I had a bad feeling," said Madiha. "I couldn't see this ending peacefully. Why would they come so late? There was more commotion. Behka was a feisty woman. From her voice, I could hear the fear, but she tried not to show that she was intimidated. She tried to persuade Milan Lukić that, now that he'd stolen her car, he should leave her alone and bring back her family. I went right to the boundary between our houses and hid out of sight. I don't know what I was doing. I wanted to protect Behka but I just wasn't brave enough to show my face and try to stop them from harming her. Do I regret that? Yes. Would I behave differently another time? I don't know. I was so afraid.

"There was more angry shouting and then a single shot rang out. I scurried across the terrace at the front of the house. Both of the Lukićes were there – but Milan had a rifle in his hands and his finger near the trigger. The gun wasn't quite horizontal but he had clearly just been pointing it. His cousin Sredoje's rifle was over his shoulder. He hadn't used it. Behka was lying with the back of her head towards me. I'll never forget the sight of her body, lying in a question-mark shape in the hall, just inside the front door."

Madiha switched her gaze from a spot in the distance and looked straight at Saša and me. "Gentlemen. Milan Lukić shot my best friend dead. In cold blood. There can be no doubt about it."

She paused.

"I think I said something stupid like 'You've killed my friend. Why did you do that?' Milan turned and looked at me. There wasn't a flicker of emotion on his face but then his look became contempt. No – more than that. Superiority. It was as if he knew he held all the power. He could do what he wanted and it didn't matter what I had witnessed – or all but witnessed.

"I'll never forget that look. And his words. 'Get the fuck out of here. You'll be next.' He didn't say 'Or you'll be next.' He said explicitly 'You'll be next.'

"Well, of course, I wanted to tend to Behka, to see if there was any sign of life. But, with the Lukićes there, I couldn't. I had to back off.

"Gentlemen, do you know that feeling, when something unspeakable has happened? And you don't want to believe that it has? And you just want to wind the clock back and stop it from happening? Mentally, I felt paralysed. I couldn't process what had happened. And then I walked back into my kitchen and I began to tremble. Great palpitations. I couldn't stop them. And I couldn't stop revisiting that sight of Behka curled on the floor of her hallway. My best friend. She couldn't be gone…"

Madiha's voice petered to a whisper. Nevena laid a hand on her forearm but said nothing.

Madiha resumed. "The Lukićes drove off again after about a quarter of an hour. When they'd gone, some neighbours came out. Before I had the courage to go back, one of them checked her pulse and put a blanket over her. As I'd suspected, she couldn't be saved. As we waited for the ambulance to come, I just wept and wept. I wept for Behka and her family, but I wept with fear too. That look on his face. 'You'll be next,' he said."

The room fell silent. Nevena, Saša and I all sensed a need to pause respectfully.

Then Saša spoke up. "Mrs Kalajdžić, you said that you'd seen the Lukićes commit other murders. That there were more killings. Can you tell us about any of them?"

"After Behka was shot and the JNA left town, it wasn't just me. Anyone could have seen it. There would be times in broad daylight, mainly on the bridges – both the old and the new – when Milan and Sredoje and their sidekicks would bundle men out of their cars. They were obviously Muslim men. Usually, they would just shoot them in the back and then hurl them over the parapet or the railings into the river. But, once – and I remember this as if it were in slow motion because it was so shocking – one of the White Eagles with Milan Lukić pulled out a long blade and, with one stroke, decapitated his victim. I was crossing the Old Bridge in my car and I didn't dare stop but, out of my rear-view mirror, I saw them tipping the man's body into the Drina and I'll swear they had placed the man's head on the parapet, as if it was funny. When I drove back a couple of hours later, of course, it was gone."

"So, do the police do nothing?" I asked.

"No, they don't. Some of them will offer acts of kindness, privately, if you come across them. Tell you to avoid a certain street or suggest where you might hide, if they know the White Eagles are on a purge. But they're probably as afraid of Lukić and his men as we are. They're the appointed ones – certainly by Karadžić in Pale and possibly by Milošević in Belgrade. By comparison, the local police are way down the pecking order."

I asked her whether she couldn't try to get away from Višegrad.

"I will. But first, I need to try to find my husband's body and lay him to rest appropriately. Then I'll think about me."

Nevena cut in. "There's a line the worst of the Serbs parrot. They say that, according to Islam, there is no obligation on Muslims to bury their own dead. That's what Madiha was told. She didn't need to get her husband's body back because the Serbs would bury him. It's rubbish, of course."

Madiha explained that she had had to cross the Old Bridge sometimes several times a day, following leads and tip-offs that might lead her to her dead husband.

"More often than not the Lukićes and their crew are on the bridge, doing their business – but what am I to do?"

"You're very brave," I said.

"Brave?" Madiha looked at me, as if it were a word she had never heard before.

"No – not brave, sir. Every time I put the key in the ignition, I'm craven with fear. I'm ashamed of how fearful I am for my own skin. But if

I laid low in my house and made no effort to find my husband, how much would I despise myself? He's gone, my brother's in hiding. Behka and her family are dead or disappeared. How could I put my safety first?"

I didn't resile from my point. "That's what 'brave' is, Madiha. That's its definition. You persisting in the face of fear. That's bravery." I hoped my insistence might provide her with a scintilla of strength at least.

She sighed quietly but she didn't bridle further. "If you say so," she said. "Thank you for your words. I know they're well meant."

Just an hour or so later, we were back in Nevena's flat. Her friend and work colleague Vesna arrived to tell us her story. She had to come to us, Nevena explained, because she lived in the street into which Milan Lukić and some of his family had moved after a Muslim police officer had been evicted from his sizeable property. She didn't want to be seen hosting visitors who weren't known around town and risk questions being asked.

Vesna was a Bosnian Serb who worked alongside Nevena as an economic forecaster. She had a bird-like look and a bird-like nervousness. Her thick woollen sweater couldn't conceal the fact that she was stick thin.

"She has a keen brain and she can spot an error on a spreadsheet from a mile away," said Nevena. "But she lives on her nerves and what she's seen has made that worse. But she's highly principled and, though she's afraid of any recriminations, she feels people need to know what's happening."

Vesna lived in Pionirska Street, an address that would acquire notoriety as a result of what she had witnessed from her upstairs bay window. One late evening she had heard automatic fire across the street. She had been too frightened to go out and investigate, but she learned the following morning from neighbours that a much-loved elderly couple had been murdered during a visit from the White Eagles, led by the Lukićes.

Vesna explained that it was obvious from her and anyone else's observations over previous weeks that the Lukićes and the other White Eagles were intent on removing from Višegrad any Muslim men of fighting age.

"It was as if lists had been drawn up and the White Eagles were going through them methodically."

The couple opposite had had four sons, now with their own homes and their own families, but Lukić and his gang had reached them on the list and come hunting them. Their parents were gunned down for refusing to reveal where they might be.

But the story she wanted to share with us eclipsed in its sheer horror even the gunning down of an elderly couple in their own homes. Recently back from work one early evening, she had heard a commotion in the street and saw the Lukićes and a band of White Eagles herding a group of around fifty people along the street.

"There were women and children. One young mother was carrying a baby. The only men in the group were elderly," said Vesna.

She said that the White Eagles kept adding to the group, fishing individuals out of homes in the street that she knew housed Muslim families. They would learn later that the core group had been from a village called Koritnik, which had been declared a Serbian village. The group had been told they were being bussed to a safe place but couldn't stay in Koritnik.

Vesna said that some White Eagles kicked in the door to a Muslim man's house who had not been seen for some days. They made the group, now about seventy strong, file inside before entering themselves. For around an hour, the door remained shut.

"Given what happened elsewhere, we think that, during that time, the Lukićes and their White Eagle colleagues were frisking them for weapons and forcing their captives to hand over any money, jewellery and other valuables," said Nevena.

Vesna said that, eventually, three White Eagles emerged with three young women and took them out of sight behind the house.

"Ten, maybe fifteen minutes later, they led them back. The three women looked terrible. Traumatised. One was crying," said Vesna. She paused. "They had obviously been raped."

Later in the evening, the Lukićes and their gang had moved the group on to a house thirty or forty metres further up the street but still in sight of Vesna's bay window.

"Milan Lukić was at the doorway of the first house, shouting at the Muslims to hurry up. I noticed none of them were wearing shoes and none carried any of the luggage they had brought from their village," said Vesna.

"The White Eagles formed a cordon to make sure no one escaped, as the captives walked towards the second house. And there was constant abuse. The White Eagles kept calling them '*balijas*' – dirty Turkish gypsies, it means – and asking them why their President wasn't there to help them. I could hear it all clearly from my house. They pushed the last man in through the front door, an elderly man, and shut it."

Vesna said there was a pause of around half an hour and then more activity. In the light cast by a street lamp and from an outhouse next to the house where the Muslim group was incarcerated, she saw Milan Lukić open the front door, light an orb-like object that he was holding in his left hand and throw it into the house before slamming the door shut again.

"After a few seconds, there was a huge explosion – but it wasn't just a blast. It was as if the bomb had ignited something. Flames filled the parts of the house I could see right up to the ceiling. There was a bitter smell of burning petrol. And then, some of the White Eagles started shooting, I presume to stop anyone from escaping through shattered windows. Then they were throwing more grenades and petrol bombs into the house and letting off bursts of automatic fire.

"The screams from the house were blood-curdling. I didn't want to look but I couldn't take my eyes away from what was happening. To be honest, already I was thinking that I needed to be a witness to what was happening. I couldn't let these people get away with it."

Vesna said that the White Eagles remained around the house for over an hour.

"It was as if they wanted to be sure every last Muslim in that house was dead. They were just focused on the task – as if this were legitimate work. No signs of concern at what they'd done. And I kept thinking about that baby that a mother had been carrying. It could only have been weeks old. And I just hoped it had known nothing, felt nothing; had died instantly.

"And, in the air, the smell of petrol had been replaced by another appalling smell. It wasn't quite like the smell of barbecued animal meat. I had to assume it was the smell of melting, roasting human flesh."

Nevena said that they had learned in subsequent days that around half a dozen people had managed to escape from the house after the initial explosion. Naturally, they were now lying low, knowing the Lukićes would want to finish them off, given what they had witnessed and experienced.

Saša asked Vesna to what degree the whole Pionirska Street episode had appeared pre-planned.

"Could it have been a movement of people that got out of hand?"

"Saša, there is no way that the events of that day could have come about other than through detailed pre-planning: the story that the families from Koritnik were to be bussed to a safe place; their being herded by the White Eagles once they arrived in Višegrad; their hand-picking individuals from houses in the street to add to the convoy; the fact that there were two empty houses ready for them; the fact that the White Eagles had prepared petrol bombs. This was all meticulously planned. And, you know, in all the events I've seen Milan Lukić involved in, I've never seen him take orders from anyone. I just don't believe anyone told him he had to incinerate his victims. I don't believe anyone told him that babies and infirm, old men had to be burned to death. He led the whole… whole…" Vesna struggled for the word. "The whole enterprise – and he did so in a way designed to terrorise his victims before their deaths and without a single indication of regret or compassion."

Vesna fell silent and I sensed that she had given as much detail as she could.

"Vesna, we're really grateful for your sharing this with us," I said. "It's an appalling story and it must have been difficult to retell it."

"Mick, it is painful – but, as I said, even as I stood and watched, I felt I might need to relive the pain multiple times to try to get justice. Heavens, I had enough to worry about before all this. I could do without it; but when people are called to account, then I'll be there to make sure the truth is told. Whatever it costs me…"

After Vesna left the flat, I felt a pall of gloom descend upon me. My hunch about the kind of activities that were going on had been proved right, but I took no pleasure in the accuracy of my forecast. I was now within touching distance of the worst aspect of this conflict: individuals going well beyond the recapture of territory they rightly or wrongly claimed to be theirs and tipping into a revelling in acts of terror and cruelty wreaked upon fellow citizens. Innocent fellow citizens, sometimes even women and children.

Eventually I broke the silence and told Saša Hugh's theories about how it was possible for human beings to inflict atrocities on other human beings. Some were psychopaths, some criminals, and some were inadequate and easily led no-marks, for the first time in their lives persuaded that they could act as they pleased.

"I agree with all that," said Saša, "but, for me, the critical element in all of this is leadership – and it can be at a national, local or brigade level. Leaders granting their men what you've already called 'permission to persecute'. Once that permission is given, it acts upon individuals in all sorts of different ways. Some guys can't believe the normal rules of civilised behaviour have been lifted. And so they test it a bit, and then a bit more, and then a bit more. And they experience a deeper level of exhilaration each time they step up the brutality. 'Hey, guys, I bayoneted a young girl in the stomach in front of her mother – and no one called me to account.'"

But Saša said that he believed there was an extra element affecting the behaviour of Milan Lukić. "From what Madiha and Vesna have said, he clearly enjoys the intimidation, the menace and, of course, the killing. He doesn't seem to have been a delinquent kid or a criminal with a long record, but I suspect he's high on the feeling that here he is – a twenty-five-year-old who, by a combination of unlikely circumstances, has found himself the most powerful man in Višegrad. Yes, he's had to show he's the toughest guy, the most ruthless, to be dishing out orders instead of taking them. Now he probably feels he has to sustain the brutality to remain top dog.

"But there's more than that. He needs to spread the culpability. He needs dozens of supporters to dip their hands in blood so that, if reckoning were ever to come, he can say that everyone did it. And it's the same with rape. I've little doubt he's raped women, girls, but that episode in Pionirska Street: I suspect he told three of his colleagues to do the business so that they were guilty of the same crime."

Saša said that overarching all these actions was another 'truth' in conflicts where one side was seeking to bring about mass movements of people.

"The brutalising of the defeated has to be so severe that the families of those murdered, tortured, raped or just driven away will never nurture ambitions to return to their homes again. It's part of the way you make a land grab permanent."

I shared with Saša Hugh's conviction that this suspension of civilised behaviour and the flouting of the requirements of the Geneva Convention could only ever be temporary; his view that the likes of Milan Lukić could not escape the consequences of their crimes forever.

"Do you think he's right?" I asked.

"I hope he's right. We have to believe he's right." Saša paused. "But I've never seen anything like this in all my years – the scale of the bombardment in Sarajevo, the individual acts of brutality here – so I'm not totally confident of how this is going to end. Particularly given how the world's so-called great powers are standing on the sidelines, doing precisely nothing."

I shrugged. "Let's not go there, Sash. Let's not go there."

We were considering leaving Višegrad. We had seen and heard enough to be clear that we had captured a prime example of the mini-wars breaking out across Bosnia. But Nevena suggested that, before we leave, we visit a friend of hers whose flat on the Drina riverside overlooked the Old Bridge.

"You might just witness something with your own eyes before you go," she said.

In mid morning, the day after we had met Madiha and Vesna, we made our way to the flat where a neat man in his early fifties in olive green slacks and a maroon V-necked sweater let us in. Nevena had told us that Dušan had been a schoolteacher but he had had to retire early due to a serious lung condition. He was a Bosnian Serb. Like her, he was appalled by what fellow countrymen were doing.

He spoke softly and in measured bursts of words, in part, I felt, reflecting a quiet, thoughtful nature, in part due to his condition. He frequently placed his right hand over his face and drew it downwards, as if mopping it with a handkerchief – a gesture of underlying anxiety of which he was possibly unaware, so natural had it become.

"Gentlemen, if it wasn't so brutal, it would amount to a spectacle. I've sat here and seen dozens killed. Often they stab them several times before throwing them into the water, sometimes they shoot them first. One method they particularly like is throwing a wounded man in the river so that they can take potshots at him from the bridge. Like it was a sport. Oh, yes. They seem to find that one hilarious."

Dušan said that sometimes it was so relentless he just had to pull the curtains and shut it all out.

"But," he admitted, "then you get a kind of ghoulish curiosity and you can't stop yourself from looking again… in case it's someone you know."

Dušan talked touchingly about his bond with young people in Višegrad, as he had taught mathematics to class after class of teenagers over the years.

"Most of them, even when it's many years since they left school, they still show me real respect. Many of them even call me 'sir', as if we were still in the classroom."

His mouth creased into a smile of fondness for the first time.

"I didn't know the Lukić boy. He was at the other school, so I never came across him. Word in the town is, though, that his grandfathers were both notorious Chetniks in the Second World War."

"Was there ever any antagonism between the boys? Bosnian Serbs and Bosnian Muslims?" I asked.

"No, no. Never. There were disputes, of course, and, you know, kids can be cruel. Pick on a vulnerable classmate. But it was never about ethnicity."

As I sipped at coffee too hot to take in draughts, the blaring of a car radio pumping out thumping turbofolk came into earshot and became louder as it approached.

"That'll be him. Milan Lukić," Dušan said. "Now you might see what he does."

Saša and I went to the window. A cherry-red VW Passat had come to a halt outside a block of flats on the other side of the bridge, a pale green Yugo behind it.

"That's them. That's Milan's car," said Dušan.

The music cut out and two men from the Passat disappeared into the apartment block. Some fifteen minutes later, the two emerged, another two people ahead of them, apparently being directed towards the red car. The Passat and the Yugo twisted down onto the bridge, the music pumping from Milan Lukić's car again. Six men got out of the cars as well as the two people who had been brought out of the flats. They were both women, one around thirty years of age, the other possibly her mother.

Dušan pointed out Milan and Sredoje Lukić. He didn't know the identity of the other four men, but all were dressed in White Eagles' paraphernalia.

Perhaps because we were too far removed to hear the exchanges between the men and the two women, it was as if the episode were happening quickly yet in slow, stark detail. The two women tried to push away their captors, looking round to see where they could run, but two of the men grabbed them by the forearms, manhandling them to the bridge parapet. Their instruction was clearly for the women to straddle the parapet as if they were riding a horse, manipulating them until they were content with their positioning a couple of metres apart from each other.

We could hear the women's screams as they realised they were sitting ducks and knew what was likely to come next. Then shots rang out. Rifle shots. Perhaps six. Perhaps eight. I could see that Milan Lukić had fired some of the shots. It wasn't clear who had fired the rest. The screaming stopped abruptly as the women's bodies jerked backwards at the impact of the bullets. Bloodstains pooled around each woman's stomach, then expanded in crimson circles, the cream material of their blouses acting like blotting paper.

First, the elder woman tipped backwards, her spine approaching the parapet, as if lowered smoothly by a winch. Then she tipped to her left and plunged down into the river. Perhaps twenty seconds later, the younger woman fell abruptly left and into the water. The White Eagle group clapped and cheered. I didn't think I had imagined pools of red surfacing in the waters of the Drina briefly before the river's currents swept them away.

"You see, gentlemen. This is their sport," said Dušan. He paused and made the hand-mopping gesture again. "Now go and tell your news organisations what's going on. See if you can do something to stop it. See if you can help me stop feeling ashamed to be a Bosnian Serb."

Saša and I thanked Dušan and headed back to Nevena's.

"Mick, we're out of here first thing tomorrow," said Saša. "It's too dangerous, and now we've seen it with our own eyes, there's no need to stay any longer. We'll go to Užice and stay with my folks and decide what to do next."

Back at the flat, Nevena displayed what could almost have been described as excitement when we told her what we had witnessed.

"I had a sense that there was a good chance of you seeing it for yourself if you went to Dušan's."

I knew she wasn't being triumphalist in her forecast; she was simply content at having fulfilled her goal of showing us the depth and the creativity of the depravity on full view in Višegrad.

It was, of course, the first time I had seen anyone killed in cold blood. I had stumbled across Delila and Azra's parents hours after their demise, but seeing the deed didn't make the experience feel entirely real. Just as Madiha had fleetingly hoped to find a way of turning back the clock and stopping her friend, Behka, from being killed after the event, so I kept imagining that the two women might not have been killed after all. I banished the thought with an expression of irritation. It was preposterous. I had seen them slain.

After our evening meal was over and the coffee on, Saša and I were sitting on the sofa a few feet apart, Nevena came behind and, standing between us, laid a hand on each of us, briefly stroking our hair.

"Boys, I'll miss you when you're gone. It's been good to have some proper company – even if just for a couple of days. I never felt alone before all of this broke out – but now…" Her voice trailed away.

I thrilled silently at Nevena's touch. Saša looked round and up at her.

"Nevena? Why don't you come with us? Back to Užice."

Nevena said nothing at first, though I had a sense that she wasn't weighing up the proposal as a real option.

"Not yet, Saša. Not yet." She was looking beyond us at no fixed point, perhaps imagining her home back in Serbia, her family. "I think I can always get out of here if I have to. They'll let me go back to Serbia if I want to. But there are people here I don't want to leave. Madiha, Vesna and others. I might have to leave them behind. But just not yet."

In my room an hour later, I picked up the copy of Ivo Andrić's *The Bridge Over the Drina* from a row of around a dozen books by the bedside.

I flicked through the pages before alighting upon a passage that recounted how the Turk in charge of building the Old Bridge, Abidaga, had ordered his men to capture the Serb, Radisav from Unište, who had led the campaign to prevent its construction by acts of overnight sabotage.

Andrić told in excruciating detail of how the men had impaled Radisav alive on a thick wooden stake, one end of which issued from his mouth. The men were under strict orders not to penetrate any vital organs as they carried out the task to ensure that they did not shorten the duration of his torture. Before all curious enough to witness the spectacle, the stake splicing Radisav was attached high on the bridge's scaffolding. He hung there pathetically, wriggling occasionally in so far as he could move at all, eliciting reactions from people on the riverbanks ranging from scorn and contempt to the deepest sympathy – a warning to anyone of the consequences of preventing completion of the works. And Radisav remained pinned there, alive, for several hours into the night, a spectacle that would have been ludicrous, had it not been so appalling. The workmen who had raised the stake pinning him onto the bridge claimed that he kept uttering the words: "Turks, Turks… Turks on the bridge… may you die like dogs… like dogs."

I thought back to the inscription on the bridge and its prayer that it might never know sorrow. The bridge had been initiated in brutality back in the sixteenth century. It had been witness to conflict over the centuries; yet here, in 1992, it was playing host to a new kind of atrocity, perhaps one as macabre as any ever witnessed before.

As soon as I settled into Saša's parents' home in the suburbs of Užice, I felt a sense of relief that quantified the weight of the stress that I had been carrying with me for several weeks. I knew that I had felt tense, but the scale of the release was more significant than I might have expected. As I pottered around the small orchard of plum and pear trees that Saša's father had cultivated, it almost felt as if I was on vacation. It took me some time, just fifty kilometres east of the Bosnia-Serbia border, to get used to the fact that the silence would not be ended suddenly by the sound of shells exploding or sniper fire. The nervous tic beneath my left eye was stilled – permanently, it seemed.

The atmosphere set by Saša's parents was a contributory factor too. His father was a cabinet maker, a man of few words, as are many craftsmen used to spending hours alone as they perfect their products. But he was clearly brimming with pride at the achievements of his son, asking questions of Saša's assignments, as if in awe of the circles he mixed in and the events he witnessed. He asked big questions about global developments and Saša responded patiently and as best he could, though some topics – how might the fragmentation of the Soviet Union play out, how widely might the borders of the European Union extend – would have required hours to do them justice. His mother was zealous in seeking to meet my every need to the extent that she appeared over-respectful. Icons typical of the lavish Serbian Orthodox churches I had entered were on several walls and tables, her faith a fulcrum in her life.

I felt privileged to have been invited into this humble, comfortable environment and I didn't think that I was overstating the extent of that privilege when I concluded that Saša would have been selective about who he invited into the home of his parents. Saša had taken to me and part of me still didn't understand why; part of me hoped profoundly that it was because he recognised in a raw, young journalist a degree not just of insight but of integrity too. But I couldn't yet be sure about that.

I felt a sense of satisfaction at being able to identify the physical attributes Saša had inherited from each parent. He resembled his mother more than his father but he bore resemblance to both. I noted a photograph on a sideboard of Saša in his teenage years with two other children, presumably a sister and a brother. I made a mental note to ask Saša about them at a later, suitable moment. Saša had never mentioned them, though, to be fair, I had never asked.

Saša and I filed our stories and there was an immediate response. Vukovar and Bijeljina had both caused a stir, but the JNA's involvement to different degrees in each assault made the brutality there feel a little more impersonal. Our first-hand experience of individuals' targeted cruelty towards other innocent individuals registered in a way that felt both new and shocking. German politicians expressed outrage, a Parliamentary question was raised and batted away in the House of Commons; but, powerful as the narrative was, it was insufficient to prompt any new European or American action.

In normal circumstances, the reporter's instinctive follow-up to such a story would be to return to see whether what he or she had written had changed anything on the ground. Might the Lukić cousins become more circumspect? Might the killing stop? But having exposed Milan, Sredoje and their paramilitary colleagues, it didn't sound like a terribly sensible choice to go back.

In the event, we were able to follow up our stories without setting foot in Višegrad again – even though we had to rely on updates from Nevena by telephone.

The identify of the two women we had seen gunned down on the bridge had emerged. They were the mother and sister of a woman who worked with a friend of Nevena's. Milan Lukić had recently visited the Varda furniture factory where the woman worked and said openly in front of employees that it was time to 'finish off the Muslims' still in Višegrad. Her husband had been abducted by a Serb neighbour he had known well a fortnight before the shootings that Saša and I had witnessed. She had no idea whether he was dead or alive.

"There's been a repeating pattern of the White Eagles taking out Muslim men and then, a few days later, going back to finish off their wives and families as well. Their arriving at her flat reinforced her fears that her husband was dead," said Nevena.

But when Lukić arrived at the flat she shared with her sister and parents, she had managed to escape with her six-year-old and eight-year-old daughters and hide in a flat that she knew was unoccupied in the same apartment block.

"So she lost her husband, her mother and sister but she saved her children. Her father had survived too. He had been too infirm for the White Eagle gang to move," said Nevena.

The second update was that Madiha had managed to escape from Višegrad on a Red Cross relief bus.

There was one final grisly update. One of the town's police inspectors had been contacted by the manager of the Bajina Basta hydroelectricity plant on the Bosnia-Serbia border, about sixty kilometres downstream of Višegrad. He asked whether the police could do something to halt – or, at the very least, slow – the flow of corpses down the Drina because they were blocking the culverts in his dam at such a rate that he didn't have the manpower to remove them all.

Saša and I would learn later that, by around the end of August, Milan Lukić would have all but achieved his goal of 'finishing off' the Muslims in the town. Barely a single Muslim remained in Višegrad and any who did were under cover and out of sight. Across the whole of the conflict between 1991 and 1995, only one town saw the removal or elimination of a larger proportion of Bosnian Muslims than Višegrad. That was a small town at the end of a valley in south-east Bosnia, called Srebrenica.

Višegrad taught me an important truth about these conflicts. It taught me that the scale and visibility of the siege of Sarajevo contained a distortion, initially invisible to the human eye: Sarajevo would be the piece of theatre staged to distract attention from all the other cruelties, killings and 'cleansings' going on across Bosnia.

We would learn later that, just months after the siege started, Bosnian Serb President Radovan Karadžić would quote with amusement a comment from one of his colleagues: "We are skinning the cat alive, while the world is watching."

And, just a year after the siege began, challenged by a British politician as to why, if the Bosnian Serb Army was so superior, it had not already taken Sarajevo, Ratko Mladić would say: "I can take Sarajevo any time I like. But I was Russian trained. And we were always taught that if you have a choice between shooting an enemy in the head or shooting him in the balls, always shoot him in the balls. It takes only two people half an hour to bury a dead man. But it takes many tens of people many weeks to keep a wounded man alive. I am very happy to leave Sarajevo as it is. The West is now spending so much of its time and energy keeping Sarajevo alive that you have none left to deal with me. While you have to go on doing that, I can go on doing what I want."

16
EARLY AUGUST 1992

Our period of relaxation turned out to be brief. Paul was in touch and said we needed to head to the north-west of Bosnia as a matter of urgency.

There had been reports of concentration camps being set up between Prijedor and Banja Luka on the back of a purge of Muslims in the area. Appearing at a peace conference in London, Bosnian Serb leader Radovan Karadžić had denied that Muslims were being mistreated and offered free passage to any journalist who cared to travel to the alleged sites to witness the truth.

Paul explained it was likely to be a race to a place called Omarska, twenty kilometres east of Prijedor, formerly an iron ore mining complex but now apparently housing hundreds, perhaps even thousands, of Bosnian Muslim and Croat internees.

"I'd suggest you put your foot down because other news outlets will be trying to get there before you. See if you can be first on the scene," said Paul.

I winced, conscious that it meant another white-knuckle ride with Saša at the wheel.

In the event, it wasn't as terrifying as our drive through back roads in the night to Jablanica on our way to Sarajevo or our off-road adventures as we picked our way down the mountainside to Višegrad. Thankfully, the roads were good and there was little need for cavalier driving from Saša.

As we made our way to the northern belt of Bosnia, Saša made plain his distaste for this part of the country and, in particular, its political complexion. It was true the drama of central and southern Bosnia's mountains and river valleys disappeared the closer we got to Omarska.

"This is the most unlovely stretch of Bosnia – light industrial, unremarkable landscape. Why would anyone stop here, when there is so much else that's breathtakingly beautiful, inspiring, across the rest of Bosnia?" he asked out loud.

And he told me of how, on the heels of victories for Karadžić's Serbian Democratic Party, the SDS, in 1990 elections, Banja Luka's leaders had established the ARK – the Autonomous Region of Krajina – and set about removing from all positions of wealth and influence not only any non-Serbs but even those they deemed not to be 'good Serbs'. This was in a city in which only half the population was Serb.

Executives whose ethnicity or face did not fit were told to resign from their positions in medium and large businesses and organisations within three days in what was described as 'a dignified and silent manner'.

"Mick, there's a guy called Radoslav Brđanin, who heads what they call ludicrously The Commission for National Levelling, and he said in as many words that if those notified didn't quit their posts, the problem 'will be eliminated' by the Serbian Defence Forces.

"Even the Rector of the university was on the list. He's a Serb but he refuses to doff the cap to the SDS so he's out on his ear.

"They're evil bastards, Mick. Evil people kept in place by the spineless. I hate this place, Mick."

"I can see that, Saša. I can see it."

As we reached the environs of where we estimated the Omarska complex was located, Bosnian Serb Army officers flagged us down at roadblocks and explained that the former mine was not under their control. The local police and the leadership of Banja Luka's nearest major town, Prijedor, were in charge and we would need their permission to access the site.

On the road to Prijedor, the story of what had been happening in the area in the last few months appeared to be being recounted by its debris: stretches of abandoned, burned-out houses punctuated by occupied, untouched homes flying Serb flags. The village of Kozarac appeared to have been particularly heavily targeted. We would learn later that its population had been near enough one hundred per cent Muslim.

At Prijedor, after a couple of hours of sitting around, we were eventually ushered into the offices of a bear-like man who announced himself proudly as the vice-president of Prijedor's 'Crisis Staff' – the Bosnian Serb entity that we would learn had seized control of multi-ethnic Prijedor in April.

Milan Kovačević, who urged us to call him Mićo, oozed such self-importance that I had actively to stop myself from laughing out loud, despite the seriousness of the situation. There was something hilarious about the contrast between how seriously he took himself and his appearance: square gold-rimmed glasses, an extravagant moustache which would have qualified as Mexican had it been black instead of fair, and sandy hair which crinkled in waves so abundantly from a left parting that it fell only just short of meriting the description 'bouffant'.

Mićo told us we were wasting our time asking to access Omarska as there was nothing to see. When Saša challenged him, insisting Dr Karadžić had given any international journalist free access to the site, he revealed that a convoy of journalists would be arriving from Pale the following day and, if we were to have any chance of getting to the mine, we would have to join them.

"Even then, I'm not guaranteeing that you'll see anything."

He told us to find ourselves a hotel and come back at 10am the following day.

As we slipped through the streets of Prijedor in the fading light, fatigued from the day's travel and the boredom of waiting around, a man in a striped apron and white boater was rolling back the awning above his shop window with a pole. 'Pavlović & Sons – Prijedor's Finest Butchers', the shop sign read.

"Oh, Saša – I forgot to tell you. You remember you asked me about my mum? Ages ago?"

"Yeah."

"Well, I checked back with my dad about where she came from and he gave me a box of documents and photos."

"Oh, yeah?"

"Well, it turns out she wasn't called Pavlović at all. She was called Pavelić."

Saša stopped in his tracks and looked across at me.

"Anything else in the box?" He spoke as if mild panic was setting in and he needed reassurance to rout it.

"Well – not much. Quite an intriguing photo of a family in Spain in the late 1950s but no explanation as to who they might be. And it turns out that my mum wasn't from near Split. She was from near Senj on the north coast of Croatia. Place called Krivi Put."

Saša now gripped me by the bicep. His panic had not been routed.

"Fuck me, Mick. This could be serious," he said. I think his complexion may have whitened but it was hard to tell in the early evening light.

"What? What could be serious?"

"It's probably nothing – but we need beer and a pen and paper. Well, when I say it's probably nothing, there's a chance it may be nothing."

Saša led the way to a café a little further down the street, ordered two beers and, at a table at the back remote from other customers, pulled his pen and pocket book out of his jacket.

"So when was your mum born, then?"

"August 1941."

"Okay. Then we've got 1889 and 1959 – when he was born and when he died. There was an older brother too. So they'd have kids when?" He was muttering to himself, as he made his calculations. "Let's say 1920-ish… Oh, Jesus! It all fits…"

I allowed a brief silence. He looked at me still more urgently.

"Were there any pictures? Pictures of your mum's parents."

"Yes – there was one I presumed was her with her mum and dad."

"And what did they look like? Can you remember?"

"Well, her mum looked like her. Sweet, fair, kind. Her dad had slicked-back black hair, but what struck me were his ears. Too big for his head. He was called Željko. Željko Pavelić."

Saša laid his elbows on the table and placed his fingers over his eyes.

"What is it, Sash? Tell me."

He looked across and said only slightly louder than a whisper, "Mick, I think your mother is likely to have been related to – possibly very closely related to – the most notorious Fascist in the history of Croatia."

The concept was so preposterous that I laughed – but without mirth.

I had never seen Saša so alarmed – not even when the bullets were whistling.

He laid his hand on my forearm. "Mick, you need to know that Krivi Put is a tiny, tiny place. About thirty-five people live there. You're either called Pepić or Pavelić, if you're from there."

He was articulating his words in a staccato fashion, as if he were speaking to a child who was a little slow on the uptake.

"How do I... how does anyone know that about Krivi Put? Well, the parents of Croatia's wartime dictator, friend of Hitler, murderer of thousands of Serbs, Bosnians, Jews and Gypsies, Ante Pavelić, came from Krivi Put. There is a chance that there is no blood link between you and him, but you know what? I think it's slim. Very slim."

It was information I couldn't immediately process. Every instinct rejected the analysis. I'd known that the Croat Fascists had conspired with Hitler and the Nazis, that they had been part of the Axis in World War II, but I hadn't heard of Pavelić. And anyway, how could my sweet, devout, kind mother be a descendant of a monster? No, it didn't make sense.

"But, Mick, you need to think about consequences. You're making a name as the guy who calls out the bad guys. In these wars, they've mainly been Serbs or Bosnian Serbs. If you're related to a Croatian Fascist leader, how do you think that looks?"

I was too stunned to speak as he continued. "Do you know, Mick, there's the site of a Second World War concentration camp called Jasenovac just an hour's drive from here. It's *the* most notorious camp in Croatian history. They say even the Nazis who visited it were shocked by the brutality. They didn't gas their victims at Jasenovac. They preferred to bludgeon them to death with axes or bricks.

"Now that Prijedor is run by Bosnian Serbs, it's possibly *the* most dangerous place for an ancestor of Pavelić to be walking the streets. No exaggeration but hundreds of ancestors of Pavelić's victims will be passing by us... now, every day."

He wasn't cross at me for my ineptitude and tardiness in teasing out my own backstory. I sensed that he was genuinely concerned for my well-being. And it began to sink in that, if he was right, then the threat to me was not in these bleak Prijedor streets – I had no beacon on my head, flashing 'ancestor of a Croat Fascist' after all – but it would be first reputational and, once out, could become material and potentially frighteningly physical.

I said nothing for what seemed like a while but was probably just thirty seconds or so. Then I said, I hoped not too plaintively, "Saša – it can't be true. It can't be."

I paused again and looked down. "If you'd known my mum…"

My voice trailed away. I knew I could conjure up no magic potion in short order that might make Saša's 'charge' evaporate.

"Look," said Saša. After his panic, there was some tenderness in his tone finally. "There's no urgent threat but, just to be safe, we need to see what we can of these camps and then get the hell out of here."

He paused for a moment. "And, if I were you, I'd have a serious conversation with your dad. He might have known nothing… conceivably."

I knew that that meant he thought it was inconceivable.

"He might even have a miraculous explanation."

I smiled weakly. "You mean one bound and I'm free?"

"Yes – something like that. But, you know, if I were you, I'd do it in person. I suspect your dad's as straight as you but he might be less than frank over the phone. Harder to dissimulate face to face."

"Yes – I think you're right, Sash."

As often, with potentially life-changing events or revelations, we fail to take in their implications instantly. Like biological processes, they drip into the bloodstream, the effects of their contamination being felt only gradually. I didn't feel like the ancestor of a Fascist dictator, but the reputational risk and the potential consequences for my physical safety, as Saša had conjectured, would firm up over time. I imagined faceless figures emerging from a thin mist to tug at my sleeve and demand a response.

However, despite Saša's forensic marrying of my family tree to a sequence of terrible events born out of the unlikely hamlet of Krivi Put, I probably wouldn't believe any of it until my father had either stood up the charge or knocked it down.

Although we had met Paul's challenge and arrived first on the scene, by dint of Mićo's delaying us, Penny, Ian and Ed from *ITN*, *Channel 4* and

The Guardian had caught us up that morning. There was a Serbian TV unit in tow as well, apparently with a brief to film the filmers, plus an armed guard of military police officers.

Before we were all transferred to a bus from central Prijedor to Omarska, the British journalists told us of how, as they had approached Prijedor, the military police guard had faked a Muslim terrorist attack on the convoy to try to frighten them and persuade them to cancel their trip to the complex on the last leg of their journey.

"The police guys leapt off their bus at the sound of gunfire and returned fire – but it was laughable. The bullets coming at us were way above our heads. If it was choreographed, there'll be no Oscars dished out," Ed said with a smile.

The bus wriggled down back roads and dirt tracks before entering the complex: a huge open yard with an ugly rust-red four-storey building at the back. It was on a scale that suggested the mining operation had been significant and its administrative requirements heavy in its time. I imagined trucks with tyres as tall as human beings lumbering and growling around the yard, clods of reddish earth piled high in their hydraulic dump bodies. Now there was only a scattering of military police and the occasional individual in civilian clothes. There was no sign of any internees.

We were ushered off the bus and left to bake in the sun. Now that we were here at Omarska, there was little chance we would allow the authorities to bore or burn us into a retreat.

Eventually we were led into a first-floor office where we met the camp commander, a local police chief dressed in camouflage fatigues by the name of Simo Drljača. He endeavoured to normalise the situation with the help of the only English-speaking member of the reception group. Nada Balaban was a squat, square woman in her late forties with a short, masculine hairstyle. She was wearing a red and candy-pink striped jacket that seemed inappropriate for the occasion.

An English teacher at Prijedor High School, her brief cameo as sidekick to Drljača would bring her international notoriety and the contempt of Muslim pupils, who believed that her justifications on air of the purpose of the camp at best condoned and at worst contributed to the deaths of their relatives. Standing behind a table covered with piles of documents, she said there were 2,500 'internees' at Omarska, being interrogated as 'possible Muslim fighters'.

To our suggestion that Omarska might be a concentration camp, she insisted, with a firmness no doubt honed in the classroom, "No. This is not a camp. This is a centre. A transit centre. Omarska and Trnopolje – both centres – not camps."

Ian, Penny and Ed had met Karadžić in Pale to ensure safe passage to Omarska and kept pushing Drljača and his translator to let us walk freely around the premises.

Balaban promised that we would have an opportunity to see some internees, but we couldn't wander around freely. "It's because of our security – and your security. Some of these people are fighters."

In the event, our exposure to Omarska's detainees was as stunted as the fake terrorist attack on the journalists' convoy earlier. We had been led down to the canteen to witness a couple of dozen prisoners jog across the yard and into the building for what we would learn later would be their only meal of the day.

In hindsight, although this was a raggle-taggle bunch of scruffy, skinny, cowed men, they had clearly been hand-picked so that we could witness prisoners still capable of breaking into a trot. As we would see at the Trnopolje camp an hour or so later, many of those incarcerated there would have fallen over, had they even attempted to run.

In the canteen at Omarska, the men appeared to have been ordered to avoid eye contact with the visiting journalist pack. They bent over bowls of grey-brown soup studded with the occasional bean, dabbing with the chunk of bread each had been given. It was fare no one would have chosen to eat, were there to have been anything resembling a wholesome alternative.

Once we witnessed how short a period of time they were given before they were moved on – just a few minutes so that all 2,500 thousand inmates could be cycled through – we understood why they had appeared to be torn between savouring their sole meal of the day, however unappealing, and gulping it down.

Back outside in the yard, the camp commander and his interpreter were intent on shutting down our inspection of the camp. 'Security' prevented our being able to see more of the conditions in which those interned lived, and the timetable of our visit required that we be transported to the Trnopolje 'reception centre', Balaban insisted.

The three journalists who had met Karadžić in person two days earlier were particularly insistent that the deal they had been offered was not being kept.

Penny Marshall from ITN said in her broadcast report that she could not say that Omarska wasn't a concentration camp from the evidence before her.

"We've seen nothing," said Ian Williams from Channel 4. "Why are you not fulfilling Dr Karadžić's promise to us?"

Mrs Balaban replied, "He promised us something else. He said you can do this and this and that – and not that." She paused. "I'm sorry. That will be all."

Given the scenes we were to encounter at the Trnopolje camp just half an hour's drive away, I had to conclude in hindsight that Drljača and his interpreter were trying simply to save their own reputations and take the heat off Omarska. There was no attempt to offer any rationale for an exercise clearly planned in extensive detail months in advance, involving the evacuation and torching of Muslim homes and villages and the transfer of thousands of individuals to a network of pre-prepared camps around Prijedor. How much easier to conceal their own activities and try to switch our focus onto more visible misery at a sister camp.

"Such comradely solidarity," I quipped to Saša.

If Drljača and Balaban had visited Trnopolje or even been driven by, they would have registered how appalling it looked compared to the Omarska complex with its inmates tucked way out of sight behind a neat yard and an office block. By contrast, Trnopolje amounted to a collection of ramshackle buildings ringed by a barbed wire fence. In plain view of any passer-by, hundreds of internees were squatting and standing in groups in the open ground, sweltering in near forty-degree heat in the midday sun.

Dozens bunched up close to the barbed wire fencing next to the road, as they registered that external observers, perhaps from beyond Bosnia, had arrived to observe their plight.

Although some of the men looked relatively fresh from freedom, with neat hair and nourished faces, the majority were visibly distressed and clearly famished. They ranged from men in their twenties to elder men in their fifties, I guessed. In short, any Muslim from the area who might be fit or savvy enough to pick up a weapon and push back against the Bosnian Serb 'coup' in Prijedor.

I had never in my life seen so pitiful and miserable a group. Bewilderment, pain, resilience – all were on show before us.

"Saša, this is fucking appalling," I whispered, conscious instantly of how inadequate my words were to sum up the situation before us.

Many of the inmates were stripped to the waist or wore scooped vest tops that revealed rib cages jutting through paper-thin skin. It reminded me of the sight of abused donkeys, fit to drop, pulling carts through the streets of Tunis, desperately trying to stay on all four legs or risk a thrashing from their driver.

Even someone without medical training could have estimated without fear of contradiction that the weakest men in the camp had been on starvation rations for a month or two. So it would turn out. As we approached the fence, our military police guard stood close enough to intimidate the inmates without preventing us from trying to enter into dialogue.

If I was close to being rendered speechless by the spectacle, Ian from Channel 4 was more appreciative of the urgency of the situation, aware that we were likely to be allowed only a few minutes to ask some questions before our minders stepped in.

"How are conditions for you here?" he asked.

A handsome young man in his early twenties with piercing brown eyes spoke across the barbed wire. "I don't know if I'm allowed to speak."

Ian coaxed him into revealing that he had arrived at Trnopolje that day after fifteen days in another camp.

"Why have they brought you here?" asked Ian.

"I don't know. I know nothing."

"Where did you come from? Did they take you from home?"

"Yes."

"Are you all from the same town?"

"From the surroundings of Prijedor. From villages. From our homes."

Ian asked if it was difficult for them. He managed a hollow laugh and said, "Yes!"

"They say that some of you are fighters," Ian said.

"I have never been a fighter."

Other inmates with a smattering of English began to volunteer snippets of information, aware now that these were British TV crews.

"Have people been beaten?" asked Ian.

"No – not here."

"In the other place?"

"I rather wouldn't talk about that."

Perhaps as a distraction, a guard inside the fence emerged with a bag containing some pieces of bread. A group of inmates peeled off to try to get a share from the lucky man handed the bag. Others were keen to offer what little information they felt they could share.

Ian persisted with his line about reports of beatings.

"How were things in the other place? Can you tell us about the conditions you were being kept in and the treatment of the people you were with?"

"Well – that's hard to talk about."

"We heard stories of people being beaten and disappearing."

"Well – I can't say much about that."

Another man, who said he had come from a camp called Keraterm, said: "Conditions were very bad. We haven't had food. Just tea and afternoon bread and soup."

"The reason we're here is we heard terrible stories about people," said Ian.

"Yeah – this story is very complicated here. You can't translate it."

"Were you interrogated at the last camp?"

"Personally, no – but the rest a little bit. The rest of the people were interrogated. I would like to say to my friends in Sweden and other parts of Europe, I'd like to say to those people it isn't good anymore. It's not life."

As this latest inmate began to open up, one of our guards stepped in and ended the exchanges. With the cameras cut, Saša managed some quiet exchanges with prisoners before we were ushered away. Yes, there had been routine beatings and executions at Trnopolje and other camps.

The killings had sometimes been retaliatory, one man said. After ten Bosnian Serb militia had been killed, the men were told one hundred and fifty Muslims would be executed in revenge.

"Come back in a few days' time to make sure I haven't been punished for speaking to you," one inmate asked Saša.

We were expecting to be put back on the bus and driven away, but those running Trnopolje camp sensed they may be able to still any concerns about mistreatment by escorting us to the medical centre where a Muslim doctor and a vet were treating cases of scabies, malnutrition and diarrhoea. But when Saša asked the doctor discreetly whether there had been beatings, with the cameras rolling he nodded almost imperceptibly. Almost imperceptibly but sufficient to be captured on film by ITN. Asked if the beatings were frequent, the doctor looked straight ahead. He dared not nod again.

Penny would reveal later that, as we were being led out of the medical centre, the vet had whispered, "It's as bad as you fear. They kill, they torture. Here – take this." And she slipped Penny a roll of undeveloped camera film. Penny let us know later that the pictures showed weals and bruises on the bodies of inmates – injuries too substantial to have been caused by anything other than blunt instruments.

Deposited back in Prijedor, Saša and I deliberated as to where next. Should we overnight in Prijedor again or move on? Miša from ITN, their experienced driver from Belgrade, warned us that, were we or the other British journalists to overnight in the area, the easiest thing in the world for the Prijedor officials would be to arrange for us all to be bumped off. It may not stop the truth getting out, but it would delay it. And they could blame Muslim terrorists for the atrocity. Saša and I headed back to Zagreb, the others to Belgrade.

I was feeling my own inexperience acutely, desperately trying to scribble down every detail I could recall for my reports but feeling shaken to the core by the exhibition of human misery that had been arrayed before us. Our inability to do anything to help these wretched people had hollowed me out.

"Sash – that kid who asked us to tell his friends in Sweden and the rest of Europe that things weren't good anymore. You and me could have met him on Interrail. How's he different from any other European? How is it he's ended up behind barbed wire in the blistering sun and we're walking free?"

"It's the way of the world," he replied – in a way that meant he didn't believe what he'd just said.

"It isn't, Sash. It mustn't be," I said.

This time, once our reports and news bulletins were published and aired, there was a significant international response. President Bush expressed his horror and said the abuses must end. Dr Karadžić said he could close the camps in two days, provided Bosnian Muslims agreed a prisoner swap.

Only the United Nations struck an ambivalent tone: "People think it's just the Serbs but that's not the case. Serb civilians who have fled or have been forced to flee Croat or Muslim-held areas also give accounts of mistreatment," their spokesman said.

I made a mental note to track down my European Community Monitoring Mission contact in Zagreb, Hugh, to get his take.

17
AUGUST 1992

We knew that we would need to return to the Prijedor area shortly to try to track down accounts of what had really gone on inside Omarska, Trnopolje and Keraterm, once the camps had been closed and their inmates relocated; but there was time for me to return home briefly and Saša urged me to use the trip to establish once and for all the truth about my Pavelić antecedence.

He had laid a hand gently on my arm to emphasise that his advice was for my own benefit and said, "Mick, don't come back from the UK without having spoken to your dad. You're better off knowing… one way or the other."

I knew that that meant that he was convinced that the Pavelić connection was real so I nodded and said quietly, "I will, I will. Don't worry."

Perhaps I would have taken on the challenge anyway, but Saša's gentle pressure made it a task I had to address on this trip home. I couldn't allow long grass to grow around it.

The question had gnawed away at me in quiet moments, but my instincts were increasingly that the name might be the same but the connection would prove to be non-existent. Perhaps my memory of my sweet, gentle mother was trumping Saša's background knowledge and calculations.

I allowed myself to bed in at my father's house and recount in some detail the story of our discovery of the camps and the haplessness of the limited number of inmates we had been able inadequately to quiz. Even he could not feign disinterest in this topic, though it probably reinforced his view that I would be better off out of this conflict. He had winced as I recounted the ITN driver's view that, had we overnighted in or near Prijedor, we may never have been seen again.

It was only on my third day at home that I raised the subject. I explained how I'd always thought Mum was a Pavlović and I told him that that was a very common name in Croatia – unlike Pavelić.

"No, no – Pavelić was your mother's maiden name. I always said it was Pavelić," he said.

If I believed that in the past he might have said 'Pavlović' knowingly, then I would be effectively accusing him of being aware of but concealing a Pavelić connection. I wasn't on strong enough ground to do that. But as I outlined Saša's account of Krivi Put and its Ante Pavelić connections, he began to look a little uncomfortable.

"So did you know about that connection? Did you and Mum ever talk about it?"

"Michael, it wasn't something we ever wanted to talk about publicly. We didn't want to set any hares running."

I smiled inwardly at the quaint, old-fashioned, rural imagery.

"It was tough enough for your mum as it was – trying to cope in a new country, improve her English – without letting anyone get any funny ideas. Start spreading false rumours, that sort of thing."

I let him talk. Silence was the best way to winkle out the truth from an interlocutor. If a person felt uncomfortable with the vacuum, they would nearly always fill it, often by sharing detail they'd never planned to share.

"Of course, it was nonsense anyway. She told me they were completely different families. There was no link," he said.

"Seems a bit implausible, Dad. A one-horse town with only about three dozen inhabitants. Half of them called Pepić and half called Pavelić. And not a name you'd find in many other places. Not like Pavlović."

His irritation was now visible. I wasn't intending to rile him; I just needed to get to the unvarnished truth.

"Michael, all I can tell you is there was *no* link. She told me the Pavelić strands were completely separate. She sketched me out family trees to prove it."

"You didn't keep those family trees, did you? They weren't in the box you gave me."

"No – no. Why would I? She sketched them out for me: dates and names and everything. But there was no link, so there was no reason to keep them."

"A shame. They could have been useful. You do know, don't you, it would put me in a difficult position, if there were to be a connection?" I paused. "I mean, I can hardly bash the Serbs if I'm related to a Croatian Fascist leader."

"Well, Michael, you need have no concern about that. And, from what you told me about those Bosnian Muslims being forced into concentration camps, it's the Bosnian Serbs who've got the questions to answer. Not you. Really… Disgraceful behaviour."

And he turned aside. And I wondered whether he was trying delicately to switch the emphasis of the conversation.

"Dad, if you know of a connection, you know you do have to tell me, don't you? Because of my job."

I was trying to sound reasonable – not threatening.

He turned back to me. "Michael, you know what I think about what you're doing. I think you're in a wild place writing about people steeped in centuries of fighting and I wish you'd just get out before some madman shoots you dead. That's what I think.

"But, if you must persist, don't worry about a Pavelić trap – because there isn't one."

"You're sure of that, Dad?"

His voice fell to a whisper. "I'm sure of that, Michael."

I wanted to tell him about Branko and Ivana, about Marta, about Delila and Azra, about Ševa and Ismail, about the mother and daughter shot dead on a bridge in Višegrad. I wanted to explain to him just how tightly bound I had become to the fate of these beautiful people. I wanted to tell him about my 'obligation' to speak out for these people and against those who failed to protect them, no matter how much that irritated or infuriated more inert colleagues or international decision makers.

But I sensed that this was not the moment to try to break down his antipathy – or was it aversion? – towards these people. It was the moment to walk away, having bagged whatever assurances he had been able to supply. Whether those assurances would bring me succour, I couldn't yet judge.

But I had completed as adequately as I was able the task that Saša had set me and that I had agreed to.

"Just one last thing, Dad."

I pulled the photo from Alicante from my jacket pocket.

"Do you know who these people are? The back of the photo says it was taken on the beach in Spain in 1958. It was in Mum's box."

He took the picture, examined it, flipped it over, and then handed it back. There was no flicker of recollection, suppressed or otherwise.

"Sorry, Michael. No idea – no idea who they might have been."

I popped into *The Times*' picture library on my way back to Zagreb and looked up photographs of Ante Pavelić. His most striking features were his slicked-back black hair and ears that looked slightly too large for his head. I snapped shut the folder of pictures and left for the airport.

18
LATE AUGUST 1992

On my return from Zagreb a week or so later, I sensed that Saša was unconvinced by the version of events I had been given. I didn't mention the details of the photos I had looked up in *The Times'* picture library. Perhaps because of his scepticism or perhaps because the urgency of the situation required us to return to the Prijedor area despite the danger, he didn't dwell upon it. I knew it was something to which we would return in due course.

He had spoken by phone to Ismail in Sarajevo and, using his party contacts, Ismail had tracked down a Bosnian Muslim who had been incarcerated with his sister in Omarska and who was now lying low in a safe house on the outskirts of Prijedor, while his wife attempted clandestinely to conjure up the paperwork that would allow them to escape the town.

"Mick – Ismail tells me that this guy can trace back his family in Prijedor for at least three hundred years. And now he has to leave – or try to," said Saša.

We found Habib Hodžić in a comfortable house in the Puharska district of Prijedor, set on its own square parcel of land and bordered by a waist-high mesh fence. The house belonged to a Bosnian Serb woman, a lifelong friend of his wife's, who had insisted that they stay with her, regardless of the risk.

"She's a diamond," Habib said, "but I owe it to her to get the hell out of here as soon as I can so she's not at risk."

Evidence of Habib's two-month ordeal in Omarska remained in the shape of a red weal around his right eye. It would weep clear liquid that he would dab away regularly. He revealed that he had also lost thirty-four kilos during his incarceration.

"Gentlemen," he said to us, "I'm almost too ashamed to let you see me in this state."

He said he had been a big, fit man prior to being locked up, and the weal around his eye had been inflicted during 'a game' the guards seemed to enjoy: spreading oil on the floor as inmates were made to run the gauntlet on their way to the canteen. As they slipped and fell, others had been struck with iron bars or fire extinguishers; he had been struck by an iron ball on the end of a length of industrial cable – a weapon purpose-built for torture.

"It could have served no purpose in everyday life," said Habib. "So, imagine it: one of the guards must have put it together the night before with the specific purpose of inflicting a potentially fatal wound on one of us. Where does that kind of creative imagination come from?"

He turned his outstretched palms skywards, as if to emphasise the rhetorical nature of his question.

"After he hit me, I really thought half of my head was missing. Then I passed out and my friends told me they'd had to drag me back to the open area where we were kept."

Ismail had told Saša that, in the past, Habib had enjoyed a relatively elevated role in the Communist Party. He had been one of the party members who organised events on the occasions when Tito made formal visits to Bosnia; but his sixteen-year role as a communications and encryption expert, ensuring that intelligence gathered on all suspect individuals in the Prijedor area reached the authorities, meant he was likely to be of significant interest to those running the Omarska camp.

Although he had been forced out of that support role to the security services by a new section manager he suspected of seeking to purge his department of Muslims as the spectre of ethnic discrimination began to rise in Prijedor and Banja Luka, he could still be useful in identifying which might be the local Muslims with terrorist backgrounds or links.

Though Ismail stressed that Habib had never been an agent or a spy, Saša and I would reflect later that Habib himself was likely to have been at least partially responsible for some of Tito's critics and opponents suffering loss of liberty and – to put it delicately – 'degradation'. Nevertheless, his was a compelling tale incapable of being dreamed up, its details beyond the imagination of even the most deranged of fantasists.

He admitted to embarrassment at how blind he and his community had been to what was going on out of sight in the six months prior to the seizure of Prijedor by supporters of Karadžić's SDS party. It emerged that secret crisis committees had been set up, Bosnian Serb policemen were supplied covertly with additional weapons, and Serb-only police stations were established.

This meant that, in the early hours of 30th April, what had been a council hung between Bosnian Muslim and Bosnian Serb elected representatives was gone in a heartbeat.

"They reckon it happened in thirty minutes without a shot being fired," said Habib. "We were so naïve. They said that they had to act to protect the area from Muslim extremists who were plotting to throw out of office all Serbs."

The developments came against a soundtrack of poisonous propaganda that increased in volume until, on the morning of the coup, Radio Prijedor began broadcasting Chetnik songs calling for a Greater Serbia and announcements were made claiming that Izetbegović's party, the SDA, was destroying the town.

"That was why the SDS, assisted by the military and the police, had carried out a military coup, they said."

Habib said that those who dared to venture outside found that all the vital entrances and exits to the town were under the control of armed Serb soldiers or paramilitaries. The local paper, *Kozarski Vjesnik*, now a mouthpiece for the SDS, began publishing a daily 'war' edition and explained that the coup had been essential because five hundred and fifty Muslim extremists were promising a 'fight to the death' around Prijedor, according to alleged intercepted communications.

"Were there pockets of Muslim extremism?" I asked.

"Well – what would you call extremism? There were people who would hit back, if provoked. And there was one guy who tried to arrange a fightback after 30th April. They called him 'Ribar' – the fisherman. He marched towards Prijedor centre with a small band of men armed with hopeless Second World War weapons. He just ended up being tortured to death in Omarska, his family were murdered and he gave the Bosnian Serbs a justification for saying that they had to put down Muslim terrorists. You might call that extremism but I call it provocation," said Habib.

After the Serb overnight coup, Muslims were forced to wear white armbands when outdoors, and to fly white flags from their homes, he said.

"They didn't tattoo us, as they did in Auschwitz, and our stigma might have been more short-term – but it was more immediately visible. It was designed to humiliate us and unnerve us."

Habib himself had first been taken to Omarska in a case of mistaken identity, but there was no relief in his being returned to his own flat. First the administrative error that had led to his being arrested was that the authorities were after his sister, Habiba, a senior judge who sat on the local bench. She and legal colleagues who had jailed considerable numbers of the town's low life over the years were among the first to be hauled into the camps in what would prove to be a thorough and systematic trawl through the ranks of the educated Muslim community. Anyone articulate enough to make a post-conflict case against the coup leaders needed to be killed or at least removed.

If there was little relief from his release because it confirmed that his sister would be among the first Omarska inmates, he also experienced on this 'dry run' to the camp a flavour of the brutality awaiting him when finally – inevitably – he would be rearrested.

At Omarska, Habib had witnessed villagers arriving in other vans from Kozarac being lined up against a wall and severely beaten before he was released. In the van that took him to Omarska, at an impromptu stop en route, one of his sister's fellow judges had been lunged at by two knife-wielding thugs he had previously sent to prison. One of them, a taxi-driver and serial criminal, Djordje Đorađević, would turn out to be one of the most notorious and unstinting persecutors of camp inmates in that spring and summer of 1992, inexplicably allowed free rein to roam from Keraterm to Omarska to Trnopolje.

Habib explained that one reason for the scale of the brutality that he and other detainees would face was that, once all Muslim and Croat officers from the police and Territorial Defence reserve had been stood down, the Serbs replaced them with any thug, criminal or Chetnik that was up for the sport. Many of these recruits made up a new 'Intervention Platoon', which carried out much of the new Serb Prijedor authority's dirty work: arrests, beatings, and killings.

"And they did their dirty work, the dirtiest work of all in Prijedor municipality, with admirable diligence," said Habib.

If Habib was spared temporarily by the one-letter mistake of identity, a frail neighbour in his seventies and one of Prijedor's most successful Muslim businessmen was less fortunate. The scale of their brutality related to the size of the prize his captors planned to elicit from him.

"They told him he'd get the worst beatings if he didn't hand over his money," said Habib. "So, he took out some money from his pocket and one of the guards said, 'Safet, you've brought only very little money to the camp. You'll have to give us some more.'

"Eventually, when I was taken back to the camp, I watched him expire on the floor. He was just exhausted by all the beatings he took. He was a lovely man. He didn't deserve that. Obviously…" Habib's voice trailed away at the banality of his observation.

Saša explained to me that, with inflation rocketing in Yugoslavia during the 1980s, anyone with any sense converted their assets into German marks and held them as cash, rather than putting them in banks where they would lose value.

"The top guys in the camps, the police and the local authority spent a lot of time trying to locate where Muslims had hidden their Deutschmarks. They then took them. If they knew you were comfortable or well off, you were in trouble in the camps. They'd beat you till you let on where your money was hidden. They would make sure they didn't kill people till they'd squeezed the last mark out of them," said Habib. "Of course, at a local authority level, Muslims' businesses were sequestered and made over to the people at the top. A lot of people will have made a lot of money."

During the period between his first and second arrest, back in his flat with no power and limited water, his wife and children secreted away in a friend's home, Habib said the propaganda being broadcast worsened.

"There were regular outright appeals for Serbs to lynch and kill non-Serbs and lies and fabrications were put out on air about leading Muslim figures. One senior consultant was accused of injecting Serb babies with poison. It was ridiculous nonsense but most leading figures from the community who were Muslim had their reputations trashed. Scarcely any of them survived their incarceration in one or other of the camps."

"So how long were you free for?" I asked Habib.

"Just ten days – then the same group of officers who had first taken me in came back."

"One of them who I'd known for some years – we called him Bato – said, 'Well, it seems you have to come with us once again. But, this time, there is no mistake.'"

Habib said that in the yard at the police station the atmosphere was poisonous. Two APCs had just pulled in and the men from them were priming their weapons and singing Chetnik songs. Habib found himself in a group that included a former police inspector, another former police officer from the criminal evidence section, an eminent Prijedor physician, Dr Osman Mahmuljin, and a boy who appeared to be no more than thirteen years of age. If the arrest of such a young boy was an anomaly, it emerged that he was there because he had approached Serb soldiers at a checkpoint to ask them to stop some of their colleagues from raping his mother and her friends.

"That kid would go missing in part of the camp and, because of his allegations, I don't think he made it out alive," said Habib.

After being made to line up and remove shoelaces and belts, Habib's group were set upon by a team from the Intervention Platoon.

"They made us run the gauntlet between them in the yard. They beat us savagely with metal rods and bars – something that I'd never seen before. I mean, I had never thought it was possible for someone to beat a fellow human being with such objects.

"And, after you've been hit hard with a metal bar for the first time, the shock as much as the pain is like nothing you've ever experienced before. You think you can't tolerate it – but you have to. And, from then on, you're cowed. Whenever you're in proximity of a guard or an interrogator, you're half waiting for the blow. Excuse the language, but it fucks up your head… But then, I suppose that's what it's supposed to do."

The group were then forced into a basement room, which Habib knew used to be where suspects were detained. Dr Osman had been beaten to the ground and couldn't walk. Habib and one of the former officers had to carry him down and lay him on a bench.

"Then we heard a scream and one of the Intervention Platoon yelling, 'The doctor didn't get enough!' And they burst through the door and beat us again. Dr Osman was beaten till he passed out. Two of the platoon kept shouting, 'We'll kill you! We'll kill you so you never get the chance to kill Serb children again!'"

At Omarska, Habib was put in a building called the Garage where there were already around eighty men and it was hard for the new arrivals to find space.

"We were practically standing on top of one another," said Habib.

He said that the only person given any real space was a man he recognised as the ousted Mayor of Prijedor Municipality, Professor Muhamed Čehajić.

"He was lying all alone near an iron door in the corner of the Garage. He'd obviously been beaten severely. They said he'd been urinating blood."

Habib said he had known the professor quite well. He had taught literature and philosophy at the best high school in town and they had lived in the same neighbourhood for a while.

"We regularly greeted each other in the street. He was a quiet, peaceful man. I once asked him, when he was sufficiently conscious to hold a conversation, why he hadn't fled Prijedor after the coup. He told me, 'I'd never had a disagreement with anyone. The Serbs took over in Prijedor and there was nothing I could do about that. I never imagined they would commit crimes on this scale. So, I stayed in Prijedor, waiting for decisions on a more global level, at the Bosnia and Hercegovina level – decisions affecting the fate of Prijedor.'"

"So, he was expecting international or at least national intervention?" asked Saša.

"Precisely."

"And there was none," Saša added – a statement rather than a question.

"Precisely," said Habib.

"So, did he survive Omarska?" asked Saša.

Habib momentarily leaned his forehead on the arch of his clasped hands. Then he looked across at Saša and me.

"He suffered terribly for weeks, singled out for particular brutality because of his status. And then, on 27th July – after we now know that word had begun to get out internationally about the camps and they were probably thinking they might have to close them – he was taken out of the camp with a group of other Prijedor intellectuals and they were killed in the vicinity of Omarska village."

When it came to Habib's turn to be interrogated, he was fortunate in that, on arrival at the interrogation room in the main administration building, he found those questioning him to be two old acquaintances from the security service.

"The sort of questions they asked me were the run-of-the-mill questions they used to ask everyone. Did I have any weapons? Did I vote for the SDA – Izetbegović's party? But the most important question for them, although they knew me well, was what my financial situation was like and how rich I was. That's what they wanted to know. I mean, they pretty much knew everything else about me," he said.

Saša asked if he had been beaten or mistreated during the session. Habib said that he had not but stressed that he was fortunate. After his interrogation, he was ordered to go to the 'pista' – the open area of the camp – rather than back to the Garage. Although there were five to seven hundred prisoners there and it meant finding ways of dealing with the blistering heat during the day and the cold at night, it was a prime location for witnessing what was really going on in Omarska.

"Every day, except on Saturdays and Sundays, people were called out and taken for interrogation. Many of them would come back bearing obvious marks of torture, beating and all the other things that were done to them. Some came back wrapped in blankets – particularly those interrogated in the White House."

Habib explained that sometimes the guards would ask on the pista for four strong prisoners and that would mean they were needed to carry out a corpse – someone who'd been killed during interrogation.

"And they usually dumped the bodies on a lawn, a meadow to the left of the White House."

So, were all of the killings carried out out of sight?" asked Saša.

"No. Most were committed in the interrogation rooms; but some were in full view of detainees, sometimes when some of the lowlifes' games of torture went too far. Sometimes, they just didn't seem to care who saw them finish off detainees.

"There was one night, when they brought in two busloads of men from Hambarine, a Muslim village. They'd clearly been expecting a lot of resistance from the village, as there were Muslim men who were mainly of an age where they could have been called up to the military, when Yugoslavia was Yugoslavia.

"A group of them were transferred to the White House, which was an ominous sign for them. In the early hours of the morning – I'm talking about around 2am – I was woken on the pista by the screams and the cries of dozens of people being brought outside. They were in such a state that none of them could stand or attempt to run away. They'd clearly been subjected to severe beatings. And then the guards just wandered between them: a single bullet to the head of anyone still moving.

"And excuse the detail but it's a sight I'll never get out of my head: when a bullet was fired, the brain would come out, first a puff of white powder and then liquid, as if the bullet had hit milk."

Habib said, though he had never witnessed the use of machine guns, he had heard second-hand reports of killings with automatic weapons in the Keraterm camp.

"I know that that little shit Đorađević was involved in probably the biggest mass killing in any of the camps over those summer months. A friend of mine, who was released from Keraterm at about the same time as I left Omarska – I bumped into him by chance in Puharska. He was locked up in a shed at Keraterm they called Room 2. Late one night, they saw Đorađević overseeing the setting up of a machine gun on a table outside the next shed. They called that Room 3. Through chinks and gaps in the walls and door, he and his colleagues could see bursts of flame – you know, the flashes that come out of the barrel of a machine gun as it's being fired. It went on from around midnight till about 2am."

Habib said his friend and fellow inmates estimated there were about one hundred and sixty men cooped up in Room 3 and, next morning, he and some of his fellow inmates had to carry the dead bodies and pile them up on the grass.

"As you can imagine, he said it was horrific. Many of the victims had had limbs blown away, but he told me the most appalling fatal wounds were to men who had had all or part of their backs blown away. He said he suspected they had tried to turn their backs to the machine-gun fire. He said to me, 'Can you imagine what kind of state we were in, mentally and physically, after lifting and carrying these corpses with innards spilling out. Some of these guys would have been our friends – but there weren't many we could identify after they'd been shot to ribbons.'

"As well as those mortally wounded by automatic fire, he said others had been suffocated in the crush inside Room 3. And then there were survivors – he reckoned about forty of the one hundred and sixty survived – but most were gravely injured.

"He said that after they'd moved the corpses into a pile, Đorađević and a sidekick had then directed a huge truck into place and another group of inmates was requisitioned to pile these bodies into the truck. It was a huge truck so all the corpses fitted in but, as a final touch, the wounded were ordered onto the back of the truck as well. So, they were lying on top of layers of dead men.

"The truck left, some of the inmates were made to hose down the yard and flush away all traces of flesh and blood and then, several hours later, the truck came back empty. They never heard what had happened to the dead and the dying, my friend said."

"So, this Đorađević – was there any reason why he set up the machine-gunning?" I asked.

"Not that we know," said Habib. "I now know he was wandering through all three camps just meting out rough justice. I saw him most days in Omarska and he was always threatening everyone. 'Balijas! You're all going to die,' he'd say. There he was – a little squit of a man with an ugly mug and eyes that pointed in different directions, swanning around the camps, for the first time in his life holding power over other people, even though he had no formal authority. And, to this day, he's a menace. I lie low here because I'm pretty sure if he saw me around Prijedor at best he'd beat me up, at worst he'd kill me or have me killed."

But Habib said that, if there was torture and ritual humiliation, the hardest thing for him to bear had been the way in which the guards and the Intervention Platoon and the paramilitaries had gone through the ranks of the most distinguished, experienced, humane, and nurturing of the Muslim community from Prijedor and its environs in the final days of the Omarska camp's existence.

"I've told you about Professor Čehajić and Dr Osman. From the very beginning, they were humiliated, taunted, degraded and physically abused – in a special way. Ordinary people like me – well, I was both picked on and at times protected because of my time working for the security services, because I know a lot of the police officers who had become guards and interrogators. But these people were singled out because of the levels they had reached in the community. I can only think the authorities wanted to remove anyone with the intelligence, influence, and articulacy to bring them to justice at a later date.

"Some of them died from beatings or were just made to 'disappear' before the end but, after word got out of the existence of our camps, you can't conclude other than that the new Serb authorities in Prijedor ordered the systematic elimination of any Muslim man of standing.

"It was a couple of weeks before the camps were closed and we realised that, as well as the daily murder of detainees taken for interrogation and spontaneous killings by guards operating on their own initiative, the organised killing of members of specific professions started."

Habib said that one night it was the lawyers, then the next night former police officers. Only four or five of the Muslims who had been in the force left Omarska alive.

"Then it was the turn of doctors and physicians. And they went through the distinguished professions like this and, night after night, groups were called in and never seen again," said Habib.

I was curious to know whether Habib understood at all the psychology of his captors.

"You said that some of the guards seemed to regard torture as a kind of game. Presumably many of them would have been law-abiding, upstanding public servants before the war. Did you even understand what flipped them?" I asked.

Habib breathed in deeply.

"Mick, no – I'm not sure that I can. The likes of Đorađević were always bullies and hooligans so, given the opportunity to practise their sadism at a time when it felt as though they could get away with anything, I'm not surprised they behaved the way they did. But there were others who underwent inexplicable transitions."

He said that there were some details that he couldn't even bring himself to articulate.

"The behavioural equivalents of hard pornography. Nothing, no one could bring me ever to describe them," he said.

"I won't go into detail, but one of the guys who was particularly fond of games of torture was a man who was something of a hero to local youngsters because he was a karate instructor and him and his three elder brothers had won multiple medals in competition. Dušan Dragić he was called.

"He was from a prominent Serbian family from the largely Muslim village of Kozarac, his father a decorated World War II hero, his mother one of the survivors of the Jasenovac camp.

"He would make much of the fact that his mother had been in Jasenovac. The unspoken implication being, I suppose, that, because Serbs had suffered there, now it was our turn. He delighted in 'games' of torture and the most notorious involved a young man bleeding to death after another inmate had been forced at knifepoint to bite off one of his testicles. Before the conflict I would never have seen him as a cruel man but – Mick, Saša – where does that kind of wickedness come from? I just can't explain it to you.

"And it wasn't just a few that were responsible. I told you about our beatings in the canteen. Lots of our jailers took part. Maybe it was a kind of contagion. Maybe a couple started it and then others were swept up into it. I don't know, I can't say.

"In terms of simple cruelty, I recall once looking out of the window of the room I was staying in at the camp for a while and seeing guards dropping a nineteen-kilo fire extinguisher from an upstairs window just to see the impact on a man spreadeagled, face down, on the ground below. It just smashed his back into pieces, blasting out blood and white stuff in a single violent puff and splatter. Of course, the guards laughed uproariously. They never concealed the fact that they really enjoyed this stuff."

Habib checked his watch and I sensed he felt he had told us enough about his ordeal.

"Gentlemen, I could tell you more. I could talk for a week about what went on, but I think I've told you enough to give you a sense of how it was, how it felt."

"Now that you're out, Habib," asked Saša, "I know you say you still don't feel safe, but do you feel any sense of relief that that part of the ordeal is over? Does the camp experience feel past and gone?"

"Saša, I think I still feel in limbo. I probably need to get out of here – out of Prijedor, maybe even out of Bosnia, however painful that might feel – before I'll feel anything like a normal human being with freedom of choice and control over my own destiny.

"You've lived your life with this set of certainties and then, almost overnight, it evaporates. And it's replaced by this environment that you have no control over. You've had these moral certainties, these rules of society you were quite comfortable in signing up to because they protected you and your family more than they restricted you and them – and then they vanish."

That last comment rankled with me slightly. Hadn't Habib and his family felt more protected than restricted in the Tito era because he had been an active member of the League of Communists? According to my father, my mother's family may not have felt the same way because of my grandfather's refusal to join the party. But – naturally – I said nothing.

"Habib, would you describe Omarska as a concentration camp? One of the people in charge said it was a transit centre – not a camp," I asked.

"Mick, a large part of the purpose of that camp was the torture and the elimination of many, many Muslims from Prijedor and surrounding areas. Many of them senior figures, thought leaders – though not all of them. That's not a transit centre. I'm not one hundred per cent clear about the definition of a concentration camp but the purpose of that operation wasn't transit," said Habib.

We thanked Habib and wished him and his family well. And then we were off out of Prijedor and out of Bosnia, sketching out our reports in our heads as we motored towards Zagreb.

If the accounts of the camps were powerful and I felt I had captured them vividly in prose, I was privately a little disappointed that they didn't receive the prominence I had hoped for when I had filed them.

There was a response in the form of letters to the editor from readers outraged by the details of the atrocities; but the fact that ITN and Channel 4 had already screened footage of Trnopolje and that images of its emaciated victims had already been shown around the world seemed to soften the power and dull the impact of Habib and others' stories of incarceration and torture.

"I've said to you before, Sash – I just feel inadequate when we're recounting at second hand events that we haven't witnessed ourselves." I paused. "Not that I'd have wanted to see much of the stuff Habib told us about in the flesh."

If he didn't share my frustration, Saša understood it. "Mick, I suppose informed people see it as layering more detail onto events that they were already aware of."

"Yes, I'm sure you're right – but this is stuff happening a few weeks ago in the shadows of so-called 'civilised Europe'. I don't know…" I let my words trail away, stood up and flicked on the kettle in the hotel room. Displacement activity.

Just ten days later, Saša was banging on my room door in a state of high excitement. And indignation.

"Mick, you're not going to believe this! Governments, diplomats, the UN – they all knew about these camps. Weeks before the footage was broadcast."

"And what did they do?" I was struggling to come to terms with what Saša was saying.

"Nothing!" said Saša. "They just ignored it… till the ITN film was broadcast."

Saša said he had called a contact of his in the office of the Bosnian President's son, who had told him that a government agency, Save Humanity, had begun collecting eye-witness reports from the displaced as early as May. A Sarajevo-based lawyer followed up, collecting his own evidence and distributing it to anyone who would take an interest.

"Mick, he said he knows that the information about the existence of camps was in the hands of aid agencies and diplomats by June. In mid May, Bosnia's Ambassador to the UN, Muhamed Sacirbey, had told the UN Secretary-General, Boutros Boutros-Ghali, about the camps. He said Sacirbey didn't think Boutros-Ghali took him seriously."

Saša said his contact had pointed him in the direction of a thinly reported speech by President Izetbegović at an international summit also in early July in Helsinki.

"There were European Presidents and Prime Ministers there. And President Bush and Canada's Prime Minister, Brian Mulroney. Izetbegović had mentioned in his speech that Bosnia had become the battleground of genocide and he said specifically that it was now 'a country of concentration camps'.

"Mick, I suppose that's our fault. We should have picked up on that. But maybe journalists, political leaders and diplomats – all of us – thought it was just Old Man Alija exaggerating for effect."

Saša said that, in mid July, an UNPROFOR commander in Bosnia was handed a list of forty-two camps registered in Bosnia and Herzegovina.

"I don't know if this is true, but my contact says that that commander went on to deny the existence of camps and held onto the information about them instead of passing it to his bosses in New York. Whether it's true or not, he says there's no doubt Western governments and the UN were well aware of reports of camps and grave abuses in those camps well before the ITN report in early August. Even if they had misgivings about the scale of any atrocities, there's no evidence that any government or international agency did anything to find out more."

"So Habib's Professor Čehajić didn't need to die? And probably countless others? That's what you're saying?" I felt a fury boiling up inside.

"Yes, I think that's precisely what I'm saying," said Saša.

"And we're not being spun a line by the Muslims in the Bosnian Government?" I asked.

"Mick, I've known that contact for years. I honestly don't believe he'd try to get me to fly a kite that might trash my reputation."

"Well, I'll tell you what we'll do: as well as putting calls in to the obvious people – the UN, International Red Cross, European Community – I'll talk to Hugh off the record. Find out whether the European monitors were tipped off," I said.

When I tracked down Hugh, he sounded happy to hear from me but reluctant to go into detail.

"It's complicated, Mick. Very complicated. It's quite a story but…" Hugh paused.

I realised that he didn't want to make any revelations over a phone line that was unlikely to be secure. But a few days later, I was sitting opposite him in the dark corner of a small restaurant not far from St Mark's Square in Zagreb's Old Town.

Hugh said it was true that there had been an awareness of the reports of camps or collection centres and of atrocities taking place within them.

"Trouble is, Mick, we're heading for a US election that Bill Clinton might win so the US certainly doesn't want to get drawn into a war at this period in time. They say it's Europe's war – which, of course, is a very convenient thing to say. And most of the European Community is reluctant to be drawn in. And the British Foreign Secretary, Douglas Hurd, is probably the most reluctant to intervene. Paddy Ashdown MP told me Hurd said to him that he thinks we should just build a firewall around the Balkans and let their people fight themselves to a standstill."

I shook my head not in disbelief but in anger. From what I had heard and observed I believed absolutely that the British Foreign Secretary could think that way.

"I just think of the people I've met in the Balkans – beautiful people, who just want a peaceful life. No different to the rest of so-called 'civilised Europe.'"

As I reflected that I was using the phrase 'so-called civilised Europe' increasingly frequently, the images of Ivana, Branko, Marta, Ismail, Ševa and Nevena jostled for space in my mind.

Hugh slipped his right hand into the inside pocket of his jacket and pulled out a folded sheet of A4. He unfolded it to the right of his plate, flattened it with his palm and looked across at me. He was not quite ready to hand it over.

"You know I said it was complicated. Well, this just proves the point. There are camps right across Bosnia, Mick – and they're not all run by Serbs. There are camps run by Serbs, by Croats and by Muslims." He paused. "And, of course, none of them are holiday camps."

Hugh turned the sheet round and slipped it across the table.

"You can use that, Mick, but don't say where you got it from. You can be confident that the UN, US and European governments, and the International Red Cross were all aware of this well before the camp footage was broadcast in early August. But remember that those numbers will be changing all the time, as people are – how can I put it? – 'moved on'. Yes. 'Moved on'. That covers a multitude of sins."

I took in what was printed on the paper – a photocopy of what looked like an official report. It was marked 'Highly confidential' but I was unable to identify the organisation that had issued it.

The document listed the number of people detained in fifteen camps across Bosnia. There were 913 in Croatian-controlled camps, an aggregate of the numbers from six camps listed, a total of 8,320 across five Serb-controlled camps, and 916 across four Muslim-controlled camps.

Hugh leaned over and laid his finger on the name of one camp – Čelebići.

"This one's interesting. It's at Konjic, sixty kilometres west of Sarajevo and a place where both Croats and Serbs believe they should hold sway. The main railway line and highway pass through there.

"The document says it's Muslim-controlled, but it's a joint enterprise between the Muslims and Bosnian Croats and it holds Bosnian Serb detainees. There are very recent reports that there's been a big, new influx of detainees there – perhaps even bumping the numbers to as high as three thousand. Bosnian Serbs who've come out alive say a lot of prisoners are kept in an old, disused railway tunnel. And the stories you were telling me about Omarska – well, if the Čelebići reports are true, then Bosnian Serbs are suffering the same kinds of beatings, torture, sexual humiliation, rape and – no doubt – killings."

Hugh pointed at another camp name, Čapljina.

"They call that the Dretelj camp. It's right on the south-western border of Bosnia with Croatia. Just a few concrete warehouses and two tunnels bored into the hillside. The Bosnian Croats have got Bosnian Serbs holed up in there. Same story: starvation, beatings, sexual assault, torture."

I shifted the sheet slightly, needlessly, with my fingertips. Initially, I had no words; but an important revelation was unfolding in my mind. I had been hostage to a serious misconception. I realised that I had incorrectly assumed that this was a uniquely Serbian phenomenon. And one limited to a minority who put the creation of a Greater Serbia ahead of the decent treatment of other ethnicities – a minority that wielded power but which was massively outnumbered by the decent Serbs like Saša and Nevena and Vesna, who would insist that this violence endorsed by Belgrade and Pale was not carried out in their name.

But, if Hugh was right – and I had no reason to think that he wasn't – then similar, mindless humiliation, torture and killings were being perpetrated by Croats and by Muslims. What might Ivana in Dubrovnik and Ševa in Sarajevo think of that? They would be appalled, I knew.

"Hugh, we've had this conversation before, but what makes people behave like that – not just towards former neighbours and friends but to anyone? My mind can't frame it," I said.

"At the risk of repeating myself, there are two broad categories: the real villains at the top of the political tree – in Belgrade, in Pale, even at the level of a town like Prijedor – who give the signals, who spell out the goals; and then there are the perpetrators, who pursue those goals. Some because they believe in them, some because they are psychopaths and criminals, some because it makes them rich, some because they like power over others, some because, for the first time in their lives, they're off the leash."

I was still letting the implications sink in.

"So, are we saying, on the basis of this evidence" – I pointed to Hugh's sheet of paper – "that gentle, cerebral Izetbegović and Croatia's Tuđman are as guilty as Milošević and Karadžić?"

Hugh made to reply but no words came out.

"Sorry, Hugh – that's a rhetorical question. I don't expect an answer," I said.

And I thought back to Saša's story about the French journalist raising the victory fist to a passing PLO armoured vehicle and a British journalist saying witheringly "There are no good guys in the Middle East."

And a thought broke that suddenly cast some sunlight across what had been a darkening mood. Yes, it was true: in the Balkans, no side, no state, no ethnicity could claim it occupied the moral high ground exclusively and permanently; but yes, there were many, many good guys. I had met them: individuals caught up in the violence unleashed. These were people who needed rescuing from a conflict for which they bore no blame.

"Hugh – Hurd is wrong. He's absolutely wrong. I don't think the silent, blameless majority can end this conflict. It needs outside intervention. And pretty quickly too."

In the months that followed, there was some good news to emerge in the wake of the camp closures around Prijedor; but, as ever, it came with qualifications and additional disturbing details that would add to the dark shadows cast over parts of northern Bosnia and create new shrines for the families of the lost to cluster around.

Paul told me that one of my contacts had called in from Croatia and asked that I give him a call.

"Have I got this right? I got his name down as Habib Hodžić?" asked Paul.

When I got through to Habib, he revealed that he was safe, having managed to escape over the border with Croatia with his wife and children.

Habib said that at several points after his release from Omarska, it had appeared touch-and-go and he had been unsure whether he would make it out of Prijedor alive. One of the Prijedor police chief's deputies had him arrested and brought in. Allegedly, the reason for his questioning had been in relation to the deeds to his flat, which, on his release from Omarska, he had found to bear a sign on the door that stated 'Occupied by a Serb soldier'.

"I was taken to the police station where it was logged that the Hodžić family were not allowed to leave Prijedor."

Habib said that his wife had already pulled together most of the paperwork required for them to leave Prijedor and leave Bosnia.

"It was clear to me that the police chief's deputy would kill me if I hung around. If not him, then one of the groups led by Djordje Đorađević or other local thugs, who were supposed to take care of the remaining Muslims in Prijedor."

But Habib said his wife managed to organise their secret departure from Prijedor through a private legal agency in Gradiška, located near a border crossing into Croatia. However, before he left, he had to renounce all the property he had and hand it over to the nascent Serbian autonomous state within Bosnia, Republika Srpska.

"Well, Habib, I know Prijedor was your family's home for centuries but I hope you and your family can now rebuild your lives," said Mick.

"Thank you, thank you, Mick. I don't know if we'll ever be able to go back. Or want to…" said Habib. "But there's one more story I want to share with you before I go. I'd be grateful if you'd share it with your friend Saša and investigate it because I think, if you do, someone is going to find the corpses of a significant number of the men who went missing from the camps on the last days of their existence in a space on Mount Vlašić."

He explained how he had heard that the son of friends of his had been among hundreds of detainees, including women and children, who had been bussed out of the Trnopolje camp as it was being shut down.

A couple of hours south-east of Banja Luka, the women and children were separated from the men and bussed away. The men were lined up on a ridge at a place called Korikanske Stijene – the Koričani Cliffs.

Habib said his friend's son couldn't recall whether he had jumped or had been pushed, but he knew that many of his colleagues fell into the crevasse below, having been shot in the back. After coming to, buried under corpses, the young man had survived, eventually climbing out of the pit into which he had fallen and, over time, he had made his way back to Prijedor. He was now in hiding.

Habib said that he hoped my and Saša's reports might prompt some investigation and excavation around Korikanske Stijene.

"Maybe not now, but somewhere down the line – in the not-too-distant future," he added.

I did my best to meet my side of the bargain with Habib, and my piece 'Are there two hundred corpses in this Mount Vlašić crevasse?' had been well received.

As usual, Saša and I had arranged for our pieces to be published simultaneously so that any glory was shared. Our colleagues in Bosnia now saw that we were a regular partnership. Given Saša's experience, this prompted the occasional bout of jealousy. I had bristled as one experienced – some might say jaundiced – journalist had said on being introduced to me, "Oh, yeah. You're the guy who rides shotgun with Saša, aren't you?"

"I'm quite capable of driving myself, thank you," I replied. Subsequent relations were cool.

Saša had praised me for my piece. He said I had turned Habib's account into a gripping story without laying on any fake detail.

"Thanks, Sash," I had said. "I'm pleased with how the last few pieces have gone down but, as I keep telling you, I'm still not used to this world where journalists aren't where the action is. Maybe that's why lots of the rest of the Press pack are still in Sarajevo. It's dangerous but you're in the story. We were close to the story in Višegrad but, if it hadn't been for ITN and Channel 4, camps might still be in place with hundreds more dying. There's no answer to it. No side wants us to witness their worst behaviour. But… well, as I say, it's frustrating."

Saša clearly had something on his mind. We had just learned that Croatia had announced that it could take no more Bosnian refugees and was shutting its borders, yet we doubted that the removal of Bosnian Muslims from areas the Serbs wanted to make their own was over.

He looked across from his winged Chesterfield leather armchair in the bar of the Astoria, he sipped at the brandy in his heavy crystal glass and said Delphically, "That's what I wanted to talk to you about. We have to ask ourselves where's the action now that the worst camps are closing? Now that Croatia is shut. They're still driving Muslims out of North Bosnia, so it's obvious, isn't it?"

"What's obvious?" I replied.

"We need to get ourselves ethnically cleansed…"

19
NOVEMBER 1992

Although I didn't share the nature of the expedition that Saša had in mind, I did manage to elicit from Hugh the intelligence that a current hotspot and a strong candidate to be the Serbs' next 'cleansing fields' was the municipality of Kotor Varoš, ninety-five kilometres south-east of Prijedor.

"It's about forty per cent Serb and thirty per cent each Bosnian Muslim and Croat," said Hugh. "So, if as looks likely, there's an attempt to move on non-Serbs, it's going to be a major operation."

In the days running up to our journey to Kotor Varoš, after the evidence of the camps around Prijedor, any doubts that lingered about the reality of ethnic cleansing were blown away by a scoop from a *Financial Times* journalist. In the dullest of publications, the latest issue of *Epoha*, the weekly magazine of Serbia and Milošević's Socialist Party, she found a news article that stated in matter-of-fact terms that ethnic cleansing was indeed a central policy goal of Serbian leaders – in Belgrade and, most likely, in the headquarters of the Bosnian Serbs in Pale too. The article was equivalent to finding a gem in a dung heap.

It read: "The region of NW Bosnia is now cleared of Croats and Muslims. Our army surrounds Muslim villages. If the Muslims do not raise the white flag, we raze the villages to the ground. Serb villages will be built there. Those people not from mixed marriages can go to Izetbegović or Croatia. Those from mixed marriages who have not fired at Serbs can choose to remain. Across most of the region, there are no longer ethnic minorities."

Habiba, Habib and his family had got out into Croatia just in time but, from what we had seen, we expected the 'cleansing' to go on. Saša reasoned that that border closure meant finding a group of the exiled on the roads south out of Prijedor and Banja Luka should be relatively easy.

Still in the 4x4 with the Bosnian plates that we had picked up from Ševa's friend on the road from Sarajevo to Višegrad, Saša admitted that we were embarking on something of a leap in the dark.

"I don't know how orderly or chaotic these evacuations are, whether we'll happen across a convoy of vehicles or refugees on foot but… well, we'll soon see. You've been chewing my ear off for so long about seeing things at first hand that I suppose we have to give it a tilt."

I smiled but said nothing. I was a little surprised to find that my regular internal struggle with fear was temporarily stilled. I had no idea what we were walking into beyond Prijedor and Banja Luka. How could you fear what you couldn't conceive?

Between Prijedor and Banja Luka, Saša and I saw more burned-out Muslim villages. If the Bosnian Serb leadership's aim in the area was wicked, they were certainly pursuing it with thoroughness and efficiency.

Beyond Banja Luka, the dull, flat landscapes began to give way to roads that twisted their way through the foothills of the Uzlomac mountain range, dense with oak and beech forests.

Around Kotor Varoš itself, there was further bomb and fire damage to properties but there seemed to be an eerie silence. After Saša pulled off the M4 towards the village of Večići and drove past empty, sandbagged trenches, we learned why.

Though the majority of people were indoors, by chatting to a couple of villagers picking their way carefully across the village square, we were able to ascertain that, after some fierce fighting, Večići was in the middle of a five-day truce. The men's gingerly passage across the square perhaps reflected their less-than-complete confidence in that ceasefire.

One of the men, probably in his early seventies, still with a large frame and more than six feet tall, wearing a flat cap, green corduroy trousers and a blue jacket, said the men of the village had held out courageously but the feeling now was that they couldn't continue to resist the shelling and the bombing.

"We can probably only guarantee the safety of the majority of our villagers and of the refugees driven out of other local villages by surrendering. And, when I say 'guarantee', that's me being an optimist."

Another man, most likely in his fifties, said the picture was less clear.

"We've heard of other villages surrendering and some of the menfolk being killed and properties being looted and burned despite their having signed a truce, so we're not sure."

He explained that there was a school of thought that the men of fighting age should break out and try to make their own way across the hills to safety rather than rely on the Serbs to keep their side of any bargain allegedly offering safe passage to all.

"One thing's for certain," he added with an asthmatic wheeze, "I'll be doing no hiking across the hills. Time's caught up with me."

He smiled ruefully and I saw in his ruddy face and his cheeks streaked with tiny blue rivulet veins a man who had enjoyed the pleasures of life – particularly out of a bottle – but who was now paying the price with fragile health. He told us his name was Harun and he offered to let us sleep overnight in a barn on his smallholding on the edge of the village.

"Just hide yourselves if the Serbs do come. I don't want to get shot for harbouring international journalists."

After a sleep that was deeper than I had expected under blankets on a pile of hay, we rose to a bright, clean, cold day and to coffee and eggs prepared by Harun's wife.

The truce appeared to be holding but, in the village, there were signs of planning and organising as the day unfolded. By early afternoon, it was clear that a plan had been hatched that would be implemented before the day was done. After Harun had spoken to friends and relatives across the village, he returned to tell us that a group would set out from the village in the evening – largely the able-bodied menfolk, but a few women were insisting on going and some teenage boys would make up part of the group too. Most of the women of the village, the children and the elderly would take a chance on the Serbs delivering them to Bosnian Muslim territory without harming them.

In the village square, Harun was able to take aside for a few moments the man who was leading preparations for the breakout group.

Ahmed nodded seriously and shook Saša and my hands firmly, as Harun explained why we were there and our wish to accompany his group.

"Gentlemen, you're more than welcome – but at your own risk. We're planning on joining up with another convoy of local men and trying to pick our own route to safety, but we don't know what it'll be like out there."

"Sure, sure," said Saša. I nodded along.

Ahmed went on. "And if I could ask each of you to help us. There will be some minors accompanying us. My boy, Ajdin, for example. He's fourteen and I don't want to leave him with the women and the elderly. I've heard that sometimes they split out the young lads from their mothers, if they're nearly of fighting age. Then they're never seen again. I can't take the risk. So he's coming along. Those of us leading the group will have to have our wits about us, so, if each of you could stick close to some of the youngsters, look out for them, then you'll be helping us enormously."

Saša and I returned to the smallholding with Harun and prepared our backpacks for the journey. We agreed that we should wear our flak jackets bearing the word 'Press' on them concealed beneath our winter jackets.

"There'll come a moment when we'll have to reveal that we're hacks – not Muslim refugees," said Saša.

At around 7.45pm, several hundred people gathered in the village square and emotional farewells were exchanged, married couples, elderly parents and their sons hugged and kissed ahead of their separation, tears were shed. The core convoy turned out to be made up of around two hundred people. They were nearly all men of fighting age, though I counted around half a dozen boys in their lower teens and about a dozen women, a couple of whom appeared to be below twenty years of age, all of them fit and strong enough to make the journey. Some had not wanted to be separated from their menfolk, Harun had explained.

Ahmed made his way out of the crowd with two boys. One appeared to be about twelve years of age but Ahmed explained that this was Ajdin, the fourteen-year-old son he'd mentioned, and the other was his classmate, Tarik.

"If you guys could keep an eye on them…"

"Ajdin, why don't you stick with me?" I said.

Ajdin nodded but said nothing. He was rangy but slight and I suspected he would pack on the muscle in forthcoming years till he resembled his tall, strong father. He had dark hair, verging on black, cut in a straight fringe, a style that said 'boy' rather than 'adolescent'. He had dark brown eyes, like deep pools that it was hard not to gaze into. I imagined that, in later years, girls would queue up to claim him as a partner. But, at this stage, he appeared nervous, uncertain, and younger physically and psychologically than his fourteen years.

"I'm Mick, by the way."

"I'm Ajdin."

We shook hands. Ajdin had the weak grip of a child. Saša was getting to know Tarik, a smaller boy with fairer hair and gap teeth. In different circumstances, his immaturity, his love of mischief but his irrepressible cheerfulness might have been more in evidence. I guessed he would be a boy who liked a prank or a practical joke, always in trouble in the classroom.

Our group left the village under a cloudless sky, the moon and the stars offering as much light as they could muster to assist this band of homeless. Even the sombre, uncertain nature of the circumstances could not prevent me from feeling a frisson of delight at the magnificence of the stellar array.

"Look at the stars, Ajdin," I said. Ajdin nodded but said nothing. I wasn't sure whether he had taken them in.

We walked north along the road for around half a mile before turning off into an uncultivated field, the gradient of which rose sharply. High above were woods and I suspected that the aim was to head for the additional protection that the forest might offer. Saša and I and our young charges were close to the back of the crocodile. It was a trail of humanity whose constituents had left their homes less than an hour earlier as local villagers but who had been transformed at a stroke into fully fledged refugees.

My level of trepidation had risen as night had begun to close in and we left the village, but the need to look out for Ajdin became a useful distraction from my more typical introspection.

Before the ascent steepened abruptly, I made out across the field another gathering of refugees, as Ajdin's father had forecast. In the distance, Ahmed and the other group leaders from Večići had a brief discussion with those leading this new group. It was hard to estimate in the low light and from afar but, at a guess, I suspected that the human convoy that would begin the ascent and pick out the potential route to safety would now be around one thousand strong. There were occasional, low-volume exchanges as instructions were passed down the line but, overwhelmingly, this was a near silent ghost army.

The route being picked out soon became steep and demanding. I kept up largely monosyllabic exchanges with Ajdin.

"You okay?"

"Yeah, fine."

"Wet underfoot, isn't it?"

"Yeah. Soggy."

I had to hold Ajdin by the hand at times to help him find a way up the incline; at other times we were both scrambling independently, almost on all fours, the slick grass resisting the grip of boot and hand.

"If somebody falls behind or gets injured, don't try to help. Just keep on moving till you're instructed to stop."

The message was passed down the line, but it was not one that I felt applied to Saša and me with our young charges.

After twenty minutes or so of navigating the slope, I wondered whether I had the stomach for this exhausting effort, but I knew I now had no option but to plough on. There was no going back. I panted for breath; Ajdin exhaled at the sheer effort required. We carried on because we had to carry on. Necessity outbid physical and mental frailty.

"There must be a better route than this!" I exclaimed at one point. Ajdin managed a laugh.

"No, no. I don't think there is."

The exchange was another step in a process of bonding between us, my reaching out gently to the teenager with instinctive but, I hoped, carefully graded diplomacy and Ajdin slowly dropping his guard and beginning to trust.

I kept Saša and Tarik in sight, anxious that they never be separated too far from me and Ajdin. From what I could register, Tarik was taking to his task grittily, showing a determination not to let the challenge defeat him; but I was concerned for Saša. He wasn't as young and lean as I was – yet he seemed to be coping thus far. A ridiculous detail niggled at me. What if Saša were to lose or break his glasses?

I was cross at myself for framing the thought and then for worrying about it, but it kept coming back, like an irritating gnat that wouldn't be swatted.

Yet, in that instant of acknowledging that I needed to keep my friend close, I realised what weight I placed subconsciously on Saša's unspoken support. I recalled my reaction a year earlier, when Saša had landed in Dubrovnik. "The grown-ups have arrived," I had thought. It was as if Saša's mental strength and experience were counterbalancing what I saw as my own vulnerability – not just in the near darkness, the cold and the damp of a field in Kotor Varoš, but across this whole, baffling series of Balkan episodes in which cruelty and compassion fought unremittingly for space.

After a couple of gruelling hours, the steepest ascent had been scaled and, though mountains still towered above our convoy, we had reached a flatter area. It wasn't the depth of the forest but there were trees scattered across the scrubland, offering some cover. A network of scouts must have fanned out from the core group, as instructions would come back from men going up and down the line.

"We have to hurry here… We have to slow down."

Then, as my watch appeared in the half-light to suggest it was close to midnight, urgent whispered messages spread like a panic.

"Don't move! Don't make a sound! Hunker down. The Serbs are very close."

I didn't understand why but my reaction was to think "It can't be true. There must be a mistake." Did I think that peril couldn't reach me?

All of a sudden, the rattle of automatic gunfire broke out and hails of bullets riffled and ripped through the grass patches near me and the other stragglers at the back of the group, each bullet sparking as it touched a surface.

I leapt and flattened Ajdin, forcing his face into the earth. I tugged and rolled him down a small incline to our left, then eased the boy towards the base of a tree where a tangle of roots might offer some cover. Around us, the others who had been near us had spreadeagled themselves as best they could in the safest spots they could find.

My heart was racing and thumping, as if it were smacking off my ribcage. I felt the fear might have paralysed me, had I not been responsible for Ajdin. Instead, I kept a close watch on the direction of the bullet hails skittering around the open spaces nearby and rapping against tree trunks, and I tried to gauge any subtle changes to the angle of attack. Where I had dived with Ajdin was a shallow hollow and, provided we kept our heads down, it seemed the bullets would slide past or above us.

During a first lull in the shooting, I found myself posing again the rhetorical question: How the hell did I get here? I knew the answer and, at the same time, I had no idea what the answer was.

I realised without fully articulating the thought that I had expected the ethnic cleansing journey to be uncomfortable, to push my physical strength to its limits; but I hadn't conceived that our party would be shot at, as if the Serbs were shooting fish in a barrel. It was the indiscriminate nature of the shooting that shocked me. I couldn't see the Serb gunmen and they clearly couldn't see us, so they were spraying bullets into the gloom, unaware of whether their targets were armed or even adult. Did they even know whether or not we were Muslim?

The hail of shots would stop and then resume a couple of minutes later, each new volley sending a new palpitation through me, each assault as shocking as the first. Now and then, I would extend my left arm to make sure Ajdin was as low to the ground as possible and to reassure him with a gentle pat or a squeeze to the bicep.

"We'll be okay, Ajdin. We'll be okay," I would whisper, and, as I said the words, I genuinely believed we would be, though I had no reason to suppose so and Ajdin had no reason to believe me.

Over time, the angle of the bullets appeared to have shifted from being pretty much head-on, straight at our group at the back of the chain of refugees, to coming in increasingly from left to right, as though the Serb soldiers were moving gradually down the hillside.

After several rounds of volleys, I heard a shriek that died in the air, around thirty metres to my right. Had the marksmen claimed their first victim? I suspected that they had.

The shooting went on for almost an hour, just short breaks of a few minutes each punctuating the volleys of bullets.

This is what it feels like when people say their nerves are shredded, I thought, but there was room for such thoughts only in the lulls in the shooting. When the bullets flew, I was flat to the ground and making sure Ajdin was too. The need to survive suppressed reflection. Every bullet landing in range killed off fresh thought.

Eventually rain began to fall and, as it fell more and more heavily, big fat drops splattering off the ground against my face, the shooting became more distant and then, eventually, the guns fell silent.

Once everyone around us was convinced that the immediate threat had gone, we got to our feet to try to gather ourselves as best we could and to assess the scale of the casualties. There were two dead from our group, which had been split off from the rest of the convoy in the melée.

"It was Ahmet Zec and his son," said Ajdin, after chatting to some of the men from Večići. "Ahmet lived in Večići and I knew his son by sight, though I didn't really know him well."

Ajdin reported the intelligence factually. He appeared too stunned for emotion at this stage. A group of men volunteered to lift the bodies and try to find at least a makeshift, temporary burial spot for the victims.

Saša and Tarik wandered over, muddied but apparently none the worse for wear, Saša's glasses intact to my enormous relief.

"Well… that was a close thing," said Saša, and he gave out a whistle of relief. I laid my hand on his shoulder. I said nothing but I raised my eyebrows in my own variant of an expression of relief.

Before long, the tail end of the group, including me, Saša, Ajdin and Tarik, was reunited with the rest of the pack and our snaking trail of weary, wet refugees continued our trudge through the night, the terrain a little easier now. As the group had reunited, more volunteers had been sought to fan out to try to make sure there were no further ambushes.

One of the leaders had told Saša that they were now confident they were on the right track to Travnik and to safety. Travnik was a

Muslim-controlled town in Central Bosnia which was welcoming those displaced by conflict, we were told.

"You see that peak up there, Mick?" Saša pointed across the valley. "That's Ježica and it's the best guide point to help us locate where we are and where we should go next."

He tugged at my sleeve and lowered his voice to a whisper.

"And you see that guy over there?" He was pointing at a thin man in his thirties with long curly blond hair. "They say he's a collaborator with the Serbs."

"So why's no one gone and filled him in?" I asked.

"Dunno. Maybe they're not one hundred per cent sure."

The time ticked by and I was beginning to feel as though we had made real progress towards Travnik, when a fresh rumour spread through the convoy.

"The Serbs! They're coming again! They've got us surrounded! Run down the hill."

The order was not to cross a flat patch down by the river. It was a minefield.

"The Serbs are trying to drive us onto it," the message came.

"Quick, Ajdin. Run!" I gave Ajdin a light push and we and the rest of our group headed off down the hill as gunfire broke out again, crackling behind us, rattling off the trees around us but, so far, over our heads.

I became aware of a couple of dozen men from the convoy, all of them armed with rifles, standing still in the midst of this tide of bodies scurrying downhill past them. They had clearly decided to stand and fight – perhaps delay the attack on the rest of our group, saving some lives by putting their own at near inevitable, fatal risk.

I kept Ajdin ahead of me as best I could but, as the incline grew steeper, we were both sliding down the grass bank as much as running. As a pocket of men took a route closer to the river, a voice rang out: "Don't skirt the river! It's mined!"

It was too late. There was a series of explosions and a man screamed. And screamed. As we slalomed part way down the hill and slithered to a halt, our vantage point offered us a view in the moonlight of a patch of land, fifty metres below, now strewn with the bodies of around a dozen men. They lay there like mannequins left prone and incomplete in a shop window, the odd limb detached from its trunk. They appeared to have died instantly, apart from the man who continued to scream to the heavens. He no longer had legs attached to his body.

"Shoot me! Shoot me! Somebody please shoot me!" He was screaming in agony.

"Oh, no! It's Besim," Ajdin exclaimed. "He's one of our leaders. Oh, no… not Besim!"

I pulled Ajdin in close and hugged him for a few seconds, then I nudged him again and we set off again down the hill. Saša and Tarik were still in sight, grim-faced, concentrating fiercely, laying their feet as carefully as they could in a scramble. All of a sudden a single pistol-shot rang out and Besim's cries were silenced. It transpired later that one of his friends had tossed him his pistol and Besim had put a bullet through his own temple.

The men offering guidance pointed our group to a stretch of the river further down, which they said was not mined. The bullets from above were dwindling in intensity and were perhaps fired from too far away to pose a threat.

The river downstream from a small waterfall was wide but it had to be crossed. Ajdin, Saša, Tarik and I formed a human chain with others and waded through the water. It was freezing cold and the flow tried to prise away individuals and whisk them down the river's course but everyone made it to the other side. It felt a little like deliverance but, given the second outbreak of shooting, I wasn't convinced that we were out of danger.

Just up from the bank of the river to which we had crossed, there was a flat area. Around two hundred of the people from the back of the convoy were gathered there, mostly the Večići group Saša and I had set off with. I picked out at the far end of the group Ajdin's father, Ahmed.

"Look, Ajdin. It's your dad. He's safe," I said.

"Oh, great! Great. Shall I go to him?" he asked.

"No, no. Not yet. He'll be busy making plans. Let's wait and see what our next instructions are."

Meanwhile, a man who turned out to be the Imam from the mosque in Večići gathered the youngsters around him and said, "Let us pray, my children. Let's pray."

Tarik and Ajdin and the other teenage boys surrounded the Imam in a circle and bowed their heads and joined in prayer – touching solemnity and a few moments of composure after their terrifying ordeal.

Saša and I were sitting side by side on a rock.

"Mick, I'm so, so sorry…" said Saša.

He was looking down at the ground, as if he couldn't bring himself to make eye contact. I couldn't process his words or make any sense of them in the context.

Eventually, Saša raised his eyes, looked at me and said, "I completely misjudged this. I thought we might find ourselves on a long footslog to Travnik. I thought it would be gruelling. I never ever thought I'd have put your life at risk. Heaven forbid that you lose your life through my stupidity and this crazy mission."

He paused and said grimly again, "I'm so sorry, Mick."

I gave him a gentle push against the arm. He managed a weak smile. My heart rate had slowed a little from its earlier, fast drum beat.

"Don't be daft, Sash! Neither of us knew what it would be like. We both decided to take the risk. Don't blame yourself…" I paused, then added with gallows humour: "Blame the fucking Serbs!"

Saša cracked a weak smile but remained sombre.

"Look, Mick – we might not make it out of this alive. There are only so many bullets we can dodge. But I just want you to know that, if I make it out and you don't, I'll never forgive myself. And I want you to know that, if you make it out and I don't, you need to be aware that you've got something special about you. And you must never change."

I had reflected recently that we had grown closer over the months since we had met, but this was a tribute from Saša that I wasn't quite prepared for. I felt a hot flush to my heart. I had difficulty in absorbing the scale of the accolade. I was speechless for a moment or two. I was the raw kid, afraid almost of my own shadow, and Saša was the experienced, brave international correspondent who had seen it all yet retained his compassion and humanity. Saša had spurned the harbour of bleakness about the human condition, the cynicism into which so many of his peers had slipped so comfortably, so glibly.

"What do you mean, Sash, 'something special'? I'm not special. I'm fearful. I'm vulnerable. I'm not sure I'm cut out for this stuff."

Unusually, Saša still continued to look down at the ground beneath him, instead of into my eyes. Had the terror of the last few hours or so diminished him temporarily? I couldn't know.

"Mick – you just get it. You know what the story is. You know what's new, you know what's an important development. And you can capture it and transmit it – from where I'm standing seemingly effortlessly. You don't struggle for the words, like I do. You just pluck them out of the air.

"But that's not it when I say 'Don't change.' You really believe in what's right. I've never once heard you compromise on what the right way forward should be. Your pieces seem to say to our leaders, our decision makers 'Your available courses of action are obvious. Don't let us down, don't duck your responsibility.'"

At this point, Saša did look up and he locked me with the most fixed of gazes.

"I want to say to you, Mick, 'Never, ever change,' but, you know what? I don't think you're capable of change. But…" And Saša paused at this point. I sensed that he may even have gulped. "Never forget: you have a special, special gift. You must nurture it."

I leaned across and wrapped my arms around Saša and hugged him tight. Saša returned the embrace. It was intimacy that would have been impermissible in a roomful of journalists in a Zagreb or Sarajevo hotel, but it was perfectly choreographed for this bleak moment in the wilderness when we were both still coming to terms with how close we had come to being shot or blown to pieces. Perhaps we were clinging to one another for safety.

We exchanged no words for some time, but I felt in those moments that our friendship was deepening to previously unfathomed depths. He had become the most important person in the world to me.

I broke the silence. "Saša, I think you're overstating it – but I really, really appreciate what you say. That's pretty much the best thing anyone has ever said to me. I'll carry your words with me through the rest of my career."

I managed a half-laugh. "No – through the rest of my life!"

Saša grinned, then showed a lightness he had not for many hours. "You fucking well better had!"

We both laughed again; but I was soon adopting a more serious demeanour. It struck me that I had been given an opportunity to ask a question that had always baffled me.

"Tell me, Saša. What was it that made you hang out with me? Invite me to go with you – like that night when we drove into Trebinje to see Arian? What made you take me on those road trips to Sarajevo and Višegrad? At first, I thought you were just doing an old mate, Paul on the foreign desk, a favour, keeping an eye on me for him. But I feel we're way beyond that now." I paused. "And I can feed off your experience and contacts – but what can you get back in return? You can't learn anything from me."

Saša looked up at the hills across the river then slowly turned his gaze to me. "Oh, I can, Mick. I can. You've got a clear way of unpacking what's happened and explaining it; you've got a strong sense of what's an important detail and what's not; you've got a descriptive touch that – as I've told you before – paints pictures with words. So there's all that – but, you know, it's not about what I can learn. I just like the fact that it all matters to you. What people do, the consequences of their decisions, the miseries people bring by their excesses. You burn with indignation like you did in those first days in Dubrovnik. You get mad at bad leaders and irresponsible leadership and gratuitous cruelty. I know it's natural to you, but I've lived and worked alongside so many journalists who've let their fire fizzle out, who've become jaundiced or cynical or just a little too self-important. I told you never to change but… you know, I don't think you ever will. And, if you don't, you'll keep on doing what we do best: letting the world know what's really gone on; holding the decision makers to account, defying them to distort events, history. That's what we're here for, and I'd rather hang with you than with any number of older and supposedly wiser hacks who've lost their passion."

"Thanks, Saša. Thanks for that," I said quietly. I was glowing so much from the dazzle of the tribute that I couldn't be sure that I had completely suppressed the smile that wanted to break out across my face. "I appreciate that. You don't know how much I appreciate that." My response felt inadequate but they were all the words I could muster.

Ajdin and Tarik had drifted back to where we were sitting, the Imam having concluded prayers. The first glimmering of dawn was beginning to break, though this was still half-light. The group leaders, some fifty metres away, seemed to be deep in discussion – a discussion from which resolution did not appear to have emerged.

High up on the hills, opposite the point at which they had crossed the river, a group of men began waving in the direction of our group. A man, who Ajdin appeared to recognise, had wandered over to the group around Saša, me and the boys.

"There's a big debate going on. The majority think we should surrender but there's a minority that want to try to escape or to stand and fight. I think, on balance, we'll surrender," he said.

The man said we had become separated from the group that we had met up with just outside of Večići, so we were down to the two hundred or so that had first set out.

"And we don't know whether those guys waving are the other part of our convoy or Serbs."

Suddenly, the crackling sound of a voice over a megaphone broke out. "Balijas! Surrender! If you surrender, you'll live. And, if you don't, you're all going to die."

Within minutes the word had drifted back, apparently authoritatively, that the choice was surrender.

As the message spread, the man with the long blond curly hair, who Saša had been told earlier was a potential collaborator, jumped to his feet.

"Surrender? I can arrange that for you. That's not a problem." And he ran off, went back across the river and fell out of sight.

"The guy who was killed with his boy – he was Ahmet Zec. They call that guy Zec too, though he's not related," said Ajdin. "He's a total shit. No one likes him."

Before long, Zec was back.

"I've talked to some of the Serbs. They've guaranteed us, if we surrender, there'll be no harm done to us and we all should be transported safely to Travnik," he said.

"What's with this 'we'?" said one of the group of men closest to him, gruffly. "You're a traitor to your own people. Why should we believe you, you bastard?"

Zec extended his arms either side of his body, as if to say 'You can trust me or not. It's your choice.' After a silence, he pointed ahead of where the refugees had crossed the river.

"We need to go that way. There's a tunnel. It'll take us to Grabovica," he said.

"If a hair on the head of one of these kids or one of these women is harmed, Zec, I will personally hunt you down and make sure you die a painful, lingering death," said the man who had challenged him.

The fact that we were surrendering gave me little sense that our ordeal was over. Might there be a double-cross? Why might the Serbs lead these men of fighting age to safety unharmed? However, I sensed that, in the short term, there was unlikely to be a further hail of bullets out of the blue.

As our group set off in the direction of Grabovica, I asked Ajdin whether he had been born and raised in Večići. Ajdin said he and his family were not from there at all but from Hrvaćani, six kilometres northeast of Večići. His was a village of around seven hundred people and it was virtually one hundred per cent Muslim. There were nearby villages which were totally Muslim, others totally Serb and one village that was one hundred per cent Croat. Yet in Ajdin's lifetime there had been no animosity between villages and their children had attended school together, striking up friendships and celebrating one another's feast days without so much as a thought of ethnic differences.

Since conflict broke out a few months earlier, Ahmed, Ajdin and their family's story had been one of perambulation, as they wandered with fellow villagers, sometimes in large groups, sometimes in smaller groups, looking for a safe place to stay but being regularly driven on, as the Serbs warned other villagers not to take in refugees from Hrvaćani. If other villages did, they would face annihilation, they were warned.

"The Serbs hated us because they claimed that as they had been trying to disarm Croats and Muslims in the area in the summer, a Serb soldier had been shot dead in our village. They claimed our village elders asked them to come the following day for negotiations but, when their unit arrived, it was ambushed and shot at."

"And was it true?" I asked.

"I don't know. I just don't know," said Ajdin. From his manner, I judged that Ajdin at least suspected that the incidents had occurred and, given his prominence in the Hrvaćani group, I wondered whether Ajdin's father, Ahmed, might have been involved in an ambush.

"So you had Muslims too fearful to offer you shelter?" I asked.

"Yes, that's right."

If Ajdin had been tentative about the detail at first, as he relaxed into my company and our group trudged south with no apparent risk of a resumed attack, his story began to tumble out of him. He spoke dolefully but without self-pity. In fact, it appeared now to be a relief for him to share his story with me.

After being bombed out of their village, a group from Hrvaćani had set off for the Croat village of Plitska, but this was just the start the start of Ajdin and his family's demoralising trek. After a few days in Plitska, the village was attacked by Serbs.

"Everywhere we went, we weren't welcome. Some Muslim villages had signed loyalty oaths with the Serbs, and so they were afraid to have us. We were informed that if the Serbs found that anybody from Hrvaćani was staying there, or if people were harbouring any of us, they would be killed. Everywhere we went, we were pushed out."

Ajdin said that a group of people from his village, now numbering about sixty in total, were in such despair that they decided to go back to Hrvaćani. Regardless of its condition, it couldn't be worse than this endless trudge from place to place, they reasoned.

Close to the village, they had come across two Serb soldiers in camouflage uniforms, carrying AK-47s. One had asked, "Where are you balijas going?" And Ajdin's mother had said they were going back to their village, Hrvaćani.

"The soldier replied, 'There's nothing left there. There's no place, balijas, for you to go other than Turkey. This is Serbia. How are you going to manage to survive there? There's nothing left.'"

Ajdin said the soldiers hadn't stopped them from proceeding but, at the village, they found a scene of devastation. His aunt's house at the southern tip of the village was completely burned to the ground, just parts of the outside walls and the chimneys still standing.

"There were cows lying in the street. They'd been shot and they were just bloated and the smell was terrible," Ajdin said.

At his own home, nearer the main street in Hrvaćani, there was a scene similar to that at his aunt's. The inside of the house was completely burned out, the furniture, the TV, all the contents had gone. His father's dog, which had been on a chain when the shelling started, was still there but he had been shot.

Although a handful of villagers decided to stay and eke out a living among the rubble, most of the group were back on the road with little idea of where to find safe harbour.

As they passed the Serb village of Savići, a group of villagers were on the outskirts with two Serb soldiers alongside them. One woman, dressed in black, whom Ajdin recognised as the mother of a Serb friend from school, came at them.

"She was really screaming and she was trying to get a gun from one of the soldiers and yelling, 'Why are you balijas wandering round here? There's no place for you, while our soldiers are dying in Večići! How dare you come and try to walk through our village.' And she was tugging at the soldier and saying, 'Give me that gun! Give me that gun! I want to kill them all!' And the rest of the group was cursing us and spitting at us."

Ajdin explained that they had eventually arrived at Večići, where Saša and I had come across them and their trek to Travnik had begun. The night before he had met Saša and me, he had overheard his father discussing with his mother whether he, Ajdin, should stay in Večići or make the trek with the menfolk. And now, here they were: Ajdin and his father, in a no man's land between Večići and the safety of Travnik, unsure as to whether they had made the right call.

Our group continued our journey as the rain resumed, until a tunnel through the hillside appeared, as Zec, the collaborator, had forecast. As we took shelter in the fifty-metre stretch, it seemed like a good place to rest and most of the convoy sat down. Like a marathon runner, I felt I had 'hit the wall' mid race. As I sat down, I realised just how spent I was. Not just physically. My head felt as if the contents of a pack of thick elastic bands had been fitted one after another around my temples along the route. A minute of relaxation here seemed to flip off one of them. If we could rest awhile, perhaps more would be released and that tension eased.

The curved brick ceiling of the tunnel was imperfect and, here and there, sprinklings of fresh rainwater would trickle down. Ajdin and Tarik cupped their hands beneath the nearest leaks and quenched their thirst as best they could. I stood up and made a quick calculation of the number of refugees sheltering there. As best I could estimate, two hundred was pretty close to the tally.

But, just as some of the fatigue and tension was beginning to dissipate, the shocking blast of automatic fire began again.

"Fuck! It's an ambush!" someone nearby shouted.

I dived down and pinned Ajdin, who was already flat to the floor. The commotion appeared to be at either mouth of the tunnel. Although the possibility of us all being mown down was real, I quickly sensed that no bullets were being fired into the tunnel at us.

But had Zec led us into an ambush? If that was my reaction, no doubt others had the same thought as well. But, just as the thought formed, Zec jumped up.

"Guys! Don't worry! It's pre-arranged! You won't be harmed."

Zec ripped off the white shirt he had been wearing underneath his jacket and tied it to a stick. He picked his way through the crowd in the direction of the far end of the tunnel. He turned and, with a wave, said, "Follow me! It's safe!" And he led the way out, the first refugees in the line behind him stepping tentatively out into the open air, unsure whether they would be met by more bullets.

The convoy emerged from the tunnel in a narrow line, two or three wide, and made its way through a small wooded area, which opened into a field. About one hundred metres away, the helmets of what I assumed were Serb soldiers were visible above a trench. I could make out four figures, though I suspected many more would be hidden in undergrowth nearby. The soldiers in the trench began letting off rounds – but, again, it seemed to be fire to intimidate and control, rather than wound.

Over a megaphone, the call came: anyone carrying a weapon was to hold it up in the air and walk slowly towards the trench.

"You will deposit your weapons on the left of the track in front of us; you will deposit all your valuables – your gold, your Deutschmarks, anything of value – on the right of the track as you pass our checkpoint. If we find so much as a needle on one of you after you've passed our checkpoint, we'll kill you."

I felt a hand grip my left wrist. It was Saša. He spoke in sharp, urgent bursts. "Mick! Quick! This is where we bail out. Take your jacket off. Show your 'Press' flak jacket. We're going for it."

I couldn't process the words at first.

"What do you mean? Bail out where?"

"Just follow me. I'll do the talking. Hands in the air."

"But I can't leave Ajdin," I said, bewildered and unconvinced by Saša's tactics in so far as I had understood them and had had time to make sense of them. It was the first time I had ever been on the receiving end of a glare from Saša. Anger bubbled just beneath its surface.

"Mick – we're saving our skins. The boys won't be harmed. Now, come!" And he yanked at my arm.

As I moved forward, I cast a glance over my shoulder. Ajdin was standing with Tarik. I believe that I read in his look in that moment sorrow and fear in equal measure. I had no words. I had either to trust Saša's instincts or stay with Ajdin and the rest of the convoy and fend for myself without my experienced, decisive, now dearest friend.

Just as, when we had been under fire the previous night and a hail of bullets had suppressed all reflection beyond survival, so I had no thinking time or space to dwell on the thought that was crystallising as I stepped away from Ajdin. Was I betraying him? Letting down Ajdin in the way that so many temporary hosts had, offering him and his fellow Hrvaćani villagers support and harbour, only to withdraw the protection when the threat intensified? I would return to the thought endlessly, tormentedly, in future days and months, but here I was, arms up in the air, Saša and me the only two men stepping out towards the Serb soldiers in front of us who were wearing navy flak jackets with the word 'PRESS' in white, block capitals blazed across our chests.

To either side of us, men in twos and threes were making their way slowly across the open area, rifles or pistols held high above their heads – a humiliation for those who had held out for as long as they could, refusing for some months to give in. Despite my terror at my own plight, I felt momentarily fraudulent. I was an observer, who, I presumed, would move on. They were living through an uprooting of their existence that would almost certainly be permanent.

As we approached the trench, Saša made for the soldier who seemed to be the most senior. I stuck close to Saša.

"Excuse me. We're two international journalists who were mistakenly caught up in the convoy. We need to see your commander," said Saša.

"Oh, you do, do you?" The Serb soldier was close to six feet two inches tall. He was wearing a greatcoat and a thick felt hat that bore the four Cs symbol. I was struck by his pencil moustache, slightly thicker than the classic Errol Flynn version but an unlikely affectation.

Saša ignored the note of menace. "Yes, I'm a Serb from Užice and Marko here's just back from the States. We're trying to tell the story of the war… from a Serbian perspective."

"Oh, really?" said the soldier sceptically. "Fact is you're with a bunch of balijas who've been trying to shoot the shit out of us for months now. You're guilty by association." He paused. "Now what about I put a bullet through both of your heads? No one would ever know, would they?"

I froze. I felt my sphincter loosen. Far from freezing, Saša sustained a calm, firm tone.

"No, I wouldn't do that, if I were you. You see I'm a personal acquaintance of the Minister of Defence in Belgrade. Your commander can put in a call to Belgrade to check out my story. Minister Panić might not be too pleased if he learned that an experienced Serbian journalist had been…" Saša searched for the word. "Eliminated. He might ask questions. Ask what happened."

I estimated that the soldier was probably not even twenty-five years of age. Saša was chipping away expertly at any solid ground he might have felt he was standing upon.

"Who's the commander? Who's your boss?" Saša sounded firmer still, as if obliging the young soldier to reply.

The soldier gave Saša a sneer. "Media scum!" he said. "Show me your papers."

Saša and I fished out our papers from our inside pockets. I was now Marko, from Novi Sad.

The soldier turned abruptly and rummaged beneath the carpet-thick cloth of his greatcoat, releasing a walkie-talkie and clicking it into action. There was the usual scrambling feedback. When, finally, he made a connection, I thought I heard him say that he had two journalists who claimed to be Serbian and who claimed to know Minister Panić.

"Do you want to bring them in?" he asked.

I felt the pressure between my temples ease as the soldier waved the antenna of his walkie-talkie to the right of where he was standing and said, "You both wait over there. Somebody'll come to pick you up. But not a word or any funny stuff from you… or else."

As we stood by the trench, the other soldiers began processing the armed men from Večići, overseeing a growing pile of rifles and pistols, and then making the men turn out their pockets and their backpacks.

After ten minutes, a jeep swung into view from the track behind the trench. Two men jumped down and, after being pointed in our direction, beckoned to us to jump into the jeep.

"In there. In the back," one said.

After the jeep had set off, Saša tried again.

"Excuse me, who's your commander?"

The soldier in the passenger seat turned. "Dušan Novaković is the commander of the 1st Kotor Varoš Light Infantry Brigade – but he's not around. We're taking you to Vojslav Kršić. He's assistant chief of staff."

"Okay. Thank you, thank you," said Saša.

The jeep made its way towards and into the village of Grabovica, turning in through the open gates of a school. Saša and I were dropped at the entrance to one of the school buildings where another two soldiers, with rifles over their shoulders, took us inside and upstairs to a first-floor office.

As we sat on standard, uncomfortable, wooden school chairs under harsh strip light and waited for the assistant chief of staff, relief coursing through me, I broke the silence.

"Smooth talking, Saša… I didn't like the look of that first soldier."

Saša exhaled. His was measured relief.

"Yes. So far, so good." Saša paused. "Timing's everything, Mick. And I just didn't fancy our chances if we'd been frisked along with the rest of them and they'd found we were wearing Press flak jackets. We needed to front it up."

It all seemed so obvious, as he explained it. I hadn't anticipated that potential pitfall.

"I just hope Ajdin and Tarik are okay. I hope they don't think we let them down."

"Mick, you've got to ask yourself whether anything we could have done would have made them safer, if we'd stayed. We need to tell the story of what ethnic cleansing's really like. We're not much use dead, are we?" There was just a flicker of irritation in Saša's response, I sensed.

"No… I suppose not."

The door handle rattled. A man in camouflage uniform and a peaked cap entered the room with two armed guards behind him. I realised I had expected a military commander with grey streaks in his hair and a battle-worn visage. The man in front of us was at the eldest in his mid thirties with smooth features, neat dark brown hair and keen dark brown eyes that spoke of not inconsiderable intelligence.

He leaned over and proffered his hand. It was relaxed formality that would have been appropriate for people meeting for the first time at a mutual friend's dinner party.

"Vojslav Kršić, Assistant Chief of Staff, 1st Kotor Varoš Light Infantry Brigade. Pleased to meet you."

His handshake was firm, as one would have expected from a military man, his articulation strikingly precise and crisp. This wasn't the kind of world-weary local hick that I had for some reason been expecting.

"I'm told, Mr Našica, that you're an acquaintance of Minister Panić. How is he these days?"

If I sensed a trap being set, Saša was not for stepping into it.

"Please do call me Saša," he said. "What with the war and everything, I've not seen him for some time – but Živi and I go way back. We met first in the late '70s, I'd reckon. I last caught up with him in Belgrade when he was appointed to head up the JNA's 1st Army District. If you're speaking to him, mention my name. I'll tell you what he'll say. He'll say, 'Oh, Saša – that old rogue!'" And Saša managed a laugh.

Kršić knew he had been outbid and that, if he had met the Defence Minister during his military career, he certainly did not have the familiarity with him that Saša did. He turned to me.

"And you, Marko? I see you're from Novi Sad."

I had never been to Novi Sad in my life.

"Yes, yes – but I left Serbia several years ago for the States."

"I can tell," said Kršić. "You even speak Serbian now with a little hint of an American accent."

"I was based in Connecticut. Filing articles for a British newspaper. But, when the Federation began to break up, I wanted to come back to see for myself what was happening on the ground."

"Ah, Connecticut!" said Kršić. "I love New England! Especially in the autumn. And don't they call it the nutmeg state and – what's the phrase? – the land of steady habits? Yes, that's it."

"They do, they do," I said. I had no idea whether either moniker was correct or not.

Saša moved to change the subject abruptly, aware that I could begin to drown if the commander across the table began asking me about landmarks in Novi Sad.

"So, sir – what's the story round here? We were driving out of Banja Luka when we came across this column from Večići. We were asking them what was happening and then we came under fire. We were carried along with the column as they fled. It wasn't till we got here that we could let your guys know who we were."

Kršić sat back in his chair, rocking it gently on its back legs.

"Gentlemen, we've been engaged in a delicate tightrope walk in the Kotor Varoš area for over six months now. We've tried to protect civilians across the whole area – civilians of all ethnic backgrounds – but, since March, in the non-Serb villages around Kotor Varoš, we've seen Muslim and Croat paramilitaries in camouflage uniforms and with automatic rifles not just guarding their homes and cafés but also actively attacking Serbs and Serb targets.

"You may know this, gentlemen, but Kotor Varoš was an Ustaše stronghold during World War II and many Serbs were murdered there. They just weren't prepared for war. In June, a soldier was killed nearby. Serbian civilians in nearby villages took it as a signal that history might be about to repeat itself.

"One of our senior officers – Slobodan Župljanin. He's commander of the 5th Company of the 122nd Light Infantry Brigade. He was in a car ambushed by machine-gun fire. He and his driver were wounded, his escort was killed and there were fifty-two bullet holes in the vehicle. This is the kind of provocation we've faced. Without our intervention, there have been times when the road from Kotor Varoš to Banja Luka would have been impassable for Serbs."

Kršić insisted that Serb units had attempted to strike deals with Muslim and Croat villages – successfully in the case of Garići, Šiprage and Zabrđe. There, villagers went about their lives unharmed, he said. But elsewhere, such as in Ajdin's village, Serb leaders had been lured into traps, offered negotiations, and then fired on when their delegations arrived.

I cut in. "Sir, we've not been there but I'm told that Hrvaćani, for example, was reduced to rubble by Serb forces. Did it really need that kind of bombardment?"

Kršić smiled but without mirth. "I think you'll find, Marko, that those reports are an exaggeration. Perhaps some tall tales from your Večići column."

I sensed that Kršić was weighing in with every ounce of his intelligence, sophistication and articulacy, each point delivered in a polished, civilised manner to paint a picture of a disciplined military force dispensing fairness and protection where it was earned; but it was one that was occasionally forced into an armed response. I had to admit: had I not heard a young teenager's accounts of his family's journey and had I not come close to losing my own life in a hail of Serbian bullets, I might have found it convincing. I did concede to myself that I had not had the presence of mind to push Habib or Ajdin or anyone else on the scale of any Muslim or Croat guerrilla or paramilitary activity prior to the launch of the now overt Serb ethnic cleansing campaign.

"But, sir, we Serbs will always be associated with ethnic cleansing after that film from the camps at Omarska, Trnopolje and Keraterm was broadcast to the world," said Saša.

I appreciated Saša's disarming description of 'we Serbs'.

"Saša, I can't account for what went on everywhere but I can assure you that, in my area, the only people who were removed were Muslim and Croat fighting men. And, when they surrendered to us, we put them on buses and drove them to safe places of their choosing."

The conversation was at risk of continuing into daylight. Saša was keen to clinch our safe passage, I sensed.

"So, sir, do you need to call Minister Panić's office or are we free to go?" Saša asked.

"I don't think a call will be necessary. I just hope that, as good Serbs, you'll be able to tell our side of the story, report on the pressures we've been under over the last few months."

Kršić asked whether Saša and I would like to be driven back to Banja Luka.

"I'll tell you what. How about a driver drops us close to Travnik? It'll be great if we can confirm that Bosnian Muslims are reaching Muslim areas safely and put that story out to the world," said Saša.

Kršić paused. I sensed that Saša had snookered him. How could he refuse the request if his account of his and complementary units' firm but fair approach was genuine?

"I can probably get you to Smet. Then, you're on your own," he said.

I would swear that I saw a glint of frustration in Kršić's eyes as he made the concession.

Twenty minutes later, Saša and I were in a police saloon car, heading south from Grabovica. Smet was a drive of fifty kilometres and there were another fifteen kilometres from there to Travnik.

As we settled on the back seat and I began to feel that we had effected our escape – or, rather, Saša had – I laid a hand on Saša's shoulder and said quietly, "You're a fucking genius, Saša. A genius…"

Saša put his finger to his lips. Best not to risk their driver or his sidekick sensing any triumphalism or trickery.

As the car rattled off at a crazy speed in the direction of Knežovo en route to Smet, I relaxed back into his seat. I registered again just how exhausted I was, but the aches and the fatigue felt as though they were seeping out of me in a consistent flow into the upholstery.

"You okay, Marko?" asked Saša. "We'll soon get you back home to Novi Sad…" I smiled and said nothing.

And, at that moment, the thrill of the prospect of writing my account of our ethnic cleansing experience rushed through me like a charge. It was the first time for many hours that I had been able to think about what the purpose of our escapade had been. My mind began to swim with ideas, phrases, details I might use. And then the thoughts came to a shuddering halt: what about Ajdin and Tarik and Ahmed and the rest of the Večići convoy? Would we ever see them again?

20

NOVEMBER 1992

Any sense of relief that I felt in the back of that car soon dissipated as we arrived in Smet and stepped out into the chill of the hour after dawn. Several single-deck buses were parked in a lot in the centre of the village and it became clear that the wretched, frightened cargo of refugees that had been put onto each bus was being released in stages – stages sufficient to allow the Serbian soldiers gathered round the perimeter of the car park to strip each individual of any cash, jewellery or other valuables that they might have bundled into bags they had been able to pack before being removed from their homes and villages.

It was a sight that a Renaissance painter might have captured to depict a crowd scene entitled 'The condemned making their way to Hades'. These were the elderly, the women and the children from villages across the area – demoralised, vulnerable, removed from the protection of their menfolk, cajoled into lines to be abused, humiliated and not so much frisked as robbed blind.

If I heard the word 'balija' again, coming from the mouth of a Bosnian Serb soldier, I felt I would scream. What was it about that insult that gave each Serb who used it so much pleasure? Surely the thrill of the taunt, its application to each and every Muslim at every opportunity, would dissipate through overuse? Apparently not. It did have a musical ring to it, I acknowledged, but I did think, "Really, guys! Get some more imaginative terms of abuse."

And I recalled the phrase 'worse *poturica* than Turk', a *poturica* being a biological Serb or Slav turned 'Turk' by Islamisation, the worst kind of traitor according to Serbian folk epics and Kosovan myth. But I had to admit to myself that it didn't trip off the tongue quite as rhythmically as 'balija'.

A soldier ten yards away from us was aggressing an elderly woman who had opened a bundle of her possessions that had been wrapped and tied in a blanket. Having taken from its contents a wedge of Deutschmark notes bound with an elastic band and some pieces of jewellery, he gestured to the thin, gold chain around her neck.

"That chain – take it off and give it to me."

"But… it's the last gift I have from my late husband."

The soldier slapped her cheek with an open palm.

"Balija! Give it! I don't give a shit about your dead husband."

I sensed Saša flinching, as if he wanted to intervene and slap him back on the old lady's behalf. The soldier realised that Saša and I were watching him, that we had seen him – an armed, fit man in his twenties – bullying a woman in her late seventies.

"You two! Next in line – behind her! Open your backpacks!"

As I instinctively went to move, Saša extended his right arm, blocking me. He gave no ground. Saša and I had put our Press flak jackets back on after we had stepped out into the car park and I was pretty sure that the soldier had registered that we had been delivered in a police car from the Banja Luka municipality.

"I don't think so, sir," said Saša. "We are Serbian journalists, covering the war from a Serbian perspective, and we have been guaranteed safe passage to Travnik by your commander, Vojslav Kršić, on the orders of Defence Minister Panić from Belgrade."

Saša paused – for effect, I guessed. "Commander Kršić was keen for us to see that Muslims were not being mistreated on their way to safe havens."

I would have sworn that Saša even risked a glare at the soldier. He took my elbow gently and eased me past.

All along the edges of the car park, refugees were being forced to open up their belongings. Bundles of Deutschmarks were placed on a low wall, alongside watches, necklaces, bracelets.

One of the more senior officers cruised up and down the wall, scooping the booty into a cardboard box. I wondered how it would be shared out.

I kept in lockstep with Saša as he strode purposefully towards the end of the car park towards the road that would lead to Travnik. Saša explained later that his hunch was that the Bosnian Serb writ stretched only as far as Smet. Get beyond the centre of Smet and we were safe, he figured.

Saša needed to pull rank one more time before we escaped beyond the ring of Serbian soldiers. The Kršić-Panić authorisation claim worked again, this time with an officer senior to the callow youth who had been menacing the elderly lady. It was a good line, but I sensed that it was as much Saša's firmness as his impressive connections that worked.

If I felt fresh relief as we appeared to put the Serb Army behind us, the respite was short-lived. Saša and I were free now to concentrate on the line of abject homeless, snaking their way out of Smet onto the road to Travnik. If they were on the road to freedom, it would have been impossible for a stranger dropped into their midst to divine it.

The convoy was a line punctuated with wailing and sobbing: the elderly unsure as to whether they had the strength to make the hours-long journey on foot or indeed what kind of welcome might await them at the other end; mothers struggling to keep their children in sight or their spirits up; and, of course, the total absence of able-bodied men draping the human trail with a pall of uncertainty and potential tragedy. A single message, unspoken, screamed out into the cold air. Had it been audible, it would have echoed and resounded endlessly, defying the woods on either side of the road to swallow it up: Will we ever see our husbands, our fathers, our children again?

The quiet of the morning was broken occasionally by the sound of shells overhead, targeted, Saša believed, at the Muslim village of Čosici ten kilometres into the valley; but the refugees so far were not targeted.

Five kilometres out of Smet, an impromptu 'border' had been constructed: a pile of boulders marking the end of Serb territory, its edges mined for good measure. I spent some time helping the elderly and women with children scramble over the rocks, a two-year-old on my hip first, then an elderly man incapable of anything beyond a restricted shuffling of his feet. I was shocked to see that he was still wearing the carpet slippers that he had had on when he was urged as a matter of urgency to quit his home and climb into a bus. I could have stayed all morning, a conveyor belt of the frail and the needy and the miserable being fed at the boulder pile.

But Saša cajoled me. "Come on, Mick. We're not the Red Cross. We can't help everyone. We need to get on." It was a call resonant with his decisiveness in quitting Ajdin and Tarik the day before. Tough but practical. Might I have to learn a lesson from him in that? I might but, for the moment, it felt counter-intuitive to me.

As we tramped on, the relentlessness of the misery around us came close to overwhelming me: the tears, the faces frozen in fear, the moon-eyed children too young to comprehend why they had been plucked from warm homes and dropped onto this near-freezing mountain road against a backdrop of occasional explosions. I had to choke off a desire to sob and I did so by channelling mournfulness into anger.

Which leader could fail to intervene in the face of barbarity that could produce scenes like this? But that was it, wasn't it? It was despair tucked away out of sight, people driven like cattle along routes that no one could access. No one but Saša and me and the refugees themselves. It was why Saša and I had to find a telephone line and put this truth out beyond the firewall that Douglas Hurd would have liked to build around the Balkans so that its people could 'fight themselves to a standstill'.

Just a couple of kilometres west of the boundary of the Travnik municipality, a Bosnian Army officer leapt out from behind rocks, momentarily shocking the convoy with a sharp shout.

"Everyone! Space out! The enemy lines are just four hundred metres away! They could shell us at any time! At least ten metres between each of you. There'll be too many casualties if you cluster together."

Without a word, the convoy thinned to a single file, only mothers with children staying close to one another. But there was no shelling, no additional trauma for these people now in clutching distance of a kind of relief. With the unexpected emergence of the officer, I sensed the nearby presence of the Bosnian Army's frontline – an invisible, comforting spirit.

And, finally, houses came into view along the roadsides. We were at Turbe, the hamlet at the western edge of Travnik.

"We're behind Bosnian Army lines now," Saša said authoritatively. "We're safe," he added. Ironic that the remark should come from a man from southern Serbia, I reflected.

The drinking fountain in the square in Turbe took on a powerful symbolism, a life-sustaining landmark at the end of a journey that many of the convoy must have feared they would not survive. The elderly, the young women with children, all queued patiently to drink and to splash clean the faces of the youngsters. Later, I would pick up a story passed down the convoy: one person had not survived. The old man in the carpet slippers, who I had helped over the boulder pile, had suffered what appeared to be a massive heart attack and had died on the roadside. His daughter accepted that the cause of death was coronary, but she put her own spin on it.

"My father died of a broken heart," she would say.

The four strongest members of the convoy nearby when he expired wrapped the man in a couple of blankets and carried his body down to Turbe. At least he would receive the burial he deserved in Travnik.

As the convoy trickled into Turbe and the numbers around the fountain swelled, a figure appeared from a side street, a young, handsome man in the uniform of the Bosnian Army. He might as well have been an angel, given his words of welcome to the people milling around.

"My name is Emir Ptica. I am with your army, and this is free territory. Welcome to Travnik. We have buses to take you the rest of the way," he said.

Some young mothers, who finally were beginning to dare to believe that their children might now be safe, reached out to touch the Bosnian Army badge with its six lilies on the sleeve of his shirt, as if it might be some kind of magic charm.

Saša whispered, "His family name – Ptica. It means 'little bird.'"

The 'little bird' methodically boarded groups of refugees onto buses to make the five-kilometre journey to the centre of Travnik. Saša and I were allocated space in what we would learn had been a renowned restaurant, Plava Voda – Blue Water. It had been temporarily requisitioned as the barracks for the Bosnian Army in the area. The refugees were housed in a Jesuit school. Some hot food and a space on crowded floors, already part-populated by previous convoys of the displaced, represented luxuries compared to the reduced expectations of their latest days.

I slept the sleep of the just, going under for several hours, despite the activity around me, as army officers milled about and chatted. I awoke to find Saša chatting with 'the angel of Turbe'. Emir Ptica was taking some downtime between convoys and was telling Saša that his job before war broke out had been as a dispatcher at the Travnik bus depot. He was proud that, just a few days earlier, he had been part of an operation that had organised the safe passage of up to thirty-five thousand refugees from another of Bosnia's former capitals, Jajce, forty kilometres north-west of Travnik.

Soon there would barely be a square metre of space across school halls, classrooms and public meeting spaces that was not occupied by a Muslim refugee from another town.

But, already, just over six months since the conflict had transitioned from Croatia to Bosnia, Emir was feeling the strain. He may have been a skilled logistics operative, he may have been wearing the uniform of the Bosnian Army, but the reassuring welcome that he offered wave after wave of refugees was masking deep misgivings.

He looked up at Saša and said, "It's got to the point now where I can't look those people in the eye, when they land. They all look into mine. But there have been so many thousands of eyes – tired, scared, lost. Every night these days is a flashback to the night before and a taste of the next night."

He looked down, as if the weight of the sorrow he was witnessing, day after day, night after night, was dragging him down; then it was as if he had snapped out of it, dug out from somewhere deep down some more resilience. He stood up, as if to go.

"Work to do. Better get on," he said.

As he turned to go, I had a thought. "Oh, Emir. By the way, if you hear of a convoy of buses coming from Grabovica, can you let me know?"

"Yes, of course," said Emir.

"I'm hoping some people that we were with might make it this far," I explained.

"I'll let you know," said Emir.

Early the following morning, I woke and stepped out into the fresh air. It tasted as if it had been rinsed clean with rain overnight. What I witnessed confirmed to me a truth about Bosnia that would prove to be unerringly sound and would draw me back time and time again in forthcoming years – during and well after the war. And it was this: once a traveller headed south from the drab flatlands in the northern belt, there was no end to the settlements tucked away like hidden jewels. After a journey across fertile plains in the south-west beyond Kupres or after a tortuous drive down a mountain pass in the centre of the country, a town or a village would emerge that would take the breath away and make me say to myself "How did I not know about this place?"

Jajce and Mostar were obvious examples but, even after my initial powerful reaction to Travnik on that cold morning, I couldn't have forecast just how powerfully I would be drawn back to that town in the years that followed. Though my heart leapt at this initial exposure to its improbable location and quirky charm, I couldn't have foreseen that I would wake up regularly in the middle of the night in my London home, well after the war had ended, and long to be back in Travnik.

As soon as I stepped out of the makeshift barracks, I was met with the sight of the real Plava Voda. The restaurant was named after a broad stream alongside it that tumbled down from the Vlašić mountain range, which all but filled the sky to the north of the town. The flow descended in small waterfall steps as the stream reached the east side of the town before finally tipping into the River Lašva.

I imagined myself on the terrace of that restaurant on a summer evening. What could be more conducive to relaxation than this permanent, soothing whispering of water, this view of water patterns on the surface shifting perpetually? Only a photograph could capture and freeze a single ripple pattern – and then that pattern was gone forever, never replicated perfectly again.

As I looked at the way in which the town was folded into the mountainside to the north, the river valley and the hills to the south, I was instinctively drawn to ascend, to pick out paths that would take me up the lower levels of Mount Vlašić and offer ever more dramatic views of how ingeniously this settlement had grown to fill a landscape that might have seemed an unlikely host to a locus of cultural, administrative and bucolic significance.

With every fifty metres scaled through the backstreets in the direction of the ruins of a huge fort perched above the town, Travnik unveiled its Ottoman architecture: the minarets and domes of mosques, the white houses with enclosed balconies that I would learn were typical of the traditional Bosnian Ottoman style.

An elderly man emerging from his front gate advised me, "Don't go beyond the fort, sir. Serbian snipers might be able to pick you off. They're up there on the mountain top."

The white walls of the fort were still intact, the handsome circular keep at its heart topped with a conical roof. It was an expansive, ambitious construction with an elevation that would have provided domination of the road and the valley below. I would learn later that it pre-dated the Ottoman Empire but the Ottomans developed and expanded it, transforming it into a fortress with watchtowers.

Back down at main street level, it was difficult to play the tourist because, even at this early hour, the streets were full of refugees looking for a better spot to squat than on a school-hall floor. I suspected that these were largely Jajce refugees, some of them with portable stoves and cooking pots. From what Emir had suggested, they had been able to gather up more of their possessions, some even yoking their horses to carts to make their escape. If their exile could hardly have been described as leisurely, it appeared that they had got out of town before the Serbs landed. It meant not only that they had more possessions, they had also escaped without the Serbs being able to strip them of their cash savings and their valuables. Travnik might be in danger of being overwhelmed by its own generosity but, small mercy, a windfall of unexpected trade was sweeping through town.

I managed to pick my way through the Old Town nonetheless to take in the Sulejmanija Mosque, its sixteenth-century exterior murals faded now. There was the elegant, slim sixteenth-century clocktower, the Sahat Kula na Musali, with numbers in a naïve style painted on its face. I saw the arched ceremonial domes above the tombs of Ottoman viziers on Bosanska, the high street, and even got as far as the church of St Aloysius Gonzage, its ornate interior tucked behind an unprepossessing entrance that looked like the façade of a local government building.

Back at the Plava Voda, Saša filled me in on Travnik's background. Implausibly, for a town of just twenty thousand inhabitants now and, presumably, several thousand fewer three hundred years earlier, it had been designated Bosnia's capital by the Ottomans in 1699, after the sacking of Sarajevo by Prince Eugene of Savoy. Equally implausibly, it had remained Bosnia's capital until 1850. And if Višegrad had claimed Ivo Andrić as its own, Travnik did too. The novelist and poet was born there and – as I would discover in downtime back in England – had captured in an inimitable novel, *Bosnian Chronicle*, the intrigues, the subtleties and the brutality of the power relationships that played out within Travnik as emissaries of Bonaparte's France and the Austrian Empire jostled for influence with the ruling Ottoman viziers of the day.

But if this mountain-valley settlement on the road between Sarajevo and Banja Luka, little known beyond Bosnia, had its own remarkable history, here was a new chapter that would continue to set Travnik apart: its leaders' generosity sublimating the risk of the town being overwhelmed by sheer numbers to an acceptance of its need to absorb the homeless and the destitute.

I drank in the spectacle and listened enthralled to its simple soundtrack: the milling around in the streets, the shouts exchanged, the polite tooting as a driver tried to pick a way for his car through the crowds without injuring anyone. And I sensed that all this activity might be presaging a gradual lifting of the pall of gloom that had oppressed the trails of refugees.

Yes, there were those they had lost – some temporarily, some permanently; but was the 'Little Bird' the first harbinger of a gentler future? There may be rockets and shells here and there in the future, more people may have to die, but could they now begin to rest, to start to reacquaint themselves with a degree of relaxation, to begin again to strengthen the relationships between themselves that had been frozen in place by fear and by flight? Perhaps.

I tried out my thesis on Saša and he wasn't dismissive of it, but he said, "Mick, there's another factor to key in and that's the elements. Before long, there'll be snowfall and, in mountains like this, it can be heavy and extended. Ironically, it might keep them safe from the Serbs for a while, but their next battle may be against the big freeze. How do so many people stay warm in an overcrowded town like this?"

I was becoming fretful about the need to file my stories but something held me back from composing them in those first twenty-four hours. I would sit down to begin the process but my mind would drift away to Ajdin. I didn't have writer's block – I never had writer's block – but, deep down, I knew my story would feel incomplete until I saw Ajdin again and learned what had happened to the rest of the convoy after Saša and I had peeled away, as some might say, 'to save our own skins'.

One of my inner voices was reprimanding me for leaving Ajdin. Another resisted: "We might just as easily have had bullets put through our temples by the Errol Flynn wannabe in the trench at Grabovica. It was a gamble. We got lucky. Or rather, Saša pulled it off."

But the debate was stilled because it wasn't long before Emir was back in the barracks.

"Mick – you asked about a convoy from Grabovica. Were they a group of women and children and elderly from Večići?" Emir asked.

"There were a couple of hundred – but mainly men of fighting age," I said.

"Well, there weren't many men, apart from some old boys – but they were definitely from Večići. Landed from Smet a couple of hours ago. We've just squeezed them into the hall at St Aloysius' Church. The Jesuit Gymnasium is full now."

I turned to Saša. "Sash! Quick! We've got to go."

"Where's St Aloysius'? I don't know it."

"I do. Quick. Let's get down there."

I picked my way through the groups of refugees in the streets with Saša trailing me, west along Bosanska and then south across a bridge over the Lašva. I found the hall adjacent to the church I had visited earlier in the day. I opened the door and saw inside what I estimated to be several hundred people: the elderly, women and children, as Emir had suggested. I sensed that this was the group that had waved off the convoy of men from Večići a few nights ago. And, again, Emir was right: no men of fighting age.

I felt a sense of mild panic. Perhaps Ajdin and the rest of the convoy had not made it out of Grabovica. Perhaps they were still there. Perhaps they had been killed. I was able to suppress the panic; something told me that the gloomiest scenario was not real.

And then I caught sight of Ajdin, standing up near the back of the hall. Ajdin had seen me and risen to his feet. He appeared to be undecided as to whether he should approach or not. I walked round the side of the Večići refugees seated in groups in the middle of the floor. Ajdin took some paces towards me as I reached the back of the hall. And then he stopped. He stopped ten metres from me and looked at me with a melancholic air. There was a hint of reproach in his expression that stopped me from approaching further.

At that moment, I noticed that Ajdin's left eyelid had drooped so that it part covered his eye, like a dromedary's. The word 'ptosis' flashed into my mind. I had known a girl who suffered from the condition. It was Ajdin's nervous reaction to his trauma.

Ajdin broke the silence. "Why did you leave me?"

I had no words in the moment. There was an awkward silence. It was probably only ten seconds, but it felt way longer to me.

"Everyone always leaves me." His voice was becoming more distressed. "Or they drive me away."

The weight of the anxiety of the last months, of being driven from village to village as the Serbs threatened anyone who might harbour the people of Hrvaćani, now risked crushing him.

"The only person I can trust in is my father… and… and…" Ajdin's inner dam broke and he jammed shut his eyes but couldn't stop the tears from streaming down his face. I moved to him quickly and held him close.

"And I think I've lost him," I heard him say, his words muffled in the cloth of my jacket.

I could feel Ajdin's sobs shaking his bony frame convulsively. His head was tucked neatly under my chin and I caught out of the corner of my eye Saša and Tarik, standing still nearby, on the fringes of the groups of refugees, observing with concern the sight of my seeking to console Ajdin.

"There, there, Ajdin. Don't worry. I'm sure he'll turn up here soon… safe and sound."

I knew that it was illogical to advise Ajdin not to worry but what else could I say? Ajdin began to regain some composure. He eased out of my embrace and looked up at me.

"No, Mick. I think I've lost him…" He paused. "You know, I'm getting used to dealing with the fear… but I'm not sure I can cope without my dad."

I put my hands on Ajdin's shoulders and, as best I could, looked him straight in the eye.

"We'll find him, Ajdin. We'll find him." I cast round for reassurance. "Saša has loads of contacts. He'll help us find him. I promise." If it was lame, it was the best I could come up with.

"Come on, let's go get some tea." And I led Ajdin in the direction of a queue for a hot water boiler, where a couple of Travnik women were dispensing black tea. As we made our way out of the clusters of refugees camped on the floor, Saša and Tarik came either side of Ajdin, each laying a hand on his shoulder, then patting him in consolation.

Ajdin and I sat along the edge of the hall on uncomfortable wooden chairs, warming our palms on our hot paper teacups. We were both looking down at our shoes.

"Ajdin – I'm sorry we had to leave you," I said, looking up and across at the teenager. "Saša just figured we'd be killed if we didn't front up as journalists and ask to be taken to their commander."

Ajdin said nothing for a moment, then replied, still looking at his shoes, "It's okay. I understand. You had to do what you thought was right… and you're not Muslims. So the Serbs aren't after you."

He paused again. "I just wish my dad had had that choice." I felt it was an observation, no longer a reproach.

I left space for a respectful silence and then asked, "Ajdin, do you want to talk about it? About what happened after we left?"

He nodded and described how, after the armed men had handed their weapons in, the whole convoy had to pass the trench where the soldiers were standing.

"More and more soldiers kept appearing from the shadows and then a whole truckload of them arrived. They were really excited and they were cheering and shooting above our heads. Some of them were shouting, 'Oh, yes! We've got the balijas!'"

Ajdin explained how everyone was made to open their baggage and backpacks and turn out their pockets as they queued to pass the checkpoint at the trench.

"Families have lost their life savings," said Ajdin. "Including ours. My mum had been worried after we heard stories that when women and children were evacuated from their villages, the Serbs stripped them of all their cash and valuables. So she handed over our Deutschmarks to my dad. The hope was that we could make it to Travnik with our money intact. In that field outside Grabovica, they took everything we'd got. And everyone else's cash and gold. They'll have picked up hundreds of thousands of Deutschmarks in a couple of hours."

Ajdin said that, after being searched and frisked, everyone was made to lie face down in the mud in three lines as Serb soldiers picked their way through the group, looking for ringleaders.

"My dad was picked out because he had an expensive pair of leather boots. He'd saved up for them because they were proper hunter's boots. A couple of soldiers made him stand up. They said, 'Where did you get these boots? You must have killed one of our soldiers to get them.'

"He said, 'No, I'm a licensed hunter. They're my boots.'

"'Oh no, balija – you've killed one of ours.' And they started punching him and one hit him with a gun butt till he screamed. I was lying down but I was trying to look. I was so scared. They asked if he had family with him and he said no. They knocked him to the ground and then moved on."

Ajdin said they had then alighted upon Hodza, the Imam who had prayed with the children earlier in the day.

"He was wearing an embroidered kufi hat and one of the soldiers who'd been beating my dad said, 'Oh, you're the one with the hat on. You're the one in charge.' And he said, 'No, my child.' He always said 'my child'. He said, 'No my child. I'm not.'

"And another soldier, who must have been told what happened perhaps by the collaborator, Zec, chipped in, laughing. He said, 'No, mate. Their leader's Besim – and he's had his fucking legs blown off!'

"And he looked around at us, spreadeagled in the mud, and he laughed and he said, 'Where's Besim? Where is he? Where's your fucking leader now?' But they beat Hodza anyway. Hit him with a rifle butt as well and kicked him."

After a while, a call came from a solider in front of the refugees for all women and children to stand up. Ajdin was going to remain prone and stay with his father but his father made him stand up.

"'I don't want to. I want to stay with you,' I said. But he said, 'No – you must get up. Get up and you'll survive.'

"That's when I stood up and I was the last boy who got up from that group. We were told to walk ahead and not look round. But as I picked my way through our men, there was just one lying on his back. It was Hodza. He had blood all over his face. I didn't see him move. I couldn't tell whether they'd killed him. And then they made us walk down the road towards Grabovica. There were about twenty-five of us: ten girls, ten women and five or six boys."

Ajdin said that, as their small group made it to the outskirts of the town, people were gathered in front of their houses.

"They were normal people. Civilians, elderly people, and they were waiting for us: spitting at us, cursing us, throwing stones at us – just like at Savići. And the soldiers told us not to look but just to walk on."

Eventually, the group of women and children reached the school where Saša and I had had our meeting with Kršić.

"In the playground, they told us to line up, shoulder to shoulder. There were soldiers in camouflage uniform, each with an AK-47, behind us. I thought, 'This is the end.' Because they had lined us up, I thought this normally meant execution."

"Were you afraid, Ajdin? Were you afraid of dying?" I asked him.

Ajdin thought, as if withdrawing the specific sensation from the recesses of a memory crammed with recent, traumatic episodes. "Yes, Mick. I was. Of course I was – but, you know, I think a little part of me felt that, if that was it, if it was all over, then it might be a relief."

Ajdin said there was an excruciating two- or three-minute wait as they listened for the click of a rifle or attempted to catch out of the corner of their eyes whether the soldiers behind them might be raising their weapons, as a firing squad would.

"And then this guy with a big hat and a greatcoat walked into the playground and introduced himself, though I didn't catch his name. He told us that we women and children would spend the rest of the night in the school and he guaranteed nothing would happen to us."

Ajdin and the rest of the women and children were taken to a first-floor school classroom and asked to pick a desk and sit behind it. An armed guard sat in the teacher's chair at the front, another on the teacher's desk.

Eventually Ajdin saw military trucks pull into the schoolyard and soldiers whipped back the tarpaulin at the rear of each truck and made the men inside step down. Each did so slowly and precisely because their hands were tied with rope behind their backs. They were led in a line into the school building, up the same staircase that Ajdin and his group had taken but up another level to the second floor, where they were distributed across classrooms there.

Ajdin said that, after a while, those in his classroom were told they could go under escort to see their men or their fathers, if they wished.

"So you got to see your dad after all?" I said.

Ajdin looked down. "No, Mick. I didn't. I didn't dare go. You see, when they were beating him up and he said he had no one with him, I was afraid that, if I went to see him, I'd get him into trouble. I was afraid for his safety." He paused and qualified: "And for mine too."

Ajdin said that one woman, a newly-wed called Hajrija, had gone to see her husband, Sead. She came back and said he had been beaten black and blue but had managed to let her know that all the men who'd left Večići and survived the trek were there in those schoolrooms.

"Now, of course, I wish I'd gone to see my dad. If I never see him again, I'll regret it for the rest of my life," said Ajdin.

The following morning, another soldier came in and told the women and boys that they were all going to Travnik and a bus was waiting for them outside the school. The bus was around two hundred metres beyond the school gates.

"They told us to walk slowly. A guard with a rifle said, 'If you run, I'll kill you. You can't run, you have to go slow.' But there were angry people on either side of our path to the bus. What do they call it? You know – running the gauntlet. None of us wanted to be first to go – but, eventually, this kid from my class decided to go."

Ajdin said the boy made it halfway to the bus before people from the crowd with sticks and axes jumped at him and clubbed him to the ground. Others from Ajdin's group followed, taking beatings themselves but trying to drag the young boy to the bus. Ajdin had held back until he was one of the last and he had to go.

"I started walking and my mind was just fixed on getting to that bus. I felt a terrible beating on my back but I just kept walking. I just didn't care. I was taking blows to my back, my backside, my legs – and I got so close.

"Then an old lady, dressed in black, jumped out and I saw the glint of a blade. It was a knife from the kitchen. You know, a proper carving knife. She grabbed me by the neck and I could feel she was trying to push the blade at it. I tried to wrestle her off but I wasn't strong enough and it flashed through my mind again: 'I'm going to die.' She was screaming, 'Let me kill one balija because two of my sons died in Večići.' And all of a sudden, a guard flipped her off me and threw me into the bus and closed the doors. I was the last one to make it."

Ajdin said that most of the women and children on the bus were crying and desperate for it to pull away. For some reason, the ignition of the bus wouldn't spark.

"And these people, from the gauntlet we'd run, were all around the bus, shaking it, banging the windows, rocking it till we felt it would tip over. And then, eventually, the engine fired and we were about to go."

Ajdin swallowed. I sensed he was trying to compose himself to recount a key moment.

"Finally, when the bus started and we started moving off, I turned round and I looked up and, on my right, on the second floor where our men and my dad had been taken, I didn't see a body but there was a hand that waved like this."

Ajdin made a slow, swinging, waving action with his hand.

"And I can't get the image of that hand waving out of my head. Was it my dad? I can't know." And Ajdin swallowed again and looked down at his shoes. I laid my right hand gently on his back.

Ajdin said the guards on the bus told them not to speak so they passed the journey in silence, but there had been one other person on the bus apart from them and the guards.

"It was that Zec guy, the collaborator. And the soldiers on our bus were saying what a great job he'd done. Somehow he must have alerted them to where our convoy was. Maybe he was giving signals with a torch, I don't know. Anyway, they were able to surround us and capture us – probably thanks to him."

Once the bus arrived at Smet, Ajdin spotted in one of the adjacent buses, in the group of over a dozen that had been penned into a corner of the car park, some of the people who had waved off his convoy from the town square in Večići.

After several hours, after each bus's occupants had been released, frisked and relieved of their valuables, he was reunited with his mother somewhere between Smet and the boulder pile marking the limit of Serbian territory.

"She's over there with two of my aunties." Ajdin gestured at a group of women in the middle of the hall. "She's distraught because I was separated from my dad. She fears the worst. And so do I."

I asked Ajdin to describe the commander who had walked into the school playground. From his description, I knew that this was not Assistant Chief of Staff Kršić. Perhaps it was Brigade Commander Dušan Novaković.

"Ajdin – listen. Saša and I were taken to meet a guy who was probably second in command in the area. He was a proper soldier. I don't believe for a minute he would have put to death your father and all the men with him. He boasted about how even out-and-out fighters – Croats and Muslims – were made to lay down their arms but then driven to safe places."

I turned to Saša, who was sitting with his elbows on his knees, munching an apple on a chair ten metres away.

"Saša? That guy, Kršić. He wouldn't let his men kill the men from the convoy, would he?"

Saša shook his head. "No, I wouldn't have thought so. He talked some nonsense but I think he's a pretty straight guy."

"So, Ajdin's dad – he should be okay, yes?"

"Well, yes. I'd have thought so."

Ajdin grinned weakly. He had no capacity for injecting that smile with any real hope, though.

I pulled my wallet from my inside jacket pocket and picked out three one hundred Deutschmark notes and one fifty.

"Here you are, Ajdin. Give that to your mum. It'll tide you over for a while at least."

Now Ajdin did smile with conviction. "Oh, thanks, Mick. She'll be really grateful. We're all really grateful. You're very kind."

Saša and I headed back to the barracks and, on the way there, managed to find a hotel with spare rooms for a couple of nights, its owner delighted to find paying guests. Once we had fetched our bags and settled in, the task of writing up our experiences began. I spoke to Paul and talked him through the story. Half an hour later, Paul called back: there would be a front-page news story, the first ever account of an authentic ethnic cleansing experience, and a double-spread inside, telling in detail the story of the convoy.

It would have been understandable for me to have felt overwhelmed by the scale of the task, given the unique and traumatic events we had been through; but instead, after I had scoped out the pieces in my head and in bullet points on paper, they flowed without obstruction and I felt the inimitable adrenaline rush that accompanied the crafting of my favourite or most important pieces.

After I had completed the front-page story and the double-page write-through, I decided to knock out as well a short think piece on my recurring theme: how was it that these people could be chased cross-country like cattle just hundreds of miles from the borders of the European Community? Perhaps that was a job for the paper's editorial writers. I didn't care. They could use it or not, as they chose.

After more than three hours, the task was complete. It took another half hour or so to dictate to the copytaker – an additional pleasure, as I could hear down the line Mary rattling at her keyboard with speed and, I knew from experience, with impeccable accuracy. And I always warmed to the little commentary she would make at the end of each piece – just as she had done when I had dictated to her the story of the orphaned Delila and Azra.

"Heavens, Michael. That's an awful way to treat fellow human beings, isn't it?" she said on this occasion.

Although it was the middle of the afternoon, I lay on my hotel room bed, grateful for this new-found privacy, and fell deeply asleep. Ninety minutes later, I was awoken by the hotel receptionist banging on the door.

"Mr Morrison! It's your editor. He needs to speak to you urgently."

I wasn't sure how long the receptionist had been banging at the door but I felt as if I had emerged from the depths of a warm, comfortable, totally enveloping, pitch-black abyss. I trembled slightly at the shock of being jolted awake.

There were a few small details that Paul wanted to check. He dared also to question a couple of my descriptions, despite my reputation for being notoriously touchy at anyone I suspected of trying to 'monkey with my prose'.

But Paul continued. "Two things. First, this is really tremendous stuff. It's vivid and it doesn't go looking for a response of outrage. The details demand it on their own. Second – you really need to come back to the UK for a bit. The stories about the camps were traumatic enough but I suspect, after a couple of days, you might crater when it dawns on you how close you were to not surviving."

He paused. "Come back, catch your breath. Spend Christmas with your family and, in the New Year, if you want to go back, then I won't stop you."

"Thanks, Paul," I said. "Thanks for the plaudits. I appreciate them. As for coming back – well, you may be right. But that lad I wrote about, Ajdin. I have to make sure he's settled before I head back. I'm hoping his father will turn up, unharmed. Just give me a few days and I'll head back."

Although it would be some time before I saw my pieces in cold print, as always, when I did, it gave me fresh thrills. The front-page article was headed 'Revealed – the brutal reality of Bosnia's ethnic cleansing shame.' Inside, the strap across the top read 'The misery of Bosnia's Muslim refugees – homeless, humiliated and shot at like fish in a barrel.' A strap below read '*Times*' man's first-hand account of deadly human traffic.' And they had published my think piece under a heading 'Where are you, Mr Hurd, as Bosnia's Muslims flee?'

I would spend some time reading and rereading, my heart warming at phrases or passages that I felt I had captured well. It was a satisfaction that was only deepened by time putting space between my creating and revisiting my words.

"Heavens – that's good!" I would say to myself privately, but always with a nod to my subjects – the victims of this 'cleansing'.

Every day I would go back to St Aloysius. The Večići refugees had now been supplied with sleeping bags and were given regular hot meals. The people of Travnik's reserves of generosity showed no signs of running out and there was plentiful produce from the surrounding area to ensure that there was enough for everyone.

Out in the streets, the air penetrated the lungs like an ice-cold drink. Saša was right: snow couldn't be far off. When I could, I would persuade Ajdin to come out and walk around Travnik to get some fresh air and perhaps take his mind for a few moments off the ill-disguised anxieties of a community without its menfolk; but as each day passed and Ahmed and the rest of the men failed to materialise, those anxieties became keener, the number of mothers and wives in tears at any given time had increased exponentially, and the only resilience toughening was among the youngsters, perhaps subconsciously preparing themselves to step into the shoes of their missing fathers.

"I have to keep strong for my mum," Ajdin told me in a backstreet near the river. "I might be all she has left." Back in the church hall later, I noticed Tarik scurrying around, fetching tea for the elderly and generally trying to keep spirits up. The class joker had had heavy responsibilities laid upon his shoulders. Overnight, he had grown up. Overnight, he had had to grow up.

On the day before Saša and I had planned to leave, I found Saša in the hotel foyer looking grim.

"Mick, I managed to get through to Kršić in Kotor Varoš. Asked him about the men. Asked where they'd gone after they'd been housed in the school. He was very evasive. He sounded shifty." He paused. "I don't think it sounds good."

The following day Saša and I said our farewells to Ajdin and Tarik, we promised to do all we could to find out where the men of Večići and Hrvaćani were being held, and then we were off in an UNPROFOR vehicle that would take us on the first leg of our trip to Split in Croatia.

From there, I was to take a flight to Paris on my way back to London and Saša would head for Zagreb.

As Saša turned away after a final embrace and headed in the direction of the railway station, I felt a pang of regret. What would I not have given to have spent the evening in the bar of the Astoria, with Saša delivering his latest commentary on the war and the world, a chunky brandy glass in his hand, the wings of his Chesterfield armchair enveloping him like a comforting, protective spirit? I didn't know how he felt but I felt irrevocably bound to him – for life.

21
JUNE 1993

"Sometimes you should just enjoy your heartbreak…"
Marta Perić

I hadn't 'cratered', as Paul had feared I might in the aftermath of my flight from Večići to Travnik but I was quieter these days. At home, I had been the garrulous one, the son and brother who always had observations to make, stories to tell from my journalistic encounters. But now, although I'd sketch out some of the details of my experience in Croatia and Bosnia, I tended to fall silent rather than fill any space in a conversation, even though there were abundant, shocking details I could have shared, from my last few weeks in Bosnia in particular. Were some of the details too graphic to share? Did I feel I couldn't do those episodes justice? Could it be that I, the wordsmith, might fail to find the right words? Surely not?

No, it was more than that: at the same time as I feared that friends and family might not be able to empathise sufficiently and that I might be irritated by any signs of a lack of interest, so I felt increasingly that this conflict was my property. I owned it; it was down to me to describe it and explain it – but not in ephemeral words in a bar or at a dinner table. Its episodes had to be packaged in my own sacerdotal tablets: finely crafted articles in an internationally distributed, serious newspaper. Should I choose, at the end of the war I could pull together every one of them. Together, they would represent *my* Bosnian chronicle – not just of the details of the war itself but, more importantly, of the people and the stories behind it. Dare I say it? An Ivo Andrić of my time. If the reflection was immodest in its audacity, I had thought it. I might be embarrassed at having framed it, but I couldn't deny it.

Paul wandered across the newsroom and laid an envelope with a Croatian stamp and a Dubrovnik postmark on the desk in front of me.

"Fan mail, I expect," he said with a smile.

"Bound to be," I replied.

As Paul wandered back to his desk, I handled the envelope with curiosity and a sense of quiet excitement that made me pause to open it. Like an unexpected love letter, better to savour the anticipation than to tear it open. I didn't recognise the handwriting, but it had the delicacy of a woman's hand. Perhaps it was an update from Marta? Yes – she was the most likely author.

The writing paper was light and delicate, its grammage only slightly heavier than tissue. The script was in biro – wouldn't Marta use a fountain pen? – and written in Serbo-Croat.

Dear Mick, it read.

> *I hope you don't mind me writing to you, but you were so kind to the people of my town in letting the world know about the terrible things that were happening to us in 1991. We are still so grateful.*
>
> *Because you both got on so well, I thought I should write to tell you that my dear husband, Branko, died in action some weeks ago.*

The revelation came at me like a mugger: unanticipated, shocking, and brutally violent. In the calm of the newsroom, I must have started visibly. A cartoonist would have caricatured me with a dropping jaw and eyebrows leaping from my face.

> *We don't understand entirely how it happened. He had been off on manoeuvres for some weeks and was in Platak, not far from Rijeka and close to the Risnjak National Park. It should have been safe territory. It was firmly in Croatian hands, but he was killed with a single bullet from a sniper's rifle. His soldier friends tell me he would have felt nothing.*

As you can imagine, I am distraught at the loss of a man who has been my soulmate over the last several years. As you witnessed, he was the perfect husband: caring, loving and always putting my needs first. I had never met such an admirable human being in my life before and I know that I never will again.

I weep for him and for myself, but I weep principally for my fatherless daughter, Nada. She had not even had her first birthday when he died and, just weeks after his death, she took her first steps. Of course, I will retain a piece of Branko in her but my heart breaks that she will have no memory of him and will never be able to grow to know him.

Everyone is being so kind to me that I want for nothing, so don't worry about me. I just felt you should know. You struck up such a good friendship with Branko so quickly and you were so at ease with each other.

I hope you have been able to stay safe in your work. Things are a little better here, but I suspect you have been drawn into other danger zones in this crazy Yugoslav war.

When it all settles down, if you are ever passing this way, do visit us.

God bless and best wishes.

Ivana.

I pushed back my chair, jumped to my feet and, waving the letter in my hand, shouted across, "Paul! Gotta go!"

"Go where?"

"Croatia… like now!"

"Why?"

I left the question hanging in the air and headed down the stairwell. I couldn't hold back the tears as I made my way down to the street. I stood outside for a moment until I was able to control my quivering bottom lip and wipe away tears that crystallised in a salt taste. The image of Ivana and Branko in their flat was sharp in my mind and, even more than one year on, I swore I could capture still the calmness that they had spun effortlessly around themselves: Ivana at peace in her unspoken adoration of her man; Branko, brimming with self-confidence and compassion, wrapping an invisible protective cloak around his bride. They were two beautiful people, like a pair of chemical elements whose combination produced a compound more powerful than the sum of their individual atoms. They had been living proof that we flourish together, we perish in isolation. Now their chemistry was undone.

I walked to a call box and rang my father.

"Dad. It's Michael. If I say something to you, do you promise you won't be cross?"

My father, nonplussed initially, said eventually, "No, Michael. I can't promise. Depends what it is."

His response momentarily took the wind out of my sails, but I ploughed on. "I think I'm going to get married, Dad… only not to Beryl."

Beryl had been my most recent girlfriend. Her name was Angie but she had gained the nickname Beryl from Beryl the Peril, the mischievous character from *The Topper* comic, because of her tomboyish preferences and intrepid nature. She and I had never fallen out. She had been a lot of fun and a good counterbalance to my innate cautiousness, but work commitments had led to our drifting apart.

"Well, who to? I mean… are you sure about this?"

"Yes, yes, I'm sure I'm sure. She's Croatian – just like Mum. She's got a daughter. Called Nada – just like Mum. Her husband's just been killed in the war. Can't you see? It's fate. I have to marry her… No, I mean I want to marry her. I need to marry her."

There was silence for a while from the other end of the line.

"Well, it sounds a bit impetuous to me," my father said. "And what does the lady herself say about it? Surely she's still grieving?"

"I haven't asked her yet. I'm just ringing you to tell you that I'm flying out to Croatia today. I'll bring her back home. Maybe not straightaway… but soon." I paused. "Dad, you'll love her. She's the gentlest thing. I need to be with her… and I think she needs me."

With Dubrovnik's airport at Čilipi still out of action since the JNA had taken it over and looted it ahead of their siege of the city, I had to fly into Split and take a hire car down to Croatia's southern tip. I had called Marta and asked her to find out where Ivana was, so that I could visit her. I didn't reveal to Marta the true purpose of my 'mission'.

On the flight out, I had tried to rehearse my script; but this was not journalism. I hoped I could be eloquent and persuasive with Ivana, but it was unlike piling words onto a blank page. I hoped that the six months that had passed since Branko's death might mean she had regained some composure and could think about the next chapter in her life, but she would have grief, personal circumstance and, most likely, reservations to express about the radical life change I would be proposing. What if she said she couldn't leave Dubrovnik or Croatia and I couldn't persuade her to come and live in London?

I felt so strongly that this relationship was the right fit that I concluded that I would marry her anyway and work out of Dubrovnik or elsewhere in Croatia, whatever the challenges that lifestyle posed.

"Are you serious?" one of my inner voices queried.

"Dead right, I'm serious," said another.

But I was aware that my tactics were proving difficult to moor, even if my strategy was crystal clear.

I had been drawn powerfully to Ivana even as I first met her, a blissful, pregnant, newly-wed. The fact that she was unattainable and that her husband and I had bonded with such facility couldn't prevent me from being smitten with her. Love didn't work like that.

Now I was convinced that fate was calling us together. I believed in fate: not in a hapless, hopeless submission to events, but an acknowledgement that, in people's lives, some things happened for reasons they could not initially comprehend. But these were coincidences that shaped our lives irrevocably. Were they divinely directed? I couldn't know – but their frequency suggested they could not be random.

It wasn't right that Branko needed to die to bring about our union; but could it be that I might repair to some extent Ivana and Branko's now broken circle of happiness? If I lacked much of Branko's self-assurance, his physical courage, and his practical skills, I could offer to match his devotion to Ivana, his assiduous care and attention, and his kindness – though I hesitated before the daunting height of this last hurdle.

I had never raised a child, but that child would receive as much love as if she were my own flesh and blood. I would nurture her in the knowledge that she needed to be shielded from the tragedy of her first year with a love so special that she might never feel a sense of loss, never spot a gap in the seamless transition from biological to adoptive father.

If I wrestled with my tactics, most of my doubts were crowded out of my mind by anticipation of the future that lay ahead for Ivana and me. My heart swelled with exhilaration at the prospect of moving from a lifestyle defined by my profession and my professional success – satisfying and privileged though they were – to one with a dimension novel to me: complete absorption in another's personal fulfilment and completion. No – in two others' personal fulfilment and completion.

As I sat in my window seat in the aeroplane and looked out at the lights of Split below, I wondered what I had done to stand on the brink of such joy.

An inner voice spoke to me, as if out loud: "Hold on, son. You're not quite there yet."

My other inner voice, the kinder, less brutal voice, the voice I preferred, swatted away the challenge.

A voice came over the tannoy. There were ten minutes to landing.

Although it was over a year since I had seen Marta, the passing of time had done nothing to loosen the bond between us. I was aware of her son and her daughter in the UK and the US respectively, but she had nonetheless annexed me to her family. Perhaps it was that, because she knew the story of my late Croatian mother, she felt I needed a surrogate. On reflection, it was probably less complicated than that: two people of different generations who shared the same values, who lived in the same house during a time of trauma for them both. Of course they would grow closer together.

The hug that we shared after Marta opened her front door to me was proof that we were to resume where we had left off.

Marta had no additional news of the circumstances of Branko's death, but she had seen Ivana several times since she had been bereaved.

"She was devastated to begin with," Marta said, "but pretty soon I think she realised she had a daughter to raise and it wasn't a job she wanted to delegate to her mother. I think she's a strong girl, Michael. She'll never get over it, of course, but I think she's going to be all right. Well, as much as she can."

Marta paused and added a comment the significance of which she was at that moment unaware. "I mean she'll never find anyone as 'good' or as 'right for her' as him."

I struggled to stay silent. I had been on the brink of letting Marta in on my plan, the words queuing up to trip off my tongue before she made that comment. But I knew that I had to give Ivana the respect of being the first to hear my 'offer', and part of me thrilled inside at the thought of coming back from Ivana's to share the news of our imminent union with Marta. I guessed that, initially, she would be speechless for a few seconds, unable to process the information that she never could have anticipated, and then absolutely delighted for us both. Two of her favourite young people coming together – implausibly.

At this point my imagination was galloping ahead of itself, like a racehorse that had thrown its rider yet continued to think it could stay in the race: it was an image of Marta in an extravagant hat at the wedding, a gentle smile playing on her lips, delighted by this unforeseen, joyous coupling.

"Really! Pull yourself together!" an inner voice said. On this occasion, it spoke well. I was getting way ahead of myself.

Marta had photographs of Delila and Azra on the kitchen windowsill. The kitchen, rather than the main living room, was where the heartbeat of her home was located, so their position demonstrated that the children were still significant in her life. She said that Delila had stayed strong and had managed to pick up at school and do well. Azra, though far from delinquent, had suffered more. She lacked concentration and drive. She could be moody.

"Mind you, Michael, that lady whose family took them in – she's a gem. They fell well there. And, as for her moving them on, as she suggested initially; well, they're going nowhere else, I can tell you. The bigger girls are great with them too.

"We can go and see them tomorrow, after you've caught up with Ivana," Marta said.

"Yes, that would be great."

The following morning I tried not to show it but I felt close to being paralysed by nerves. Marta had arranged for me to go round to Ivana's mother's house at around 11am and the time dragged by. I had to force myself to eat toast and drink several cups of coffee when I felt like neither. I filled the time by recounting to Marta some of the tales of the last few months. Marta was particularly struck by the story of Ajdin and the ethnic cleansing episode.

"Really, Michael, we're creating a generation of children who'll be mentally scarred for life. We can't go on like this," she said.

Eventually, I found myself at the front door of a comfortable, detached home in the outskirts of the north of Dubrovnik. As ever, I had preferred to walk rather than take a taxi. By the time I was on my way there, I had given up trying to rehearse any lines. Far from feeling joyful and hopeful, I felt jumpy and irritable. I wanted to be with Ivana and, at the same time, I wanted the walk to take forever.

My heart was thumping and my stomach seemed to shift slightly as the door opened and Ivana stood before me. As usual, her straw-coloured hair, which would have been shoulder length, was parted in the centre and tied back. The large round pale blue eyes, the thin lips, the clean, simple features came at me like a flood. I hadn't forgotten what she looked like but, in the flesh, it was almost overwhelming. The only difference was that her whole aspect was overlaid with an air of fatigue. She was wearing a simple charcoal-grey dress.

"Ivana, I'm so sorry…"

Neither of us knew quite how to break the spell of our brief paralysis on either side of the threshold. We ended up stretching out our palms and touching fingertips, like two Scottish country dancers about to embark upon a reel.

"It's lovely to see you, Mick. I never expected you to come so far, so soon." She smiled a slightly embarrassed smile, looked down at her feet in vivid turquoise mule slippers. "You didn't need to," she added.

"Of course I did. I really did."

Ivana invited me in and introduced me to her mother, standing in the half-light of the hallway.

"Mick, this is my mum."

"Very pleased to meet you, Mrs Lovrić."

She was smaller than Ivana and my judgement was that, physically, Ivana took more from her father, whom I had not yet seen. I shook her hand. I suspected that her spectacles, with their black upper rim, and her platinum crinkled hair gave her a sterner look than she merited. She wore a maroon merino wool cardigan and a predominantly maroon pleated tartan skirt.

We walked through the hall and into a sitting room that was filled with bright January sunlight. It was the comfortable home of an affluent, middle-class family. Nada had pulled to stand against one of the sofas, a pile of wooden bricks on the carpet nearby.

"Now that she's on the move, we can't leave her for long," said Ivana.

Nada's hair was darker than Ivana's, closer to Branko's. She would be brunette rather than blonde. I wanted to lay my hand on her hair, conscious that, at that age, a child's hair would feel like the finest spun silk. She lifted her right hand in my direction.

"Ba!" she said. It was definitely "ba!" and not "Da!".

I crouched down to her and said, "Now aren't you a lovely thing?" Ivana's mother asked if I would like coffee. I lied and said that I would.

Ivana coaxed me into an armchair at ninety degrees to the sofa, while she sat in the middle of the sofa, Nada still leaning on it at her side. I didn't need to broach the subject of Branko. Ivana addressed it upfront. There would be no elephant in the room.

She told me that her expectation had been that he would defend the city until the siege ended and then go back to his work.

"But he was drawn into the army because he wanted to defend his country. And he started to go away on operations beyond the region. Sometimes I was minded to ask him not to go, to stay at home. But I knew that for him to miss some of the formative weeks and months of his daughter's life, the pull of fighting for his country must be really strong. He didn't talk about it much but I could sense he saw it as duty. And, with the ceasefire being signed and things settling down a bit in Croatia, I figured the risks probably weren't that high. I managed not to worry too much, while he was away."

Ivana paused. She looked up and into my eyes. "And then the news came."

Her mouth crumpled, her eyes pooled with tears, but she didn't cry. She was too far from me for me to reach out and touch her.

"You know, Mick, I just couldn't believe it." A tear or two did now spill but Ivana was managing to control her emotions. "It sounds as though it was such a random incident. So senseless, so unnecessary." She paused again. "But that's it, isn't it? It's all so senseless."

She reached out and stroked Nada's hair. Ivana's mother returned with a tray of coffee and, having distributed the cups, sat down on the sofa between Ivana and me. Hers was a presence I hadn't schemed into any tactics I had been able to come up with. I doubted I could make a pitch with her in the room, but I didn't feel as if I could ask her to step outside. So I blundered on.

"Ivana, do you know what you're going to do? About the future?"

Ivana placed her hands together in her lap and looked down.

"I've been thinking a lot about it – since things settled down, after the funeral and all of that and there's a friend of ours – Ante. Well, he wants to look after me… Me and Nada."

"But – who is he?" I wasn't sure that I had managed to conceal my shock.

"He's called Ante Koštro. He works on the land. A lifelong friend of ours."

As she spoke, an image of a small, squat man with a dark moustache and beard, a crumpled haircut and sleepy eyes flashed into my mind. It was Ante, the farmhand, the owner of Sherlock the donkey, with whom I had scaled the hill to the Fort.

"What?! Not little Ante – the guy with the donkey?" I said. I hoped it wasn't too obvious just how horrified I was at the prospect. My beautiful, gentle Ivana with a farmhand!

"Yes, that's him. I've known him since we were kids. Branko too. We were all at school together. He's a kind, kind man."

My tactics were scrambled, my strategy was in tatters but, through the haze of my panic, I managed to reason coolly that, if I didn't remove Ivana's mother from the room, I would have no possibility of clawing back the situation. I would have boarded a plane to Split, cranked my hopes up high, only to let a man with a donkey and a severe-looking lady in a tartan skirt put a bomb under my hopes and dreams. It might be brutal, even potentially rude, but I had at least to take away the obstacle that was Mrs Lovrić.

"Mrs Lovrić, I hope you don't mind but would it be possible to have a few minutes in private with Ivana?"

If Ivana's mother was surprised or affronted, she didn't show it.

"Of course. I'll take Nada out of your way too," she said.

Perhaps she had been expecting it. Perhaps she had been trying it on out of curiosity, hoping to hear what I might have to say. She lifted Nada and slotted her round her right hip. She closed the door to the living room behind her. I looked at Ivana. My heart was thumping again, as it had done as I stood on the threshold before the door was opened.

I leaned my forearms on my legs and clasped my hands together and said softly, "Ivana – I know that this might sound a little strange. It may not be what you were expecting but… don't do that… Don't go with Ante. It's not right for you."

Ivana looked at me with bemusement, as if I were speaking a language from the another part of the galaxy.

"No, Ivana. Be with me instead." And I fixed her eyes so that she knew I was serious. "You and me. That's what's right. After the tragedy, that's what's meant to be."

Ivana gave a single, sharp laugh. But it wasn't mirth or derision. It was utter shock.

"Mick?!"

"I know it might sound out of the blue, but I know it's right." I paused and allowed my eyes to dip from hers to her lap. "I've always loved you, Ivana. Pretty much from the first moment. It's terrible that we're where we are because of what happened to Branko – but I'll make the future so much better for you… I'll do anything for you… I'll do everything for you…"

Ivana issued another whispered 'Mick', this time overlaid with what I took to be incredulity. If I had brimmed with love for her in the past, she had never spotted it. While Branko was around, why would she? And now she was scrambling to recompute our relationship, I sensed.

Still in a whisper, Ivana said, "Mick… I had no idea."

I hoped that the shock might jolt her out of her Dubrovnik horizon and make her consider that she had endless alternatives – and one compelling alternative in particular.

"We'll buy a house in a nice part of London. In a few years, find a good school for Nada. I promise neither of you will want for anything. I'm going to devote my life to making you feel loved and cared for."

All of a sudden, Ivana's expression switched from shock to discomfort. She raised her right eyebrow quizzically.

"You want us to move to London?!"

Her tone revealed that the proposal had been so unexpected and so radical that, rather than jolting her out of the only environment she had known, it had plunged her into waters so uncharted that she was in danger of panicking.

"It would be a great, new beginning for you. For you and Nada. For all three of us. Some say it's the finest city in the world. You'd love it."

Ivana looked up at the ceiling and then back down again. There was still a look of shock and bewilderment on her face.

"Mick, I couldn't... I can't... I can't leave here... And you and me... Well, I'd never thought of it."

"But, Ivana, why would you have thought about it? All the time you were with Branko – I used to watch you and I envied you both. How much you loved each other, how complete you were as a couple. But now Branko's..." I hesitated. "Now Branko's gone, I'm going to try to make you feel as special as he did."

There was no apparent dropping of her guard or easing of her alarm. I sensed that I had been too hasty in painting my idyllic image of Mick, Ivana and Nada Morrison in a characterful house on the fringes of Hampstead Heath.

"Ivana – it doesn't have to be London. It could be Zagreb. Or Split. Or here... Or anywhere. I just need to be with you and to make sure that what's happened is the last awful experience you ever have."

I needed to leave some space for Ivana to redial our relationship, for it to dawn on her that radical could be good; it wasn't always frightening or disconcerting. There was silence. I didn't fill it, and nor did she for a period that felt like an age but was probably no more than thirty seconds.

"Mick, it just won't work," she said eventually. "We're from worlds apart... I can't go and live in London. All I've got is here." There was another pause. "And you and me... Well, I'm really flattered, Mick. I really am. I had no idea."

She looked up and into my eyes, prompting a pang to my heart. "But we really don't know each other. You might think you know me – but, really, you don't. I've known Ante for years. He's like a brother to me and Branko."

If I had expected some obstacles on my route to persuasion, Ante, the donkeyman, was never one that I could have dreamed up or catered for. I knew that she was saying that she knew what she'd be getting with Ante. No surprises. He would be no Branko, but he would be solid, reliable.

As for Ante himself, although he had paid a high price in losing his best friend, he would be gaining a spouse beyond his wildest dreams. He would be grateful to God for every second he had been allocated to spend with Ivana. In the school playground, she would have appeared untouchable: a friend but out of his league in the contest that matches man with woman and woman with man. And now, here she was, falling into his arms.

I spoke softly. "You don't need a brother, Ivana. You need a different kind of love to make you complete. I promise you: you can learn to love me." I paused. "You'll have no option." I smiled at her. "I'll bombard you with love."

Ivana shook her head and looked aside. She had been drifting from a blissful past into an inferior future, but it would have been a secure future. And now I had stepped onto the scene. I hoped I had set dynamite sticks into the very foundations of her assumptions.

She stood up and walked beyond the chair I was sitting in and, her back turned to me, gazed out of the window. I sensed she was now reaching a conclusion. Might those fizzing dynamite sticks have burned to the end of their wicks and blown her into a completely different future?

She turned to me, her arms folded. It was a bad sign. Folded arms meant defence. They didn't signal letting me in.

"Mick. This is so lovely of you. I'm really flattered – but I can't… I just can't."

I walked to her and laid my fingers gently on her biceps.

"Ivana – you can." I tried to sound gentle firm. She moved to my side so that my hands fell from her.

"I can't, Mick. I can't let Ante down for something I don't know is real."

"Oh, it's real, Ivana. Don't have any doubts about that. Would I have jumped on the first plane after I got your letter and dashed here, if it wasn't real?"

She looked down at the carpet and I sensed that she had no appetite for challenging my claim.

"Mick – I'm pretty much settled in my mind. After all I've been through, I just need some certainty. I can't take a gamble on a completely new relationship. I really can't."

Her tone was such that I realised the question was no longer up for debate.

She added with finality, "My parents are going to buy us some land – for a proper smallholding. I don't think we'll want for anything."

An image of Ante, Ivana and Nada in the sunshine outside a newly built villa in the countryside north of Dubrovnik flashed into my mind. Sherlock was munching grass, Nada was stepping happily among chickens and Ante was carrying out one of the multiple practical jobs that I with my urban upbringing and middle-class background had never needed to learn to master. Ivana's back was to the person taking in the scene – in this case, me. I couldn't see what kind of expression was on her face.

When I thought back to our exchange two days later, I sensed that seeking to undermine Ante was not likely to prove productive. I felt sure that Ivana knew her choice of a life with Ante was suboptimal, with all the cold, mathematical calculation with which that term resounded, but my pointing this out was more likely to entrench her in her position than to win her to my side. Although I could have tried harder to persuade her that swapping Ante for me was not a gamble, I didn't think I could have made her see it that way. I was a gamble; Ante wasn't. She knew precisely what she'd be getting.

However, even months later, I couldn't take the next logical step and concede that it could be the case that Ivana had called it right; that she had made the right choice. I couldn't concede that Ivana and Ante would make a better couple than Ivana and me.

As I had left her house, I had dangled one final string before her. Was I kidding myself in thinking that there might be a slender chance that she might reach out and grasp it?

"Ivana, I'll be here in Dubrovnik for a few days. Think about what I've said and, if you have even the slightest doubt, even the slightest temptation to change your mind, just ring Marta and I'll be round. Even if you don't want to change your mind but just want to talk about things – just call, eh?"

"I will, Mick. I will."

I leaned into her, kissed her left cheek and gave her a gentle hug. She didn't stiffen.

As I made my way down the drive, she shouted, "Come and see us before you fly out."

I turned. If it was well meant, the comment was nonetheless crushing. It suggested finality, not room for a rethink. Nada was holding onto Ivana's left leg. I winced internally. The child I had wanted and had drafted into my future was slipping away from me.

Beyond the garden, back out in the street, I felt my cheeks hot with embarrassment. If I hadn't blushed in Ivana's presence, I was making up for it now. And, as my inner voices squared up to one another to deliver their conflicting verdicts, I felt gloomily that, on this occasion, the kind, generous, supportive voice that tried to build me up was about to be routed by the brutal, critical, unforgiving voice that was forever seeking to diminish me.

"You complete idiot! You made a complete fucking fool of yourself in there! What did you expect? Flying over a thousand miles to a woman you hardly know and proposing to her! You're not just an idiot – you're a naïve idiot."

My embarrassment would surge to a point at which it felt like shame, and then it would subside, as my more generous side defended my motives before surging again.

Back at Marta's, the thought of not revealing what had happened soon evaporated. It felt right to tell her. What's more, might it have occurred to me subconsciously, or perhaps consciously, that Marta might just pick up the phone and suggest to Ivana that I might be a better long-term bet than kind but dull Ante? It would be a direct request too far of Marta, I knew; but perhaps she'd make the call anyway or pop round to Ivana's mother's home and reinforce my case without my asking her.

Marta was clearly shocked by the ambition of my pitch to Ivana, but she was totally supportive. In fact, she was thrilled by the idea of my making the offer.

"Mick, I didn't see it myself – but now you suggest it… Well, I think you'd make a lovely couple. I know Ante – he's a kind boy. But really, she deserves better than that."

I mooched around the house. I hated the word 'depressed'. I wasn't depressed; I was deeply disappointed and, to an extent, humiliated. And I could get no rest as the recollection of our conversation rattled around my head. I went into Marta's living room, usually an unbreachable, inner sanctum, the room kept for important visitors. But there weren't many important visitors – just friends, and friends were much more at ease in Marta's sun-drenched, south-facing kitchen.

After leaving me for a while to lick my wounds, Marta wandered into the living room, where I was sitting in a plush indigo and crimson armchair, staring ahead of myself, focusing on nothing, beating myself up and then being easier on myself. She stood above me and ran her fingers through my hair in a way that my mother might have done.

"Poor Mick," she said. And then, as if I were a third person being discussed by two observers out of my earshot, she said, "His heart is broken into pieces. And he's wondering how to put it back together again."

Marta crouched down by my chair and put a hand on my arm. "Listen, Mick. I'm not saying I've felt what you've felt but I've had my dreams shattered in the past as well. Many years ago now, but what you need to know is that sometimes you should just enjoy your heartbreak."

At first, the words made no sense to me. Or, rather, I understood each word. I just couldn't understand what they meant when strung together in a single sentence.

"What do you mean, Marta? 'Enjoy your heartbreak.'"

"These times are amongst the most intense of your life, Mick. As you get older, you have different satisfactions. Me and Nasko, we grew to know each other so well that, at times, we didn't even need to speak to be able to communicate with each other. But I think back and, in a way, I envy you that raw emotion of your twenties. You're looking for the right person and your emotions are careering around. Even the setbacks are vital. They hurt – but it's good hurt."

Marta paused for a moment. "You wanted Ivana to complete you; but you wanted to provide her with a caring, loving future. I happen to think you're right: that she'd be better with you than with Ante. I just think it was too much of a shock to her."

"So, do you think I messed up? Do you think I went about it all too quickly?"

"Mick, I think you had to. You didn't – she didn't – have four weeks to work up to it. You did what you did. You had the right motives, generous motives. I just think, in the end, it was too big a change for her."

She paused. "But it was dashing; it was bold. Not many people would have reacted in the way you did. You were prepared to make her a big offer. I think you're blaming yourself because it didn't work out." She paused again, then said forcefully, "Don't!"

Marta went on. "You've made a beautiful offer. You've been pushed back. Your heart is broken. Enjoy the heartache – because it proves you have the capacity to love again."

The comment demanded some space in which to expand and pulse outwards. For some moments, I was speechless as I absorbed it.

Eventually, I said, "Marta – she may drift away a little, through distance and time, but I'll always love her. I always will. She should be mine... We should be together."

Marta patted my arm again. "I know, Mick. I know."

As the afternoon drifted into evening, I dwelt on the phrase 'Enjoy your heartbreak'. If I would take some time to heal, I thought I might be beginning to understand what Marta meant.

I would see Ivana twice more before I left. The day after my unsuccessful pitch, I had gone to visit Delila and Azra at their foster parents' home. I was thrilled to see them, and I found them more or less as Marta had described them: Delila confident and chirpy and apparently unruffled by the traumas of the previous twelve months or so; Azra a little more remote and, I feared, having lost some of that constant questioning and curiosity about life that had touched me back in late 1991.

There had been one significant addition to the household: a cute bichon frise on which Azra focused most of her attention, giving her an excuse for not engaging more generously with adult visitors. And I learned something new: the Serbo-Croat for bichon frise was 'bichon frise'. I would never have guessed.

My time with the girls cheered me up temporarily and, when I returned to Marta's, she said that Ivana had phoned.

"I don't want you to get your hopes up, Mick, but I think she feels it's only right that she show you Branko's grave before you go home," said Marta.

The following day, Ivana drove to Marta's and took me up and out of the outskirts to a cemetery on a hillside north of the city. From there, there was a distant view of the Old Town and, some way to the west, a sight of a sliver of the Adriatic. If a chill wind was whipping through the cemetery that day, the sun was bright again. It was a lovely spot and I imagined Ivana sitting by the tombstone in the weeks and months and years to come and perhaps finding some peace.

I imagined her sitting alone on the grass by the grave, her arms looped over her knees, chatting to Branko, updating him on Nada, on the smallholding, on how much she missed him. She wouldn't say to his spirit or to the winds that carried away her words that it wasn't the same, swapping her soulmate for their loyal, reliable friend – but it would be written in bold between the lines. I felt a pang to my heart at the thought of her silent pain. That was what it was about: her pain, not mine.

The headstone was cream with brown, etched lettering: Here lies Branko Komlenac, killed in action on 10th November 1992, at Platak, aged 25. Much-loved husband, father and son. 'You died for your country, but you are always alive in our hearts', the inscription read. And the stonemason had managed to reproduce in a small, circular etching at the top left-hand corner of the headstone a copy of a portrait of Branko that I recalled from their flat: a handsome man, thick dark hair swept from right to left across his brow, with piercing eyes. It was a nice touch, I thought.

I persuaded Ivana to go for lunch with me at the Hotel Argentina for old times' sake – my old times rather than hers. I kept the conversation ticking over with tales of Delila and Azra and those surreal episodes during the siege when the Argentina's management had attempted to operate business as usual as shells and rockets whistled overhead and guests occasionally had to scuttle for cover from the terrace.

Ivana laughed occasionally and any tension that had been created between us two days earlier was beginning to wind down, though I didn't kid myself into thinking that the shock of my proposal that we uproot to Hampstead had evaporated completely.

The second and the last time I would see Ivana for some time was on Marta's doorstep, as I prepared to set off on the drive back to Split. Marta had clearly conspired with her so that, as I prepared to say my farewells to my surrogate mother, a knock came at the door and there was Ivana, in an orange anorak with a fur-trimmed hood standing on the doorstep, in her arms Nada tucked up warmly in a knitted hat and gloves.

"Mick, we've just come to say goodbye and thank you for making such an effort to come all this way. And when this is all over, you must promise to come back and visit us."

I was slightly taken aback and found no obvious words. I was thrilled to see her, though.

As I reflected privately that it might stick in my craw to come back and witness Ivana playing happy families with Nada and Ante on a smallholding just out of town, I heard myself reply, "Of course, Ivana. I promise. I promise."

In the car along the coast road back to Split, I felt calmer, even if I was still nursing an emotional wound that was hypersensitive to the touch. I had managed largely to mute the brutal voice in my head that tried to diminish me and I wondered whether what I had left was a tale with which I would regale friends and family in months and years to come: of how a lovelorn bloke in his twenties had flown across a continent to offer his soul to the woman of his dreams… only to find that a man with a donkey had got there first. A Croatian fairy tale of sorts.

And then I turned back to gloomy for a moment. Well, it might be funny at some point in the future, I thought, but, at that moment, all I felt was a deep lovesickness and an inability to believe that Ivana and I would never be together.

I plugged into the dashboard machine what looked like a home-recorded cassette that had been tucked in the driver's door. It must have been left by the last person to rent the car. A line of trumpets blasted out in unison. The song opened unusually with a chorus. It was the Beatles' *Magical Mystery Tour*.

And I smiled and wondered, "Where to next?"

22

SEPTEMBER 1993–MARCH 1995

Initially I had felt a little hurt when I told Saša of my failed pursuit of Ivana and he had chuckled and said, "Mick – you're priceless! Only you could cross a continent to propose to a woman who's just lost her husband and had no idea you held a candle for her. You're a hopeless romantic!"

But his smile had been benign and I sensed he was enjoying what he saw as my raw optimism. I weighed my hurt in the balance against the words he had said to me as we fled Serb bullets on a dark night between Večići and Grabovica. There was no doubt which words carried greater weight. I decided there was no need to sulk.

There were more urgent challenges to address as well. If it had looked as if it were game, set and match for Bosnian Serbs after they had mopped up around seventy per cent of Bosnian territory, Saša and I were sensing that the military balance was shifting unpredictably and that the new complexion of the Bosnian map might not be set in stone. There had been alliances between Bosnian Croats and the Bosnian Army to drive Bosnian Serbs out of some areas. Now there were report of Croats turning on Muslims and vice versa. And, in the domain of our old friend Tarik Begić, in the Bihać pocket in the north-west corner of Bosnia, Muslim was turning on Muslim.

Once the break-up of the Federation was complete and the conflicts were over, the tally of misery in this corner of the former Yugoslavia would prove to have been sky high: more Muslims would have been killed in the Bihać pocket in the course of the war in Muslim-on-Muslim attacks than were killed by Bosnian Serbs.

Although Hugh had already alerted me to strife in that area, Saša had a scoop fresh from the lips of Petra, Tarik Begić's assistant, who Lucy and I had met in the castle at Velika Kladuša and who I was convinced had 'history' with Saša. Perhaps even contemporary history.

"She said it was getting a bit hairy in the Bihać pocket," Saša told me, "so Old Man Begić told her to get the hell out and she's staying for a while in a flat he's got here in Zagreb. Had a nice spot of dinner with her the other night in a restaurant in the Old Town," he said.

"I'll bet you did!" I said, trying to sound prudish but concerned that I might just sound envious.

Saša said Petra had told him that Begić had not only cut all ties with President Izetbegović and been removed from the seven-strong Bosnian Presidency, he had created his own party, the Muslim Democratic Party, and then launched an 'Initiative for the Establishment of the Autonomous Province of Western Bosnia'.

"Petra says he now has a military greatcoat and a peaked cap. He's a proper pocket-sized general! All five feet five of him!" And Saša laughed, conscious that he had understated Begić's height by a couple of inches for comic effect.

"It's complicated, but I think what he wants to do is set up his own fiefdom and try to show Izetbegović an alternative way of protecting his people. Alija is resisting an ethnic carve-up of Bosnia but Begić thinks it's already the reality on the ground. So why not cut some deals to keep your own people safe?" said Saša. "Now it's got to the point at which Begić's forces are fighting the Bosnian Army."

I shrugged. If it was hard enough already to explain to a non-Yugoslav readership the causes of and developments within the conflicts, how could you even begin to explain this Muslim-on-Muslim violence?

But, if Begić was infuriating Izetbegović, the news from Sarajevo was not all bad. And one day Saša brought news from the heart of the Bosnian Government.

"Mick, I've had one of the guys in the President's office on the line. They're all pretty upbeat in Alija's team. What's that expression you have in English about the worm?"

"You mean 'The early bird catches the worm'?"

"No, no. Something about turning… Yes, that's it: 'The worm is turning.'"

Saša said that not only had they begun converting every manufacturing operation in Muslim areas of Bosnia into weapons production, they had also begun to receive significant amounts of cash from overseas that they could use to buy weapons on the international market in defiance of the arms embargo imposed across the region.

"This guy told me they've given a Bosnian passport to a billionaire from Saudi Arabia. He's from the family that tends to win most of the Saudi state's infrastructure projects. He goes by the name of Osama Bin Laden."

Some time later, I was up early and went down to the breakfast room.

"So, are we good to go – after breakfast?" I asked.

"Sure," said Saša.

After Saša's claim that the worm was turning in favour of the Bosnian Army and relaxing some of the grip held by the Bosnian Serbs, I had managed to get through to Ismail in Sarajevo, the retired chemistry lecturer with the bear-like, mild-mannered son, Ševa.

Ismail told me that Bosnian Serb heavy weaponry had been moved back from the hills around the city after a NATO ultimatum following a bombing of the Markale market in Sarajevo in which 68 people were killed and 144 wounded by a 120-millimetre mortar. Afterwards, life had been a little easier; but it was far from back to normal.

The bombing had stopped but the siege frontlines remained. There was the odd sniping incident, but people had taken to the streets again, the trams had started to run, businesses had begun to reopen and small quantities of domestic supplies were making it through a new UNPROFOR-protected route from the airport. Prices were falling, as the grip of the black market loosened.

"It's hard to feel happy but we do at least feel relieved for now. It's as though our death sentence has been commuted to life imprisonment," said Ismail.

I asked him whether President Izetbegović was feeling more optimistic now that he and his family didn't have to dodge mortar attacks on their homes.

"Well, not really, Mick. You see he feels that Karadžić has got what he wanted all along. We always said you couldn't carve up Sarajevo into ethnic districts. It's a cosmopolitan city. But now that's precisely what we've got. And, what's more, the Bosnian Serbs don't even have to police their own frontline. The UN is the thin blue line keeping the sides apart. The city that you couldn't divide has been divided."

But Ismail had further news. Ševa had mentioned to Saša and me that he might sign up to the Bosnian Army if, as was likely, his hopes of studying for a chemical engineering degree were put on hold. Now I learned that he had indeed signed up and he was now travelling extensively, taking part in the fightback against the Bosnian Serb Army wherever he was needed.

"It turns out he's good at this soldiering lark," said Ismail. "Apparently, he's a crack marksman – though you know him, Mick. He's a gentle soul and he's not wild about shooting people – any people. But I think he thinks needs must."

When Ismail revealed that Ševa's next escapade was an exercise out of Travnik, I asked whether there might be a chance of our meeting up with him before his mission began. Plans had been laid and that was where Saša and I were headed now.

Travnik packed a kind of charm very different to that at which I had thrilled over a year earlier because these were among the months of the year during which the town was deep in snow. I was relieved to arrive in one piece, given that the conditions didn't seem to curb Saša's cavalier instincts behind the wheel. The winter tyres and chains round each wheel did at least offer some comfort.

The snow was dry and crunched satisfyingly underfoot as we made our way to the makeshift barracks by the Plava Voda. Mount Vlašić stretched to the sky behind the town, a dazzling white expanse. The streets were still congested, as a significant number of refugees, marooned far from their homes, continued to eke out some kind of life in Travnik. Ajdin and his mother and aunts were long gone.

"I'll be interested to hear from Ševa what they're up to at this godforsaken time of year," said Saša.

"Yes, he said the conditions were part of the plan, though he didn't go into detail."

I felt my heart leap as the officer on the desk at the barracks reception called through on his phone and, a couple of minutes later, Ševa emerged. I had never let Ševa drift far from my thoughts as the conflict had unfurled, and I had regularly wondered just how he and his father were coping with what had seemed like an endless siege in Sarajevo, but I felt quite emotional to see again in the flesh this kindly giant of a young man.

The excesses of his shovel-beard had been trimmed back, no doubt out of military necessity, and I estimated that he was perhaps fifteen kilos lighter than when we had first met. His embrace was as firm and enveloping as ever, though it was strange to see him in his camouflage fatigues instead of in the long coat he had always worn in Sarajevo, his hands usually thrust deep into its pockets.

In a café on the Bosanska, Ševa explained how he and his father and mother had continued to cope, as the siege had played out, until he had volunteered for the ARBiH and had begun his training.

Ševa explained that his transition from unofficial street warden in their part of Sarajevo to one of Alija's army had seemed natural.

"My dad never expressed a view either way. I think he was worried for my safety but, as at every stage in my life, he's always left it to me to choose my next step."

And Ševa went on to explain how, over a period of a couple of years, the Bosnian Army had been transformed from a ramshackle bunch of amateurs armed with hunting rifles to something resembling a professional army. He placed much of the credit at the door of Rasim Delić, the army's Chief of Staff. Saša and I had once met him in a hut in Visoko at a military complex north-west of Sarajevo where he had explained to us his ambition of a Bosnian Army's fightback against the Bosnian Serbs. I smiled inwardly at my recollection of Delić's big cowlick of a haircut and his slightly dopey air as he had explained to us the rapid expansion of his forces.

But Ševa confirmed that Delić was far from dopey. He had begun a process of instilling in his troops professionalism and discipline from the moment he headed up the army in June 1993.

"To be honest, parts of our army in Sarajevo, the 9th and 10th Mountain Brigades, were run by mafiosi. And he kicked them out. He even tried to get a grip on a unit made up largely of foreign combatants from hardline Islamic groups in Africa and the Middle East, the Muslimski Brigade. It was a signal that everyone in the ARBiH was going to respond to orders at all levels. And he flipped another switch. Realised he couldn't keep up morale if all we were doing was defending ourselves. He got us on the front foot. Initially, we were harrying and just generally trying to be an irritant to the Serbs but then he built us up and up – strategically, tactically. And, when we won a victory here, made up some ground there, we began to think we could turn things round."

Ševa admitted that, as if by magic, equipment and weapons and proper uniforms had begun to appear, where previously the army had been scrabbling around.

"We didn't ask where the funding came from but, as I told you back in Sarajevo, we knew Alija had his 'alliances.'"

But, given that it was Ševa's sensitivity and humanity that had attracted me to him, I was keen to know how he had taken to his new role as a marksman. Had it been an inevitable rite of passage that he could see coming or did it happen in a rush? And how did he feel when he first shot a man? I knew I could ask Ševa directly without his taking offence.

"Mick, you know, nobody has ever asked me that, though I think about it constantly. I'd done the training and they told me I had a good eye and a steady hand, but I'd never shot a man. And there we were, in the hills north of Višegrad where it was very mixed territory: we held some villages and they had others. And our mission was to take back a village that had recently been overrun. I knew that some of our men were approaching through the forests to the west and I figured they would be quite close. And I saw through the rangefinder a Bosnian Serb fighter on a rock above the road that led into the village. I couldn't see our guys but, all of a sudden, I saw him raise his weapon and point. He would have been about half a kilometre from me.

"Mick, it must have been a split second but I'll swear a complete thought went through my head: I have to shoot that man or he will shoot my friends. And I knew nothing of this man, of his circumstances, his life, his family – but I knew I had to shoot him. And I did. I can't be sure but I think my bullet entered his left temple. And he was gone."

"And excuse the question, Ševa, but… what did it feel like? Shock, horror, elation perhaps?" I asked.

"Shock and then a little burst of elation. Elation at the fact that you hit the target. You have to make instinctive adjustments to your targeting to account for elevation and what we call spindrift. And, when you get it spot on, initially it feels good. You've mastered a skill you'd been taught technically but never used practically.

"And then you chase away the elation. You're a little bit ashamed of it. It seems inappropriate. And then there's the dawning. A dawning of the implications of what you've done. A husband, a father, a son has gone – and it's down to you. And then you keep trying to bury the thought. You say he copped it to stop my friends from copping it."

"But I don't suppose you can bury it completely, can you?" I doubted that Ševa would ever get used to being a terminator.

"No, Mick. You never can. And, you know, I haven't killed many times but, when you do it again and again, it doesn't get easier."

Ševa looked at the floor, and I wondered whether there might have been some shame in that gesture. I wanted to tell him he had nothing to be ashamed of – then thought better of it. He didn't need me to tell him that. Instead, I left some space for a piece of silence to expand and to give us all a moment of reflection.

I was already writing the story in my head: the gentle student, who aspired to be a chemical engineer, rationalising his role as a sniper taking out the enemy in the wilderness of Bosnia's mountains. Naturally, I would fold into my story that intriguing word he had come up with – 'spindrift'. I had to look it up to learn that it meant the slight rightwards trajectory of a bullet in flight caused by a gun barrel spinning its projectile clockwise.

Ševa went on to explain why he and several thousand other ARBiH men were in the area, readying themselves for a push that seemed so audacious that it almost amounted to the foolhardy. A ceasefire had been nominally agreed at the beginning of winter, but Ševa said that, for the Bosnian Army, this had been largely an opportunity to regroup and plan some still more effective attacks on the Bosnian Serbs. His understanding was that Croatian forces were adopting a similar approach. Hunker down, strengthen, and then strike back.

Ševa explained that there was a powerful symbolism about Mount Vlašić – physically and psychologically a barrier that separated territory held to the north by the Bosnian Serbs and Bosnian Army-held space from Travnik south.

"The main target is to take control of Serb-held radio transmitters on the top of Mount Vlašić. If we pull it off, it'll be a hammer blow to the Bosnian Serbs. It's not even so much the transmitter itself. It's the audacity of the enterprise in conditions that the Serbs will never believe we'll brave," said Števa.

He explained that as many as twenty-one thousand Bosnian Army troops would be involved directly and in support.

Števa said that the three thousand troops at the apex of the assault were being provided with white winter camouflage uniforms, and hundreds of tons of ammunition, fuel and food supplies had been stockpiled.

"Close to the frontlines, our guys have been building barracks, field hospital facilities, bakeries and improved roads. We've had daily exercises and battle simulations. At squad and company level, each individual has been made aware of his responsibilities," he said.

Števa said that the Serbs would never expect an assault in bitter winds, high snowdrifts and poor visibility. The conditions would also undermine some of the Bosnian Serbs' defensive capabilities and ARBiH men would be able to creep unnoticed through no man's land, with the depth of the snow enabling them to scramble over Serb minefields unharmed.

It sounded preposterous, unrealistic, and immeasurably perilous. I imagined networks of little white ants clambering over the mountain. There was almost something humorous about it. Yet from Števa's demeanour after his weeks of training, it appeared he and his fellow officers believed in the plan implicitly.

"Just one question, Števa," said Saša, his brow furrowed in what I took to be incomprehension. "Is the prize really worth the risk? Let's say you get to the top of Mount Vlašić and let's say you seize the transmitter. What then? I don't know. I just fear lots of casualties from an escapade that might not achieve what your commanders hope it will."

In the face of Saša's scepticism, Števa was as imperturbable as ever.

"Saša, we're confident that we've now trained to an elite level and that the assault will be so shocking to the Bosnian Serbs that, if it's successful – and I believe it will be – then it'll be a huge blow to their morale. Psychologically, for our forces, it will be massive."

My heart leapt a little at the sight of this admirable man, brimming with enthusiasm at the details of a military campaign that would have appeared alien to him just two years earlier, when he was close to the end of his high school career and hungry for study. I didn't believe Ševa had changed temperamentally at all. The framework of humanity and integrity that his father had constructed around him, as he grew from boy to man, was incapable of being unpieced.

Yet an image I would have found unlikely when I first met him popped into my mind: it was Ševa dressed from head to foot in a white outfit with a zipper from chin to waist, a hood tied tight around his head with wisps of ice-encrusted beard poking out. He was on the incline leading up to the summit of Mount Vlašić and he was tussling with a Bosnian Serb assailant.

Ševa had drawn a knife from a pocket on his right leg and was calculating how urgent was the need to draw its blade across the Serb's neck and spill shockingly crimson blood in the snow. The image faded out before the scene reached a conclusion.

Thirty minutes later, Saša and I were saying farewell to Ševa and wishing him Godspeed.

"It might be a dumb thing to say, Ševa, but stay safe," said Saša. "Make it 'au revoir' and not 'adieu'. Okay?"

"Okay," said Ševa quietly, and he bear-hugged us in turn, first Saša, then me. I asked myself bluntly whether I thought it likely that I'd ever see Ševa again, and my conclusion was that I would. I just hoped that my inclination towards optimism and my own illogical sense that, come what may, I myself would survive the war, was not deluding me and leading me to be too positive about Ševa's likely fate.

At 4.30 the following morning, Ševa's unit made its way out of the back of Travnik and began their ascent. Saša and I had decided to stay in Travnik for a while, hoping that the officers left in the barracks in the town would keep us updated as to how the campaign unfolded. There was talk too of a joint Croat-Bosnian Army assault from the Travnik area before long to reclaim from the Serbs another of the several towns that, throughout history, had acted as temporary Bosnian capitals – in this case, Jajce. Saša suggested we might follow behind such a thrust, were it to appear likely to be both practical and relatively safe.

After Ševa's units had set off, we learned that ARBiH mountain brigades had early successes, overwhelming unprepared Serb outposts. Then the fearsome Muslimski Brigade was fed into the fight. I could barely get my brain around the idea of these men from Ethiopia, Egypt, Saudi Arabia and Iran scaling a mountain deep in snow.

And then the intelligence dried up. We couldn't establish whether the campaign had gone disastrously wrong or whether the Bosnian Army was keeping a news embargo on its progress to reduce the risk of the Serbs being alerted.

After a few days of radio silence, UN relief workers in Travnik passed on reports of Bosnian Serb civilians fleeing from villages around Mount Vlašić – including 1,200 from the town of Imljan, twelve kilometres north-west of the mountain. The UN reported claims that Bosnian Croat forces were helping in the push with artillery support.

There followed a full two weeks before Brigadier General Mehmed Alagić was announcing that, after days of vicious fighting and temperatures as low as -25°C, his forces had captured the summit, two thousand metres above sea level. Bosnian TV broadcast images of jubilant Muslim troops dancing with joy in deep snow around a Bosnian flag.

Back in Travnik, Bosnian Army representatives were non-committal about claims that victory might not have been absolute. There were reports that the Serbs had trashed the communications facility that had been a principal target of the assault, rather than allow it to be captured intact. There were reports too of Bosnian Army casualties from a less successful parallel assault on the 900-metre Stolice TV transmitter in the hills east of Tuzla.

The more mixed the news from these latest attacks, the more frequently I went to the barracks in Travnik to ask about the safety of Ševa. His mission had been the more successful, though not without reports of vicious fighting en route to military success.

I would approach the officer at reception. "Any news of casualties from Mount Vlašić, please? I'm looking for my friend, Ševa Ljevaković."

"Sorry, sir. We can't release details of casualties."

"Yes, but couldn't you just check the list and tell me that he's not among the casualties?"

"No, sir. Sorry. Can't do that."

Though I drew a blank each time, I kept going back, hoping that a change of shift might bring an officer whose guard would drop. I consoled myself with the thought that there was no information either way.

The days ticked by and, though reports of an early assault on Serb-held Jajce appeared to have been premature, Saša suggested that we head there anyway to see how the land lay, given that three other international journalists had landed in Travnik and were up for the trip. The plan was to drive towards Jajce and see how far the Bosnian Croats had been able to nibble into the land the Bosnian Serbs had taken shortly before Saša and I had first landed in Travnik after our ethnic cleansing journey.

23
LATE MARCH 1995

Santiago from *El País* was probably only a decade older than me, but I felt callow by comparison. He was a large man with luxuriant black hair and neat beard, stylishly matched that night with a black polo-neck sweater that I suspected was spun with merino wool. His chestnut eyes seemed to exude wisdom. How did a man in his thirties know so much and yet reveal his erudition with such grace, such modesty? Facts and finely weighed analysis seemed to tumble out of Santiago effortlessly and without ostentation. I could have listened to him all night.

As Santiago gave me a crash course in the causes and implications of the Spanish Civil War, Saša was squeezed between Bryan from *The Washington Post* and Étienne from *Le Figaro* on the other side of the restaurant table.

The plan was for the five of us to set off for Jajce the following morning in two cars. I had already agreed to accompany Bryan and Santiago in Santiago's vehicle, while Étienne would travel with Saša. I was hoping – and expecting – Santiago to be a more relaxing driver than Saša. I hoped that Saša didn't realise that I had volunteered to accompany Santiago in large part to avoid another of his white-knuckle rides.

Saša was clearly looking forward to returning to Jajce. He was the only one of us to have been before and he was explaining enthusiastically to Bryan and Étienne its fairy tale location, ringed by mountains 400 metres above sea level, the town forming the backdrop to a waterfall with a dramatic thirty-metre drop.

After explaining that a fourteenth-century walled city crowned Jajce's hilltop and that it had been home to Bosnia's last kingdom and king – Stjepan Tomašević, put to death as the Ottoman Empire expanded northwards – Saša paused in his geography and history lesson to lean across towards me and say, "Mick, I'll be interested to see whether you prefer Jajce to Travnik, when we get there."

"If we get there," I cautioned. There was no guarantee that rumours were true that the Bosnian Serbs' grip on the town had been loosened.

The *Washington Post* correspondent, Bryan, to Saša's right, was a genial, intelligent individual with none of the brashness and sweeping certainties that I occasionally found in some of his fellow Americans. Étienne, to Saša's left, lacked the 'seen it all, nothing new in this' tired cynicism of some of his French journalistic colleagues.

I recalled the dismissive Frenchman who'd shared my car in Dubrovnik and who, as Montenegrin wild men rampaged through idyllic Adriatic villages, opined that all mountain people were the same the world over. And the thought that I had had at the time returned: how tedious life must be for a know-it-all.

Yet there was still something irritating about Étienne. He was a slight man with cadaverous cheeks and the fragility of a hypochondriac always on the lookout for the next chill that might assault his kidneys or the next foodstuff to challenge his digestive system.

"Glad I'm not travelling with him tomorrow," I thought, before reprimanding myself for my lack of generosity.

The evening drifted on. I was in a state of warm contentment. These were among the best moments for a journalist: with colleagues, shooting the breeze, subconsciously relieved at being between the latest scare and whatever challenges tomorrow might bring. I wanted the evening never to end.

The following day, the bright edge that in the previous few days had given the snow above Travnik a sky-blue hue had been shut out by a thin ceiling of cloud.

In the hotel car park, Saša was dispensing advice. His hunch was that the town of Donji Vakuf, about halfway along our sixty-five-kilometre trip and where the road west turned north, would still be very much in

Serb hands. Everyone was to leave him to do the talking with the Bosnian Serb officers if there were checkpoints there.

"And, Santiago, you'll need to put your 'Press' banner in the corner of your windscreen so it's clear we're media."

Santiago nodded and rummaged in the boot of his Land Rover for the panel and some duct tape. Five minutes later, we were nosing out of the car park, Saša's 4x4 leading the way. Beyond Turbe, where Saša and I had arrived on foot from Smet and met Emir, 'the Little Bird', the road followed a ridge beneath towering hills of dense forest, just a scattering of humble homes by the roadside.

'Donja Trebeuša' read the signpost, then 'Gornja Trebeuša'. Lower Trebeuša and Upper Trebeuša, I mused, relieved to be in the hands of Santiago with his more restrained driving style and happy to be able to take in the landscape instead of clinging to my seat. The road curved away from the ridge and the woods gave way to breaks in the cover. I looked in the direction of Donji Vakuf, marvelling at views of hillsides, rolling and folding as far as the eye could see.

Saša's 4x4 was still in sight, perhaps seventy-five metres ahead of Santiago's Land Rover, when I noticed a hairpin bend sign, and the 4x4 disappeared from view. Santiago followed, easing into the bend. As the vehicle completed its 180-degree turn, Saša's car came back into view. The Land Rover had had Saša's vehicle in sight for just ten seconds when a tearing, roaring sound followed by a trail of white smoke emerged from trees on the left, high above the road, several hundred yards away. There was a huge explosion, and a shell made a direct hit on Saša's vehicle. The 4x4 burst into flames as it was lifted off the tarmac and flipped down a ravine to the right of the road.

"Holy Mary, Mother of Jesus!" yelled Bryan.

I heard myself scream at the top of my voice: "NO! NO! NO! PLEASE, NO!"

Santiago slammed on the brakes and guided the Land Rover to a swerving stop behind a crater in the road where the shell had hit Saša's car.

"Get out of the car! We might be next!" Santiago shouted.

The smoke trail from what my friend Hugh judged later to have been a Serb 20-mm anti-aircraft shell hung in the air and began to dissipate.

I felt as if an electric charge that my body could barely tolerate was coursing through me. Sheer physical pain. But I knew I had to stir myself and get out. I flung open the back passenger-side door and threw myself out of the Land Rover to the ground. Santiago followed on the other side, descending more carefully. Bryan had eased himself out and was standing with his arms aloft, as if in surrender.

But I was not surrendering. I scampered, head ducked low, in the direction of the ravine. "SAŠA!" I screamed the name at the top of my voice. Despite my panic, one thought jabbed away at me: could Saša have survived? Might there be a miraculous outcome?

I reached the fringe of trees that bordered the road. There was a steep decline and I could see straightaway that the car was not intact but that it had scattered in pieces, having tumbled between the trees and was now lying in chunks perhaps fifty to seventy-five metres down from the roadside. I stood up and raised my arms skywards. "SAŠA!" I screamed the name again. It was a dawning, not a revelation: no matter how much I willed it, how loud I screamed, I couldn't bring Saša back.

In that moment, the fastness of my bond with Saša was laid bare. I couldn't frame the thought in anything but a cursory fashion, but I couldn't now imagine a life without Saša. It would be a reflection that would come back in relentless wave after wave in forthcoming days, weeks, months. This man, who had nursed me through my early months in a war zone, had become an essential fixture in my life. But the detailed contemplation was yet to come. Here, now, looking at chunks of metal strewn down the steep incline before me, I sunk to my knees.

"SAŠA!"

I dug my hands into the clay by the roadside and squeezed until I could squeeze no harder.

"No, no, no – it can't be," I said, now more in a whisper than in a cry. And then I felt a boiling rage surface. I stood up. I flicked some of the clay from my hands. I turned slowly and began pacing metronomically across the road in the direction of the source of the shell. I could feel my teeth gritting. I said out loud but without risk of being overheard, "You fucking bastard, I am going to kill you."

And I strode towards the owner of a weapon I couldn't see. I would find the Serb who had killed Saša and I would strangle him with my bare hands. My rage blocked out practical considerations. The soldier would be carrying a pistol. I had never strangled anyone. How might I do it?

I had covered thirty metres. The space had in no way dimmed my rage. I shouted out loud, "I am going to fucking kill you!"

There was a sound of boots on the ground, running from behind me. All of a sudden, there was a cry: "MICK! NO!"

A strong arm came from behind and locked my neck in an elbow. It was Santiago. I couldn't match him for strength and he quickly pinned me to the tarmac.

"Let me go! I'm going to kill him," I pleaded.

Santiago's right knee was on my chest, his arms were pinning mine to the ground. The handsome face with its chestnut eyes was close to mine.

"Mick, listen." He spoke firmly. "No more deaths." Then his tone softened. "Okay? No more deaths."

I tried limply to push free but Santiago was too strong and I had run out of determination. Instead of resisting further, all of a sudden I felt a paralysing weakness, then I crumpled into tears.

"He can't be... It can't be..."

Santiago allowed me to sit up on the tarmac. Smears of clay from my hands had stained Santiago's windcheater. I cast a glimpse in the direction of what I presumed to be an anti-aircraft missile launcher. I didn't think that the soldier who had blown up Saša and Étienne would pick me off too. Perhaps I should have been more afraid.

Santiago led me back to the Land Rover. Bryan put an arm around me before Santiago eased me onto the back seat and clipped my seat belt into its socket. I felt a fatigue that was absolute and a sorrow that was so overwhelming that I had to keep pushing away its content as best I could. The sobbing had eased but tears continued to stream. Each time my brain sought to assert its own logic and tried to compute the fact that Saša was gone, I would push it away. Try to reset.

Santiago swung the Land Rover round and headed back towards Travnik. No Bosnian Serb soldiers had emerged from behind their gun. They had made their point: no outsider gets beyond here. Santiago's foot was down. We were speeding away. The venture had been catastrophic but I would reflect later that it had been no one's error of judgement. This was just what war did.

Back in Travnik, I couldn't rest.

"We need to get Bosnian Army units out to bring back the remains," I insisted to Santiago.

Santiago reassured me. "Mick – me and Bryan will sort it all out. You need to rest. I promise. We'll sort it all out."

I fell onto my bed. After a while, I realised I needed to get under the sheets. I took off my clothes. Exhaustion tipped me into a deep sleep. Hours later I resurfaced and, for a moment, I didn't know where I was. Then I located myself in Travnik and the dreadful realisation began to piece itself together. I wanted to drift back into unconsciousness but the truth firmed up, like a picture out of focus gradually sharpening into a stark, horrific, hellish landscape.

The worst thing that had ever happened to me had been my mother dying; but her demise had been forecast and counted down. This was a wrenching. And the pain of the transition from reflections of 'it can't be true' to 'it is true' was a multiple of any emotional hurt I had ever felt before.

I got out of bed, pulled on jeans and a sweatshirt, sat down at the desk and wrote the story of the death of my best friend. It wasn't just that the graphic detail was fresh in my mind or that my emotions were raw; it was a catharsis – incomplete, inadequate, but an instinctive response, my first step towards coming to terms. It would be months before I 'came to terms' but it was a first step, a means of preventing my descent into an even deeper well of despair. And my written words began the process of making it real.

Once I had dictated them to Mary, the copytaker, and she had offered her sincere condolences and her usual expressions of concern for my well-being – lovely, caring Mary, I would give her a tight hug when I was next back in the office – I knew that the remote hope that this wasn't real, that Saša wasn't gone, had evaporated. I had to deal with the reality that Saša was dead.

I stood up from the desk and walked out into the streets of Travnik.

It was late afternoon now, though dusk had not yet set in. The thin ceiling of cloud had slid back and there was some weak, late winter sun playing on my face. I didn't know where I was going. I would just wander. I endeavoured to keep looking up at the mountain and the sky rather than at my feet.

And there he was: his stride instantly recognisable, his bulky frame back in camouflage fatigues after I had imagined him in a pure white snowsuit. It was Ševa. Back from the front and clearly unscathed.

"Mick!" He fanned out his arms in delight at the chance reunion. I felt a surge of joy – and then devastation. I stopped in my tracks. Ševa walked towards me. He realised something was wrong. I tipped my head towards the ground and the vale of tears broke again. Drops splashed dramatically into the trodden snow.

"What is it, Mick?" His arms fanned out again, this time in concern.

"Ševa… He's gone… Saša's gone." I was gasping for air between words.

"You remember he said to you, 'Make this au revoir – not adieu'?" I paused. I couldn't get out any more words for a moment.

"Well, they killed him… I was there and I saw it. The Serbs blew him away on a mountain road on the way to Jajce."

And again I broke into convulsive sobs. My eyes jammed shut, I felt Ševa enfolding me in his big, consoling arms and holding me close. I relaxed into the embrace. I had felt like a leaf in the wind. After some moments in Ševa's embrace, I felt I might be able to grow again.

And two thoughts surfaced. First, my coming across Ševa had laid bare the scale of the challenge I had inherited: to each mutual acquaintance I met I would have to break the news of Saša's death. It was a daunting responsibility – yet, at the same time, a unique privilege.

I thought of Nevena in her flat in Višegrad and I knew that that was a call I would have to make before long. And I would track down Begić's assistant, Petra, in person. How much had she meant to Saša and how much he to her? I had a hunch that there was a mystery there to be unlocked.

But as I absorbed the significance of this fresh obligation, another even bigger question was coalescing. If I had never felt more damaged than here in Bosnia and in Croatia, might what really mattered be that I had never felt more vital? Might the words even be 'more fulfilled'? And that word 'damaged'. It took me back to Marta and her advice to me, after I had been spurned by Ivana, to 'enjoy my heartbreak'. Could there be such a thing as 'good damage'? Would I ever wish I had never witnessed the dead parents of two orphaned children, the pitiful refugees in the camp at Trnopolje, or Saša being taken from this world? Strangely, I would not.

I wished that the forces that had created those tragedies and dramas had never existed, but if these were events I could never have prevented or reversed, it was right that I had been there to chronicle this 'damage'. For once, my inner voice gave me some credit – unchallenged. I had integrity; these events mattered; I was right to try to bring them to international attention and to stop them from happening again. And it didn't matter that that might be a vain hope.

I was British to the core but, in the space of a few years, these people – Saša, Ivana, Marta, Ševa – had gone from being unknown to me to becoming the most important people in my life. It wasn't simply that I had spent more time in Bosnia than Britain lately. It was the depth of my empathy with these people. Yes, they had faced traumas unimaginable to the citizens of London, or Manchester, or Newcastle. But was something more profound going on? Had the axis of my meaningful life shifted from England to the Balkans – and to Bosnia in particular?

The following day, Santiago and Bryan were able to assure me that Bosnian Army officers would go to the spot beyond the hairpin past Gornja Trebeuša where Saša and Étienne's remains lay, such as they were. And, no, I couldn't accompany them.

I had scarcely given a thought to Étienne, whose tragedy for his family would be as profound as that for Saša's family and friends. But I swept away the concerns. I had only enough emotional capacity to deal with Saša. I barely knew Étienne and, if I hadn't warmed to him, it wasn't as if I had wished him ill.

The thought tried to gain traction in my mind that, had I not disliked the way Saša drove or had not found Santiago's company compelling, I could have been in Étienne's place in that 4x4; but the thought wouldn't land. What happened happened. My conviction not that I was indestructible but that death would not reach me during this war might be nonsensical but, so far, it had held.

Before long, a fresh dilemma began to nibble away at me: I had their number in my contacts book; surely it was my duty to call Saša's parents and explain what happened? Again, my inner voice was gentle with me. It was not right to let his parents know via a phone call from 275 kilometres away. It would be too brutal, however sensitively I could couch it.

I walked into the Travnik police station and explained the situation. Might they be able to call the police station in Užice and ask them to send an officer round to explain what had happened? The officer behind the desk agreed that that would be the best way to deal with the situation. And, no, I shouldn't make the call to Saša's parents myself.

I imagined the Serbian police officer sitting them down in the front room of their comfortable home. They would be likely to suspect the worst as soon as he arrived at their door. Their grief would be unimaginable. I winced at the thought. But I accepted that I would call them in a few days' time, not just to express my condolences but to ask if I could attend the funeral.

My mind turned to thinking about the coffin and I couldn't head off the thought: what might be in there? Having seen the carnage from the roadside, I doubted that it would be anything resembling an intact corpse. And would they be able to differentiate between the remains of Saša and those of Étienne? Most likely it would be a jumble of body parts, if the conflagration had left anything that merited such a description. So I may well attend the ceremony unconvinced that much of Saša was inside the coffin.

Instead, I would travel back to the scene of Saša's death in a few months' time or after the war was over and create a home-made shrine on the fringes of the ravine beyond Gornja Trebeuša. Would the shrine identify Étienne too? I swatted away the thought. My concern was Saša's memory. And I made a vow I was unsure I would be able to keep: that I would make a detour and visit that spot every time I returned to Bosnia.

Paul on the foreign desk had been on leave when I had filed my story about Saša's death and I had been too distraught to track him down. When, a couple of days later, we did catch up, I could sense that Paul was perhaps as cut up as I was.

I suspected that they had painted several cities red together in their younger days and I wondered fleetingly whether I had been too tame a comrade for Saša by comparison. More likely, Saša had been happy to slow down a little after hitting his forties. I knew too that Saša had drawn some unspoken satisfaction from being able to teach a keen, idealistic, young journalist some of the tricks of the trade.

Never far from my mind was the episode that I suspected was the most significant in our relationship: when Saša had feared we might not escape with our lives from our ethnic cleansing experience. I could hear him still, saying mournfully, 'I'm so sorry, Mick.' His plea to me, should I be the survivor, never to change, never to lose my idealism, never to stop confronting leaders with the evidence of their sins of omission or their fundamental errors of judgement touched me to the core with each fresh recollection.

Paul urged me to come back to London straightaway and take some time out. I said I would rather wait and see when Saša's funeral would take place. Better to try to get my head straight after Saša had been laid to rest, I reasoned. And there was no possibility of my not attending the funeral.

I did derive some pleasure from bringing together Santiago, Bryan and Ševa in the restaurant that we journalists had visited the night before Saša's death. Hence, Ševa's story of his brigade's audacious ascent of Mount Vlašić in the snow would make it to readers in Spain and the US as well as the UK. Each journalist's story would contain the words 'gentle giant' without their being clichéd. Each story would recount Ševa and his colleagues' struggle with the elements and description of their exhilaration at accomplishing their mission.

Ševa was relieved that he had not had to add another Bosnian Serb to his list of victims and that he had never felt in mortal peril. Naturally, he rued the loss of some colleagues but the boost to morale that he had forecast to a sceptical Saša had been realised. Momentum in this war was now with the Bosnian Army rather than Mladić's men, he insisted.

I took a ride back to Zagreb with Santiago. I never thanked Santiago explicitly for saving me from a likely fatal confrontation with a Bosnian Serb gunner. Regularly, in later months and years, I would begin to wonder how the episode might have concluded, had Santiago not pinned me to the ground; but the scene never played itself out compellingly in my mind. I never believed that 'what-ifs' were helpful in self-understanding and my mind didn't frame them easily; though on the occasions when I did manage to let that particular film reel play on, it was hard to see how the episode would have concluded other than by my being taken out either by the anti-tank gun or by the gunner's pistol.

A few days after returning to Zagreb from Travnik, I managed to track down Tarik Begić's assistant, Petra, who happened still to be in the Croatian capital. We agreed to meet in a café off Vukovara Street without my having to reveal the real reason why. She probably expected a fishing expedition relating to Babo and the trail of Bosnian Muslim fatalities for which he was now partly responsible in the Bihać pocket, but when she came through the door, she beamed me a smile, as if she sensed this would be meeting a friend rather than fending off an inquisition.

I was overwhelmed all over again by Petra's exceptional beauty and particularly those large green almond-shaped eyes. Her hair, which had been tied back in office mode when Lucy and I had met her at the castle in Velika Kladuša, was untied, a bluey-black mane long enough to fall two-thirds of the way down her back. It had the sheen of hair shampooed in the last couple of hours. I basked smugly and unashamedly in the glow from this exotic, curvaceous yet trim companion, as other men in the café swivelled to take her in and crave her company.

Once coffee was served, I thought it best to be upfront about the purpose of his mission.

"Petra, it's lovely to see you, but I'm afraid I asked you here because I've got some bad news."

"Oh, really?" She held still the coffee cup that she had been lifting to her lips.

"Yes – it's about Saša Našica. The AP journalist. I think you knew him."

"'Knew' him?" She put down her cup. "Oh my God – he's not dead, is he?"

"I'm really sorry, Petra – but I'm afraid he is."

And I proceeded to tell her what had happened. Petra retained her composure but her eyes pooled. After some time, a tear and then another escaped from her lids and spilled onto the table. She listened quietly to my account of his sudden demise.

"I don't know how well you knew him, Petra, but he mentioned you one day, and I hope you don't mind me saying this, but I sensed you were someone special to him."

Petra looked to the side but clearly without focusing on anything or anyone. I paused. I was tempted to jabber but resisted. Petra turned back to me.

"Mick, thank you for letting me know. I can't take it in – but you're right. There was something special about us. It was probably about ten years ago now, but we had a relationship. Lasted around a year."

She fished in her handbag, took out her cigarettes and said, "You don't mind, do you?"

"No, no."

After exhaling her first blast of smoke, Petra went on to reveal the details which bore out the hunch I had long held: that she had been more than just another of Saša's 'conquests'.

"When I first met him, Mick, I thought we were made for each other. Whether it was here, or Belgrade, or Paris, we were quite a couple. People would stop and stare. And, you know, Mick, I could be wild back then, but I thought I might spend the rest of my life with that man."

Petra explained that, while she was aware of his reputation as something of a ladies' man and friends had warned her that he would never settle down nor prove reliable, she wasn't daunted.

"You know, I'm not being arrogant when I say that ten years ago I was capable of seeing off most of the competition. For looks and style and – how can I put this delicately? – passion, you would have had to have gone a long way to outbid me."

I smiled. "I'll bet!" I said, I hoped not too awkwardly.

"But it wasn't just about being out and about and having fun. He had such a tender side too and, when we were alone, say on a car journey, I just felt at peace with him." She paused. "And I felt he felt the same."

"So why did it not last, Petra?"

"Your telling me about his passing away just now. Well, it took me right back. I didn't understand it but perhaps I do now. He just kept saying he might not always be around for me. And I knew he didn't mean he couldn't or wouldn't settle down. I think he really loved me. I wasn't sure back then, but I think I'm sure of it now: I think he knew he would die in action. And he didn't want to leave me a widow.

"'I might not always be around, Pet,' he'd say. And I'd tell him not to be daft. But he'd just shake his head and go quiet. He'd talked previously about nearly coming to grief in Damascus, about losing his best friend Steveo in Beirut, but he was never explicit about expecting to be killed."

"The thing was, Petra, he was always the coolest judge about where to go and where not to go. Early on in this war, I was all for heading for Vukovar, when things blew up there. He virtually forbad me from going. He said it was too dangerous. And he was right. So he didn't take risks – and then, when he was blown away, it was in the stupidest, most random circumstance. He wasn't being rash. We weren't being rash."

"Mick, maybe he just sensed it. I don't know."

"I never felt that he did. We had this saying, the pair of us. We'd talk about going to a hotspot and we'd always laugh and say that we needed to find a way of going there 'without getting our heads blown off'. And, even when we came closest to dying together as part of a Muslim convoy being shot at by Bosnian Serbs, he magicked a way out of the situation in a way I could never have framed."

Petra shook her head in a gesture of regret. I sensed despondence was not far away and I imagined her later, alone in a Zagreb flat, no longer feeling she had to hold back the tears. But, for the moment, she was holding up. Even the death of her lost love was not going to break her, I sensed.

"And you know, Mick, what saddens me is we could have had ten years together. Ten fabulous years. And – just imagine it – what would our kids have been like? Either dazzling – or totally incorrigible!"

We both managed a laugh.

"But just think, Petra. You'd have been left now with, say, an eight-year-old and a six-year-old. It would have been tragic for you, for them, to have lost him."

"But you know what, Mick? I'd rather have had those ten years. Rather have had those children." Petra paused. "I say that but… Hell, how can I know?"

She paused again. "But it's not as if I've spent my time moping around. As soon as I realised he wasn't about to be a fixture, I moved on, focused on my work."

"And did you find a man to take his place, Petra?"

"No, not yet. I've had relationships. I've not lived like a nun but, although I didn't mope, maybe he spoiled things for me. Maybe he was irreplaceable. Maybe that's why I never settled down."

"Well, he was certainly special. I'd just known him for three-to-four years but here, now, I can't imagine never seeing him again. It's not really landed with me that he's gone."

Petra stretched her right hand across the table and laid it on top of my hands. Her tears having dried, she smiled.

"I feel for you, Mick. We've both lost him – but to have seen him killed. I don't envy you that nightmare."

I frowned in concentration. "Petra, I hope you understand what I mean, but I was mulling it over the other day and, in a strange way, I'm glad that I was there to witness his last moments. Part of me feels that it was better that I was there right behind him and saw it happen, rather than his dying and I wasn't there and somebody else told me. And I'd never know quite how. Does that make any sense?"

Petra thought for a moment. "Yes, I think it does, Mick. I think it does." She squeezed my hands again.

Three days later, I was in Užice where Saša was laid to rest. I was told by Saša's younger, more portly brother, who was a lecturer in politics at Novi Sad University, that the tradition in the Orthodox Church was to have an open casket so that people in attendance could pay their final respects. Understandably, Saša's casket was shut.

"Normally, Mick, the priest pours oil and sprinkles earth in the form of a cross on the body of the dead person, as he says 'Wash me with hyssop and I shall be pure, cleanse me and I shall be whiter than snow.' And then the coffin is closed," said Saša's brother.

On this occasion, the priest had poured oil and sprinkled earth on the coffin lid. I didn't dwell upon it but I reflected again on what kind of mix of Saša and Étienne might be wrapped inside.

The service had been spare and solemn with a focus on the vanity of life on earth for anyone without a living faith in Christ. As was the tradition, the sole eulogy was from the priest and, knowing Saša was not religious at all, despite his mother's deep faith and her icon-rich house, I regretted somewhat that no close friend of Saša was asked to conjure up in words the true spirit of my friend.

However, at the *makaria* afterwards – a fish dinner known as the mercy meal – Saša's family were attentive hosts, making sure I wasn't marginalised in this extended family grouping. Saša's mother seemed to be holding things together with the support of her faith; his father looked a little sadder than when I had last visited and he had bombarded his son with questions about international affairs. Now, he sustained a largely silent dignity. My heart ached for this couple and I hoped I had succeeded in letting them know just how much Saša had meant to me and what I felt was unique about their son.

Saša's parents insisted on my staying the night. The following day I said my farewells, promising to return, if I was ever in the area. I took a car over the border to Sofia and then flew back to Britain.

24

JULY–DECEMBER 1995

It felt as if the endgame might be in sight in Bosnia now that the Bosnian Serbs were feeling the heat, their actions being disowned even in Belgrade.

A contact in the Serbian capital that I had inherited from Saša told me, "As the war has gone on and sanctions have degraded their lifestyles, you'll hear more and more educated people in Belgrade complaining about the *prečani* – the Serbs who live outside of Serbia. 'Why should we suffer because of them?' people say."

"So much for the Greater Serbian dream, eh?" I said.

So, although I had gone home after Saša's funeral, as Paul had suggested, I was soon back for the dénouement. I owed it to Saša and to myself to see this through.

In the event, the worst atrocity of the conflicts took place just as much of these dirty wars had done: completely out of sight of objective journalists, just a few crews of tame, pro-Serbian propagandist TV journalists anywhere near the action.

I had watched on a TV in a bar in Travnik as a young Muslim man, who had made the sixty-five-kilometre trek from Srebrenica to the safety of Tuzla, told his miraculous survival story. Hundreds of Muslims from his home town had been lined up and gunned down in a field near the village of Gbavći Donji. He had had to extricate himself from hundreds of corpses and creep slowly and under cover of darkness to safety. General Mladić's promises in person that he and his fellow villagers would be part of a prisoner swap proved to be hollow.

The full scale of the horror of Srebrenica would only emerge later.

The International Committee of the Red Cross would estimate that, after virtually the totality of the Bosnian Muslim population of around thirty-eight thousand people in and around Srebrenica had been removed from the area between 12th and 16th July 1995, a total of 7,079 Bosnian Muslims were killed in fighting, were executed, died fleeing Bosnian Serb attacks or were otherwise unaccounted for.

I had no Saša to turn to to express my frustration at our failure as a Press corps to get the story – though 'frustration' seemed like an inadequate word.

However, as General Mladić was seeking to secure the eastern strip of Bosnia so that Bosnian Serbs could claim those key locations in any peace settlement, he was unable to protect Serbs in the north-west of Bosnia and over the border in Croatia's Krajina.

Rumours of a major troop movement were what had drawn me back to Zagreb and, when deployment became military action, it amounted to an attack on a massive scale by the Croatians. Despite the fact that Serbs and Croats had lived largely peacefully side by side in the Krajina for centuries, Croatia's President saw it as necessary finally to drive Krajina Serbs out of his country altogether. This was *Operacija Oluja* – Operation Storm.

After the Bosnian Serbs' shameful ethnic cleansing episodes in Bosnia, Storm would turn the tables, amounting to the largest single refugee crisis of the war, with 120,000 Serbs driven from Croatia in the space of around ten days.

Embarrassingly for General Mladić, whose exploits with the 9th Corps of the JNA based in the Krajina Serbs' capital of Knin had led to his promotion to head of the Bosnian Serb Army, Knin itself was routed in a day, its population falling from 35,000-40,000 to around 500-600 in less than twenty-four hours.

My Belgrade contact shared a theory with me that President Milošević had hung the Krajina Serbs out to dry, so desperate was he to end the war, end sanctions against his country, and secure the gains made for Serbs in Bosnia.

But I also recalled a steer Saša had given me back in 1994, when President Clinton first began to be drawn into the war after a US-driven ceasefire between Muslims and Croats in Bosnia.

"Mark my words, Mick. Part of this deal that has produced a ceasefire between the Muslims and the Croats in Bosnia is that, over time, the US won't stand in the way of President Tuđman clearing the Krajina Serbs out of Croatia. Tuđman thinks he's nearly got the lot: independence from Yugoslavia and Belgrade; the European Community cosying up to Croatia. Why would he want to leave one-third of his country occupied by Serbs – even if they have been there for five hundred years?"

As usual, Saša had been right.

After Srebrenica and Operation Storm, a mortar fired by Bosnian Serb forces into an area near Sarajevo's Markale market square in late August 1995, killing thirty-seven people, finally flipped the switch and a massive NATO air campaign was launched: over two weeks, 3,400 sorties and 750 missions against fifty-six ground targets decimated Bosnian Serb military capability.

In the months that followed, the Dayton Accord was struck at the Wright-Patterson airbase in Ohio, creating a single Bosnia and Hercegovina state made up of two statelets: the largely Muslim-Croat Federation of Bosnia and Hercegovina, accounting for fifty-one per cent of total territory, and the largely Serb-populated Republic Srpska, accounting for forty-nine per cent.

The outcome was a victory for Bosnian Serb ethnic cleansing, said critics of the deal. Bosnian Serb insistence on a partition of Sarajevo was rejected, but towns 'cleansed' of Muslims, such as Višegrad and Srebrenica, would fall within Republika Srpska under the terms of the deal. The Presidency of Bosnia and Hercegovina would rotate every eight months among three directly elected members – a Muslim, a Croat and a Serb – over a four-year period, rendering coherent, sustained political and economic development plans in Bosnia elusive.

25

JANUARY 1996

"Not everyone is who they say they are and not everyone is who they think they are."
Ray Massingham-Byrd

Two episodes stood out for me in the run-up to the Dayton Accord that would finally end the war.

First, Paddy Ashdown, a British politician with a military background and probably the best grasp in Parliament of what had happened in the former Yugoslavia, had told me that he had been in informal discussions with the British Commander of the UN Forces in Bosnia, Lieutenant General Rupert Smith.

General Mladić risked being the last leader standing, typically defiant in the face of NATO – in fact rather enjoying the odds stacked against him. So, as leaders resisting details of a peace deal caved in one by one, it was important that, in the midst of a huge show of force, a specific message was sent to him.

"Mick, we agreed that the thing to do was to carry out airstrikes not on Mladić's home village but on the cemetery where his father was buried. And NATO did just that," said Paddy.

The second episode was related byŠeva, who I had reached by phone after signatures were dry on the agreement and Ševa was back home in Sarajevo.

He said he had been part of a push by Bosnian Army brigades in the run-up to Dayton which was closing in on Prijedor, Banja Luka and the villages nearby from which thousands of Muslims had been driven – some after a stint in camps like Omarska.

"Mick, we could have taken Prijedor, for sure, and even Banja Luka was wobbling. Bosnian Serbs had started fleeing. They were afraid of being caught up in the last knockings of Operation Storm. And then the order came. We were to stop. And if we didn't stop, we'd be bombed by NATO. And then we were demobilised," said Ševa. "I'm not sure that Alija's Government in Sarajevo wasn't complicit in that. Maybe they just wanted an end to the war – so they were prepared to give up Prijedor and Banja Luka. I don't know but, for us on the frontline, making headway – well, frustrating is hardly the word."

"So what was that about, do you think?" I asked.

"I can only imagine that they were already firming up which areas would be Bosnian Serb and which Bosnian Muslim-Croat Federation. It was galling, after everything we'd been through – but there wasn't much we could do about it."

After 1995 had tipped into 1996, I was in the House of Commons select committee corridor. Heavily patterned, old-fashioned dark carpets firm underfoot; dark panelled walls; historic portraits and scenes hanging in large frames; chunky old brown radiators that would gurgle occasionally; the reassuring sight of a police officer outside each clutch of committee room doors.

"What a gig!" I reflected. While their colleagues chased down drug dealers or strove to unmask paedophiles, these members of Her Majesty's Constabulary were keeping order across a corridor about the length of a football field – just in case a member of the public might turn unruly while exercising his or her democratic right to attend a select committee and to listen to ministers, MPs, economists, or other experts expounding their views about the latest topics under the political microscope.

The police officers' toughest challenge was usually acting as quasi-bouncers, licking into shape the queues for popular sessions, holding the members of the public at bay until a select committee chair decreed that it was time to bring in the expert witnesses and let the open session begin.

I was scouting for the next likely topic to focus upon, but I had found little inspiration. Though I was reluctant to return to dodging bullets and shells and trying to piece together the truth behind strife in a part of the world beyond the Balkans, the implications for the future shape of the EU of the forthcoming 1996 Inter-Governmental Conference didn't quite seem to fit the bill.

Stepping out of the European Legislation Committee session into the corridor, I froze at a sight that I had been unprepared for and one that I could never have envisaged would affect me so profoundly. Former Foreign Secretary Douglas Hurd was walking down the committee corridor, chatting to a young, cerebral-looking assistant, and heading in my direction.

The benign, grandfatherly figure, regarded as a voice of moderation and sanity in a Conservative Party wracked by division over Europe, had unexpectedly prompted within me what I could only describe as fury. I knew that I had to speak calmly but I knew too that I couldn't let Hurd walk by without reprimanding him for his sins of omission and commission over a four-year period as Foreign Secretary – a period that that had ended by coincidence one week before the Srebrenica massacre began.

I found myself whispering under my breath, "Saša would still be alive, if you had done what you should have done."

And then Hurd was beside me, just six feet away. I beckoned to him, raising an arm. "Mr Hurd – er, excuse me."

Up close I could see that his fleecy snow-white untameable hair had something of a day-old chick about it. His face was mottled, with tiny burst blood vessel lines set across a sallow skin palette. His teeth spoke of neglect or poor dentistry and the heavy plastic frames of the spectacles that were his trademark appeared to show a couple of decades of wear and tear. I had to acknowledge, as he chatted to his young charge, that Hurd's eyes spoke of generosity and openness, as if it were important to him to encourage those just embarking upon their political journey.

But now he was stopping in front of me.

"Yes?" he replied brightly, clearly unperturbed by my flagging him down while he was in conversation.

My mind risked jamming as the items on his charge sheet ticked up. How could I make my point succinctly? I doubted Hurd would hang around for a forensic examination of his failings.

"Er, I'm Mick Morrison. I'm with *The Times* and I've spent the last four years covering the wars in the Balkans," I said.

A scintilla of alarm registered on the former Foreign Secretary's face, though not enough to banish his predominantly benign air. I wasn't sure whether it was the fact that I was a journalist, the fact that I had raised the former Yugoslavia, or both.

"Oh, I see," said Hurd. "That would have been a tough assignment, I imagine."

"Yes, it was, Foreign Secretary." The redundant job description had just popped out automatically. "I mean former Foreign Secretary."

I tried not to sound flustered. I pressed on as calmly as I could.

"I hope you don't mind me saying this, Mr Hurd, but I think you called the conflict wrong at every stage."

There. It was out. I had said it. And rather elegantly, I thought. There was something of a stunned silence as Hurd imbibed the depth of the charge.

"I just couldn't let you walk by without letting you know that I think you were one of the principal obstacles to the war ending one, two or perhaps even three years earlier than it did. My best friend – another journalist – died about a year ago and, if you hadn't opposed intervention for so long, he would still be alive today. I think I'll find it hard to forgive you for that."

Hurd and his Defence Secretary, Malcolm Rifkind, had faced down early US and UN pressure to lift the arms embargo, thus cementing in place the Serbs' decisive superiority in conventional heavy weaponry. It had left the Bosnian Muslims fighting mortars with hunting rifles until they found their own ways of circumventing the blockade. Britain dissuaded the US from active intervention till the very end. The then chairman of the US Senate Foreign Relations Committee, Joe Biden, described European policy on Bosnia as a 'mosaic of indifference, timidity, self-delusion and hypocrisy'. London and Paris had vetoed Bill Clinton's plans for a lift-and-strike policy in 1993 – removing peacekeepers and hitting the bombers and besiegers with air power. Hurd had led the opposition to the involvement of NATO and, while he was careful usually to concede that the Serbs bore the greatest responsibility for initiating war, I had found a dangerous whiff of moral equivalence about his statements, as though Serbs, Croats and Muslims bore more or less equal responsibility for years of suffering.

If I had jolted Hurd unexpectedly out of ministerial retirement and back to the Balkans, he had behind him years of experience at the dispatch box, having to field questions and criticisms of his and his government's policy decisions without pre-sight of them, so he was hardly likely to be fazed by me.

He leaned in gently towards me, looked me squarely in the eyes and said, "Let me say, first of all, I'm so sorry to hear about your friend. I know more journalists died in those wars than in any other in living memory, so you have my deepest condolences." There was no doubt he spoke with sincerity, not spin.

"He was a great man, Foreign Secretary. He died needlessly." I couldn't stop myself from calling Hurd 'Foreign Secretary'. No matter.

Hurd went on. "But you say the war could have been stopped years earlier. I'm not sure that's true. Given the terrain, given the weapons being used for most of the killing, given the way in which civilians and military, Croats, Muslims and Serbs, lived side by side and the likelihood that military action of this kind would immediately bring to an end the humanitarian activities of the Red Cross and UNHCR, we and our allies came down against the intervention option each time it was considered."

At this point, Hurd sharpened his gaze, raised his eyebrows and said, "It would have been easy, I always felt, to increase the casualties without stopping the conflict."

I pressed on. "As soon as Britain and the French reinforced UNPROFOR last summer, as soon as the US insisted on a concerted airstrikes programme, all sides were forced to the peace table. You could have done that in 1994, 1993 or 1992. Correct me if I'm wrong, but didn't you personally hold out against this kind of intervention for four years?

"And, Mr Hurd, Paddy Ashdown told me that you told him that the people of the Balkans were prone to internecine violence. That the West needed to build a firewall around them and let them fight themselves to a standstill."

Hurd took a half step back, as if bruised by the charge. His brow was furrowing now. Irritation seemed to be surfacing and banishing the benign.

"Mr Morrison – I can assure you. I never said that."

Hurd's assistant stepped in and inserted an arm between me and the former Foreign Secretary.

"Excuse me, sir, but Mr Hurd is on his way to an important meeting. I'm afraid he hasn't got time for this."

One of the corridor policemen began to stir.

"Everything all right, sir?" he called over to Hurd. Was he craving a bit of excitement in that rarefied environment or just ensuring that any potential incident would be nipped in the bud?

"Well, perhaps I could come and discuss it with you in more detail in your office sometime?" I suggested.

"Yes, of course. Just put in a call," said Hurd. And then he was off with his assistant, turning the corner at the end of the corridor that led to the Parliamentary Press Gallery where, I would learn later, he was addressing a Press Gallery lunch. A *Times* colleague would tell me that Hurd had not had to field a single question about Bosnia at that lunch. So much for my personal crusade to put the Yugoslav wars centre stage.

I had thought I would go and visit Hurd and discuss what happened and what didn't happen in detail, perhaps persuade him to give an interview on the record in which he could defend himself against the charges levelled against him. But I never did contact him. I couldn't turn back the clock and make Hurd and the British Government change their positions retrospectively and I doubted I would have elicited any admissions of serious or serial misjudgements anyway. Would I have been happy if Hurd had been able to invite me then and there to the House of Commons tea room to talk it all through? Yes, I probably would. But he hadn't, and I had other business to attend to beyond the Houses of Parliament anyway – business I considered to be more important than a conversation with the former Foreign Secretary.

A few days earlier, I had contacted Oxfam and asked whether they could track down one of their former Directors of Press and Media, Ray Massingham-Byrd. Two days later, Mrs Massingham-Byrd had called and she agreed to my visiting them, after I explained where I had met her husband and, briefly, what had happened since.

"I'd just like to explain to him how he set me on my way. And I'd like to share some experiences with him. I'll be interested to hear his take on where I've ended up… on war, on politics. All of that," I had said.

Mrs Massingham-Byrd said that her husband was now on a home kidney dialysis machine, so his mobility was limited.

"But it's not intrusive. You can chat to your heart's content, while he's plugged in!" Mrs Massingham-Byrd laughed. "That's what we call it: plugging him in!"

I took the train from Charing Cross to Tunbridge Wells and a taxi from the station to an attractive detached tile-hung house set in a plot of about an acre, with tall pine trees at the back and an immaculate lawn at the front, mowed into diamond shapes.

"This is a beautiful house you've got, Mrs Massingham-Byrd. And I love the lawn," I said, after shaking her hand on the doorstep.

"Thank you, Mr Morrison. We were lucky to buy it way back when house prices were low. Ray used to do the lawn himself, but we have a gardener to do it now. Ray makes sure he keeps it looking immaculate."

She paused. "But you must call me Maggie."

"Oh – okay. Then you must call me Mick."

She was a neat, slight woman with straight shoulder-length grey-blue hair that was clearly now her natural colour. It was parted at the side. She wore blue Perspex-framed glasses that spoke of someone artistic. It didn't surprise me to learn later that she had been a Classics lecturer at the University of Kent at Canterbury. There was a bust of Euripides on a sideboard in the hallway.

"Ray! Mr Morrison is here," she called.

"Bring him through, bring him through."

Ray was sitting in an armchair with his back to French windows through which light streamed, picking him out like a sunlit saint in a stained-glass window. The fringe of pine trees lined the bottom of the garden behind him.

He was connected unobtrusively to a machine on a trolley by his chair and it was clear I needed to go to him rather than expect him to get up.

"Mick Morrison. Lovely to see you again," I said. We shook hands firmly.

It had been six or seven years since I had met him and I felt that he looked perhaps ten years older, his medical treatment no doubt taking a toll; but he was bright-eyed and alert.

Although I had explained to Maggie over the phone how I had met Ray, I wanted Ray to know how he had inadvertently set me on a course that I had never contemplated before, one that had completely changed my life.

"I think I might have just stayed in the north-east or, at most, come to London and been a general reporter. But, after I met you and you mentioned the historic events you'd experienced at first hand and you talked about them with such calmness, well I couldn't really get it out of my head. I felt I was totally ill-suited to war reporting – I was cowardly and more introvert than extrovert. Or rather, I *am* cowardly and more introvert than extrovert." We both laughed.

"But then I got a break: the war in Croatia broke out, my mother was Croatian, so I had good Serbo-Croat and, would you believe it? The *Times*' man in Zagreb broke his ankle playing five-a-side football and, at the age of twenty-four, there I was. Didn't have a clue. Frightened to death and in the middle of all sorts of crazy stuff going off."

"You find your way, though, don't you?" said Ray. "Busk it at first, copy what the others do – and then, after a while, you realise they've got no idea either!" And we laughed again.

I explained how, early on, I had met Saša and immediately had a touchstone.

"He was completely the opposite of me: brave, experienced, brilliant contacts book. And, when it started, I was sent to him by my foreign editor and we got on well enough but, you know, after a while, we pretty much did everything together. We were like the Odd Couple. You couldn't understand how we'd palled up – but it worked."

I was conscious that I was now looking over Ray's shoulder, as if fixed upon something specific in the garden; but I was focused on nothing – just being drawn into reflecting on what it was that made the dynamic between Saša and me work. The dialysis machine at our side beeped regularly and soothingly, as I fought to control my sorrow.

"I asked him once why he hung out with me. He had all the contacts and the ideas about how we might track down a story, who we should talk to. I thought I might be a bit of a drag on him, you know, but he just said that 'I got it'. I knew what the story was, when it was significant, and when it was trivial. And he loved my writing. He'd listen in as I was dictating to the copytakers. And he would say 'How do you do that?' He'd say 'I was there but I never could have described it the way you did.' And I'd say to him 'You're the agency man, Sash. Bang, bang, bang – get it over quick. That's what you're good at.'"

I turned back to Ray, unfixing my gaze from the distance.

"But he was so inventive and so well connected. He could always find a way of chasing down a story, making sure it didn't run into the sand. To be honest, it seems so obvious now – but what it was was that we shared the same values. And we were both driven by the need to tell the story so accurately that the leaders and the decision makers who got it wrong – through cowardice, laziness or misjudgement – would be called to account. It sounds pompous – but that was us."

I checked my flow. "But I don't need to tell you about that. I went back and read some of your cuttings after we met. I suspect you felt the same."

"I did, I did," said Ray. "It always struck me that that was the whole point of war reporting."

"Trying in an idealistic way to make sure the same mistakes weren't made again, you mean?"

"Precisely. It's a high-minded aspiration, but why would you risk being shot at, if it was only to gild your own reputation?"

"But, Ray, there's a lot of them out there who seem to me just to want to show how brave they are. There's a lot of them out there who just want to say 'Seen it all before.' I never understood that," I said.

Ray nodded. "Mick, if I'm right in reading between the lines, you talk in the past tense about Saša. Did you lose him?"

I nodded. "Yes, I did. He was up ahead of me in a car on a mountain road between Travnik and Jajce and I watched as a Serb anti-aircraft gunner just blew him to smithereens."

I paused. "It was the worst thing that has ever happened to me."

"Oh, Mick, I'm so sorry to hear that."

"Tragic irony, eh? A Serbian guy who hated what Milošević and Mladić were doing, and he's blown away by a Serb gunner, who probably thought he was a Brit or an American or German."

I shook my head and tried to stop tears from forming in my eyes.

"But you know, Ray, there was just one area where I think I would have to disagree with Saša – and I feel a little heretical in saying it – but he used to quote a former colleague, who had worked on my newspaper before my time, covering the Middle East beat for many years. You may have known him – Robert Fisk."

"Yes, yes. I knew Bob very well. Scoundrel – but a great journalist!"

"Well, Saša told me that he used to say 'There are no good guys in the Middle East.' And Saša liked that idea. He was suspicious of people who, because they hated Israel, thought the PLO could do no wrong. He was suspicious of people who saw Israel as doing nothing worse than defending itself against Palestinian terrorism.

"I think Saša was suggesting to me that the same applied in the former Yugoslavia. I don't think he meant ordinary people. He meant the leadership. But, you know, Ray, throughout my time in journalism – and, okay, it's not many years – I've always struggled with sweeping statements like that. It's caused me problems with news editors. They say to me 'Sum it up in a sentence,' and I say 'I need a paragraph at least', because, I don't know about you, but for me, capturing the nuance was what was important.

"I meet journalist after journalist who think it's clever to take absolutist positions about situations, regimes. It always seems to me that they have a template that they feel they need to stick on a situation. It has to fit their blueprint, or it can't be true. Well, that can't be right, can it? The complexity of the situations that arise is the most interesting aspect of them, but it makes describing them terribly difficult. You really have to work to deconstruct them and then explain how the elements have combined. And, if I'm proud of one thing, it's that I tried to do that at every stage, in every episode I covered over the last four years. And sometimes I had to fight with news editors but, usually, by telling the war through its impact on individuals, I would land what I wanted to land – have printed what I wanted to be printed."

I checked myself again. "Sorry, Ray. You know all this. I'm on my soapbox and I'm in danger of ranting."

"No, no. I can feel your passion. And it takes me back," said Ray.

"But, you know, Saša's line about there being no good guys? Well, could I honestly say the Bosnian Muslim who tried to cut deals in his own north-western patch of Bosnia, Tarik Begić, didn't begin with good motives? Even though, over time, he set Muslim against Muslim and set up detention camps? Could I say that Izetbegović wasn't a good guy, though he ended up colluding with some terrorist organisations from abroad and gave them space to unleash some terrifying violence on their enemies? I'm not sure I could.

"And these were wars that no one would have wished for – well, hardly anyone – yet I witnessed their bringing out some extraordinary instincts in people. There was a Muslim guy from Sarajevo who was just seventeen when I met him. The war stopped him going to college and getting a degree – but it turned him into a community leader and then a brave solider, attempting to recover territory that had been taken from his 'brothers'. There was a mechanic from Croatia who was needlessly and tragically shot by a sniper, leaving a widow and a daughter – but not before he fought against the odds to try to keep Dubrovnik safe for its citizens. So, I'm afraid I have to part company with Saša on that. Sometimes good people have to do bad things, even if bad people only do good things by accident."

"That sounds dangerously like a sweeping statement, Mick!" We laughed again.

We went on to exchange views about the provenance of aggression on an unimaginable scale in wartime: the government-controlled broadcasters pumping out propaganda steeped in hatred, designed to instil fear in their people and to provoke distrust which, ultimately, led to neighbour-on-neighbour violence; the incomprehensible creativity of acts of cruelty in which some participants seemed to revel; the criminals for whom war was an opportunity; the no-marks given permission to persecute, to rape, to kill.

"But I almost find it harder to understand what drives soldiers to rocket Sarajevo or snipe at its citizens," I said.

"Huge-scale bombardments on innocent people. That takes some explaining. And I remember being told that Mladić was captured on the airwaves telling his men to bomb Sarajevo's citizens 'to the edge of madness' – or to shell that district 'because there aren't many Serbs there'. That takes some explaining.

"But, you know, Ray," I added, "the most frightening episode for me was something that I experienced myself. It showed me the way events could drive reasonable people to vengeance – and vengeance on a scale of violence they would never have contemplated before."

And I told Ray of how, after seeing Saša killed, I had turned and walked towards Saša's killer with every intention of strangling him with my bare hands.

"I don't know what would have happened, Ray. Of course, he'd almost certainly have shot and killed me; but I honestly felt that, if I had got to him, I would have killed him."

I paused. "How can that be? I was someone who never had a single fight in the playground at school. I try not to slice a worm in two when I'm digging the garden. And there I was, wanting – seriously intending – to kill someone."

Ray thought for a while, before saying Delphically, "Not everyone is who they say they are and not everyone is who they think they are."

It was a comment that paused the conversation again, as I sought to drink in its implications.

Then Ray broke the silence. "So what stopped you from throttling the Serb gunner, Mick?"

"What stopped me? A thirteen-stone Spaniard from *El País*! He jumped me from behind and drove me back to Travnik." We laughed again.

Ray made a mini cathedral arch by pressing the tips of the fingers of both hands together in front of him.

"I witnessed something similar, Mick – at one step removed. When I was in Beirut, I was friendly with a university lecturer, a Maronite Christian. I visited him a couple of days running but his wife said he was away with his twenty-two-year-old son. When he eventually came back, he said to me, 'Ray, one of the Druze militia in Chouf killed my father, my son's grandfather. We went to kill him. We tracked him down and caught him in a back alley and shot him.' Mick – these were intellectuals. How could that happen?"

I shook my head. "I could never have understood – until that day they shot Saša." I paused. "I know I couldn't have killed – but I wanted to. Northern Ireland, the Balkans, Beirut – maybe we're closer relations of brutality than we like to think."

Ray nodded. "I did wonder sometimes whether the curtain separating both sides of our personality is, in fact, a wispy, fragile thing. And that if it's torn down, it can unleash unspeakable violence, sometimes neighbour on neighbour. And then take a long time to put back again."

The evening was beginning to close in. We had talked for over two hours. Sunlight was fading and it was time for me to head back to town.

"Listen, Mick. Do send me copies of some of your cuttings. I'd really like to see them. It sounds as if you've had a fascinating few years."

"Yes, I will, Ray. Fascinating – but terrifying, bewildering, life-changing too. I thought I hated the near perpetual fear I lived under but, you know, when I came back home, while the war was still on, I couldn't wait to get back. Part of it was that I felt as if it was 'my' war. That I somehow owned part of it. Or might play a part in halting it… Ridiculous, I know, but…"

"So do you know where you go from here, Mick? More wars, or a job on the foreign desk?"

I thought for a moment. "You know, Ray. More people and stories. People battling for a better life – but preferably without guns going off. I've been reading around and I've got a hunch that might be completely without foundation but I'm wondering indigenous people – maybe in South America. Bolivia perhaps. Might they have a chance to be heard at last? I don't know."

The taxi came; I was whisked back to Tunbridge Wells station. I would send Ray the cuttings of which I was most proud. I hoped to go back and visit the Massingham-Byrds again, but I suspected that I might be drawn to other parts of the world and that word might come eventually that Ray had passed away before I had had time and opportunity to return. Regardless, I would never forget Ray and would always be grateful that he and his wife had welcomed me into their home. But, given my first encounter with Ray, it was unsurprising to me that I had found them to be such a delightful couple.

As the train pulled onto Hungerford Bridge, Douglas Hurd came back into my mind. Where might he be that evening and would the chance meeting with the man from *The Times* have registered with him in any way? Was he perhaps at that very moment in a restaurant in the House of Commons, weighing in his mind what I had said to him earlier? I hoped that he might be, but I suspected that he wasn't.

26
APRIL 1996

With Saša gone, part of me was tempted to bury with him the potential link between myself and Ante Pavelić. No one else knew apart from my father and, clearly, he would never speak to anyone about it. But one night about a year after Saša's death, on a current affairs programme on TV, up popped the man who had probably saved my life on the road between Travnik and Jajce – Santiago. I was unsurprised to see that, in the interim, he had been appointed editor of *El País*.

I called him in Madrid and a month later I was being shown into his office. If he looked at home there, he was still brimming with the humility and self-effacement that I had found so attractive when I first met him.

He took me to what was acknowledged as the oldest restaurant in the world, Casa Botin. It had been in continuous operation since 1725 and had been famously name-checked by Hemingway in the final scenes of his novel *The Sun Also Rises*, in which its central character, Jake, drinks three bottles of Rioja Alta. It was fabulous: history, atmosphere, and, provided you liked suckling pig, superb food.

We talked about Bosnia, about the European Union, and about the current state of Spanish politics but, before we moved to the dessert course, I pulled out of my jacket pocket the photograph from 1958 featuring the family on a beach at Santa Pola, Alicante, and slipped it across the table.

"Tell me, Santiago. Does this photograph mean anything to you?"

I could have photocopied the picture and put it in the post to Santiago but something had made me shell out on a plane ticket and take it in person. If the photo had any significance, I needed to be there when Santiago inspected it and hear the words that fell from his lips. I needed the instinctive reaction – not a considered verdict in the post after inspection of a photocopy.

"Where did you get this?" Santiago asked neutrally.

The question put me in a difficult position, as I wasn't sure I wanted to alert another senior journalist to my Croatian antecedents at this stage. But I didn't want to lie to him either.

"I found it at home in a pile of documents."

Santiago had no idea that my mother was Croatian, so I was accurate in what I said, if a little vague.

"This is actually a very famous photograph, Mick. It's a picture of the late Croatian Fascist leader, Ante Pavelić, with his wife and two of his children. I suspect his third child was behind the camera. It was taken a year before his death in 1959.

"He'd been in exile in Argentina and he was seriously injured in an assassination attempt there in 1957. Franco offered him exile in Spain, provided he made no public appearances."

The forces of dates, circumstantial evidence and the location of the photograph among my mother's personal effects were combining to overwhelm my breakwater of intuitive denial. It *couldn't be*, I had concluded. Oh yes it could.

"I happen to think it's an excellent photograph, if you know the background," said Santiago, blissfully unaware of its implications for me.

"You can see the wind is really strong by the way the palm trees' branches are tilting. And there's old man Pavelić and his wife looking dapper and elegant. Unruffled. It's not quite a look of defiance in his eyes but there sure isn't any whiff of regret or apology. And his kids: they look pretty cool. Nice clothes. And I don't know about you, but I read into their faces pretty much total composure. They'd been in exile in Argentina with him but I see two young adults without any doubt as to their right to a place in society."

Santiago turned over the photograph.

As he did so, I said, "I can read where it was taken but there are some words there I can't make out."

Santiago put his hand in his jacket pocket and pulled out a small, drum-shaped object. It was an eyeglass that photojournalists would use to examine the fine details of a picture. He looked at the faded words through it.

"Here," he said, offering me the eyeglass and the picture. "I can make out the words but they mean nothing to me."

With the eyeglass, I could read clearly. There, written in my mother's hand, were the words 'Praujak i porodica'.

They spoke themselves out loud in my head: "Praa-ooyak ee porro-deetsa". Great-uncle and family.

So there we were: my mother's grandfather, Josip, had been the brother of the Croatian dictator, war criminal and mass murderer. The inscription in her handwriting and its place in her document trove scarcely spoke of shame or an act of disavowal.

Devastation isn't instant. It is incremental. I could feel it building up. I feared it might build till I was fit to burst.

27
MAY 1996

As I headed back to the north-east to confront my father with the evidence of the Pavelić connection, I had stressed repeatedly to myself that I mustn't be angry or aggressive towards him. I presumed that my mother had shared her secret with him, but I couldn't be sure. What if the blood link was as incredible to him as it had been to me? Calmly laying out the facts and letting him fill in the gaps in his personal journey from the early 1960s to his marriage, to her death, to the current day would be likely to be the most successful way to reach a conclusion as to how I had ended up here. It would also be respectful.

On the train north I had recalled the myth about the birthplace of his own Irish ancestors that he had trotted out so casually and incorrectly when I was a teenager. And I recalled too my near blind rage at the inaccuracy. It wasn't that he wasn't a truthful man, but he clearly placed the sanctity of facts at a level some way below the pedestal on which I placed it. Perhaps my principal goal was to understand what kind of expediency trumped this specific truth and persuaded him to conceal it from me – if indeed he had.

When I pulled out the photo again and laid it on the kitchen table between us, he momentarily raised his eyebrows in a gesture that I took to mean 'Oh no, not that again!' I ignored his reaction and spoke factually and calmly.

"Dad – you see this picture from Mum's box? I took it to a friend of mine in Madrid. A journalist. He said it was quite a famous picture. That it was Ante Pavelić and his family, a year before he died in Spain."

I turned over the photo.

"I couldn't read it at first but, when you look closely, Mum's written on the back 'Praujak i porodica'. That means, in Croatian, 'Great-uncle and family'."

There was a pause. He didn't fill the silence. He looked at me as if he were waiting for my next thrust.

I spoke softly. "I know you told me you didn't know. That there was no link – but did you know? Surely she didn't take the secret to her grave?"

He looked at me balefully, as if he was calculating how much to reveal. And in that instant the dynamics of our relationship flipped. For two and a half decades I had willingly accepted his moral authority. There had been no question around it. Now here he was transformed into the supplicant in our relationship. I wasn't comfortable with it.

"Michael..." My name gave him space to arrange his thoughts. He might have feared after my last visit that one day I might return with a fresh charge, but it was more likely that he thought the trail would go cold, that he hadn't prepared for this moment.

"Yes, of course she told me about it. But we made an agreement very early on that we would never speak to anyone else about it. Not even you and your brother. Our view was that it was such a remote thing that no one need ever know. And, if we were upfront about it, we would just be asking for trouble. Trouble from anyone who might not have our best interests at heart."

But who were these people 'who might not have our best interests at heart'? It sounded to me like an old-fashioned position adopted from a society long gone – one where the watchwords were 'Keep your heads down' and 'Know your place'.

He went on. "As I said to you last time, it was tough enough for her anyway. In a new country with no friends apart from me, a language to master. She didn't need any rumour mill to start spinning, did she?"

"But, Dad. Did you not think – when I went to *The Times* and then to Yugoslavia and she had passed away – that she couldn't be harmed, but that it might have a material impact on me?"

I was still managing to sound composed. He rubbed his forefinger below his bottom lip in a sawing motion.

"You won't have been aware of this, but I've read every one of your pieces. I promise you – every single one. And I could feel your passion about what was going on. I'd rather you'd not been there, but you were. To be honest, to me your pieces were like letters home. I was able to locate you."

The revelation put a squeeze on my heart. He looked down at the floor and then back up again.

"I just felt you didn't need to know this. You didn't deserve to have this piece of history making you feel you had to temper what you were writing. I mean, think of it, Michael. This was the brother of your great-grandfather. It wasn't even your great-grandfather. And do you know what your great-grandfather did? He was a professor of Latin and Ancient Greek. A gentle, educated man. You might share some of your great-great-grandparents' blood with Ante Pavelić – but that's all. It's irrelevant, Michael. It really is."

I sensed his increasing anxiety.

As calmly as I could, I said, "Well, I'm not sure it's irrelevant. I'll have to front up about it – but there's another angle that's troubling me. The fact that she kept this picture and that she wrote on it that it was her great-uncle. I hate to say this but it doesn't sound as if she was ashamed of him. I get no sense from the photo and where I found it that she was appalled by what he did. Am I missing something?"

He looked aside momentarily, then confided, "Michael, you would never have witnessed it but, gentle soul that she was, the only thing that would make her blood boil were the communists.

"I remember at a party once, there was some smart alec – an Englishman, younger than us, a bit wet behind the ears – and he was mouthing off about Tito. Saying what a brilliant man he was. The only person who could have held Yugoslavia together after the war and still manage to keep the country out of the clutches of the Soviets and the Western bloc.

"Well, your mother just took him on. Told him he knew nothing about life in post-war Yugoslavia and that anyone who said that Tito was anything other than a cold-blooded murderer didn't know what he was talking about. Because she looked so sweet and gentle, he didn't know what had hit him. She gave him both barrels. He was speechless.

"What this fellow didn't know was that your mother's favourite teacher, a young history teacher, was shopped to Tito's secret police when she was in sixth form. He ended up being incarcerated on Goli Otok. Do you know about Goli Otok, Michael?"

"Yes, I do, Dad."

Goli Otok was the island off the north coast of Croatia that became the most notorious penal colony of the Tito era. It is estimated that anything between four hundred and four thousand inmates were killed there, exile to it prompted by as little as slack chat in a barroom.

"Well, your mum's teacher – nice, liberal guy, inspirational educator, in his late twenties – he ended up there, literally breaking rocks, and he never came back. She never forgave Tito and his gang for that.

"Perhaps that made it easier for the family and those with a similar take on Tito to downplay what Great-Uncle Ante did. Maybe say some of it was propaganda. I don't know…" His voice trailed away.

I had experienced what my father had called at her funeral his late wife's, my mother's, 'uncomplicated integrity'. I loved the expression because it seemed to capture so neatly what she was. But how could this Pavelić secret co-exist with such sweetness – which was all I had known of her?

My father resumed. "Michael, I know it might sound trite but we don't choose our families. And we don't necessarily agree with them or take after them, do we? Every family has its black sheep, doesn't it?"

"I get what you're saying, Dad, but it still troubles me. She was given that photograph just before or more likely just after he died. Years after his atrocities. I can't help thinking the inscription, its place among her documents… Well, it almost speaks of a certain fondness, doesn't it?"

My father shrugged – as if this were a take that he hadn't before contemplated.

"I don't know, Michael. She was born in 1941, he was fully engaged then in leading the war effort. My hunch is she never really knew him. By 1946 he was on the run."

"But did she ever talk about him fondly?" I asked.

"Not really. It was all pretty neutral. She shared the secret with me early on. I think she was even expecting that I might send her back home because of it. So she was taking a risk by letting me know. But I loved her so much… I'd never have sent her home."

I had never heard him say that, though it was obvious from how they had interacted. I felt another firm squeeze on my heart.

He went on. "Then we agreed our position, that we'd never mention him to anyone else, and he became a topic we barely touched upon. It was only in her anti-Tito moments that you could have divined any political views and not even the best sleuth could have tracked things back to Ante Pavelić."

"And tell me, Dad, did you consciously or subconsciously encourage us to think she was called Pavlović?"

"Once, when your brother pronounced it wrong, I admit I saw no harm in failing to correct him. I saw no harm in people thinking she was something other than a Pavelić."

I shook my head gently in disbelief at the revelations of the last few moments, but I was content that I had kept my word, spoken calmly, and not rounded on my father for his well-meant if misguided duplicitousness.

I said quietly, "Dad, you know I'll have to front up about this, don't you?"

"What? With your editor?"

"Well, I haven't fully thought it through yet but maybe with the readers as well."

"No, Michael. You really don't have to go that far. You reported events as you found them. This had nothing to do with your reporting."

"Well – put it this way, Dad. Is it better for me to front up and reveal the connection or do I spend my career waiting for some bright young thing to unearth the link and 'out' me?"

A look of concern flashed across his face. "If you do that, in no time they'll be at my door. Journalists. Asking for photos of your mum. Writing it up in the local rag."

He paused, then apologised. "I'm sorry, son. This isn't about me. I just don't believe you have to compromise the reputation you've built up… Painstakingly and at great personal cost, if you don't mind me saying."

He paused again. "Don't do it, Michael. Keep your head down. No one needs to know the secret. Just you and me."

"I don't know, Dad. I'm going to have to think about it… And if I have to go public, I'll let you know in advance. You can jump on a plane to South America and avoid the paparazzi!"

I was almost smiling now. Perhaps it was a kind of relief that everything was out there. Certainly, I needed time to let everything sink in.

But I had been right not to lose my temper with him. The dynamics of our relationship had been restored. He was no longer supplicant. I understood the warped, out-dated logic that he had deployed in keeping the revelation from me, even if we lodged the sanctity of facts in utterly different locations.

One thing I did know now: contrary to his assurances on my previous visit, I had been caught in the Pavelić trap. I had to work out whether there was a way out.

28

JULY 1996

In the space of less than five years, I had gone from raw, inexperienced rookie, beset by fear, unsure whether I had what it took to be a war reporter, to one of the newsroom's leading lights. The British Press Awards meant that the younger reporters would chat to me in the hope that I might bestow upon them something resembling the halo that they saw glowing above me. I liked to encourage them, though I wasn't particularly comfortable with the renown.

In the war zone, even when the conflicts were winding down at the end of 1995, I was still terrified, still wracked with self-doubt but, looking back, I now realised that my sense of fury at what was being done and to whom it was being done had enabled me over time to crowd out some of the fear. If the necessity to call out sins of commission and omission didn't trump self-preservation, that sense of feeling obliged to report on these events that had grown over time had conveniently taken a little of the edge off my initial terror.

Paul had patted me on the bicep and called me 'maestro' when I had returned to the newsroom after my BPA 'gong'. I couldn't deny a flash of pride at the accolade but, after my father's revelation, it added to my sense of foreboding about what I had to tell him. With a nomination for the International Press Awards in a couple of weeks' time under my belt, my task was particularly daunting. *The Times* was counting on me to deliver a double: awards at the British and now the International Press Awards.

Saša and I had always resolved problems and laid plans with the assistance of alcohol. You couldn't beat a bar as a place to think things through, so here were Paul and I in the corner of an old-fashioned Wapping pub, as I spelled out my story and outlined what I planned to do to fix my dilemma.

"I think it's pretty clear, Paul. I've either got to quit the business altogether, or I've got to front up," I said. "I can't sit here hoping no one'll find out and carry on as normal. Not now that I know the truth."

I had conceded privately that my relationship with the truth now appeared set to damage me. Cue the voices in my head holding another debate.

"Why couldn't you do as your father did and, on this occasion, let expediency win out? Just this once."

"A principle isn't a principle if you only apply it when it suits."

The latter voice came at me with the solemnity of a pastor from the pulpit – and I knew that that voice had won out.

"Well, you're not bloody quitting, mate. I can tell you that," said Paul. He smiled. "I didn't spot you and nurture your talent only for you to walk off into the sunset. No way!"

So – walking away was forbidden.

"Well, what about this? I've been giving it a lot of thought and here's where I am. How about I write a mea culpa article, outing myself, explaining that I wouldn't have reported anything any differently but that it's only right that I reveal my connection to a Croatian Fascist dictator? That I say I was zealous in pursuing others' stories, even when it proved hugely damaging to them, but I was remiss in failing to check out my own."

"You what?!" Paul was clearly shocked by the proposal. "Do we really need to go that far?"

He paused.

"Like your dad said, it wasn't even your great-grandfather. It was his brother. I mean, is anyone ever going to unearth the connection? I doubt it."

I didn't respond to Paul's question. Internally I'd already decided that the likelihood of the secret being unearthed wasn't really the point. Yes, we did need to go that far if I was to continue in the profession.

"But here's the next bit, Paul."

I hesitated on the brink of a proposal that I knew he would hate.

"You have to publish my article a few days before the International Press Awards – so that the judges can take it into account. The worst thing in the world would be to win and for people to say later that it should be taken off me."

Paul looked aghast.

"Jeez, Mick! You're banged on for an award. You *can't* do that!"

His 'can't' sounded tortured and plaintive simultaneously. If I didn't disappear into the sunset, he could see my second gong doing precisely that.

"You know what, Paul? It's not a question of 'can't'. I think I have to."

I knew at that moment that I was setting myself perhaps the most difficult journalistic challenge I had ever faced. Writing about Saša and my ethnic cleansing episode hadn't been easy, but once I had embarked upon it, it had flowed, the words tumbling onto the paper, my joy at capturing the drama and suspense swelling with each completed paragraph. But I suspected that this would be different.

And just as nearly five years earlier, almost despite myself, I had heard myself volunteering to go to the Balkan war zone, so now I was emerging from the editor's office, having persuaded him of my way of thinking, yet setting myself the toughest of tasks.

In the event, it wasn't so tough. It was clear what had to be said. It was simply a question of structuring it and writing it in a fashion that was as compelling as a powerful news story.

I worked the piece so thoroughly that, by the time it was ready to hit the printing presses, I could quote by heart whole sections of it.

These were wars that were inconvenient to many Western leaders and I make no apology for naming those I thought guilty of sins of omission. In the case of the former Yugoslavia in the first half of this decade, failure to act was almost as serious as the actions of those who led the violence. Why? Because both led to thousands of unnecessary extra deaths – including the death of my very best friend.

But, of course, the piece was really about me.

However, as I was calling to account the inert Western leaders, the mass murderers, the torturers, those who before long could find themselves facing charges of genocide at the Hague Tribunal, I learned that I had been remiss in researching my own backstory.

As mass murderers, torturers and perpetrators of genocide go, few can match the horrific record of Croatia's friend of Hitler and wartime dictator, Ante Pavelić. In the last few months I have discovered that my Croatian mother was a Pavelić. She came from a tiny hamlet called Krivi Put, the same tiny hamlet that Ante Pavelić's parents hailed from. You see, Ante Pavelić was a relative of mine. He was my great-great-uncle. It was a secret both my parents kept from me and my brother; but I don't blame them. I blame myself for not being as rigorous in researching my own legend as I have been in researching others' stories and then calling them out publicly.

I can honestly say that I would not have changed a single detail in any of my reports during the collapse of Yugoslavia, had I known then what I know now, but perhaps I would have written with less piety and more modesty.

To the descendants of perhaps more than three hundred thousand Serbs, Jews, Muslims, Roma and anti-fascists who died as a result of Ante Pavelić's policies, I offer my profound apologies for the horrors for which my ancestor was responsible. My journalism over the past five years, I believe, bears witness to the fact that I abhor everything my great-great-uncle stood for. Nevertheless, this is my 'mea culpa'.

To those descendants and to my readers, I hope you will find it in yourselves to forgive me. I plan to continue reporting but I shall do so chastened and more circumspect, yet with undiminished zeal.

I have always cherished 'the truth'. What I have learned is that sometimes 'the truth' as we perceive it at a given moment is only part of the picture. There is always more context and background to learn.

The response to publication was like a huge wave unfolding in slow motion. Most of the broadsheets were relatively respectful, though the *Daily Mail* predictably crowed at 'award-winning journalist who missed his own scoop'.

It was only after a few days, by which time reports had reached the Balkans, that the more venomous coverage broke.

'Pious propagandist with blood on his hands,' declared one Serbian newspaper with nationalist leanings. 'Flayer of Bosnian Serbs was covert apologist for Jasenovac,' another said completely fictionally, referring to Croatia's notorious wartime concentration camp. A Croatian newspaper highlighted criticisms I had levelled against Croatian President Franjo Tudman: 'Tudman critic's shameful past.'

A little later the death threats began arriving. Gruesome warnings landed in envelopes with Belgrade postmarks – for example that I'd be garrotted if I ever set foot in Serbia again. Others promised to track me down in the UK and bump me off. The contents of others I couldn't possibly repeat.

But when Paul offered to hire me a minder for the International Press Awards ceremony, I declined.

"Just send Doddsy along with me," I said.

Doddsy was the twenty-stone *Times* photographer that no one would mess with – not even a knife-wielding Serb.

In the event, the judges didn't give me top prize for the international category in which I had been nominated. They did, however, create an extra award – a special commendation.

As I picked it up onstage, I was tempted to describe it to colleagues and guests in attendance as the 'Best Reporter with connections to a Fascist leader' award, but I resisted the temptation and shared the joke at the bar with Paul later instead. He thought it was quite funny and I hoped he'd forgiven me for seeing his expectation of a more formal prize for our newspaper disappearing over the horizon.

It was only after my mea culpa was published and the awards ceremony was over that the full effects of what I'd learned began to register with me. I did feel unfairly bruised by circumstances that I would have been hard-pressed to have foreseen, but a worse effect was attitudinal. The fervour with which I had gone about seeking to skewer those I had thought bore responsibility for Croatia's and especially Bosnia's woes hadn't gone, but it had been shackled by a sense that I needed now to be more defensive.

As I had said in my article, 'Less piety, more modesty.' But the switch put a handbrake on my indignation. I felt I couldn't mount a soapbox so confidently now that a bloody past – not *my* bloody past but *a* bloody past – had been revealed to the world.

Sometimes I would lick my wounds – *This is so unfair!* – but more often I would accept that this was now my truth. No point in swearing allegiance to the god of truth and then ignoring your own.

33
2006–2018

For some years afterwards Bosnia continued to haemorrhage talent. Thousands of the brightest youngsters were leaving, weakening ineluctably its chances of pulling back from the brink and trying to learn to thrive.

My Sarajevan friend Ševa had become one of the reluctant émigrés. As soon as he had been able to, he had enrolled at the Institute of Technology in Zurich to study chemical engineering and, after his Master's degree, he had been scooped up by the international pharmaceutical company Bayer and was living in Leverkusen in Germany.

"He keeps saying he must come back to Sarajevo – that he owes his country," his father told me. "But I tell him not to be so silly. He put his life on the line and now he needs to take his chance to get on.

"You should see it, Mick. He has a beautiful apartment, a lovely German wife, and I have two grandchildren – a boy and a girl. Ševa now speaks fluent German."

"And I bet he's lost none of his poise and calm. I imagine he would make a great father," I said.

"No – he's lost none of that, and you're right, he's an exemplary husband and parent." I imagined Ismail glowing with pride at the other end of the line.

"I keep meaning to fix up to visit him, Ismail. I must do it," I said.

"Yes, you must – you must."

I had been more assiduous in following up my invitation to Marta and in chivvying her to come and visit England from Dubrovnik. My heart had swelled as I had spotted her coming through customs in an old-fashioned but expensive maroon trouser suit and matching hat, hair visible at the sides now snow white. I had chaperoned her round London and the Chilterns' sights and restaurants, and the bond that we had tied back in the early 1990s had stayed fast.

The news of Ivana was limited but reassuring. She and Ante had found their smallholding and, from what Marta could gauge, were living happily there, though Nada had acquired no half-sisters or brothers. I wondered whether it meant that Ante was Nada's stepfather but that there was no passion in her parents' relationship. It was none of my business, but I couldn't deny the emergence and the ownership of the thought.

Marta's news of Delila and Azra was more mixed. "Mick, something never quite clicked about their story and it was only after Delila was in her twenties that I understood what had happened. I was always surprised that Delila certainly – and to a lesser degree Azra – were not as disturbed as I'd expected them to be about their experience on that day when the bomb hit the house. Well, Delila came back one summer from medical school and she told me everything.

"She said that her father had been a brutal man, violent to their mother and, on occasions, to the girls too. She said to me, 'Marta, that sight in my parents' bedroom – I'll never forget for the rest of my life. And my poor mother – I grieve for her. She didn't deserve that kind of life or that kind of end. But, you know, when I saw he was dead, even at the age of seven, I felt nothing but relief. Relief for myself and Azra but for my poor mother too – freed from a life of misery and humiliation.'

"She said that she would be eternally grateful to her foster family. She still stays with them when she's back in Dubrovnik. And she decided she would devote herself to the caring professions. She qualified as a doctor and had stints in Africa before she came back to Croatia for good. Then she studied and qualified in child psychiatry. She's a lovely lady, Mick. She's flipped her troubled past and has thrown herself into easing others' cares."

In contrast, Azra had not fared so well.

"I think she did catch sight of her parents in that bedroom and I'm not sure she's got over the horror of it all. Delila told me that she dropped out at sixteen and kept going missing. She developed a heroin addiction and Delila thinks she might have occasionally taken to prostitution to feed the habit. She says, in the past, Azra would pop up, usually asking for money, and then disappear again. Delila says she's not heard from her for over a year now."

I imagined the sweet child I had scooped up from her bombed-out home and fast-forwarded fifteen years, considering how she might look, imagining those give-away blue half-moons beneath the eyes that can often identify the heroin addict.

"Marta, that's terrible. I was going to say I can't believe it – but, you know, I can."

"Of course, because of her training, Delila knows not to give her money to feed her habit. She's a strong lady but she doesn't have to spell it out for me to know that there's a big, Azra-sized hole in her life. I just hope Azra pulls through and can make something of her life," said Marta.

I had also managed to retain contact with Ajdin, the fourteen-year-old I had tried to guide through the nightmare that had been the ethnic cleansing episode from Večići to Travnik.

Ajdin had met a girl, married, and moved with a group of relatives to St Louis, Missouri, settling not far from the Bevo Mill neighbourhood known as 'Little Bosnia'.

Since leaving for the US, Ajdin had had his worst fears confirmed, though he had had to wait around fifteen years until witnesses at the trial of Ratko Mladić in The Hague had revealed what had happened.

Vojslav Kršić, the young, polished assistant chief of staff of the 1st Kotor Varoš Light Infantry Brigade, to whom Saša and I had been taken after breaking away from the Večići convoy, had revealed that his commander had told the officer in charge of security that none of the men from Večići captured and taken to the school in Grabovica, including Ajdin's father, were to be harmed. In fact, before he left Grabovica, the general had threatened to shoot his security chief if there were any lapses in security.

However, tensions had been running high, with some of the Bosnian Serb soldiers convinced that friends or family members had been killed by Bosnian Muslims from Večići and, after Ajdin and his group of youngsters had been bussed out of town, uniformed Bosnian Serb officers from the 2nd Battalion of the 22nd Brigade and the Kotor Varoš Brigade opened fire on the adult detainees and, according to one witness, "just mowed them all down".

Between 150 and 160 men were killed, subsequent evidence revealed – twenty-five in the school's sports hall and 120 to 130 in fields in nearby Duboka and Maljava, locations to which the victims had been taken by truck. All victims had been wearing civilian clothing and, in all but two cases, they had died of gunshot injuries, usually to the head.

"Mick, people talk about the need for closure and although, after a few weeks of my dad failing to turn up in Travnik, I never really sensed that he had survived, some people might think I now have closure. I'm not sure I would call it closure," Ajdin said in a Transatlantic phone call.

"When the bus pulled away from the school in Grabovica and I turned and saw that hand waving from one of the windows, I still want to believe it was my father's hand. I see that hand in my dreams.

"I've made a new life over here and it's a good life. I'm grateful for it. But, every day, I have to put on a show. I have to pretend that everything is okay. But it's not okay. I didn't need to lose my dad. And that war has ruined my life because I did lose him prematurely, needlessly. But I'll plough on and pretend that my life is not ruined – for my kids, for my wife. And you're the only one I've told this: that every day is a battle to conceal my sorrow, my despair and, yes, my anger – because I know you won't tell my family. I don't mind if you tell your readers. In fact, I'd like you to."

I picked up various other strands. Perhaps the most astonishing comeback was from the cat with nine lives, Tarik Begić. Begić had been convicted of war crimes against Bosnians loyal to their government in a court in Croatia in 2002. His twenty-year sentence was reduced to fifteen on appeal and he was released in March 2012, having served two-thirds of his sentence.

With typical chutzpah, Begić stood for office in 2016 and was elected Mayor of Velika Kladuša. At least the people of Velika Kladuša knew precisely the nature of the character they were electing.

I often thought of his assistant, Petra, and her moving story of rueing her failure to persuade Saša to take her down the aisle. I longed to meet her again, bump into her perhaps in a street in Zagreb, but she had slipped out of contact and was lost to me. I suspected that, wherever she was, she would still be grieving for my late best friend.

I myself had moved on and, like Paul and like Ray all those years earlier at *The Daily Telegraph*, I was now sending others to hotspots and trying to elicit from them graphic stories of strife, while keeping them safe. And, in the years running up to 2018, thanks to ISIS, there was strife of a kind that I thought at least matched and probably outstripped the worst barbarities of the Yugoslav wars of the 1990s. And then I banished the comparison. There could be no league table of atrocity.

Eight years earlier I had married Lucy. We had drifted out of touch but had met by chance at a reception at the international affairs think tank in Mayfair, Chatham House. Lucy had looked genuinely pleased to see me and I felt us automatically but actively lock out of our orbit the other guests as we updated each other on our movements since 1996 over glasses of near-antiseptic white wine.

After our catch-up, there was a pause that I felt I needed to fill, only for Lucy to gaze down at her wine glass and then look up intently at me.

"You know, Mick… You saved my life. I'll never forget that, and I'll always remember you…" She paused again, then laughed. "Well… obviously!"

It was my turn to look down, then back up again. "Lucy, I may have saved your life – but I could have cost you your life. I wasn't brave or clever. I just got lucky…"

"Well, I suppose I just got lucky too but… Really. I mean it. I'm grateful. Really grateful… Sorry. That sounds like a bit of an understatement. But you know what I mean."

"Yes, yes. Of course."

I felt a flash of irritation as a silver-haired man in his seventies crashed the conversation and spoke to Lucy. "Excuse me, madam, but you asked a question about Venezuela during the session…"

But even that interruption proved fateful. I slipped Lucy my business card and mouthed to her as I left, "Give me a call. We'll have a longer chat." And she did give me a call. And we did have a longer chat.

On the morning of our wedding, I had found myself alone for a few minutes and my thoughts returned to Ivana and of how different things might have been. I loved Lucy but I still loved Ivana too. It was proper love, I was convinced. Not a crush or an illusion. If I didn't think of Ivana every day, every thought of her absence still contained the pain of a wound so tender that time could dull it but never kill it. I didn't feel any sense of guilt towards or betrayal of Lucy, despite my critical inner voice trying its best to make me do so. No – love was like fear: it descended and there was nothing to be done to keep it at bay.

The truth was you could love more than one person, but you could only devote yourself to one of your loves. And I was now choosing to devote my life to Lucy. There. I had said it. The decision was made. Debate over.

And I visualised a meeting sometime in the future at which Lucy and I and our children would visit Ivana and Ante and Nada in Dubrovnik. And that would set the relationships in stone for us all. Love vectors might shoot from me in Ivana's direction. Dare I hope that some might shoot in my direction from Ivana? But those vectors, like all geometrical concepts, would be invisible, harmless, creating no disruption to two families now not just settled but robust. My ongoing love for Ivana hurt no one; my devotion to Lucy was absolute.

I had told Lucy of my unsuccessful mission to Dubrovnik after learning of Branko's death, and she had categorised it as a 'sweet story'. She hadn't laughed at my impetuousness, nor had she described me as naïve. I sensed that she appreciated Ivana's misgivings at making a drastic life change just months after the love of her life had been taken away, but Lucy had the delicacy not to spell this out. I sensed that she sensed that this had been an important episode in my life and was not one to be derided or, perish the thought, diminished. Oh, how I loved the precision of Lucy's reading of others' motives and feelings.

She had been delicate but firm too in dissuading me from naming either of our boys Saša. The name was more often a girl's name in Western Europe, even if it tended to be a boy's name in Russia and Central and Eastern Europe, she said. As parents, we shouldn't lumber either of our children with a Christian, or 'given', name that would invite teasing and mockery in the playground in those sensitive early years, however distinguished its pedigree or deep its associations.

After her first veto, I had turned away, grumbling, "Bloody hell, it's hardly 'a boy named Sue', is it?" But I knew she was right. She did agree to call our second boy Alexander, a diminutive form of which was Saša but, in what was for her a rare finger-wagging moment accompanied by a stern look, she said to me, "But you're never to call him Saša. Okay? He'll be Alex and nothing else." I bagged the concession and agreed. Over time, I sensed that her insistence was less about playground taunts and more about her feeling it unfair to set one of our children against an inimitable, statuesque figure in her husband's past.

Just before I had set out solo on my latest trip to Bosnia, we had been sitting in the kitchen. She was trying to plan for school holidays and I was only gently resisting. I had learned that when she suggested something practical, she was usually right and, in the last year or so of our marriage, instead of adopting a default position of saying no to any suggestion, I had tried actively to say yes unless there was a good reason not to do so. And she was right that it was better to plan ahead, now that they knew the school holiday dates.

"I think for our main holiday we should go on a road trip through Bosnia, Lucy. You know, get the boys to see what it's really like," I said.

Lucy raised her left eyebrow in a way that I knew and loved, even though it meant pushback.

"Mick! They're seven and five! They need sand between their toes, splashing in the sea, kicking beachballs. Not hours in a car on mountain roads."

"I suppose you're right…"

"Mick, you *know* I'm right."

Lucy paused, and then said in a way that I felt was so suffused with affection that my heart gave out a little ache, "Bosnia's really captured part of your soul, Mick, hasn't it? And it's not going to give it back, is it?"

I let some silence fill the gap. I had known I was 'captured' for quite some time and, what's more, I didn't want Bosnia to give back that part of my soul. I wanted it to stay there – to remain encamped. At least until things took a turn for the better. Perhaps then it could occupy a different part of my soul. Where there was sorrow and where there were harsh memories of cruelty and torture and killings never far from my recollections, perhaps over time Bosnia's unique charm, its resilient, welcoming people could diminish the dark and create only radiance. It seemed like a remote ambition.

And I thought of Ismail and Ševa and Ajdin, and the sadness that hovered over them in their quiet moments. They deserved a fresh chapter in which their beautiful, lush country could occupy its rightful place. They would be gracious and generous hosts, opening their towns and villages and homes to visitors, who would say "How is it that we didn't know about this magical place?"

As I pulled out of this reverie, the face of Yugoslavia's President Tito gazed at me from a fridge magnet. Lucy knew it was a feature not to be moved or removed. And I asked myself whether I had placed it in my kitchen as a silent act of defiance against my late mother.

30
1996

About a month after my mea culpa had been published, my phone in the newsroom rang.

"Mick, it's Santiago here. How are you?"

My heart swelled. Given my respect for him, for his knowledge, for his journalistic experience, for his humility, I felt privileged that he had thought of me and made time to put in a call. Yet I could never have anticipated what he was going to say.

"I'm not too bad, Santiago. As you'll have seen, I had a bit of a shock to the system. But I hope I'm working it through."

Santiago told me he was truly sorry about the situation I'd found myself in.

"But, you know, Mick, I thought you made a brave choice. So many journalists would have ducked it and hoped no one would find out."

It was interesting. The word 'brave' had haunted me throughout my short career. I had never felt brave at any stage. If anything, I had felt craven; yet Santiago was only the latest of a few people whose views I respected who had used the word and attributed it to me. My heart swelled again at the plaudit, deserved or otherwise, from a man I admired deeply.

"But listen," said Santiago. "I'm not one hundred per cent sure why I'm calling you to tell you this but I've discovered that one of my reporters has been quietly nurturing a relationship with one of Ante Pavelić's surviving children. A daughter. She's living in a flat in Madrid and she's done a deal with him that she'll tell him the whole story, hand him a bunch of her father's papers, but he's only to publish a story about her once she's dead."

I whistled down the line in amazement.

"Mick, he hadn't even told me. And when we read your story, he was afraid I might sack him for not revealing her presence in Madrid before she died, but he knocked on my door and explained the situation to me.

"He said to me, 'I don't know if Mick would be interested but I can ask her if she'd be prepared to meet him.' So I don't know whether you'd like to take up that offer… Or whether you'd prefer to obliterate her and her strand of the family from your memory."

He paused and I didn't fill the space.

"I just thought I should tell you and offer you the opportunity."

The fact that there was a living relative – not just any relative but a daughter of the dictator – hit me with considerable force. Perhaps deep down and perhaps also between the lines of what I had written in my mea culpa, I had tried to put distance between myself and my ancestor's outrages. If there was a daughter still alive, then it made those outrages feel significantly more recent. They were undeniably within living memory.

Santiago's voice resumed down the line. "Mick, if you do want an introduction – and we have no guarantee that she'll agree to meet you – what you need to know is that she is a one hundred per cent apologist for her father. There is not only no remorse, there is defiance. Her father did no wrong. His motives were misunderstood and atrocities laid at his door were propaganda from his enemies. You'd have to be able to deal with that kind of talk."

Santiago's qualification altered my instinctive reaction to his offer in no way. I had to meet this woman. At least I had to try to meet this woman.

I was able quickly to establish that the daughter in question was Višnja, Ante Pavelić's eldest child. In the photograph that had so intrigued me among my mother's documents, her younger sister, Mirjana Ana, had presumably been behind the camera. Višnja was the striking figure on the right of the group of four. Her short hair was tousled by the wind, the sleeves of her crisp white blouse were rolled up, her hands thrust into the pockets of what looked like a checked skirt. She had something of the strong black eyebrows of her father but appeared to have been spared his big ears with their pendulous lobes. She was wearing something just short of a smile but her expression spoke of a breezy confidence.

31
1997

By the time I came to the foot of the stairwell leading to the flat of my first cousin twice removed, Višnja, I had been through the whole gamut of potential introductions and lines of questioning. I had shredded all but one. And I had concluded that mine was not a journey of investigative journalism.

It was counter-intuitive to me not to be looking for a story from so unusual an encounter, but an account of our meeting was not only beyond the parameters agreed within Višnja's rules of engagement, I also had little interest in reporting an elderly woman's attempts to justify or deny the actions and atrocities of her father that had been so comprehensively documented elsewhere.

Santiago's journalist, Pablo, who had established the relationship with Višnja, had warned me of just how intolerant she was of alternative views. He told me that the only scintilla of doubt he had ever detected had been one day when, appearing particularly weary, she had admitted, "It was very difficult to be this man's daughter. Very difficult."

I had just one question which, were she to answer it, might shine a torchlight into a corner of my past. I acknowledged that her answer could be reassuring or devastating.

The staircase leading to her flat on the Avenida de Concha Espina, just a stone's throw from Real Madrid's Bernabeu Stadium, was poorly lit and clearly rarely swept. I imagined this woman in her late seventies or early eighties toiling up the stairs with her shopping, her mindset over the years shrink-wrapped into the narrow space of her deadening obsession with her father's reputation.

Given her insistence to Pablo that he write nothing until her death, Višnja's seemed to me an exercise directed at no one, publicised to no one, yet consuming her entirely. The word 'futility' formed in my mind but it wasn't a word I would use to her.

I reached the third floor, located her flat, and knocked at the door. It took her perhaps two minutes to unlatch the door. I was shocked to see the degree to which the plain but handsome woman of my photograph had shrunk. She was tiny and wizened.

"Miss Pavelić," I said. "I hope you were expecting me… I think we may be related."

She blinked from behind thick spectacles. Having looked average height in my photograph, I estimated she was now just five feet tall.

"Come in." She beckoned me into her sitting room. We shook hands rather formally. I hadn't been keen to kiss her and she had not looked for an embrace. I sensed that she was as tense as I was.

There were files piled high across five or six tables. The smell of dust was all-pervasive. She pointed to an armchair. I sat down.

On a small stand-alone table by my chair was another black and white family photo. Artfully posed, it showed the same foursome that featured in the Santa Pola picture, parents seated in front, grown-up children standing behind. Ante and his son, Velimir, were smartly dressed in suit and tie, Ante looking off abstractedly to the left of the camera, fingers of his right hand against his temple, his black eyebrows shockingly bushy, his ears huge and flaccid, Velimir looking off right, the very picture of a young, vain intellectual. Ante's wife, dressed in a formal coat with big buttons, had a hint of pursed lips about her. I couldn't put my finger on it but something about her expression spoke of a lowly status in this family.

But I sensed that the photograph was placed where it was, impossible for any guest to miss, so that he, she or I would see Višnja in her prime. She was even more strikingly handsome in this photo than in the Santa Pola shot. Yes, there was something plain about her clean features but she was looking straight into the camera with an air of utter self-confidence. Her hair was cut stylishly short and she wore a necklace of pearls. I took the photograph to be Višnja's saying "I may be old and wrinkled now but I was beautiful and strong once."

She saw me looking at the photograph – as she had clearly intended – and said, "That was taken just months before my father died." I could find no response to that statement.

"Aunt Višnja," I said. I had thought about the correct form of address in some detail before my visit and had decided to meet head-on our shared bloodline. "Your father's brother, Josip, was my great-grandfather on my mother's side. Did you know my mother, Nada?"

Her face brightened in so far as it could. I sensed it hadn't seen a smile or produced laughter for some time.

"Ah, little Nada! How I loved her… You know, I think she and I were soulmates."

EPILOGUE

RATKO MLADIĆ – Commander of the Main Staff of the Bosnian Serb Army

On 22nd November, 2017, Mladić was found guilty of all eleven charges laid against him. The charges ranged from genocide, murder, extermination, and terror, to deportation. He was sentenced to life imprisonment. He was one of seven of the 161 people indicted by the International Criminal Tribunal for the Former Yugoslavia (ICTY) in the Hague to be given a life imprisonment sentence. In June 2021, his third and final appeal against the verdicts and their terms was rejected. The Chamber of The Hague Tribunal described Mladić's crimes as "among the most heinous known to mankind".

SLOBODAN MILOŠEVIĆ – President of Serbia within Yugoslavia, President of the Federal Republic of Yugoslavia

Milošević died of a heart attack in his prison cell in the course of his trial at The Hague on 11th March, 2006. Charges for which he was indicted included: genocide; complicity in genocide; deportation; murder; persecutions on political, racial or religious grounds; inhumane acts such as forcible transfer; extermination; imprisonment; torture; wilful killing; unlawful confinement; wilfully causing great suffering; unlawful deportation or transfer. His trial had begun on 12th February, 2002, at which he defended himself. After his death, he was found guilty of 'joint criminal enterprise' in trials of other defendants: by the ICTY at The Hague in 2007 and by its successor body, the International Residual Mechanism for Criminal Tribunals, in 2021.

FRANJO TUĐMAN – Croatian leader, who successfully pushed for Croatia's secession from the Yugoslav Federation

Tuđman had been a member of the Partisans, led by Tito, who fought against the Croatian 'Ustaša' forces that allied with Hitler in World War II. As time passed, his Croatian nationalist sympathies hardened and he received a two-year jail-term in 1972 for subversive activities. He is said to have been spared a much harsher sentence because of Tito's personal intervention, acknowledging his time as a committed Partisan.

He became Croatian President in 1990, after putting together the outline of a national programme with Croatia becoming a nation state. He served as President until his death in 1999.

In May 2013, the International Criminal Tribunal for the former Yugoslavia concluded that Tuđman had shared in a joint criminal enterprise of the ethnic cleansing of Bosnian Muslims as part of the means of creating a united Croatia. On appeal that view was reaffirmed in 2017 without his being accused of a specific crime.

RADOVAN KARADŽIĆ – President of Republika Srpska in Bosnia and Supreme Commander of the armed forces of Republika Srpska

Karadžić was indicted in February 2009 after over a decade on the run. He was found guilty in March 2016 of eleven counts of genocide, crimes against humanity, and violations of the laws or customs of war. He was sentenced to forty years imprisonment. On appeal in March 2019, his sentence was extended to life imprisonment.

The son of a Serbian nationalist 'Chetnik', Karadžic was a psychiatrist and poet before co-founding the Serb Democratic Party in Bosnia in 1989.

In 2021, he was transferred to the UK to serve the rest of his life-sentence and is being held in prison on the Isle of Wight.

ALIJA IZETBEGOVIĆ – First president of the Presidency of an independent Bosnia and Hercegovina in 1992.

Izetbegović was an Islamic philosopher and author, who founded the Party of Democratic Action. He served two prison sentences for his Islamic writings and activism. The second, based on allegations of hostile activity based on Islamist ideology, was reduced by the Bosnian Appeal Court on appeal on the basis that "some of the actions of the accused did not have the characteristics of criminal acts".

He led Bosnia through the 1991-5 conflicts, serving as President until 1996. At that point, he became a member of the rotating presidency established after the peace agreement at Dayton, Ohio. He remained in office till 2000 and died in 2003.

MILAN LUKIĆ – Leader of Bosnian Serb White Eagles paramilitary group in Višegrad

Lukić was sentenced to life imprisonment in July 2009, after being convicted of crimes that included: the killing of at least 132 identified men, women and children; murder; and torture. His leading role in the Pionirska Street and Bikavac house-fires in which more than one hundred Muslims were burned alive was described by the ICTY as exemplifying the worst acts of inhumanity that a person may inflict upon others and "ranked high in the long, sad and wretched history of man's inhumanity to man".

The head of the Association of Women Victims of War, Bakira Hasečić, claimed to have been raped by Lukić at knifepoint and claimed rape victims were let down by the failure of the ICTY to charge either Milan Lukić or his cousin, Sredoje Lukić, with rape or sexual abuse

In December 2020, the Hague Tribunal rejected a request by Lukic for a revision of his life sentence.

SREDOJE LUKIĆ – Cousin of Milan Lukić and member of White Eagles paramilitary group based in Višegrad

Sredoje, a former policeman, was jailed for 30 years after he was tried jointly with his cousin at The Hague, a sentence reduced to 27 years on appeal. He was convicted of charges that included murder and aiding and abetting persecutions on political, racial and religious grounds. He was found to have contributed substantially to the deaths of fifty-three people trapped in a house in the Pionirska Street fire.

RASIM DELIĆ – Chief of Staff of the Bosnian Army

Delić was regarded by many as the leader who began to turn the tide more in favour of the Bosnian Army in the fight against the Bosnian Serbs. A former Lieutenant-Colonel in the Yugoslav National Army (JNA), he was charged with failing to prevent or punish the cruel treatment of twelve Bosnian Serbs at the hands of a unit comprised of members of the Mujahideen.

He was sentenced to three years in prison at The Hague in September 2008 but he died of a heart attack in his apartment in Sarajevo in April 2010, while on provisional release and while appeal proceedings were taking place.

ACKNOWLEDGEMENTS

My desire to chronicle the details of the fall of Yugoslavia was born in the streets of Sarajevo in 1996 just months after the end of a near four-year siege when, as a political journalist accompanying the then UK Prime Minster, John Major, on a visit to British troops, I witnessed the devastation of the city.

Desire became compulsion as I began reading two outstanding books, Misha Glenny's *The Fall of Yugoslavia* and Ed Vulliamy's *The War is Dead, Long Live the War*. The extraordinary story of the 1991-5 conflicts was one I had to tell, even if my ambition to ensure that these never became Europe's forgotten wars was lofty, though honourable.

I have produced an extensive bibliography of all the books and sources I used but the sections from Alec Russell's *Prejudice and Plum Brandy* were particularly helpful in relation to the details of the siege of Dubrovnik. The CIA's two-volume *Balkan Battlegrounds: A Military History of the Yugoslav Conflict, 1990-1995* represented a superb treasure trove of detail as well. Transcripts of the hearings at the International Criminal Tribunal for the former Yugoslavia in the Hague also provided me with multiple authentic stories from the period.

I would particularly like to pay tribute to the late Liberal Democrat leader, Paddy Ashdown, who, as the Parliamentarian with the deepest knowledge and closest personal experience of the conflicts, shared his thoughts with me just months before his death. I thank him for recounting a wide range of insights and experiences as well as his somewhat shocking conversation about the Balkans with former Foreign Secretary Douglas Hurd.

My friend, Meti Salihu, provided first hand experience of the Yugoslav National Army's descent upon Dubrovnik and Alis Martin, of the Chatham House think-tank, shared her experiences of working for the United Nations in Croatia and of how life was under Tito for a family whose head refused to join the Communist Party. Oxfam's GB Bosnia Country Representative Usha Kar provided valuable detail of life in Tuzla and described the tension and sense of hopelessness of Bosnians during the conflicts, wishing they could go back to their pre-strife, multi-ethnic ways.

I am enormously grateful to my two most assiduous readers, as I sought to turn initial drafts into two novels of substance – this book and my previous work, *Goran's Dilemma*. They were Ray Hedley and Sue Dolton and, at times, I asked far too much of them.

Thanks too to my wife, Sophie, and to my children, Alice and Mark, who may at times have been bewildered by my obsession with the 1991-5 conflicts.

And thanks to my publishers, Troubador, whose professionalism has been unstinting during the publication of both of my novels to date.

BIBLIOGRAPHY AND SOURCES

The Fall of Yugoslavia, Misha Glenny (Penguin)
The War is Dead, Long Live the War. Bosnia: The Reckoning, Ed Vulliamy (The Bodley Head)
Serpent in the Bosom – The Rise and Fall of Slobodan Milošević, Lenard J Cohen (Westview Press, Perseus Books Group)
Yugoslavia – A State that Withered Away, Dejan Jović (Purdue University Press)
The Death of Yugoslavia, Laura Silber and Allan Little (Penguin)
The Yugoslav Wars of the 1990s, Catherine Baker (Palgrave)
Balkan Battlegrounds: A Military History of the Yugoslav Conflict, 1990-1995, Vols I and II, Office of Russian and European Analysis, Central Intelligence Agency (CIA Washington DC)
The Balkans 1804-2012 – Nationalism, War and the Great Powers, Misha Glenny (Granta Publications)
Ratko Mladić – Criminel ou Héros? Milo Jelesijević & Ljubodrag Stojadinović (Editions Le Verjus)
The Butcher's Trail, Julian Borger (Other Press, New York)
Prejudice & Plum Brandy – Tales of a Balkan Stringer, Alec Russell (Michael Joseph Ltd)
Balkan Odyssey, David Owen (Harvest, Harcourt Brace & Co)
The Balkans in World History, Andrew Baruch Wachtel (Oxford University Press)
The Balkans – From the End of Byzantium to the Present Day, Mark Mazower (Phoenix, Orion Books)

Balkan Ghosts – A Journey Through History, Robert D Kaplan (Picador, St Martin's Press)

Swords and Ploughshares – Building Peace in the 21st Century, Paddy Ashdown (Phoenix, Orion Books)

Burn This House – The Making and Unmaking of Yugoslavia, Edited by Jasminka Udovički and James Ridgeway (Duke University Press)

The New Bosnian Mosaic – Identities, Memories and Moral Claims in a Post-War Society, Edited by Xavier Bougarel, Elissa Helms and Ger Duijzings (Ashgate Publishing)

The Autobiography – A Fortunate Life, Paddy Ashdown (Aurum Press)

Tito and His Comrades, Jože Pirjevec (The University of Wisconsin Press)

Tito's Secret Empire – How the Maharaja of the Balkans Fooled the World, William Klinger and Denis Kuljiš (Hurst & Company)

Inescapable Questions – Autobiographical Notes, Alija Izetbegović (The Islamic Foundation, Leicester)

Eastern Approaches: The Memoirs of the Original British Action Hero, Fitzroy Maclean (Penguin)

Bosnia's Forgotten Battlefield – Bihać, Brendan O'Shea (Spellmount, The History Press)

The Modern Yugoslav Conflict 1991-1995 – Perception, Deception and Dishonesty, Brendan O'Shea (Routledge, Taylor & Francis Group)

My War Gone By, I Miss it So, Anthony Loyd (September Publishing)

Besieged – Life Under Fire on a Sarajevo Street, Barbara Demick (Granta Publications)

Bosnian Chronicle, Ivo Andrić (Apollo, Head of Zeus Ltd)

The Bridge Over the Drina, Ivo Andrić (The Harvill Press)

Madness Visible – A Memoir of War, Janine di Giovanni (Bloomsbury Publishing)

They Would Never Hurt a Fly – War Criminals on Trial in The Hague, Slavenka Drakulić (Abacus)

In Harm's Way – Bosnia: A War Reporter's Story, Martin Bell (Icon Books; Penguin Group)

Unfinest Hour - Britain and the Destruction of Bosnia, Brendan Simms (Penguin)

*Saviours of the Nation - Serbia's Intellectual Opposition and the Revival of

Nationalism, Jasna Dragović Soso (McGill-Queens University Press)

The War in Croatia and Bosnia-Herzegovina 1991-1995, Edited by Branka Magaš and Ivo Žanić (Routledge)

Endgame: The Betrayal and Fall of Srebrenica, Europe's Worst Massacre Since World War II, David Rohde (Farrar, Straus and Giroux)

Anatomy of a Massacre, David Binder, Foreign Policy, No 97 (Winter 1994-5)

Black Lamb and Grey Falcon, Rebecca West (Canongate)

Case transcripts from the International Criminal Tribunal for the former Yugoslavia, https://www.icty.org/en/cases

YouTube excerpts of coverage of Omarska and Trnopolje camps: https://www.youtube.com/watch?v=w6-ZDvwPxk8

House of Commons debate on Bosnia, 25/9/92 (Hansard)

Enclave, Photographs by Wade Goddard (War Photo Ltd)

This book is printed on paper from sustainable sources managed under the Forest Stewardship Council (FSC) scheme.

It has been printed in the UK to reduce transportation miles and their impact upon the environment.

For every new title that Troubador publishes, we plant a tree to offset CO_2, partnering with the More Trees scheme.

For more about how Troubador offsets its environmental impact, see www.troubador.co.uk/sustainability-and-community